Yucca & Ivar

By DeAnn Price

A Tale of Vampires in Hollywood

© COPYRIGHT2009 BY DEANN PRICE. ALL RIGHTS RESERVED.
PUBLISHED BY PRICE PUBLISHING, JUNE, 2009.

ISBN 978-0-578-02890-3

Price Publishing – DeAnn Price
P.O. Box 222
Overton, NV 89040

Without limiting the rights under copyright reserved, no part of this publication may be reproduced, stored in or introduced into a retrieval system, or transmitted, in any form, or by any means (electronic, mechanical, photocopying, recording, or otherwise), without the prior written permission of both the copyright owner and the above publisher of this book.

This is a work of fiction. Names, characters, places, and incidents either are the product of the author's imagination or are used fictitiously, and any resemblance to actual persons, living or dead, business establishments, events, or locals is entirely coincidental.

This is book dedicated to my mom
for her unwavering support,
encouragement and patience.

I have never met a vampire personally, but I
don't know what might happen tomorrow.

—Bela Lugosi

Marisol

One

There was a light breeze blowing the gauzy drapes around. I'd never been to this place before as far as I knew but I thought I recognized it from somewhere. The familiar place was both beautiful and terrifying at the same time. It was a high-rise apartment with windows on two sides; an older building evidenced by the 20 foot ceilings, concrete floors and old fashioned pulley windows. One big room is all that I could see. It was dark except for the light streaming in from the windows from the full moon and city lights. Tonight, I saw there was a pentagram painted on the floor and several items were placed inside the star shape. As I moved closer I could see that one of the items—the item closest to me—was what appeared to be a dead rat.

Even though the rat gave me the creeps I slowly moved forward to get a better look. Another item I could identify as I got a little closer was an old skeleton key. I continued toward it and kneeled down next to the pentagram to get a better look and just as I placed my hand down on the red circle I noticed that the paint shined as though it was still wet. When I lifted up my palm it was covered with… paint?

Right at that moment one of the windows slammed shut so quickly it sounded like an explosion. A second later another window slammed shut, then another. When I tried to turn around to see what was happening I realized I couldn't—the space I was in was so small that lying on my back as I was now, the ceiling was just inches above me. I pounded my hands, pushing against it as the wet paint splashed red prints above my head. I tried to scream but nothing would come out.

Of course I knew I was dreaming at this point. I knew it when I moved closer to look at the rat. I knew it when I reached out to touch the bloody omen that always seemed to find a way to present itself when I had this dream or some semblance of it. What I couldn't understand is why I fell for it every time. Just once, it would be nice if it didn't end up with me in some small, enclosed place silently screaming. It's so cliché.

Then the phone rang and pulled me more fully into consciousness. A dull buzzing stayed in my head for a minute before I slowly open my eyes. I had to roll over to the other side of my futon to grab the ancient blue Trimline phone that has been my bedroom phone since 6th grade.

"Hello," I answered hoarsely.

"Are you up?" It was Gavin, my brother, best friend and biggest pain in the ass.

He never really got completely past the impulse to make me pay for what he considered I'd gotten from life that he hadn't. Usually he would correct himself once he realized he really didn't feel that way anymore.

"Hey, I'll pick you up and take you to work if you run a couple errands with me," he offered.

It wasn't really a question since I knew full well he would be on my doorstep within the hour no matter what I responded. "What are we doing?"

"I just have to pick up a couple of things for tonight... so it's for you too," he rationalized. Though Gavin was a master manipulator, he wasn't even breaking a sweat on this one since he knew it wouldn't be hard to get me to agree. Even though it seemed innocent enough, somehow I was sure I'd be sorry; both sorry and not since I voluntarily threw myself into Gavin's misadventures on a regular basis.

"I need at least 45 minutes to get ready. I still need to shower," I reasoned.

"30 minutes," click.

The label asshole could easily be used to describe Gavin and has been by me, and I'm sure others on several occasions, but he could also be described as witty, clever and sardonic; in a good way. You were never bored when you hung out with Gavin and I didn't know anyone who didn't wish he was their close friend—mainly because you never had more fun with anyone else.

I put down the Trimline and figured I better get a move on. It was a little after 9:00 and luckily I didn't have to be to work until 3:00 in the afternoon. Swing shift was the best time for the psychic business. I myself was mostly a medium, which means I get information from and communicate with spirits and beings beyond the human realm. It sounds a lot cooler than it is. I mostly get called on to give psychic readings. There's really no way to describe what I do without sounding totally hocus-pocus, so I usually don't tell people what I do unless absolutely necessary.

The only reason I use this annoying ability I have to make a living is, crazy enough, people actually pay good money to speak to dead people or find out if the latest guy is "the one." It's better than waiting tables or working at a department store for minimum wage. I also really like my setup at my job and I have a fondness for my boss, Suzanne. Suzanne is a psychic but mostly she's a business woman. Suzanne gets her information in somewhat the same way I do, passed on by ours or other's guides, but I get a load of other useless information that Suzanne doesn't seem to. Personally, to me it seems like my guide could pay a little closer attention to the things going on in my life and pay a little less attention to other people's issues. My life seems to waiver between general mess and modest disaster most of the time. I'm sure it's all about character building or something.

Coffee is what I needed right now. I got up and padded across the wood floor of my little bungalow to the kitchen. It was pretty small so it took maybe ten steps to go from the bedroom, into the living room and around the left to the kitchen on the South side of the apartment. The small bungalow I rented on Ivar St., just above Yucca St. in Hollywood was built sometime in the 1920's. It was like a tiny little house. My unit shared one wall with the neighbor to the North side but all the other units in the courtyard complex were individual bungalows. There were several windows on the South side of the unit overlooking a very scenic view of Hollywood.

I loved what I considered my little town and Gavin and I grabbed this apartment from my friend as soon as I heard she was moving in with her boyfriend. Two people could live here but it was really just big enough for one. So after a short time Gavin found another place and moved out. Luckily it was before either of us killed the other.

I sipped my coffee as I looked out at my personal view of the Capital Records building contemplating that today would've been my last day on the bus. Typically, I'd been walking the one block down Yucca to Vine St., jumping on the RTD down Vine to Santa Monica Blvd. then walking the two long blocks to the strip mall newly built in front of the Hollywood Cemetery. This is where Suzanne had her Psychic shop and where I divine the dead and try to glean the future. Suzanne was better at the future than I was.

Tonight after work Gavin is supposed to pick me up so we can go pick up my new car. New is a relative term as my limited budget only allowed me to get a black, gently used 1968 Volkswagen Beatle. It was beautiful to me. This was the year it had the cool looking rounded bumper. I'd put down a deposit and gotten a receipt from the seller. Today was Friday, payday, and I'll be making my final payment tonight and get the keys. No more bus and better yet, no more relying on Gavin. Complete independence. Although I'm sure this just meant that I could get myself to the grocery store, work and the Laundromat. I was fairly certain that we would still be going out in the evening in Gavin's much cooler car.

I showered quickly and got dressed. Suzanne had a strict dress code; absolutely nothing conventional allowed. Luckily my wardrobe meshed perfectly with the atmosphere of the shop. I have to say that I wasn't dressing in black mini skirts, fishnets and torn t-shirts for some pseudo-psychic effect, my taste was more music influenced. Anyway, it was a good thing I didn't work at the bank.

As I was using my lip brush to paint on the blood-red lipstick I was fond of I noticed the humming of the mystery entity. I recognized the guides of most of my neighbors and they usually gave me my space unless there was something they considered urgent. This one entity never seemed to have an agenda but sent me messages on a regular basis. I didn't think she was an earthbound spirit. Most earthbound spirits were usually confused or disoriented but this one just seemed bored. She would hum to herself and sometimes send me picture puzzles. She seemed a little too happy to find someone close by who could hear her. I couldn't quite place who she was attached to though.

This ability I had did come with some strings attached. It was rare to find an entity that could send me words. Usually they used the myriad of memories and pictures stored in my brain to play a virtual game of charades but with pictures or concentration puzzle of sorts of what they were trying to say. I've always resented uninvited entities using my mind as a virtual toolbox to compile what they invariably thought of as their very urgent message. I was getting a little better at blocking them. My childhood was pretty much a nightmare of mental invasion.

Today when the mystery female entity felt me engage she sent me a little mental bouquet of purple Irises. That was nice. At least she was a cheerful entity.

Just as I was finishing my makeup Gavin honked the horn of his boat of a car. I would be annoyed at the honk but there wasn't much guest parking around here. As it was, I had to get rid of a whole pile of stuff that was stored in my one car garage to make room for the VW. The complex was situated on a hill so the driveway ran under my windows on the South side and my garage was underneath the unit. I would have to start using the back stairs up to the kitchen door instead of the front door now that I would be parking in the garage.

"Honk… honk… honk!" So much patience... I grabbed my bag and ran out the front door, locking it on the way out.

I ran through the courtyard, down the steps blurting out "morning" to my favorite neighbor Julian on the way out. He got up early on the weekends to work on the garden that he had brought up to the level of spectacular. I think he was probably everyone in the complex's favorite neighbor for that reason. But for me he was also a great friend and confidante. He always had the best advice.

"Don't forget, bar-be-cue tomorrow. Tell Gavin to bring all his hot friends," Julian said as I passed. Of course he meant all his cute rocker-boy friends. Julian always wanted most what was unattainable. As far as I was aware, all of Gavin's friends were straight but I was always on the lookout for Julian.

"Of course," I shouted as I ran past.

I think Julian's real name was Julio, Julio Rodriguez. He was Hispanic, Cuban actually. Julian was a decade or two older than us but he had a young attitude and groomed himself better than a golden era starlet and it showed. He worked as a makeup artist on a long–running soap opera.

Gavin was at the bottom of the walk waiting for me in his '68 Ford Thunderbird. It was a striking car for sure—shiny black with a black landau top. This was the year the car grew in size and had the suicide back doors. It had the feel of a cross between a limo and a hearse.

When I got in the stereo was blasting Judas Priest. You never knew what would be playing when you got into Gavin's car. It was never a repeat.

"WHERE ARE WE GOING?" I had to shout over the music.

"To hell for sure," Gavin shot back as we pulled down the street into our day. I was wondering if he might be right. It was odd that moving through the city towards unknown adventures that would most likely mean some type of danger or, at the very least, mild trouble would give me a warm, comforted feeling. But that's the feeling that washed over me as I sat in what I considered my seat in the large, hulking ocean liner of a car.

Gavin and I had a rough, sputtering start to our relationship. We never had the chance to do childhood things together or go to the same school. We shared the same father but had different mothers. Normally this would not be such a scandal but none of the parties involved knew about each other except for my father. In fact, Gavin and I were of approximately the same age so that might tell you something about the awkward circumstance of our relationship.

I had the distinction of being the child of the legitimate family, if you could call it that. My mother was married to my father although he was only around sporadically. It's now crystal clear where he was a lot of the time. I sometimes wonder if there might be other siblings out there somewhere. In any case, all the cats came out of the bag when Gavin and I were seventeen and my father decided it was time to leave my mother and move in with Gavin's mother. During the year and a half of that arrangement is when we learned about each other, and my dad even thought it was a good idea to throw us together to "get to know" each other. We instantly hated each other and since Gavin has a sadistic streak, this turned out to be quite a bad idea.

Up until that point I'd led a mostly uneventful, mild life of good behavior. Gavin took it upon himself to broaden my horizons which meant getting me a fake ID, taking me to clubs and getting me all the drugs and alcohol I was willing to try. With the recent destruction of what was my safe, sheltered life I was pretty willing and ready to experiment with things that would numb my brain. I also found that certain drugs and drinking had the added effect of pushing out intrusive messages from the other side. It was a win/win for him and me. Gavin had the pleasure of corrupting the perfect child of the legitimate family that should have been his and I got to punish my dad for his illegitimate dalliances that destroyed mine. I think, looking back, that I was really just turning my anger inward; inclining more towards self-destruction. I think Gavin eventually realized that and became torn between resentment and some protective instinct. He never let me get too far.

Since our dad was married to my mom, Gavin had always thought of himself as the man of the house. This position probably also had a hand in forming his personality and why he eventually took on the responsibility of me. Even though I was the same age as him, because of my mostly sheltered life up until then, I really didn't have the street smarts he did. Our relationship had a seismic shift the day my mother committed suicide.

When my father left her, my mother went into a deep depression and drank a lot (more than usual). I know it was wrong to check out the way I did but I was probably not far off from the depression that she was feeling and didn't have a clue how to handle it. I also had the devil sitting on my shoulder. This may have been part of what influenced Gavin after she died to, without hesitation, move into the role of my guardian and not quite as cruel constant companion.

By that time there were also obvious similarities surfacing with us and a real bond forming. The second sight had come from my mother's side but to look at us you would think we were fraternal twins; he was blonde, I was blonde, both tall with the same exact blue eyes. That was always the first guess when people found out he was my brother and the same age. Of course that was the polite first guess. Saying "Oh, your father was a philandering ass hole?" was probably not really an option. Although that was Gavin's most common answer.

By the time we got to Sunset and Highland I knew where the first stop was. There was a guy who lived near Guitar Institute who was his pot dealer. Gavin was pretty hyper and pot really just made him come back down to everyone else's level. He smoked way more weed than I did.

I chose to wait in the car while he got buzzed into the building and rode the elevator up to make his connection. He left the engine running but I turned the metal way down. I'd had enough of that.

Metal wasn't really Gavin's thing either but he liked to think of himself as very eclectic. Sometimes he would choose things; music, fashion, just because it was the very last thing he would really choose. It was like he was choosing to have ironic taste. This is probably what kept him on the cutting edge. Local rock scene guys and even some celebrities looked to him as a trendsetter and emulated him. I guess this was part of the reason he was so successful at what he did.

These days he was a music manager. Gavin had impeccable taste but no real musical talent. He'd started out when we were in Orange County throwing clubs at local bars and nightclubs, which grew into booking bands for the clubs, then eventually managing the bands. It was a natural progression that suited his personality and strengths perfectly. It also fed his ego which I didn't think could get any more inflated than it already was—incorrectly.

Just then Gavin was back and had gotten the stash he went in for. "Check this out." He threw a baggie in my lap. There wasn't much in there but it smelled really pungent and looked sticky with red hairs in clumps. It looked scary strong. This is the type of pot that sent me shivering in the corner with paranoia. I preferred generic Mexican dirt bud myself. Just enough to mellow me out and quiet the mental intruders.

"Can we listen to something else?" It came out less annoyed than I felt.

"What's wrong? Can't relate to the acid-wash rock?" He answered sarcastically.

"Not really," I replied.

"Fine," he huffed, but I don't think really he minded.

"Do you have any of Brett's tapes?" I asked casually.

"Oh, please. Apparently, I'm more likely to get him the cover of Tiger Beat magazine then get him a record deal. Every single chick that gets in my car wants to hear Brett," he said as he pulled the Judas Priest tape out.

"He's your client. Isn't that a good thing?" I insisted.

"I guess." He fished around in the backseat and found the cassette I asked for and popped it in the player.

Oh. This was something new. I closed my eyes to let it sink in while Gavin drove on to our next unknown-to-me destination. The only reason I would want to listen to Brett's music while riding with Gavin was that he always got the new stuff first, obviously. Otherwise, to me, it always seemed to be too intimate of an experience to listen to Brett Carson with my brother. I knew there were lots of girls who were in love with Brett Carson but I couldn't help being one of them. At least he knew my name and we'd had a few conversations. I didn't have any illusions about being any more than his manager's sister but that didn't change how I would continue to feel in his presence—which was usually flustered and tongue-tied. It was completely involuntary. After a conversation or two I learned that if I didn't look directly into his deep blue eyes I would be able to maintain a little more composure and not sound like a complete idiot.

So I only allowed myself to gaze uninterrupted at his perfect face during his live shows. Even small club lights for acoustic performances would make it virtually impossible to see the audience while he played. And he was concentrating on his playing, of course, not to mention that it seemed OK to stare when someone was performing. In any case, that was usually the only time I let my guard down anymore.

I turned around and grabbed the plastic case for the cassette. The cover had a new promo photo of him. Gavin was really holding out on me. He was almost painfully handsome. He had long, dark brown hair that when loose came to just below chin level; long enough to get most of it in a ponytail while some pieces fell forward for breathtaking effect. Coupled with his incredible cheekbones and longish sideburns, the style gave him a rugged, authentic look.

His clothes were rural-chic; jeans, boots, suede jacket. He'd recently started to incorporate more urban-looking pieces; a black trench coat, some jewelry and a pretty cool black leather blazer. He had a natural easy going nature that didn't feel affected. I'd noticed some of the guys who showed up at the gig emulating his look. None of them held a candle to the real thing. I think Gavin resented not always being the most admired person in the room. He better get used to this if he wanted to be successful at his chosen profession.

Gavin was definitely savvier than Brett. Gavin had discovered Brett playing at an open-mic very shortly after Brett had just arrived from up north. He'd been a Northern California farm boy, basically—not unintelligent by any means, just new to this crazy scene. I guess that's why, as long as I didn't look him directly in the eye for more than a second or two,

I found it easy to talk to Brett. I was usually the one to explain what was going on and detail the things that Gavin was too impatient to go over.

Step two (through about twenty) was dropping off club flyers to all the vintage clothing stores and hipster restaurants with Brett's gig announcements for tonight and next week. We stopped for lunch at one of the restaurants we stocked with announcements. Several people stopped by the table to chat with us. No matter where Gavin went there was invariably someone there he knew or who knew him.

The last stop was Gavin's girlfriend Heather's. I groaned when we pulled up. What was I supposed to do here? She didn't like me very much and the feeling was mutual.

"I'll just be a minute. I need to smooth things over," he said as he put the car in park. He was always needing to smooth things over with Heather. They'd been together maybe six months and had broken up at least six times. It was very apparent that their relationship depended on the intensity of constant anger and conflict to survive. Gavin was a bright guy; surely he could see it for what it was, and was not. I'm pretty sure he didn't care and was just getting out of it whatever he got out of it for now. Gavin wasn't really a long-term relationship kind of guy.

I decided waiting in the car was actually OK with me this time. It would give me some alone time with Brett's new tape. I could even indulgently dwell on the new tape case if I wanted to without feeling like too much of a groupie.

After about forty minutes of sheer bliss, Gavin came slamming into the front seat again, clearly more agitated than when he left. This was not unexpected. He popped in a Black Flag tape.

My watch was telling me it was time to get to work. "I have to get to Suzanne's," I reminded him.

"I know." We peeled out with a squeal, I'm sure for Heather's benefit, and eventually made our way down Santa Monica Blvd. toward Suzanne's place. Her shop, "Suzanne's Psychic and Séance," was strategically placed in the strip mall in front of the Hollywood Cemetery. Gavin once told Suzanne she was a hearse chaser. She said that "if you were going to sell fishing gear, wouldn't you put yourself near a lake?" Anyway, we also sold metaphysical books and Wicca supplies so she did OK.

Gavin pulled in through the alley behind the building to let me in the back door. There was a wrought-iron fence between the mall and the cemetery but I had a key to the gate into the cemetery and usually spent my breaks trolling around the grounds. I reminded Gavin that not only did he have to pick me up to take me to get my new car after work, but also remind him about the bar-be-cue tomorrow.

"Who are you bringing?" I asked nonchalantly. He knew I liked Brett but if I pushed it too much he would be certain to embarrass me by saying something in front of him so I usually tried to play it somewhat cool.

"Yes, Brett's coming," he answered, not fooled. So much for my cool.

"10:00 tonight, yes?" I confirmed.

"Yes," he said with exasperation.

I slammed the door shut as he pulled away. I used my key to enter the back of Suzanne's and braced myself for the wave of sandalwood and patchouli that was eminent. There were really many more scents than just those but these were the standouts. I was never sure how Suzanne's Dachshund, Dino, could stand to be in the place with his sensitive nose being assaulted on a daily basis. He was obviously very devoted.

I peeked in the curtains of both the séance and reading rooms to see if she was with a client. No one was in either room. I dropped my stuff in the reading room, which I guess you could say was sort of like my office, and closed the door again. By then I could hear her up front ringing something up at the cash register.

"Do you want some extra candles? It may take several attempts for the incantation to hold," Suzanne advised the customer.

"... OK. Give me a few extras." The customer didn't really have an air of confidence. I didn't know this person but she was probably getting her shopping list from a "Wicca in a Nutshell" book if I had to guess.

I'd never really seen magic work but I held a healthy respect for the couple of serious practitioners who came by for supplies every so often. I had my own first hand knowledge of the other side so who was I to question that there might be other things that drew from other, unknown dimensions.

"Arial called in a list. Can you start putting it together while I get ready for my 3:00?" Suzanne asked me.

"Sure," I said. Arial was one of the few serious witches to which I was referring.

Let's see... Eye of Newt (just kidding), male and female representation candles, commanding powder, coffin nails (seriously), 2 black altar candles, conjure oil, personal candle, Mars oil, brown object candle and parting incense.

I wasn't exactly an expert but it seemed like she was trying to get rid of someone. Arial lived at the Fontenoy on Whitley Ave. just down the street from me. I'd never been inside but it was a pretty cool old tower building with a lot of history and one of those title signs on the top of the roof; like the Hollywood sign. I knew she lived on the 11th floor because her apartment number was 1103 on her checks. She must have a really great view. Her checks also revealed that her real name was Dorothy Long. I can see how Arial would be a better witch name than "Dotty" or "Dot." Although I think she kind of looks like a Dotty.

Just as I had finished compiling everything on her list the entry bell rang for the front door and Arial strode in. She was a tiny little silver-blond woman with wide hips. I'd guess she was probably in her mid-30's. She dressed appropriately witchey; flowing skirts and scarves. It probably had more to do with disguising her hips than anything. Her hair was cut in a severe asymmetrical bob and she always, always had a nervous smile plastered on her face. It didn't really make her scary because I think Arial was genuinely just a cheerful person but I was sure that the smile would remain even if she was unhappy. She giggled a lot and it actually sounded like a cackle when she did. Her voice was on the helium side and she had a fairly strong valley girl accent.

"Hey, Marisol," she strode in, her Stevie Nicks skirt flowing behind her.

"Hey, Arial. I have your stuff ready." I put the bag on the counter and she began digging through her gigantic bag for her wallet. "Are you having neighbor trouble or something?"

"I am, actually. The unit two floors above me has… rude houseguests and I think it's time for them to go," Arial looked up at me from her bag long enough to punctuate "go."

"Are they noisy?" I asked.

"Only at night," was her answer.

"Well this should do it. Or you could just bang a broomstick on the ceiling… Oh, no slur intended."

This sent her off into a good cackle. "I think these people need a serious push. Besides, I'm too short to reach the ceiling." She couldn't stop another series of giggles.

"Well, good luck. Let me know if you need anything else…" I said, then I remembered, "Oh, here's a flyer for a show my brother's promoting tonight," I handed it to her.

"Thanks Marisol, I'll try to make it," she looked at the flyer with interest and seemed to be pleased to be included. At that she breezed out of the store still giggling to herself a little.

As the afternoon wore on, a couple of customers came by and bought books and incense and after Suzanne finished with the one client she had booked for the evening she said she was going upstairs. Suzanne lived in an apartment above the shop. Sometimes she stayed and worked on the books but I usually locked up at night. If she left she would come back down and give me a break around seven. I didn't have any appointments tonight and, so far, no walk-ins.

When my break came I grabbed some chips and a soda at the liquor store a couple of doors down and went back and let myself into the cemetery. I walked back and grabbed a bench near one of the mausoleums. After I finished my chips I dug around in my bag for a pack of cigarettes. I didn't smoke as a habit but I liked to smoke on occasion.

During the day this place would be awash with tourists looking at the gravestones and plaques of Hollywood's elite dead. People like Rudolph Valentino, Cecil B. DeMille and Jayne Mansfield were buried here. But it was past visiting hours for the masses and now all that remained were a couple of maintenance people and some squirrels. It really was a beautiful place with expansive lawns, manicured gardens and gothic-looking buildings, albeit slightly decaying—you might say like an aging starlet, but I still loved it.

When you've grown up in cookie-cutter suburbia— if you're like me—you treasure any places or things that carry history, and the style of that history with them. It was nice to feel a sense of permanence rather than the neglected transience that I identified with most of Southern California.

I closed my eyes and let my mind scan around the area for entities. It was actually a good way to avoid danger. I would usually get some kind of a warning if there was a possibility of that. A picture from some movie I'd seen with some scenario I might want to avoid would pop into my head or a general feeling of unease coming from a certain direction.

Nothing unexpected tonight, but there they were; the brother and sister displaced spirits that always reached out to me when I was here. At least I assumed they were brother and sister, that's how I thought of them. They were two smallish, pale teenagers, male and female, both with dark hair and large, brown eyes. From the pictures they dug out of my head, they looked very much alike. Unfortunately for me I had just seen The Shining and now they were using images from that but changing them to boy/girl twins and making them a little older. I really needed to stay away from horror films.

In the beginning they were rather insistent; urgent desperate pleas to find a way to release them from their self-imposed prison. I would see painful attempts to claw their way out of the casket they now rested in and pictures of them digging their way through the dirt to the surface, like other horror films I'd seen. This was especially hard for me to witness since I'd always had a touch of claustrophobia.

I tried to direct them to let go of their earth-bound connection to no avail. As time passed they'd come to realize that I must not hold the key to their release. It's too bad they couldn't see that they were the only ones that could help themselves. I wish there was some way I *could* help them.

As I sat there and smoked I thought about picking up my car in two hours. Maybe Brett would need a ride somewhere after the gig. Brett didn't have a car; he'd been here only a short time. He caught a ride to LA originally from a friend who was coming out to become an actor but he said he hardly ever saw him anymore. I'm sure he didn't have a problem finding people to drive him around, although I couldn't see him asking for it. Gavin would give him rides but he was somewhat obligated by being his manager. I think it made Brett feel a little better that Gavin was getting paid.

I let myself out of the cemetery and made sure the gate clicked closed so it would lock.

When I got back, Suzanne was sitting behind the register reading a romance novel. It was slow tonight. Dino the Dachshund was curled up on a purple velvet pillow in the corner. "Hey, if you want to leave early and pick up your car I can close up tonight if you want."

"Wow, really? …I'll have to call Gavin to come get me early; no guarantees there… last time for that!"

"Call him, I don't mind," Suzanne said as she stuck her nose back in the book.

"Thanks Suzanne." I dialed Gavin's number and he surprisingly picked up almost immediately.

"Hey Gavin, Suzanne's letting me leave early. Can you come get me and take me to pick up my car now?" I said quickly.

Gavin paused then said, "Actually, that works out better for me because I have some more promoting to do before tonight. Do you want to go with me?" he asked.

"No, I don't think so. I want to go home first before going out. I think I'll drive myself so I can leave when I want," I said with satisfaction.

"OK, fine," he couldn't complain about this one time.

Before I knew it I was back in the T-Bird on my way to pick up my "new" VW. I'd bought it from a Mexican guy who lived on St Andrews Place near Wilton. Suzanne had let me cash my check tonight (she had a safe in the floor of her closet in the office) so I could pay the guy cash. I knew how to drive a stick but Gavin had to show me where the reverse was on this one. "Push, right then down." It took a few tries.

Once I got home I drove down the long driveway and had to get out of the car to unlock and open the one car garage that had once been my storage unit. I pulled in and parked my little car in the compact garage and closed the door behind me. I didn't bother to lock it since I would be going out again tonight anyway.

Since I left work early I had a little time to get myself put together. I pulled out a delicate, black cotton vintage dress with a tight bodice that looked like something you might have worn in the 40's, although it was a bit more sheer than would have been acceptable then. I also wore a full spaghetti strap slip with black nylons that had a seam up the back, a red vinyl belt and a pair of vintage lace up heels that I'd found at the Salvation Army.

Once I was settled on what to wear I decided to take a bubble bath. I drew it hot in the purple porcelain tub. The bathroom still had the original matching tub, toilet and sink in deep purple. I lit some candles, sunk down in the bubbles then I let my mind relax and listen to what was out there tonight. It was stronger when they were trying to contact me but I could sense what was out there within a certain distance. When I closed my eyes it "looked" like colored… you could say emotion tinged energy, if that makes sense. Think of a mood ring.

Julian was there and had someone with him, probably a date. The mystery entity was suddenly there and sending me Irises again. But something was not right. She was also sending me some odd pictures of what looked like some kind of radar equipment and pictures of my car where I'd just parked it—weird. I sent her a couple of pictures of the Riddler from Batman but I didn't get anything after that. Maybe she was just acknowledging the most recent thing in my memory, maybe she thought I was being a smart ass, who knows, I had to get ready.

I put on some Max Factor-style makeup and rolled my hair into a Veronica Lake-type style that would go with the dress I'd chosen and had a beer while I waited to leave at the perfect time. I didn't want to show up early. I usually rode with Gavin so I didn't know if I would have trouble getting into the Troubadour. I hope he remembered to put me on the list. I wasn't sure I had the same virtual all-access pass that Gavin seemed to have invisibly tattooed on his forehead.

At 9:30 I decided it was time to go since Brett wasn't the headlining act and I didn't want to miss him. The headliner was probably someone more electric than what Brett was, but I'll bet more people showed up for him than any of the other acts. I left out the back door and locked the door behind me.

Once I got there, parked and had my club securely in place, I found there wasn't much of a line yet. I'd never stood in line before. Luckily, the cashier was someone who recognized me right away and let me in. It was pretty crowded for so early but I could see that Gavin had commandeered the corner booth for our group. This would be the perfect spot for Gavin to hold court and promote his other client's gigs. Gavin had three other acts that he managed. All the rest were bands; one Rockabilly, one Punk and one Ska.

I squeezed into the booth, pulled out the vintage Bakelite cigarette holder I'd found at a swap meet and dug around for a cigarette in my black velvet clutch. Some heavy metal poser sitting with us who had hair that was way too big lit my cigarette with a Zippo.

"Thanks," I smiled politely.

"No problem," he said with a little too much swagger. That guy looked like he would be about five foot four if he stood up. With the heels I had on that would put him at about breast height.

I was scanning the room, both visually and with my mind to see if Brett was here yet. I couldn't see him but I sensed his presence somewhere in the building, probably back stage. I always recognized his main guide by his musical, warm vibration and I always made a point of greeting him so he would feel free to contact me whenever he wanted to. I'm pretty sure I was the only one of his fans who could kiss the ass of his guardian angel.

There were lots of other energies back stage, of course, but one had a dark red intense aura. I know, I hate to use that term but there's no other way to put it. As soon as I reached out for more information I got resistance, weird, but I wasn't going to get distracted.

I must be right on-time because the rodies were just breaking down some act and putting up a simple double microphone and stool in the center of the stage in front of the ancient piano; all that Brett really needed. I ordered a vodka-tonic from the cocktail waitress and sat back and listened to Wall of Voodoo play on the house sound system while the table conversations argued over this band and that.

I looked up just in time to see Arial up front scanning the crowd, looking for us presumably. When she finally looked toward us I waived her over. Once she arrived at the table I started to introduce her to Gavin.

"Arial, this is my brother Gav…" he cut me off.

"I know Miss Arial. Hey, have a seat. How do you know my sister?" He shot a look to one of the rocker posers to get up and let Arial sit. He responded like Gavin was the mafia boss.

"I didn't know you two were brother and sister—although, you can totally tell," She said with a giggle.

Arial then slid in next to me and said, "She's my supplier."

Gavin gave her an intense and worried look. He cocked his eyebrow at both of us "Excuse me?"

"No, not for what you think." This sent her into a fit of high-pitched cackles that took her a minute to suppress. "I'm a regular customer at Suzanne's."

At this point I was at least two steps behind in the conversation. "What did you think I supplied? How do you guys know each other?" I wanted to know.

Gavin paused, looked at me then looked toward Arial. He looked like the cat that swallowed the canary. Arial answered me, "…I'll tell you later."

She pulled out a long, brown cigarette and one of the denizens at our table lit it for her.

"So are any of the opening acts any good?" she asked.

"That's really who we're here for. You're just in time," I said.

"Cool," she said as she took a long drag on her cigarette.

Just as the waitress brought my drink and got Arial's order, the invisible MC—whose goal must have been to sound as bored with his job as possible—announced Brett's set and he came out on stage. I was glad to see the lights go down because I always had a self-conscious feeling when Brett was on stage; like everyone knew my biochemistry kicked into high-gear in his presence.

I would, as usual, act like it was no big deal and try and seem as uninterested as possible, all the while wishing I could think of a reason to leave the table and try to get up closer to the stage. Right then I couldn't think of one; I had a drink, Arial was waiting for hers and going to the bathroom would mean leaving the room entirely. As long as Gavin kept his mouth shut and didn't try to embarrass me I would make due with my current seat.

One of Gavin's favorite pastimes is to see how frequently he can embarrass me in front of as many people as possible with his insinuations. A couple of times he did it in front of Brett and I was mortified but I completely ignored him and gave him holy hell afterwards. Since then he's backed off being too obvious but still subtly pushed us together when he could. You would think I would be OK with that except that it's painfully obvious that he's completely out of my league.

"Hey, he's pretty good looking," Arial said, stating the obvious, "and I like that whole sort of Dylanesque thing he's doing," she added.

"Yeah, I'm talking to a couple of A&R guys about getting him his first album deal." Gavin effortlessly sounded nonchalant but this would be a first for him too.

The cocktail waitress brought Arial's drink but the waitress never bothered to pull her gaze from the stage to look at us except to check her tip. I decided it was time for another cigarette.

Since he's only an opener he finished up his set after about six heartbreaking songs. Almost all of them I'd heard before but I couldn't see getting tired of anything he played any time soon. Once he was done, Gavin wordlessly excused himself to go check on his investment. I knew they had to lock his stuff up in the trunk of the T-Bird before they could come back and join us.

Since he was gone and the noise level was such that you could hold a conversation again, I took the opportunity to fish for information. "So what was that between you and my brother?"

"Oh, sometimes I sell a few hallucinogens; just mushrooms and some acid when I have it." This widened the big Cheshire cat grin on her face.

"That explains it." Gavin would have left that out of our conversations mainly because I would've wanted him to share and he would be too stingy. So, perhaps the spell casting business doesn't pay too well. Or maybe selling acid paid for her to sample her own goods for free or a small profit. This would explain some of the strange conversations we'd had from time to time over the phone. Most of the time Arial was giggly but she was mostly lucid. Sometimes, though, she would be off on Jupiter somewhere.

Just as I was putting out my cigarette, Gavin emerged from backstage with Brett trailing him. As they slowly made their way to the back of the club, stopping several times to greet people and for Gavin to introduce Brett, I visualized Gavin as the fat-cat politician. He was totally in his element.

Brett seemed slightly uncomfortable but gracious as he met each fan (girl after girl) who came to see his show or came to see one of the other bands and liked his set. He could really have his pick of any of these girls. They all displayed the signs of interest; flipping hair, sticking out their breasts, licking their lips. My vantage point and the loud music made it a study in body language.

As they arrived at the table Brett greeted me personally, "Hey Marisol," he flashed a heart-stopping smile.

"Hey Brett… great show," I said somewhat casually, I thought. I never wanted him to think of me as a groupie. I could only meet his gaze for a split second and suddenly I had what I could feel was too much of a smile on my face. Who was I, Arial? *Act casual.*

"Hey Brett, this is my friend Arial," I added. Brett gave her a greeting none of us could hear because at that moment a new song started and the decibel level had increased with the new Bauhaus song.

Just as Gavin slipped into the booth across from me, a ripping feeling of dread washed over me. I locked eyes with Gavin hopefully conveying a warning and he could see immediately that something was up.

"What is it?" he asked, barely audible. Gavin slid in closer to let Brett sit down.

"It's nothing… It's fine," I smiled. Not wanting to look like a metaphysical freak in front of Brett was my motivating factor here. Of course, sitting next to Arial didn't reinforce that perception.

"No, I felt that too. Something's coming," she said ominously. Count on the witch to back me up with normalcy.

At that moment I could hear them. Two very loud Harleys were pulling up outside the club; no mistaking the growl. The flashes I was getting of were violent and confusing. At the moment I reached out with my mind the information stopped although I could still sense two individual guides and the same dark red energy surrounding them. When they came in they had that generic biker look; one in jeans and the other had leather pants on, t-shirts and vests. One was quite tall, maybe six-four and had a long blonde ponytail and the other was shorter but more buff and had a shaved head. The bald one was wearing sunglasses. Neither of them had any jewelry or tattoos or jackets or even helmets. Maybe the helmets were out on the bikes, I wasn't sure but the one who wasn't wearing sunglasses, the blonde, had dark brown eyes but they seemed to flash a gold glow when his eyes passed our direction as he looked around the room. It wasn't completely dark in the club but dark enough for the glow to be unnatural for anyone but a cat or wolf. I looked back at Gavin who was looking at me with actual concern, like I was going to lose it or something.

Once the blonde one noticed me and a couple other people staring at him he pulled on a pair of Ray Ban Baloramas. Brett had turned around at this point and was looking at me expectantly too. What did he think I knew?

Arial started whispering in my ear. "I think they're here to see the next band."

At that moment Arial put her hand on my shoulder and turned me around to look at her so our eyes met. *"They can hear me if I speak out loud. They're dangerous."*

My eyes opened up twice at big as they were a second ago when I realized that Arial had spoken to me *in my head* and not out loud. I was dumbfounded and I'm pretty sure my jaw had dropped open at that point.

Arial squeezed my arm and widened her already large grin then continued the unfathomable conversation.

"They are my upstairs neighbor's houseguests. I've never seen them in person." She seemed very certain in my head, which was odd since she was saying she'd never *seen* them.

I looked over at Gavin and Brett who were still staring at me and Arial. I needed to break the strange tension.

"Do you know who the next band is?" I said loudly, looking at Gavin.

Brett answered, "Yeah, um, they're some synthesizer band from Germany. I guess sort of like Kraftwerk. They're called Hecate's Revenge." He had to lean in for us to hear him over the music. He looked happy to be helpful. I was always happy to hear his voice.

I could tell Arial was suppressing the urge to burst into nervous laughter. Her face was pulling into the wide Cheshire cat grin again but looked strained. I reached over and pulled one of her brown cigarettes from the pack and handed it to her. She took it and let me light it for her exhaling gratefully.

I thought I'd try to do what she was doing; shoot a question into her head. So I looked at her and thought directly at her. *"What does that mean?"*

... I waited but nothing; no recognition. Oh well, it was worth a shot.

The creepy newcomers had taken a seat at a round table near the front. They weren't speaking to anyone, not even to each other, and sat quite still while they waited. They shooed the cocktail waitress away. Normally there's a two drink minimum but I wouldn't have pushed it either if I were her.

"Hey, can you give me a ride home? I got dropped off by a friend," Arial asked.

"Sure," I said. Arial lived near me, I knew, on Whitley.

"Did you want to wait and see the next band?" I asked Arial. Even with the new, sinister threat I wasn't ready to leave just yet for obvious reasons.

"Sure, for a little while. I'm curious..." Arial squinted toward the stage.

By then the rodies had set up the band's equipment. The lights changed and once again, the mostly disinterested, invisible MC made his introduction.

"All the way from Berlin, welcome Hecate's Revenge."

When they entered, the three members found their places behind their various electronic setups. One member had on sunglasses and I assumed this was the one they had come to see play. He had a very short buzz cut of blond hair and was tall and thin. His hair and skin glowed white in the stage lights.

Once they started to play their strange, intense, loud music I took the opportunity to whisper in Arial's ear.

"Can I ask you something now?" I asked.

"Whisper," she whispered.

"You can't be serious," I whispered back.

"As a heart attack," Arial emphasized.

"What are they?"

Arial backed up from me and looked me in the eye. *"Do you really want to know?"* She actually wasn't smiling now.

I just stared at her not knowing how to answer. The truth was I really didn't want to know right at this minute.

"I'll tell you later. You'll probably find out soon enough," she said in my head.

"Hey, this is really cool and all but Brett and I are going to split. I promised Heather I'd stop by before it got too late," Gavin said impatiently.

I looked up but not at Gavin, my eyes betrayed me by going directly to Brett instead, locking on his eyes. Then I forced myself to look at Gavin.

"OK… Arial, are you ready to go?" I looked at her.

"Yeah, I've heard enough," she admitted.

The four of us got up leaving the table to the grateful few hangers-on that remained.

We all followed Gavin toward the front of the room, through the long hallway and out the back-stage door passing fairly close to the table where the two biker guys sat. I couldn't help but look back once we'd passed them to see the front of their faces. They both turned their faces toward me but the actual direction of their gaze was obscured by their sunglasses. Their faces were expressionless. A wave of the dark red energy washed over me and left me feeling drained. I think Arial felt it too because she gently pushed me forward toward the back of Brett. I was forced to gently push on his back or run into him. This made him do a quick glance backward at me. I'm sure he didn't mean to send me into an instantaneous blush but that was the effect.

"Sorry," the proximity sent a rush through me and when he turned I took a step back.

"No, you guys go ahead of me," always the gentleman. His hand brushed across my back as I passed.

We filed backstage without being stopped and quickly exited out the back door. My car was parked next to Gavin's. There was a spot next to him when I arrived.

"Hey, the bar-be-cue starts tomorrow at 5:00." I said to Gavin because I was obviously a complete coward.

"Hey Arial, do you want to come to a bar-be-cue tomorrow? It's at my house," I said as she caught up.

"Yeah, OK." I looked back at the guys and landed on Brett. I was intending to do the normal thing and ask if he was coming but I just sort of froze when I was looking directly at him.

Thankfully, he saved me, "Hey, I'll see you guys tomorrow," he smiled at me as he got into the T-Bird. "Nice car Marisol."

"Oh… thanks," I said awkwardly although I wasn't sure if he heard me.

Arial and I got into the VW, and after fiddling with the club for a minute, we were off. It was a bit strange because for a while we were following Gavin's car. Brett shared an apartment on West Hollywood Blvd. with a few musician friends and that was the route I took toward Hollywood, and mine and Arial's apartments.

"That Brett guy likes you," she said as though it was an absolute fact.

"No. He's just very polite. He's *so* way out of my league," I corrected.

"Hey, I could make you an attraction potion... but I really don't think I need to," she said, confident in her assessment.

"It's OK. Even you're probably not that good of a witch," I assured her.

"Oh, you'd be surprised," she smiled.

"I'm sure I would. *By the way*, how did you *do* that?" As if to say this should've been our first topic of conversation.

"Oh, that only works on people with enhanced receiving skills like you. I've been working on my transmission skills for years but I've only been able to do it with eye contact so far," Arial explained.

"Well I heard you loud and clear," I assured her.

"Well that's good to know. Cool," she seemed pleased.

"I tried to send you back something but you didn't look like you heard," I said.

"Sorry, transmitting is a different skill than receiving and I'm not a good receiver. You're a really strong receiver though," she seemed sure.

"Hmm." At that I turned left up Whitley Ave. from Hollywood Blvd. and stopped across the street from the Fontenoy, her building.

"Hey, thanks for the ride and the invite. Tomorrow sounds fun. 5:00, right? He likes you!" Even though I knew it wasn't true I couldn't bring myself to disagree this time. I liked the idea too much.

"It's 1812 Ivar; just up from Yucca. You can't miss it."

"Got it—see you tomorrow." I waited for her to get into the building before I drove off, although I pity the fool who crosses Arial.

I drove home and parked the VW in its nighttime sleeping place. After washing off all my make-up and putting on one of my favorite oversized concert t-shirts, I crawled into bed with mostly warm feelings about my experience this evening. Tomorrow would be a good day, I could feel it.

Two

I woke up on Saturday gradually and naturally, without the phone ringing or a crazy nightmare; my favorite way. Slowly I realized it was Saturday, the day of the bar-be-cue. Just as I was going to open my eyes the mystery entity was sending me flashes again; of Irises, electronic equipment, dust flying around, a rat, danger and my new car in quick succession. There goes my relaxing Saturday morning. What the heck was she trying to tell me?

I quickly pulled on a pair of cutoff shorts and some flip-flops and ran down the back stairs to check on my car. I unlocked the padlock and opened the old garage door. Nothing had changed; exactly as I'd left it. I took a minute to walk around the car. The garage was small and had unfinished, exposed wooden frames on the sides, open rafters and a finished, stucco rear wall. I'd used the rafters and added some plywood for box storage and a few things were stacked on the two by four cross boards. Other than that the garage was clean, as was my car.

I closed the door and locked it again. Maybe that entity really was a ghost and just terribly confused. I so didn't have time to mess around with her charades this morning. The entire Hollywood music scene was going to be stopping by my house tonight and I needed to get ready.

I ran back up the stairs and threw my long, blonde hair into a ponytail and started to throw things into cupboards in the kitchen. I cleaned the sink and counters, straightened the living room and went into the bedroom and made my bed then jumped in the shower. When I was done I quickly pulled on an old pair of 501's, a little t-shirt and my old, white vans and started to pull candles out of the bag of stuff I'd bought at Pick'n Save a couple of days ago. I already had a lot of candle holders I'd picked up over the years so I got quite a few candles and a few more tea candle holders as well as some velvet pillows for my couch and some sheer valances for my windows.

When Gavin and I had first moved into this apartment we scoured the yard sales for vintage furniture and furnishings. Nothing matched but it all fit together and into the space quite well. Since Gavin was sleeping in the living room at the time we invested in heavy drapes for the windows. We'd bought thick, velvet drapes for the living room and bedroom and also a pair for the opening to the kitchen. That way Gavin had privacy and could sleep past dawn. I usually left the drapes for the kitchen door tied up to the sides these days but kept them because I liked the way they looked. Gavin had taken his futon when he moved but I replaced it with an antique, wood framed couch with gold fabric that I liked better anyway.

The wall of the living room opposite the front windows was completely filled with built-in bookshelves and had a feaux-fireplace. In these I had stored all my old books and records, my stereo and plenty of knick-knacks, lots of candles and some framed photos. I'd pretty much stored away all the photos of my "family" in the garage boxes but in my senior year of high-school I'd gotten an old Nikon camera and learned to take and develop black and white photos. These days I would just take the film to the lab for processing but I had a lot of great photos of friends and places I loved that I'd taken over the past few years framed in the bookshelves and on the walls.

I ran around to the different rooms placing candles into all the holders and adding tea candles to areas that would be dark without the lights on. I went out front to see if anyone was around and found Julian putting the finishing touches on the little bit of gardening he had to do.

Julian had a proud mother hen look when he was pruning or otherwise primping his garden area. This morning he was wearing short-shorts and Nikes with little, short tennis socks and a light, flowy poet shirt. He had great legs, tanned easily and loved to show it off.

"Hey Marisol, help me wind these twinkle lights around the trees," he asked when he saw me.

"OK... Hey, did you get charcoal yet?" I asked.

"No, I still have to go to the store. Do you want to come with?" Julian replied.

"Yeah, OK. I bought a bunch of outdoor tea light holders. Let's put these out too," I said as I started to pull them out of the bag.

We spent an hour wrapping lights around trees and putting candles into cardboard holders with little star and moon cutouts and placing them all around the complex. We put candles going up the stairs in the front and I put candles on every step on my back stairs. I was curious to see the effect from the street below. I would have to wait for tonight.

Julian and I got into his big, old Cadillac four door and drove down to Ralph's and got a bunch of hamburgers, hot dogs and some chicken and sides like potato salad, etc. Gavin would be having someone bring by the keg later today. A lot of the people coming would be his invitees so he needed to contribute.

After we got back and had shoved all the food into our small refrigerators Julian helped me move the huge speakers for my sound system to point out the windows and into the courtyard. I had a pretty good system complete with a turntable I'd brought with me when I moved out of my parents house. Gavin would be bringing some music with him if he ever got here, it was getting late.

After the keg arrived I had some time to get dressed and ready. I decided to stick with the 501's and exchanged the t-shirt for a black wrap-around sweater and a pair of leopard print creepers. I teased my hair up a bit and pulled it back with a black, thick, stretchy fabric headband. I pulled out some long bangs and pieces around my face and put on some makeup and jewelry. This was a bar-be-cue after all; I didn't want to look like I was trying too hard, even though it was completely calculated.

Most of the neighbors pulled out their lawn chairs and placed them around the courtyard and I put a few downstairs in the driveway where the grilling would take place. Julian pulled a large bar-be-cue out of his garage and started the charcoal with a mass of lighter fluid and flame. The sun was starting to go down so some of the neighbors and I were getting ready to go around and light all the candles.

The Department Store girls, as I called them, appeared to only be decorating their own bungalow. These two girls, Tanya and Polly, pretty much kept to themselves except when it was in their own interest to participate. I guess all of our available band friends coming to a bar-be-cue was a good enough reason to at least pretend to participate. They both worked at the Broadway make-up counter and lived in the 2nd bungalow on the hill side, just behind David.

David was a single, Jewish guy studying to become an accountant. He thought he was cooler than he actually was but family money and confidence could sometimes get you far. He lived in the front unit on the hills side in front of the Department Store Girls.

There were also the college guys just behind the Dept. Store Girls. They liked to dress very conservatively; sportswear, polo shirts, and would probably stick out like a sore thumb tonight with all mine and Gavin's friends, but they were nice guys and would enjoy the parade of pretty girls coming through their house tonight.

On the view side, there was the doctor up in the front unit but he was never around. He was pretty young for a doctor so he must be an overworked intern or something.

On the other side of Julian was The Countess. That's what we called her but Carol Sterling (who knows if that was her real name) was a starlet back in the day. These days she was retired from her union wardrobe studio job and hung around the complex in her fantastic silk wraps and beaded hats. She liked to take walks and tool around on the bus but really she liked to gossip. The truth was she fit right into our little community like a glove. I told her we would probably be making noise tonight but she was fine with that and I knew she would probably hang out with us for a while then turn in early. Although I was never up that early, Julian said she liked to take her walks at about 6:00 in the morning.

The unit adjacent to me was currently vacant. People had moved in and out while I'd lived there but no one had stayed for very long. This was on the no-view; dark side of the complex so maybe there was no incentive to stay.

The Countess had the keys to the vacant apartment so she could show it to perspective tenants so we opened it up for the party and placed several dozen candles and as many big pillows around on the wooden floors. Julian brought up one of those giant wooden spools to use as a table. This would be convenient if the number of people got out of control. In

Hollywood, no matter how many people you invited, other people would somehow find you if you were throwing a party. It was inevitable.

The sun was starting to set in that spectacular, smog induced panorama of colors that Southern California was known for. A couple of people had already started to show up and the candles and twinkle lights made the place look magical, if I do say so myself. Finally, Gavin showed up and parked blocking the driveway with his big car. I was downstairs helping Julian and the College Guys with the grilling by refilling their beer when they ran out.

"Are you really going to park there?" I asked Gavin.

"Yeah, but I'm leaving soon to pick up Brett," he said as he opened his door to get out.

"Then where are you going to park?" I asked.

"Same place. I'm not walking up that hill and leaving my T-Bird in that dark parking lot," he said as he closed his drivers-side door.

"Whatever. So why are you here now?" I asked.

"I knew you'd be freaking if I didn't show up soon and you're not answering your phone," He said as he opened the back suicide door to retrieve something.

"Oh… yeah, I've been down here and all around," I admitted.

"Let me go put these down then I'll be gone."

Gavin grabbed his handful of LP's and ran around the front of the complex and disappeared down the walkway. When he came back he had a red plastic cup in his hand and got into his car to pull out.

"*Beer* in the car? Really?" Dumb shit.

"OK, Mom," he said sarcastically.

"I'm not bailing you out," I protested.

"Yes you are," he said with certainty.

"Whatever."

He was right, of course I would, which is why I was within my rights to protest. He backed out of the driveway slowly and then pulled down Ivar toward Yucca, then turned right.

Over the next 30 minutes or so a lot of other people started to arrive. Food was being consumed and the keg was getting pumped on a continual basis. Everyone had a red plastic cup in their hand. I went back to my unit and found the guys from Gavin's rock-a-billy band looking through mine and Gavin's albums.

"OK, you guys decide," I said as I walked in. I was happy to have one less responsibility.

"Hey Marisol; great party," the pompadoured lead singer said as I walked by.

"Thanks." I kept going back to my bathroom. I counted 12 tea candles in my bathroom alone. It definitely gave the place a magical glow. As I was coming out of the bathroom I found Gavin was back and in my living room with the band. The Department Store Girls were here too talking and laughing and generally flirting with them.

When I came around the corner Brett was just coming out of my kitchen. He already had a red cup in his hand.

"Hey, Marisol, the place looks amazing," Brett said as he walked over to me.

"Thanks," I couldn't suppress a smile. Brett had been here before but not for a while. He came by a couple of times right after he'd just met Gavin and me. Gavin was just starting to rep him at the time. He hadn't been here since Gavin had moved out and the place was just mine.

"You could see the candles on the stairs from the street below," he said as I took a breath to compose myself.

"Oh, I was wondering how that would look. I haven't seen it from there," I really was curious.

I noticed that he had brought his guitar with him. "Are you going to play tonight?" I asked hopefully.

"Oh, only if there's a few people who want to play. Gavin told me to bring it," he said in an offhand way.

"Hey, I brought this for you; sort of a house warming," he said as he pulled something from behind his guitar case.

He handed me an unwrapped album. It turned out to be Tom Waits. I couldn't believe he'd brought me a gift—and it wasn't a bottle of Jack Daniels like most guys would bring. I had to struggle to keep it light.

"Wow, thanks for the um, 'getting rid of Gavin' gift." I couldn't help my big smile and even ventured to glance up at him quickly. When I did his eyes were locked onto mine. I had to walk backwards to make myself break away. I went to put the record on the player.

When I looked up again I found that the Department Store Girls had descended on Brett and were attempting to flirt up a storm. Brett had on the same polite, humble expression he always had when girls threw themselves at him. He was laughing at something they said, though. The thought of Brett and the Department Store Girls made me want to tip over some of the candles onto their bungalow.

I decided it was time to mingle rather than stand there and turn green. When I walked out into the courtyard David was attempting to talk-up a couple of groupie girls in mini-skirts and bustiers. I was pretty sure this was a futile attempt unless David had some musical talent he'd been keeping a secret.

Julian and the Countess were discussing the finer points of silk chiffon. The college guys and some of their college friends had a clutch of lawn chairs in front of their bungalow near the keg. The rock-a-billy band and Gavin had taken over the empty apartment to smoke a joint and there were various girls and guys milling around the grounds. I walked in between mine and Julian's bungalows and looked out at the driveway where they were bar-be-cuing. There were even more people down there. It's a good thing we bought lots of hot dogs.

I noticed Arial was down there flirting with one of the guys from the Ska band Gavin managed. I could see more people coming up from the already pretty full parking lot below.

I had John, one of the College Guys, refill my red cup at the keg and decided to make my way back toward my unit. Even though the Rock-A-Billy guys were gone the place had refilled with other people. Someone had put on my new Cramps album. I spotted Brett surrounded by more groupie girls and other people I didn't know were gathered in my kitchen. I went back to my bedroom, which had a sign on the door saying "no admittance" to retrieve my camera. I put in some fast film and went out to capture some candids.

I went straight outside and shot a slow picture of Julian and the Countess. It might be a little blurry. I held still but they weren't completely still since they didn't know I was taking it. I decided to move out toward where the streetlights would give me more light than the candles. On my way I shot a picture of David and the groupies, also one of the college guys who held still for me since there was no way to approach without being noticed. I went out front and used Gavin's car hood to hold completely still and shoot the crowd at the grill. I took a few different shots there as the light was better with the addition of the city and street lights. Different people would move around and come into view as I waited and shot.

I had a thought to shoot up at my apartment from the driveway. I moved into the crowd, said my hellos, and pointed my camera up at the stairs. It did look great with the candles there. I shot a couple of pictures. I panned the lens over to the left and saw that Brett had escaped the groupie girls and was standing where I was earlier; between the units looking out. He looked directly at my lens and leaned down on his arms over the railing and gave me a little, sideways smile. I quickly zoomed in and shot three pictures in succession before dropping my camera, smiling awkwardly and pretending to look for another target.

"Hi Arial," I said as I saw her.

"I saw that, he likes you," she insisted.

"Why, because he let me take a picture of him? Hardly," I clarified for her.

"Let's go upstairs and make him jealous," she said and grabbed my arm.

"Yeah, good luck with that." She let off a conniving cackle at her own idea, disregarding what I'd said.

Once we got upstairs I saw Brett was coming out from between the units and heading for the keg. Arial saw the Ska boys who'd made their way upstairs and went straight for them. I knew that one of the Ska boys, the drummer, had a thing for me anyway but there would have to be interest for there to be jealousy.

"Hey Paul, you know Marisol, right?" That was the one.

"Yeah, Hey Marisol! Are you coming to our next gig?" he breathed in my face. He'd had just enough beer to be standing a little too close and invading my space. I guessed this was part of Arial's plan.

"Oh, you know, I'm required to go to all of Gavin's gigs," I said trying to keep it light. *Oh shit*, did Brett hear that? I wouldn't want him thinking I only went to his gigs as an *obligation*. That couldn't be further from the truth.

I stole a glance at Brett and saw that he was filling his cup at the keg. I think he was looking but I'm not sure if he was close enough to hear. I don't think he saw me look though because Paul was sort of all up in my face. Brett was looking more at Paul. He didn't look happy. I guess that was good.

Gavin came out of my apartment and called to Brett. At that Brett turned around and walked back toward my unit after a quick glance toward our group. After a bit more small talk I heard guitar music coming out of my door. I excused myself and grabbed Arial's arm and steered her toward my unit.

Brett was sitting in the velvet chair with his guitar and there was another musician on the couch with a guitar and a guy with a Congo drum beside him. They were playing something classic-rock sounding and Brett was singing with the other guitar player. I think it was some old Neil Young song. We walked in slowly and I tried to retreat to the darkest corner of my living room but the whole room was evenly lit by the candles. There was no way to hide myself behind stage lights here. If I was going to watch he would be able to see me… oh well… it was, after all, my apartment. Arial and I settled on some pillows in the far corner of the room to watch.

Although I knew he could see me he was mostly too engrossed in the song to look. Once the song slowed down and got a little bit more intense he did look over at our side of the room a couple of times. Toward the end of the song he pretty much kept his eyes on mine and I was too riveted to look away. After one more song he let the other two guys play without him and got up to go into the kitchen.

Arial kicked me like this was some kind of a cue for me to follow him in there. Really, it would just be me stalking him.

"Will you get me a glass of water please?" she asked loudly as a guise. I just stared at her, frozen. "Really, I'm parched," she grinned.

Hey, it was my kitchen. I should be able to go in there anytime I wanted, right? "OK, fine."

When I got there Brett was leaning against the sink, looking out at my view, like I did every morning. He had a glass of water in his hand. There was no one else in the kitchen; the party had started to thin out.

"Hey." *Act casual*.

"Hey," he said back. He looked up at me then looked back out the window. "This is really an amazing view," he complimented. I stepped up next to him to look out.

"Yeah, you should see it really early in the morning…" *Shit*. That totally sounded like a come-on. I could feel my face turning bright red. He turned to look at my embarrassment. He was really close. Somehow looking out the narrow window put me right next to him.

"I mean… you know… the sun's coming up then…" Brilliant save.

"I'd love to see that," he said with a little bit of amusement. He turned his body slightly to face me. He had a bit of a smile left from my verbal stumbling and looked directly into my eyes. He was so close I thought I could actually feel the gravitational pull. I tried to look away but somehow I could not bring myself to. I was holding on to the sink but I found that I'd turned toward him too. I didn't remember telling my body to do that.

When I started to back up a little he reached out and softly took a hold of my wrist which made me suddenly take a breath. Had I been holding my breath? He reached his other hand up to my shoulder and pulled me closer to him. He was only inches away now. My breathing was becoming erratic at this point.

He was impossible to resist at this proximity. Without thinking about it I was leaning towards him. His hand had slid over onto my cheek and then his lips were on mine.

Suddenly I was lost inside the secret, slow motion ecstasy that was the kiss. There was nothing else. It was a good thing that we were leaning up against the sink because I forgot there was a rest of me until his hand moved from my arm to slide around my waist and pull me closer. That caused me to take a breath and open my eyes. His blinked open then he continued the kiss in earnest. He moved both of his arms slowly around my back and I slid my hands up over his forearms and all the way up over his shoulders, feeling every curve of his muscles on the way. We both shuddered and pulled back for a minute. I let the full force of his gaze sink into me until it burned.

At that moment, the third time, the kiss became more urgent and he pushed me against the sink forcefully. This made us both gasp audibly and in my mind I was ripping all the clothes from his body.

I couldn't see how this could go where it was going in the present circumstances. After a particularly long and deep kiss we took a breath. "There are people in my living room," I reminded him.

"Right…" he barely acknowledged as he was kissing my neck then sliding his lips down my throat and along my collar bone.

I was making incoherent sounds at this point. He then let his lips trace back up my neck to bite on my earlobe. He was holding my head with both his hands then kissed me so deeply and exquisitely that I'm sure I forgot to breathe again.

He stopped abruptly with a groan and grabbed my hand and started toward the living room. I expected a roomful of people but when we got there it was empty and the door was closed. Even the curtains were drawn. God bless Arial. We looked at the empty room with the dozens of glowing candles for a split second then Brett continued on to the bedroom.

Once there, he stopped and turned and we were kissing again, then we let our knees fold under and onto the futon. He untied the bow of the wrap-around sweater as I unbuttoned his black shirt. They hit the ground together. I undid his belt, I didn't have one, and then we unbuttoned each other's 501's. We laid down to pull off our shoes and boots before our pants and within seconds the vision I had in the kitchen (and on many, many other occasions) was a reality.

It went on all night and into the morning. Even after we would finish and normally you would want to stop or take a breather or get some space, I never felt that way and it seemed like he didn't either. We did sleep on and off but one sight movement, any small return to consciousness would start the whole process again.

Early in the morning, just after we'd woken each other up again, the room started to rumble and shake. We were having an earthquake… literally. It lasted only a few seconds and wasn't very strong but definitely an earthquake. We tensed together until it was over.

"That was a metaphor if I ever saw..." he started. We kissed and then remembered why we'd woken up in the first place.

Mid-morning he got up and started the shower. We'd had sex three times already so I was sure he was feeling depleted but once the shower was going he came back to get me. Since we were pretty spent we took our time in the shower and got into the soap and lather aspect of the experience. He filled the big purple tub with bubble bath and we sunk down and luxuriated in the hot water. I was laying my head on his shoulder running my hand down his perfect, smooth chest hair that ran in a V down toward his stomach.

He tilted my face up to look at his and kissed me once sweetly. "Why do you always look away when I look at you?" He asked.

You could not have torn my eyes away at this moment. "I… you… it makes it hard for me to form complete sentences. Apparently it still does," I confessed.

"It was giving me a complex. I thought it was because you didn't want to lead me on… like that drummer, maybe" He smiled a little and let his hand slide down over my stomach and hip but never left my gaze.

I gave him a look of incomprehension. "Not even close," as I leaned in and did my best to lead him on. When I was done I slid back onto his chest and went back to following the pattern of his body hair with my fingers. "I'd have to know you were interested before I could think about weather I was leading you on," I added.

"How could you not know I was interested? I thought I was totally obvious… although I guess I sort of gave up for a while until Gavin clued me in," he admitted.

"He didn't! …I guess I really can't be mad at him." How could I be mad at him for this?

"Don't' be. He's the one that gave me hope. And he's your brother. He should want to kick my ass right now," he laughed.

"In case you hadn't noticed, he doesn't exactly treat me like a hot house flower," I pointed out.

"No… I guess that's true. Sometimes he irritates me in that way. He should have more respect," he said, a little agitated.

"We have a strange and sordid history," which I was sure he knew.

"I know… but still…"

At that point he started to get distracted as I lifted up my knee and wrapped it around his hip and lightly brushed my lips up his neck to his ear…

After we finished our bath and were just coming out of the bathroom wrapped in towels I heard voices from the courtyard.

One knock landed on my door and a voice, Julian, said "Don't bother her. I'm pretty sure she got laid last night," he said quietly.

We paused in the hallway and I snickered. Brett wrapped his arms around my waist from behind and was getting ready to pull me back into the bedroom.

"You know I *should* be helping them clean up." I didn't sound or feel very convincing. He was walking me backwards into the bedroom. I wasn't resisting.

We crawled back into bed and laid very close facing each other; so clean our hands and feet were like prunes. I was sorry we'd washed away the scent of him. I began to look for it in the fold of his neck. "We've washed away your incredible smell," I breathed.

"…And yours," he agreed. He began looking for it down my chest then between my breasts.

"I do have to go to work today, you know," I reminded him.

He began kissing his way down my stomach and dug his tongue into my belly button. He kissed down a little further then looked up at me.

My mouth fell open. Why was he stopping?

He came back up and kissed me on the mouth. "I have to give you a reason to come back to me," he teased.

"Ugh. I can't think of one reason that would keep me away," I said truthfully.

"You do know it's 2:00 now, right?" He reminded me.

Alarm, "Really? … Shit."

I popped up and threw on my Asian silk robe. It's one thing to be naked in bed. It's another to be running around naked in front of him.

I grabbed a cute pair of underwear and a matching bra and ran around behind the tri-fold screen that obscured my extra wardrobe rack in the corner. I threw on a pair of tights and a shift-dress then ran in the bathroom and blow-dried my hair. I pulled the sides back and clipped it in the back. With the shift-dress it was sort of a sixties look. I quickly put on some makeup and tossed more makeup into my handbag. I had a feeling I would need to reapply.

I came back into the room and Brett was up and had his jeans back on.

"Hey, no, you should just stay. Stay here and wait for me," I pleaded softly.

I tried to convince him. I knew I'd have to at least reapply my lipstick.

"You don't have a gig tonight, right? Your guitar's even here so you could write if you want… or just sleep," I suggested.

"You want me to stay?" He whispered through my lips.

"Stay," I breathed back softly. After another round of convincing he laid back down on the futon and put his hands behind his head and gave me a sweetly satisfied smile.

As I was putting on my Beatle boots to finish getting ready I noticed the camera on my tall dresser. I turned and gave him a smile before I grabbed it and took a picture of the most beautiful man I'd ever seen.

"I wish I'd seen that camera when we were getting in the shower," he teased.

"I guess I better hide it," I retorted, but I just put it back up on the dresser.

I grabbed my bag and turned back to him. "I have to go now."

As I started to back out of the room he got up and followed me slowly out into the living room. The room reeked of wax and smoke and beer but I really didn't care right now.

I was backing into the kitchen, toward the door down to the garage—he had grabbed my hand at this point—but stopped at the sink where it all started.

I knew why he stopped. He put his hand up to my face like he did the night before and kissed me slowly. "Would it freak you out if I told you… I love you?" He didn't wait for my answer to go back to kissing me.

"Yes… but in a really good way," I said, breaking away very briefly.

"It's not like we just met," he reasoned.

"Huh-uh," I didn't want to break free to answer.

Finally, I did have to leave. I backed out letting go of his hand last. "Don't leave," I ordered.

"Where am I gonna go?" he said as he leaned against my refrigerator and smiled back at me.

With that, I was out the back door and down the steps to the garage that held the VW. I sailed into work and once I got there I couldn't remember one bit of the drive.

IRIS

Three

There was movement. Not much will wake a hibernating vampire except fire, movement and of course, blood. Lack of oxygen will not wake a hibernating vampire; we are not breathing anyway, not yet. Our skin is impervious to the elements and our temperature is inconsequential.

As I was sliding back into the black oblivion that was my current existence, I heard a squeak and some shuffling above my head.

I was laying flat on a padded, satin surface and was some three feet above the ground on the platform I had made for myself before beginning my self-imposed sleep. I had to remove the memories of the carpenter upon completion of the job. No one but my sire knew where I slept and he would be waking me on my pre-requested revival date.

The moment I identified the rat, without any thought or plan, my hand shot over and had the varmint in its grip. The hunting instinct and speed were still there after twenty years, although I wasn't sure exactly how much time had passed in my entombed sleep chamber, probably less.

I instantly sunk my teeth into the rat to drain it and felt it go limp after too short a time. It was at this moment that my eyes popped open and I sat up to take in my new awareness.

No one had come to awaken me. I was alone except for the rat carcass that I then threw in the far corner. Just past my feet on the far wall there were pieces of plaster and plaster dust. They had fallen from what was approximately a six inch hole in the wall leading to the rafters between my space and the garage next door. I could not see all the way through to the other garage but I could hear more squeaking. I fished two more rats out through the cracked plaster and drained them quickly.

My mind was now expanding into its fuller awareness. Although I could see fine in the dark, I pulled on the string that lit the single, bare light bulb above my head. This illuminated the intricately striped and flowered wallpaper that I had added to my sleep chamber as a last touch. If this was going to be my home for a twenty-year duration, I would be lying in style. The satin and velvet bed-platform was adorned with lace ribbons and a goose down pillow covered with golden silk.

Under the raised bed area was the seafarer trunk with my most important belongings and valuables. This I had brought with me from

Europe and is all I now possessed besides some real estate and what was stored in a safe deposit box. Most of my other assets were lost when the market crashed.

Apparently, I had awoken early. Was it not yet 1950? I'd gone to sleep in 1932 and did not plan to reawaken until 1952. Now that I was awake, my thirst was ignited to the level of a forest fire by the filthy rat blood I'd fed on. I needed to get out of this tomb now.

I fished in my cleavage for the skeleton key that would unlock the two-way lock in the ceiling trap door. You could use this key from either side of the door. Heinrich would be able to unlock the door from the other side once he removed the wood camouflage piece with a similar key of his own. As I slowly lifted the door open and out from the hinges I could tell there were things being displaced by my action. Someone was living in my old apartment. Heinrich had said he would have the apartment vacant at the time of my reemergence but my awakening was sudden so I couldn't expect things to go according to plan.

I silently lifted myself out of the chamber and into my old bedroom. The current occupant had a full-length mirror on a frame in one corner that caught my attention. I was still wearing the blue satin cocktail dress, stockings and low heels with a single strap across the top that I had put on the day I laid down. I had on a pearl choker, a pearl and diamond cocktail ring and my hair looked almost exactly as I'd fixed it on that day; delicate finger waves of brunette hair cut to my chin framed my heart-shaped face and large green eyes. My eyes still held the liquid eyeliner I'd applied on that day.

As I looked around the room I noticed that not much had changed in the way of fashion or furnishings. The style of bed was unfamiliar but I recognized a lot of the clothes thrown over the dressing screen and the men's denim trousers strewn on the ground.

It was just past dusk or I would have felt the pain upon entering this room, regardless if the shades were drawn. I caught glimpses of the twinkle of lights at the perimeter of the window shades.

I had been standing completely motionless for several seconds when I remembered again that this was not my apartment and that perception was reinforced when I heard a clink of glass coming from the kitchen. Seven footsteps moved this person into the living room and I heard a *cush* when they let themselves down onto some type of upholstered furniture. There was a squeak of skin against wood and then the music started. It was like nothing I'd ever heard. Guitar music for sure, but more insistent and tribal than the Spanish singers I'd heard. It was not unpleasant.

During the ten seconds it took for this to transpire I had formulated a rough plan for getting close enough to him to take his blood without alarming him in advance. I wasn't ready for screams and a crowd. I could smell and hear he was a man and alone so most of my plan would be improvisational.

I silently closed the trap door in the closet, removed and replaced the wood camouflage piece while I locked the trap door and quietly replaced the items that looked like they were displaced by the opening of the door. I tucked my hair behind my ear, put the skeleton key in my brassiere and stepped out into view in the hallway. I staggered just a bit. I'd learned from the speakeasies that a drunk, pretty woman could get away with almost anything.

Once he looked up and saw me he was alarmed. "Whoa, what are you doing there? I didn't know anyone was still here. Do you know Marisol?" he asked as he put down his guitar.

"Oh my gosh, I must have drank too much. Where am I?" I put my hand to my forehead and feigned uneasiness. With only the blood of three small rats in almost twenty years I probably did look a little green.

"You must have been at the bar-be-cue last night. Where did you come from just now?" He puzzled.

"That sounds familiar. I think I was in the closet," I staggered. It was not a lie.

"I guess it's a good thing you didn't wake up earlier or it might have been awkward… Do you have a way home?" He inquired thoughtfully.

"I'm not sure; I guess I can call a cab," I said absently. I was wondering around the room, taking in the strange assortment of things, trying to look disoriented. There was a rather modern-looking phonograph on the Pullman in the front room and some phonograph records there. There were candles and framed photographs. There were some white square things with writing on them; I wasn't sure what they were. I picked a couple up and absently twisted one of the little wheels; the Sex Pistols, the Dickies… Who were these people, Bohemians?

"I'd be happy to call you a cab. What's you name?" He asked.

"Iris, Iris Stein," I told him, which was true.

"Hi Iris. I'm Brett," He said as he got up. He started to move toward the kitchen, probably to go call my cab, when I moaned and grabbed the bookcase and feigned like I would faint.

"Hey… are you alright?" He stopped and asked.

I groaned and steadied myself on the bookcase and quickly cocked an eye to take him in. He was definitely a handsome guy. I was going to enjoy drawing blood out of his jugular vein. I could see, hear and smell it pulsing in his neck in that split second.

All the curtains were drawn to the courtyard. Only the view side of the bungalow was open to the city. The noise and light emanating from the windows was more intense than I expected but any human would be too far away to observe anything that might transpire here. There was privacy from unwanted eyes without adjustment. Sound would need to be managed.

I was leaning over the bookcase on my arm and I started to heave like I might throw up.

"Oh, hey, hold on," he implored. The handsome human ran into the kitchen, pulled out what sounded like a pot and brought it back in for me to regurgitate into. I stopped heaving and he put it on the floor beside me.

"Are you going to be OK? Do you want to go to the bathroom or something?" He suggested.

"No, I'm OK now," I said quietly, still leaning. He was standing approximately four feet from me now. He seemed awkwardly concerned and perhaps wasn't sure what to do next. I would solve this dilemma for him.

Faster than he could blink I had my hand around his mouth and sunk my canines into his pulsing jugular vein. I drew hard and the salty, thick fluid sprayed against the back of my throat. I couldn't swallow fast enough. How long had I been dormant? The thirst was overwhelming.

He struggled to yell through my hand which was effectively muffling the sound. Strong for a human; he was no match for me. I easily lowered him to the ground without letting my hand off his mouth or my mouth off his neck.

I pulled him close and had him wedged between me and the bookcase. It was nice to feel a man's body beside mine again; however against his will it was. The smell of him was intoxicating. He smelled like sex. Too bad that sex had not been with me.

My head was euphoric and every part of my body tingled with the influx of warm nutrition. I could feel my heart beat stronger and the liquid return to my eyes. I was not thinking about how much time had passed as I was warming and swooning with the blood until I realized he was unconscious.

I pulled off him and looked at his colorless face while his blood was still dripping from my mouth. I had not planned to kill this human man; he was much too attractive to waste that way. I licked the wound to encourage it to heal and listed for his heart.

It was faint and very slow and uneven. I had gone too far. How long was I really asleep? I dropped him on the floor and backed away. I was pacing silently. What should I do? If I didn't bring him back to life he would surely die without a transfusion in the next five minutes. Since that was highly unlikely, I had to decide weather or not I wanted to take on the responsibility of a new scion. That did not turn out well last time.

But, this human had a gentle feel to him and, although attractive, not exactly my type. Maybe it would be OK if I kept my distance. After a couple of seconds of contemplation, and having made my decision, someone ran up the back steps and turned a key in the back door.

Faster than the flutter of wings on a fly, I was standing and ready, leaning against the entrance to the kitchen. I could smell the newcomer was male and I had taken a flirtatious position. At the last minute I remembered to lick off the remaining blood from my mouth and teeth.

"Hey," he said with a flirtatious smile of his own. The human male dying in the front room had indicated that the apartment was currently occupied by a person named Marisol. This guy—another very attractive male—was no Marisol. His smell was similar to the female smell permeating the apartment; perhaps a relative. "I'm a friend of Marisol's," I lied.

"Hey, Friend of Marisol. I'm Marisol's brother, Gavin," he said as he closed the door, leaned up against it and took me in. "So I guess Marisol's been holding out on me," he said with a mischievous grin.

"My name is Iris," I purred. No, it actually looked like this Marisol had been holding out on me.

"So, Gavin, do you live here too or do you just burst in here unannounced when the mood strikes you?" I prodded.

"Is that a problem, strange girl I've never seen in my sister's apartment before?" He shot back.

"Just wondering. Are you German? You look German," I reflected.

"Half German, why?" He looked puzzled.

"No reason. Too bad you weren't here earlier," I said a little vindictively.

"Why, what happened earlier?" He puzzled again.

I didn't answer him. I wasn't steering this conversation in the right direction. I was letting this attractive, tall, blue-eyed German ass hole distract me from my objective; which was getting him out of here as quickly as possible. If I didn't act on my decision about the human dying in the front room soon, that decision would be changed for me.

"Marisol's not here right now. You could call her later," I suggested.

He was looking at me suspiciously. "That's OK. I just came by to pick up my records and maybe my client if he's here."

He started walking toward me like he would stride right by me. I stopped him with a gentle hand to his chest and my wide, innocent green eyes.

"Is there something else I can do for you?" He asked with a mischievous smile.

Mmm, the smell of this delicious German was intoxicating. I could make a meal of him and not even feel that bad about it. On the other hand I could hear the dying human's heart slowing down and I was running out of options. Draining this guy would only compound my problems and I knew I wouldn't do that anyway, at least on purpose.

In the time it takes the filament of a light bulb to flicker I had both his wrists secured behind his back with my right hand and his mouth covered with my left. I was also had my right leg wrapped around his legs. He was completely immobilized and after struggling for a second he realized that fact and gave me a shocked and angry look.

I pulled his face to mine. "You cannot move or speak unless I let you. You know this, right?" I said a little sternly, but not too threatening.

He attempted to free his mouth and I squeezed his wrists uncomfortably. He let out a muffled squeal.

"Look, I don't want to hurt you but you must not run or scream if I release you, do you understand? I will not hurt you if you do as I say but if you scream, your friend will die and I will be gone before you can blink, is that clear?" I said evenly. I wanted him to agree of his own free will for some reason.

After a second of thought he nodded once, curtly. I let go of his hands and he backed up a couple of steps into the kitchen and struck a bit of a masculine pose. I couldn't help but smile a little at his obvious discomfort at being overpowered by a woman. "What friend is dying? Is it Marisol? Who's here?" He demanded.

"No, your sister is not here. It's her attractive, male lover. He said his name was Brett," I related.

"Shit. What have you done to him? Who... *what* are you?" He looked surprised but not completely shocked.

I considered my options. There weren't many since I would be needing his blood anyway.

"I am..." I opened my mouth a little to expose my teeth, "a Vampire... do you believe me?" I spelled it out, looking for signs of recognition, if not acceptance. Most people knew what a vampire was even if they didn't believe they existed.

"You gotta be shitting me," he said without hesitation.

"I am not shitting you," I emphasized. I was glad this part wasn't going to take all day. "Stay here and keep quiet while I save your friend. If you scream, he'll die. You cannot get away from me," I hoped this much was obvious.

Faster than the German would be able to see, I was at the dying human's side. I sliced open my wrist with my canine and pushed it to the dying man's lips. Once some of my blood had slid down his throat and he began to involuntarily draw on my wound, I looked up at the German who had followed me into the front room. Why was he not more afraid of me?

There was renewed wide-eyed shock on his face when he saw what I was doing up close. "What are you doing to him?" His voice was calmer than his face.

"Making him like me. It was that or death," I admitted, looking for his reaction.

"Why?" He asked, without questioning the truth of it.

"I was thirstier than I thought," I confessed.

"Where did you come from?" He asked, his curiosity growing.

"I was slumbering... What year is it?" I was quite curious about this.

The German's sky blue eyes held mine. "1980," he said looking for my reaction. He looked like he might be still weighing my sincerity... or my sanity.

"Saints alive!" I exclaimed loudly.

"What?" He looked a little amused.

"Oh... I mean... you've gotta be shitting me?" I corrected with a smirk.

The German finally coughed out a laugh at that; then he was serious again. "Is he going to be OK?"

"Yes. His heart is speeding up and once he goes through the process he will be transformed," I told him.

"What year did you think it would be?" he returned to his curiosity.

"My guess would have been somewhere between 1945 and 1951," I answered honestly.

"So… you overslept then?" This was more of a statement.

"You could say that," I replied flatly.

"Shit…" The German started to pace. "Shit…" He must have finally gotten to the acceptance part of my admittance. "What does this mean…? What is the process?" He said more to himself then me. "I didn't think vampires were actually real. I mean I know Marisol can do what she does and I've heard rumors, of course but shit… shit," he continued to pace and observe my actions.

"Calm yourself before you have a coronary. Your heart rate is up to 160," I informed him.

"You can hear my heart beating?" Silly question.

"Yours and his and all your neighbors…" I gestured nonchalantly with my free hand.

"I can smell that you've had spicy food today, you've recently had quite a pint of beer…" Although, he still smelled what I would describe as yummy.

"Smell too. What else?" He asked, intrigued.

"That's enough," I said to myself and my unconscious scion. I ripped my wrist away from the handsome, greedy stranger. He moaned loudly when I did.

I licked my own wound clean until it stopped bleeding and started to close. "I'll put him in the bedroom," I told the German, and then I easily lifted the newly transforming vampire over my shoulder and walked him toward the bedroom at a normal human speed. I wanted to show the German my strength but not scare him.

He… Brett was starting to moan and groan from the transformation and I could hear his stomach complaining.

"Maybe I'd better take him to the bathroom first," I decided.

When I changed course the German followed me. Once I gently set my new vampire on the bathroom floor in front of the commode he immediately regurgitated his stomach contents into it. It wasn't much. It smelled like eggs and toast and stale beer; all tinged with blood.

"What's wrong? Is there something wrong?" He looked disturbed.

"No. This is normal. He had to expel the human food," I explained.

I picked him up and carried him into my old bedroom and put him on the bed then came back out into the hall. The German backed into the living room and let me enter.

"Why are you here?" He asked somewhat suspiciously.

This was not a short story. I indicated for him to sit down on the armchair and I sat on the couch. He crossed his legs then crossed his arms over his chest.

"I won't hurt you. Although I might ask for a donation…" I said as I smiled seductively at him again. I'm sure I would, in fact.

"Why would I give you my blood? I don't want to end up like Brett," he said defiantly, although I could tell he was not impervious to my charms.

"That was an accident. I didn't realize I'd been sleeping for almost 50 years. I'm usually not that clumsy," I said defensively, which was true.

After a minute of contemplation, "So what happened? Did your alarm clock not go off or something?" He asked.

"My sire did not come to awaken me. I fear for his existence," I said with concern.

"Where were you sleeping?" he asked, curious again.

"That's none of your business." He put up one eyebrow. The handsome German did not like me deflecting his questions. That was too bad for him.

"So, why are you here?" He demanded.

"I own this building," I told him, again defensively. This surprised him. "I was near by when some movement awakened me," I elaborated.

He had a look of realization. "The earthquake," he suggested.

"That would make sense. I have experienced other earth movements throughout my hibernation. I usually go right back to sleep," several, in fact.

"Why didn't you this time?" he asked.

"There were some tempting rats within reach," I replied.

"Eeoo" He made a nasty face.

"Actually, I agree, eeoo. Brett was a much tastier meal" I said a little mischievously. He was staring at me with obvious fascination.

"How old are you?" He looked intrigued.

"How old are *you*? Don't you know that's a rude question to ask a lady?" I couldn't help flirting with him.

"I'm 22," he offered.

I paused and decided to tell him the truth. "I was born in 1879 in Switzerland and came to this country and this life in 1898 on a ship from London," I told him, looking for his reaction.

"So you were… 19," he calculated.

"Yes," I agreed.

"You look like you're from the 20's," he observed.

"That was a good time for me," I said.

"When did you go to sleep?" he asked.

"In 1932, a couple of years after the stock market crashed. I lost a lot of money. I was depressed for other reasons. It was as good a time as any to go to ground," I replied. For some reason, I was happy to answer any question he threw at me.

"Do you have to sleep?" he asked.

"Eventually; at least every 100 years or so," I related.

I wasn't sure why I was being so honest with this human. It was maybe because I just woke up after 48 years and my sire had abandoned me or was perhaps gone forever, I wasn't sure. But, there was something about this human that I couldn't resist. He was taking this all rather well.

"So, how many questions do I have to answer to get a donation from you?" I gave him what I knew was a pretty irresistible smile.

"Why should I give you my blood?" He said with a twinkle. So he was a bargaining man.

"Because your friend will need more and I will need more to give it to him. If I take it from him, that would defeat the purpose," I answered, like it was the most logical conclusion.

"What's in it for me?" He said with a sly smile.

"Your friend's existence isn't enough for you?" I leaned forward to answer.

"I'm glad he's going to live but what's in it for *me*?" He leaned in too.

"If you'd like, you can have a little of my blood." I tempted him. Of course, he couldn't know this would be mostly for my benefit. I would know if he betrayed me… yet there were easier ways…

He cocked that same eyebrow again. "Why would I want that?"

"It wouldn't be enough to turn you, of course, but enough to give you an… experience," and a bond to me.

"Hmm, what kind of experience?" He had sat back to contemplate.

"Oh, enough questions. Are you game or not?" His smell was really making me want him. If he says no I might have to take it without his consent.

"Maybe, but…" He started.

While he blinked I'd put myself into his lap, draped over the arms of the chair he was sitting in.

By the time he realized I was there I was stroking his neck with my pearly hand and nuzzling in his smell. "Mmm, you smell good for a German," for any human, really.

He started for a second then his reaction changed to something different. His breathing became accelerated and I breathed in the welcome addition of adrenaline to the mixture. "What's wrong with being German?" He protested.

"I'll tell you later" I breathed. "Don't be afraid." Although, I could tell his reaction had more to do with desire than fear.

I secretly pierced my tongue between my two left canines and leaned in and kissed him deeply. Once he realized what was happening and started to respond appropriately I quickly pierced his tongue the same way. He gave a start for the small pain but recovered quickly. It was turning into quite a delicious kiss.

With all the kissing and swallowing the excitement was starting to increase. I could clearly sense his excitement as I was sitting on his lap. I couldn't resist taunting him a little by squirming just a bit and pushing against him. He was letting his hands wander.

I stopped it suddenly and turned to straddle him, hiking up my dress a bit to do so. "That was for you; this is for me." I pulled his shirt back and sunk my teeth into a juicy vein in his shoulder. He gasped even though I knew there wasn't much pain; my teeth are razor sharp.

I was moving on him to keep his blood pumping hard and fast. I was more in control this time. I wouldn't go too far.

When his excitement level got to the point where I knew there was probably a new bargain forming in his head, I stopped.

I licked the wound clean so it would heal fast and licked the blood off my lips and teeth so I wouldn't look too much like a monster to him.

"How do you feel?" I checked his face.

I could tell from his facial expression that he was trying to come up with a polite way to say he wanted to fuck my brains out.

"You'll live," I pronounced. I gingerly got up off him, adjusted my dress and started toward my old bedroom. When he realized where I was going he followed me.

"What are you going to do?" He demanded.

"What do you think I'm going to do?" I said with an innocent smile. I'm pretty sure his mind was still back on the chair.

He actually blushed with a defiant look on his face, which was an accomplishment. This made me smile wide.

"More of my blood will ease the process." When we got in the room my new scion was groaning and rolling around the bed in obvious discomfort. "There's no easy way," I knew.

I sat down next to him and sliced open my wrist again with my canine and put it to his mouth. I picked up his head and put it in my lap. "Well, I hope I like you, you're mine now," I said as I stroked his hair back from his face.

"What do you mean?" he asked.

"I am his sire; he is my scion—child, forever." He *was* spectacularly beautiful and will become even more so once the transformation is complete.

"Do you have other… offspring?" he asked, clearly uncomfortable with the term.

"I did," a long time ago, I thought wistfully.

"Wha..." he began to say.

"Another time," I stopped him. I did not want to think about burning children at this particular moment.

I continued to stroke his hair as he took the blood from my wrist.

"How long will his… change take?" he asked.

"About 24 to 48 hours, depending," was my estimate.

"Shit. We can't stay here. My sister will be home just after 10:00," He looked alarmed.

"Isn't your sister his lover? Perhaps she'll want to join him," I thought logically.

"NO!" Apparently he didn't think so.

"OK, I got it. …So, where do *you* live?" I asked, as an alternative.

"Can he be moved now?" He asked.

"Better now than later," when it gets more complicated.

"I don't want to know what that means. Let's go," he ordered. Somehow, he still seemed to believe he had some authority here.

I pulled my wrist from my new vampire's lips. He was quiet now and peaceful but not yet conscious. He had so much of my blood in him now that I could sense I would come to love my new child; in the right way. There seemed to be a lot of internal beauty and kindness there.

"We should put more clothes on him," I suggested the obvious. He was only wearing a pair of denim trousers.

"OK… yeah," he agreed. The sexy German fished around on the floor and found a black shirt and handed it to me to put on him while he put socks and boots on his feet. My new scion, Brett groaned a bit while we jostled him around even though I tried to move him as little as possible. I remember the agony.

"I'll carry him," The German said. I could tell he was starting to feel the effects of my blood inside him.

"It would be easier for me to carry him," I replied as though it wasn't obvious.

"Uh… OK, you carry him," when he realized that this was the most logical conclusion.

I picked him up with all the strain of lifting a handbag and tried to hold him in the most comfortable way possible for him. I finally settled on letting his head drape over my shoulder like a sleeping toddler. The German was watching me do this and I finally had to say "let's go," and make a motion with my hand.

He led us out of the bedroom and once we were out in the front room he grabbed the guitar that was next to the couch and put it into its case and brought it with us. We exited out the back door and, after he locked it behind us, we descended down the stairs to his double-parked car. I laid my new scion down onto the ample back seat and walked around the back of the car and got in the passenger side. At the same time, the German was stowing the guitar in the trunk. I couldn't help but let my hand glide across his shoulders as I passed him. He was very much my type.

Once he got in I said "this car is very modern and sleek."

"Actually, this car is 12 years old… but thanks," as he cocked an eye at me.

"Big trunk; that could be handy," I was thinking.

"I don't want to know." At that he backed down the driveway and out into a new world… for me.

Four

"Oh, wow, you live at the Fleur De Lis? This place was brand new when I was here last. I knew a couple of dancers who lived here." He wasn't entirely listening to me. He pulled around back and parked in the alley in front of the back entrance.

"You'll have to bring him in here and I'll go park. I'm on the ground floor, unit 107, right down the hallway to the right," he instructed.

He took two keys off his keychain that were attached to the car ignition and gave them to me. He held one up, then the other. "Gate key, door key. Try to make it look like he's walking on his own if someone's there—actually even if they're not, my neighbors look out their peepholes," he looked serious.

"Got it," I said with the same serious tone. I got out of the car and opened the back car door, which opened backwards like a car from my early days, and pulled my new scion out. I grabbed him by his waist and let his head lay against my head; he was quite a bit taller than me. He was probably almost six feet tall, not as tall as the German but much taller than me. His feet barely touched the ground as I held him in place as I walked.

When I got to the back door of the building I looked back and the German was still there and watching me. I inclined my head as if to say go park the car and he pulled down the alley and out onto the street to park.

Once I'd let us into the building I walked swiftly, but not too swiftly, back to unit 107 and opened the door. The bedroom was the first room off the hallway and I gingerly deposited my new vampire onto the German's large bed. Then I went back into the main room and waited for him to get back. Just then the phone rang and I decided to pick it up. It didn't look like any phone I'd ever seen but it was the object ringing. "Hello," I said genially.

"You need to push the 9 button to let me in the front door," He sounded a little frustrated. I thought about that for a moment and did as he said. It made an interesting sound. I tried return to our conversation but the phone had gone dead so I replaced it in its carriage.

I hadn't locked the front door to the apartment but when the German came in he locked it behind him.

"You know, by locking the door you're locking yourself *in* with two vampires," I teased.

"Yeah, that occurred to me. But I don't think you want any of my friends popping in unexpectedly. Oh, and don't answer the phone anymore," he directed.

"I like that phone. It's so sleek and modern; like your car," I observed.

"Right, sleek and modern," he looked amused again.

The German… Gavin went and sat on his couch as I wondered around the room taking everything it. He seemed as completely absorbed in my reactions as I was in my new surroundings.

"Hey, do you have a phonograph?" I asked as I noticed some records on a shelf.

"Yeah, but we call it a record player or turntable now," he corrected me.

He walked over and lifted open a pretty, wooden bureau from the top and placed a record inside. I followed him over to look over his shoulder.

"Hey that's so…" I started to say.

"I know, sleek and modern." He looked amused again. "Actually, it's pretty old. What would you like to hear?" He looked up at me.

"I don't know. Play me something new," I wanted to see what I'd missed.

He was flipping through his impressively large collection of phonograph records. I guess it might be difficult to pick out something for someone who'd missed almost 50 years of music progression.

He put something on the… turntable… and flipped some switch and the arm swung around and played on its own.

"Wow." He laughed a little at my being so impressed.

The music started to play. It was guitar based with a deep, soulful singer. "Does everyone listen to guitar music now?" I wondered.

"A lot of modern music is guitar based now. What are you used to listening to? Swing bands, jazz?" he guessed.

"Yeah, I love a good jazz band. I used to dance the Charleston all night long," I reminisced. I started to demonstrate a little of my Charleston but he took my hand, swung me around and led me into a fox trot, which fit the music better.

"So, how long will your blood make me feel this way?" He looked energized, to say the least.

"How do you feel?" I asked, although I could already tell.

"Incredible," he answered as he let his hand slide down to the small of my back and pulled me up against him. I couldn't mistake that he was feeling incredible. He was a pretty good dancer and even with his obvious excitement he didn't miss a step.

"Who is this music?" I inquired after a while.

"His name is Elvis Presley," his face was close to mine when he answered.

"He's pretty good," I'd decided.

"That's the consensus," he said as he swung me around and dipped me when the music hit a crescendo. He started kissing my neck.

"I should have *you* in this position," I giggled, which did seem like a good idea.

"If you like," he conceded with a sly smile. He lifted me up slowly and started kissing up toward my chin then lifted my head to plant one on me. He was an excellent kisser; even without the yummy blood exchange. He picked me up, I was pretty light at five foot four, and brought me over to the couch, presumably to have his way with me.

When he put me down I asked, "Do you have any restraints?" I had something else on my mind.

"Um… I'm really not into that kind of thing generally… but whatever you want…" He said, slightly surprised, as he laid down with me on the couch and was kissing from my shoulder up my neck.

"They're for my child. When that newborn vampire wakes up he's going to be *very* thirsty and unless you want to be his first, rather messy meal…" I started to explain.

"Oh." He stopped and looked at me full on. This turn in the conversation had taken him back to the reality of our circumstances.

"I have some packing straps in the trunk of my car," he offered.

"You might want to go get them," I suggested.

The German dashed out and down to the street and had apparently lodged the front door to the building open with something because he was back fairly quickly with the straps, although not as fast as I would have been.

"Keys," he put out his hand for them. I pulled his keys from my cleavage and handed them to him.

"What should we do?" He asked then.

I looked around the room and thought about how to do this with a human in the room. I pushed a chase lounge over toward the window where the radiator was. "We can lay him here and tie him to the radiator and by the time he figures out how to free himself I will be able to restrain him," I calculated.

"Are you sure?" He looked a little worried.

"Is anything really sure?" I don't think I was instilling confidence.

I went to the bedroom and picked up my new vampire scion and brought him to the chase lounge and laid him down. I ran the strap through the metal loop and put it around his waist. I knotted that into place and tied the other end to the radiator as securely as I could.

"That should be enough to hold him until he comes to his senses." The German didn't look too sure.

He sat down on his other couch and after a few minutes he looked resigned.

"Hey, I'm going to make myself something to eat," he said suddenly. "I would offer but… you can come watch me eat if you like," He offered.

"OK, you should keep up your nutrition," I said selfishly.

I sat at the little table in the kitchen while he put together some dead creation with bread and meat and cheese and other disgusting things.

"You know, people have said how we eat is abominable but if you think about what you humans eat it's quite disgusting really. You eat dead animals, things you pull out of the dirty ground…" I pointed out.

"Please, I'm trying to eat here," he said with his mouth filled with the rapidly disintegrating mess. I'm sure my face reflected my opinion.

"At least when we take blood the person or animal is still alive and we can usually leave them alive," I defended.

"Usually, huh?" Again, with the full mouth.

"In most circumstances, yes. Can you say that about the poor pig you're eating right now?" I was leaning pretty far back in my seat by now.

As he ate his assembled creation I watched him. I'd watched humans eat before but I was fascinated for some reason. It seemed like a lot of work to go through for nutrition when you could just drink what you needed.

"So, are you going to tell your sister about her lover?" I asked him.

"We don't know that he's her lover," he stated ignorantly.

"Yes we do," I corrected him.

"Oh… how do you know?" He inquired. I just tapped my nose to give him the gist.

"Hmm… well that would have been their first time so maybe she won't notice," he said, ignorantly again.

"Really?" I said in a flabbergasted way. Men had obviously not gotten any smarter over the years. "He was in her house alone so obviously she asked him to stay and wait for her to return," I pointed out.

"Hmm… I don't really want her mixed up in all this," he protested.

"You'll have to think of something to tell her… and it's kind of not your judgment to make. It's my child's decision weather or not to tell his lover what he is," I pointed out.

"His name is Brett. Calling him your child just sounds creepy," he made a face.

"OK. It will be Brett's decision about what to tell his lover about himself when the time comes," I reiterated.

"You're pretty easy going about telling people what you are," he observed.

"I may seem easy going but don't mistake that for what would happen if you started to tell a lot of people. The powers that be would find you and keep you quiet; take away your memory or kill you," I tried to sound frightening.

"And who are the powers that be?" He didn't look frightened.

"It's not important for you to know. You'll just want to remember to keep your mouth shut," I warned.

"Will anyone come after me for just knowing?" He asked, more curious.

"Only me… now that you know I can come and have my way with you anytime I want now." I gave him a slightly menacing smile.

This caught his attention. I'm sure we had different ideas of what having my way would mean but I had a feeling I would come around to his way of thinking at some point.

The German was cleaning up his plates in the sink. "It would be nice for me if you would remove the disgusting food particles from your teeth." I wanted to add; after that horrifying display.

He just smiled at me wryly.

We both exited the kitchen. He went to ostensibly clean his teeth and I went to go check on my new scion.

He was still resting comfortably; shuddering now and then with the quakes that came with the change. It would still be a while.

The German returned from the bathroom. "Call your sister and give her some reason why her lover will be gone when she returns," I insisted.

"Yeah, OK… Maybe we're going on a short tour for a couple days…" He fabricated.

"Whatever that means," Maybe a tour of the countryside…

"Gavin is a musician and I am his manager. I get him gigs and manage his career," he explained.

"Oh, we had that in my day. You're a mover and shaker, right? Are you in a criminal organization?" I surmised.

"What? No," He sounded insulted but looked amused.

"In my day, men who managed speakeasies and musicians were in crime syndicates," I reminisced.

"I'm just your run of the mill business man," he corrected me.

"If you are, then you are starting out early in business. You must have a knack for it," I said appreciatively.

"That's what I'm told," he said a little arrogantly.

I paused and thought about the old days. "Do they still have speakeasies?"

He looked thoughtful for a minute. "Prohibition was abolished in 1933," he said.

"Wow, I missed it by one year," I mused.

"What does it matter to you? You can't drink alcohol, right?" He deduced.

"No, but I can drink from a drunk and feel its effects," I said slyly.

"Really? Hmm… It would be bazaar to see a drunken vampire," He looked amused again.

"Yes, but it can be dangerous too, for obvious reasons," I warned.

"I can imagine," He still looked amused.

"… Call your sister," I reminded him.

"Yeah, I should call her and leave a message before she gets home and I have to actually talk to her," He calculated.

"Who will you leave a message with? Are the bungalows still on a party line?" I wondered.

"No. They have little machines that take messages for you now," he explained.

"Wow… hmm" He smiled and shook his head like he thought I'd just fallen off the turnip truck. Maybe I had.

"He went over to the sleek, little phone and tapped on a few of the numbers then put the phone to his ear. I heard a beep and a woman's voice. I looked up at him but he shook his head and said "it's like a phonograph," then a bell rang and he started talking.

"Hey Mar, I had to come by and pick up Brett. I booked him a couple nights in San Diego so he said he'd see you when he got back. I'll call you later." Then he hung up.

"I feel sorry for her. She's going to think that her lover wouldn't even bother to call her about this himself," I frowned.

"Well, that's the best we can do right now, right?" He reminded me.

"Yes, I guess you're right," I had to admit.

At that, the German let out a yawn. "Are you tired? Do you want to sleep?" I asked him.

"It's only 8:30 but I could sleep actually… Is it safe?" He looked only slightly concerned.

"It's still early in the process. I wouldn't worry yet. I will stay on guard since I don't usually sleep unless I'm hibernating," I explained.

"Don't you sleep during the day?" He asked.

"No, I can if I want to but I mainly just need to stay out of the sun entirely," I explained. He looked like he was going to ask another question so I answered the most likely one that came next.

"It would cause me great pain and eventually it could kill me," I further explained.

"It's a good thing I have these thick drapes then," he said, trying to be helpful.

I looked at them and considered. "That may not even be enough. Do you have any rooms that don't have windows?"

"I have a pretty big walk-in closet," he offered.

"Show me," I insisted.

"I have the biggest apartment size in the building. The closet is as big as the bathroom," he boasted.

It was quite large and well away from the windows. "This will do. We can tape down the window coverings and stay back here for the most part," I surmised.

"Right… I'll probably need to leave during the day," He informed me.

"That's fine, just lock us in," I instructed.

We walked back toward where we came from but I stopped at the bedroom door. "Do you want to lie down for a while? You said you were tired," I said as I leaned against the doorway a little seductively.

"Sure," He was angling for this all along. He led the way into his bedroom. Now that I looked closer, his bed was actually bigger than any other bed I had ever seen.

"What is this bed?" I asked.

"It's called a King Size." He sat on one side of the bed and flipped on a table lamp and looked up at me.

"It's so big…" I dove onto it and rolled around. So many new things... He slid down onto the bed beside me and snuggled in close and put his nose into my neck. He pulled me in tight to him. I have to admit, he smelled incredible. He was still feeling incredible too.

"The bed's pretty big too," he bragged. I'm sure he thought that was pretty clever but he wasn't wrong. Fifty years was such a long time…

"What's the use of all this space when you're going to take up all of mine?" I teased. He knew I didn't mean it when I couldn't help pulling his shirt up and exploring his back with my hands. Soon I was exploring his mouth with my tongue.

He stopped for a second to tell me "Ask before you bite, OK?"

"If I have to…" He didn't say no when I did.

Five

A couple of hours later I was fishing around on the floor for my under-garments and put on a shirt I found in the closet—I still had on my stockings and garters, my German had insisted, and went out into the main room to check on my new vampire child, Brett. I left my deliciously naked lover snoring loudly in the large bed.

I looked around the big main room. The polished concrete floors and tall domed shaped windows gave the room a cathedral-like look. It was ironic for someone like my German to live somewhere that reminded me of a church, but that was the case.

I opened a linen closet and took out two large, thick blankets. I went into the kitchen and found some strong-looking, silver tape. I carefully taped the blanket over the openings to the kitchen and main room from the hallway preceding the walk-in closet where my new scion and I would be spending the day.

There. This would be enough to create an entrance area so my German could come in and out without bringing in unwanted sunlight. I also closed the drapes in the main room and taped them to the walls to get a little more complete coverage there. I could probably venture out into the apartment for short periods without too much discomfort. My new vampire would stay in the closet. It would be more painful to him for a while.

I was flipping through his record collection when the small phone rang again. He had said not to answer it so I just stood there and listened to it ring. After the fifth ring there was a click and then I heard my German's voice. "Hi, this is Gavin. Leave a message." *Like a phonograph.* Then there was another click and a woman's voice could be heard. "Gavin, it's Marisol… Pick up the phone…" I looked up and my German was standing at the entrance between the bedroom and the main room wearing only his underwear. He indicated that I should just wait and not do anything. "Gavin… Ok, well call me from San Diego. I hope Brett's shows go well… OK, bye." There was another click and then he walked over to the box that was talking next to the small phone and pushed one of the keys. A voice announced "No messages."

I felt bad for her but I decided to leave it alone.

"Let's put Brett into the closet now. I don't think he's going to be moving any time soon. I'll lash him to myself during the daylight hours," I reasoned.

"I'm not sure if I like the idea of that," he looked a little chagrined.

I just flashed him a smile. I walked over to my scion and untied the strap from the radiator then picked him up and brought him into the closet.

"He'll be OK in here for a while…" I said then left him in the closet and walked out into the hall. "If you like, we can go back to bed for a while," I suggested with a smile. I didn't have to ask him twice. When I walked toward him he picked me up to straddle him and walked me back into the bedroom.

We stayed in bed all night, even though he slept quite a bit of the time (humans) I was able to entice him to wake up a couple of times. By the time daylight was approaching, I left my gorgeous lover in the large bed and put his shirt back on. I left my dress on a chair and my jewelry and the key to my sleep chamber on the nightstand where I'd deposited them earlier and joined my new vampire in the closet. I laid down, wrapped the strap around my waist and tied it to me, curled around him and allowed myself to drift into a mindless suspense.

The passage of time does not register when in a state of suspension so the next awareness I had was my German shaking me awake. The light was already on and he had probably tried to rouse me with his voice first.

"Hello? Rise and shine… or rise and dark actually," he said, amusing himself.

"The day has passed?" I asked. I usually could tell when it happened.

"Yep, well very soon, it's about 8:00," He reported.

"Good. That was uneventful," I said, relieved.

"Thanks," he said, referring to last night playfully.

"The *day* was uneventful," I specified.

"Glad to hear it," he smiled.

It was clear by my thirst that another day had passed. It would take a while for my satiation to be back to the level it was at before hibernation.

"Can I entice you into the bedroom?" I said as I got up and removed the strap from my waist slowly like it was clothing.

"Do you want my body or my blood?" It didn't look like he cared either way.

"Do I have to choose?" I took his hand and led him into the bedroom. I softly pushed him down on his back on the big bed and I made a show of removing the shirt of his I was wearing and crawled up the bed to straddle him, then I used my best breathy voice as I leaned over and whispered into his ear.

"Such a big, strong man can surely spare a little blood for a teeny, tiny little vampire." He was such a pushover. I was thirsty but I went in for the kiss first. It was wet and long and drove both our desires to a higher level. When I finally bit down into the juicy vein in his shoulder all of our desires were being satisfied at the same time.

I was licking his shoulder clean while he dozed off for a while. After a time my thoughts were drifting to my more immediate responsibilities. We had an important matter to attend to.

"Gavin?" I nudged him.

"Mmm," he mumbled, not really paying attention.

"We need to find a donor for Brett," I told him.

"Right now?" He didn't look like he wanted to move.

"If we're going to leave him alone it should be sooner rather than later," I explained.

He opened his eyes a little and looked up at me. "Can't we take him with us?" He suggested.

"Hmm" That wasn't such a bad idea. Weighing all the options, it was the least risky. "Is your trunk empty?" I asked as I recalled it.

"It has his guitar in it right now, remember?" He reminded me.

"Right, we can move that to the back seat," I thought.

"Isn't that a bit sadistic? Putting him in the trunk?" He looked at me questioningly.

"Actually, no. He should be completely safe in there. He doesn't need to breathe, it's optional for us. He can't hurt himself in there and he won't be able to hurt anyone else either," I explained to him.

"Won't he freak out if he wakes up in there?" He looked a little worried.

"Probably, but I'll know when he does," I said confidently.

He looked intrigued. "How will you know?"

This would be fun. "Because he's my scion; he's literally made of my blood. When someone, vampire or human, has had my blood, the more they've had, the more I know their feelings and thoughts," I said with relish. I'm sure I had a smug look on my face. I had given him a little more of my blood last night.

He cocked that one eyebrow up that I love. I could make a hobby of plotting out ways to make him do that.

"Are you trying to mind-fuck me?" He said with a little distrust and some amusement.

"Ooh, I'm not sure what that means but it sounds intriguing," I said, amused.

He stared at me for a good, long minute trying to figure out if my enhanced insight into his psyche was a good thing or a bad thing.

"I've only given you enough of my blood to know weather or not you're lying to me… or if you want me; not that I couldn't figure that out without the blood bond," I said to reassure him.

He decided to move on. "So, he'll be OK in the trunk but if he wakes up you'll know, right?" he said to recap.

"Right," I confirmed.

"No wonder you think the vampire who made you is dead. He should know that you're awake now, shouldn't he?" He deduced pretty astutely.

This made me a bit melancholy. "Yes, I will have to find out what happened to Heinrich soon. My scion takes precedence though." I got up and started to get dressed.

"So, do you know where we might find a willing donor?" I asked.

"I know several places but this is the kind of thing that might get around," he responded tentatively.

"Oh, I can make them forget," I said to assure him.

Gavin paused at this. "You're not going to make me forget are you?" He looked genuinely concerned.

"I don't want to…so don't make me," I said just to tease him. "Are you going to get the car?" I changed the subject.

"You know… I love that dress on you… and off you… but you might want to change into something a little more appropriate for where we'll be going," He said carefully.

"All my other clothes are back in the trunk in my sleeping chamber," I explained.

"Come 'ere." He got up, put on some underwear and grabbed my hand and led me into the big walk-in closet where my new scion was still curled up.

"What size are you?" He was looking at me trying to visualize.

"Size?" He surely didn't want my measurements so he could tailor me a dress on the spot.

"Never mind. You're about the same size as my sister but a little shorter…" He decided.

He pulled out a pair of leather trousers and a fuzzy, black sweater. "You want me to wear men's trousers… like Marlene Dietrich?" I loved being decadent.

"You'll fit in better that way," he instructed.

We took the clothes back into the bedroom. I took off my dress again. This seemed to distract him a bit. He kneeled down next to me and ran his hand up my leg. "Unfortunately… you won't be needing these tonight," He said as he slowly unclipped the garter straps from the stockings I had on, sliding his hands down softly to remove my stockings. As he undid the clasp on the garter belt and took it off he began kissing my stomach and moving his hands up over my derrière. I had obviously given him just enough of my blood to make him insatiable. As much as I did not wish to stop him from his current pursuit, I ran my fingers into his hair and tilted his head up to look at me. "We probably should stay focused right now," I said reluctantly.

He slowly stood up and as a concession; I pulled him in for a passionate, wet kiss.

He looked at me for a second then bent down again. He held the trousers for me to step in to. I did with both feet then he pulled them up and buttoned the one button and pulled up the zipper. They fit like a glove. He tucked under the too-long pant legs and put my own low heals back on again. Then he stood up and pulled the fuzzy sweater over my head. It was very low-cut in the front.

He quickly pulled on a pair of black denim trousers and black cotton shirt with no buttons that he pulled over his head and black boots. I sensed a theme here. While he finished getting dressed I stepped back into the bedroom and put my chamber key into the built-in pocket of the trousers. Men always had all the advantages.

He came in and took my hand and brought me into the bathroom. He fished around in a drawer and pulled out a silver hair clip and was going to fasten it somewhere in my hair. I stopped him with my hand.

"What's that made of?" I asked.

"Sterling Silver," He stated casually.

"Not a good idea," I warned.

"Oh, good to know," he said as he put it back in the drawer. Instead he just moved my hair around to shape it around my face. "You know, your hair looks like it's made of silk," he said appreciatively.

He stepped away from me and pointed me toward the mirror.

"What do you think?" He asked.

"I don't know… It's… interesting," I admitted.

I looked at myself from different angles. "Do women really dress like this? Don't you think it looks a little masculine?" I suggested.

He put one hand around my waist and ran one hand over my derrière again, this time encased in the leather. "I don't think anyone will be mistaking you for a man tonight," he said with absolute conviction.

"If you say so," I conceded. I could tell he was getting ready to get carried away again so I grabbed the hand in front of me and led him out of the bathroom.

"You know, these clothes don't smell like your sister…" I said with some suspicion.

"Why don't I go get the car and pull it around back?" He deflected.

I gave him an indulgent, wry smile. It's not like I didn't feel the little pang of guilt coming from him the moment he brought out the clothes. "When I hear you I'll bring Brett out," I let him know.

He handed me the apartment key and went down to procure the sleek black car. I went over to check on my scion. He had started to moan again but he didn't need my blood this time. We would find him a nice, healthy donor. When I heard the car pull up quietly behind the building, I gently lifted the new vampire and arranged him in what looked like a standing position. I locked the door on the way out and placed the key in my other pocket. Wearing trousers had the additional convenience of letting me take longer, freer strides. I could get used to how they felt, if not how they looked.

Once I made it outside, my German already had the trunk open and ready. I gently placed my scion inside and he closed the lid.

"It doesn't feel right," he said, a bit contrite.

"He will be fine… I will know," I said to assure him.

We got into the front seat of the car and drove down the alley to the street.

"Where are we going to find willing donors for Brett?" I wanted to know.

"Leave that to me… Brett had willing donors even before he needed them," he said a little cryptically.

"What do you mean?" I puzzled.

"He's sort of a local celebrity. Girls are always throwing themselves at him," he mused.

"That will be convenient for him later," I offered. He just laughed at that.

"Will this place we're going be very dark?" I asked.

"Mm, I guess, why?" he asked, curious.

"In darkness my eyes can be a little revealing of my nature," I told him a little ambiguously.

"It's pretty dark here," he said, referring to the car.

"There are more lights on the streets now, which I'm finding pretty convenient. But if you and I were in that trunk together right now, you would see," I said slyly.

He was looking over at me trying to visualize it.

"It's like a cat," I explained.

"Oh, huh," He seemed satisfied with that answer. He reached over and fished in his glove compartment and came out with a set of dark glasses for me.

"Thanks!"

"I want those back, they're Persols," he protested.

"So debonair…" I said sarcastically.

Just then we turned up Sunset Blvd. and were making our way West. "Wow, is this really Sunset Blvd? It looks so different," I'd observed.

We parked at a space right on Sunset. I put the dark glasses on the top of my head and we got out of the car. My German stopped to put coins into a metal post at the head of our car.

It got me thinking… "Are you rich?" I asked.

"Hardly," he admitted.

"We should go get some of my money tomorrow," I said practically.

"That sounds like a plan," he agreed. He grabbed my hand as we walked up toward a place called The Rainbow Bar & Grill.

"We don't want anybody who's had too much alcohol," I warned him. My new scion wasn't ready for that.

"That's too bad. That would have made it easier," he mused.

When we got up to the front there was a line of people waiting, I presumed, to get in. My German did not put us in that line but walked directly in the front door, greeting the man at the front by name. "Steve, this is Iris," he introduced us.

"Hi Iris," the doorman said as a greeting.

"It's a pleasure to meet you, Steve," I replied. My German snickered for some reason then we walked in past Steve into the dark bar & grill. I immediately put on the dark glasses. He whispered in my ear. "Just say Hi. You don't need to be so formal," he snickered again.

It was excruciatingly loud in this place. I think the sound was meant to be music but it just sounded like noise to me. It reminded me a little of some improvisational Jazz I had heard before, only louder.

He stopped at the second booth in our tour of the establishment to speak to the patrons sitting there. "HEY JEFF, MARCY, GUYS; THIS IS IRIS," he shouted. They all mumbled their greetings.

"HI," I shouted to the mumbling patrons. I would do my part to adapt socially. My German was talking with the one named Jeff about his booking business and the others were talking amongst themselves. I decided to speak to the artificially black-haired girl sitting at the opposite end of the table.

"MAY I HAVE A CIGARETTE?" I asked loudly.

"SURE," she shouted back. She didn't smile but she did give me one of her cigarettes and lit it for me with her big, silver lighter. This got an inquisitive look from my German. Why couldn't I smoke? It didn't really do anything for me but it was good for appearances.

"WHAT'S WITH THE SUNGLASSES?" she asked.

The cigarette giver evidently thought her gift gave her a free question.

"I HAVE A GLASS EYE. I'M A LITTLE SELF-CONSCIOUS," I shouted sarcastically over the music. That will shut her up. My German glanced over at me trying to restrain himself from laughing. I grabbed his hand and squeezed it to remind him that we had a mission here tonight besides his schmoozing. He took the hint.

"See you guys latter," he said as a means to exit. We stopped at a couple of other tables with much the same results. By the time we had circled around to the other side of the room I was becoming a little impatient.

"What are you looking for, exactly?" Apparently I wasn't privy to his master plan.

"Actually, there's what I'm looking for, right there," as he zeroed in on someone. We strode over to the next table and a somewhat plump girl with bleach-blonde hair greeted my German with surprise. It didn't look like she was used to his attentions. "Hey Sandy," he said with a friendly tone.

"Hey Gavin!" she said enthusiastically.

"Sandy, this is Iris," he indicated me.

"Hi," I said, still conforming to the new social order.

"Hi Iris, nice to meet you!" She seemed happy to be talking to us.

"Sandy, Brett's going to be doing a sort of impromptu show tonight at a private party and he told me to go and get some of his most loyal fans to bring to the party. Are you interested?" he asked.

"Sure, when is it? What time should I be there? Can I bring a friend?" She was clearly chomping at the bit.

"Actually, Iris and I were just heading up there now. Do you want to ride with us?" He offered.

"Sure! Hey Lisa, I'm going to a party with my friend Gavin. Do you want to go?" She'd turned to Lisa.

We both cringed at this. I could handle them both but it would be easier to have one person this time.

"No, go ahead," she thankfully declined. Her friend Lisa was chatting intently with a tattooed boy with several piercings on his face.

Sandy followed us out of the bar & grill and got into the back seat with the guitar.

"Is this Brett's guitar?" She looked as though she wanted to have sex with the case.

"Yeah, actually we have to pick him up first; that's why we had to leave right away," Gavin spinned.

"Cool!" It looked like she was going to explode with happiness. My German pulled out of the parking spot and turned around at the light to head back toward Hollywood. He looked at me tentatively a couple of times. I don't think he knew where he was going yet.

We started driving up Franklin Avenue and he turned left once he got to Beechwood Drive As we were climbing the hill he suddenly got a look on his face that made me think he had an idea. Just past the Beechwood Café he made a left turn onto a small street and pulled into a large, vacant lot behind the café. My German turned around and said "We'll wait here. Iris is going to go get him," he said truthfully.

"OK." She had a look like she thought it was a little strange but she didn't look frightened… yet. She was still hopeful that she would be getting close to Brett soon. She actually had the right assumption there.

Before I got out of the car I turned toward her and looked her in the eyes. My sunglasses were on my head and it was pretty dark in this empty lot so she reacted with a start at this. I gazed hard into her eyes and locked her there. "You know, Gavin really appreciates your devotion as a fan…" I was slowing her heart and breath as I spoke. "What you're doing for him tonight is a great service," I continued. Her mouth had fallen open and she was going deeper. "When we drop you off you won't even remember you saw us tonight," I suggested. Her eyes were at half-mast and she was completely under at this point. "You're going to remember you went to a fun party with some people you can't remember and had a great time. Then someone else you don't know and can't remember from the party dropped you back off at the Rainbow Bar & Grill," I fabricated.

When it was done I looked up at my German and he started to ask... "Have you…"

"I've never done that to you," I said with absolute sincerity.

He looked relieved, then curious. "Why didn't you?" always questioning.

"Where's the fun in that? Why would I want to break your spirit when I could just restrain you?" This made him smile.

"Stay here," I ordered. I got out of the car and went over to the trunk. I pushed the button that opened the hatch.

Brett, my newborn vampire child, was curled up in a fetal position shivering. I sat down on the edge of the opening and reached in to take a hold of his wrist and move the hair out of his face. He was quite pale now and was cool to the touch.

"Brett, my child... It's time to wake up." I was stroking his face and calling his name. Eventually, his eyes popped open and he looked at me. "There you are," I said warmly into his eyes.

He jerked back involuntarily at the sight of me. With his new sight, my glowing eyes and skin would be an alarming vision to someone who was unsuspecting. I kept a hold of his wrist and tried to soothe him.

"Brett, it's OK. I'm here to help you," I soothed. I looked hard into his eyes. I couldn't hypnotize him but eventually the blood tie would spark some recognition.

He kept his unnaturally glowing eyes on mine; such a deep, spectacular blue. Now that I had his attention I slowly brought my hand back to stroking his hair back. After a minute I lifted his head up and his body followed so he was sitting up. He left my gaze for a split second as he took in his surroundings at an unnaturally fast pace. "Who are you?" He asked. He looked terrified.

His own voice seemed to startle him. "My name is Iris… I am the one who has changed you into what you are now," I explained slowly.

"What am I now?" He asked, startled. This was the million dollar question.

"You are an immortal, blood-drinking being… You are a vampire," I said with more than a little pride.

I could see his razor sharp mind was reeling at the unbelievable truth of this answer. I watched him swallow and touch his skin to test this theory. Before he could jump up and try to overpower me I gently took his face with my free hand and locked him in my eyes again. "Listen to me, you must try to remain calm and do not act impulsively. I am looking out for your best interest and I will anticipate your every need," I implored.

He looked both frightened and enthralled.

"You wouldn't want to hurt anybody would you, or get lost?" I asked, knowing his answer.

"No," he confirmed.

"Then you must listen and obey me. I am your sire," I conveyed my authority.

"OK," it was undeniable for him. His eyes had not left mine. There was the blood recognition, the trust. I moved his legs over the edge of the trunk opening but did not stand him up yet.

"Good boy," not trying to be condescending, but assuring. "Now I'm here with your manager, Gavin and another friend. They are not like us, you and I, and you must not take blood from Gavin, do you understand?" I directed.

He paused to swallow. "Yes," his eyes were wide.

"The other friend we brought— her name is Sandy—she has graciously agreed to let you take some blood from her. You must not take so much that her heart will stop, do you understand?" I instructed.

"Yes," he seemed to be giving in to the trust of our blood bond.

"I will let you know when you've had enough," I continued.

"OK," still locked in.

"Now, this is Gavin's car. Do you recognize it?" I asked.

He jerked his head around and back quickly. "Yes," this disoriented him a little and he blinked hard. I held his gaze for a minute before continuing.

"Let's you and I go get into the back seat with Sandy and she can give you some of her blood. Would you like that?" He didn't know this was actually a stupid question, of course he would.

"Yes." He looked at me like he was surprised by his own answer.

"OK, let's go," I said as I pulled up on his hand he jumped down on to his feet and froze and moved his eyes around in very quick motions. It takes a little time and blood to become fluid.

"This way," I directed. I held on to his arm and he let me lead him to the back seat door. I opened it backwards and led him gently down into the car before me. Gavin had pulled the guitar into the front seat with him. Once my new vampire saw and smelled the human blood he let out a low growl and gnashed his teeth at Sandy and then at his own manager but I was holding him tight.

"Whoa Brother, not me, I gave at the office," Gavin smiled at him to lighten the mood.

My new vampire had a look like he was surprised by himself. Gavin grabbed the guitar case and got out of the car to put it in the trunk in place of Brett.

Once Gavin was gone, my scion's attentions were drawn to the girl next to him. She had watched all this transpire with a mostly detached look but now that the object of her affections was looking her way, her expression became a little more interested.

I reached across and took a hold of Sandy's arm and brought it to my teeth. I made a quick incision and drew a little blood while he watched. His eyes became very wide and his mouth fell open as his immense thirst overcame him, ignited by the smell. I put her wrist to his mouth and he immediately began to drink. He groaned with the relief of it.

"Good boy," I encouraged him. I let him drink for a while then decided to try something else.

By then my German had gotten back into the car. He uttered a one word observation: "Trip…"

When I pulled her arm from his lips, the look he gave me was first annoyed then fascinated.

"Can I show you something else?" I asked him rhetorically. He watched intently as I slowly moved myself over him to sit in Sandy's lap. I first licked the wound on her arm to clean it and start the healing process. Then I moved Sandy's hair out of the way and sunk my teeth into her jugular vein and began to drink. I could not see my scion from this angle but I assumed he was watching closely.

After a minute I stopped drinking and licked the wound in an exaggerated way so he would understand and looked at him for acknowledgement.

He was completely engrossed. "Do you want to try?" I asked, knowing the answer.

"Yes," he said with conviction. He was a little less shocked by this new admission.

"Move back," I indicated that he should move back into the space where I was originally and I scooted Sandy to the center between us. I was about to start explaining when he suddenly leaned over and sunk his teeth into her jugular on his own.

"Good!" I looked up with a big smile on my face to see my German was smirking back at me.

"He's doing so well!" I was feeling like a proud parent.

I went back to listening to the girl's heart. It was a little slow. Better to err on the side of caution. I stroked my new vampire's hair out of his face soothingly. "Time to stop," I commanded softly.

He looked up at me with his deep blue eyes without letting go of the girl's vein.

"Time to stop Brett, OK?" I said a little more sternly.

He suddenly released the girl with his mouth. He paused then licked the wound clean.

"Good, that will help her heal," I commended.

He looked at me then up at Gavin. When I began to speak he looked back at me.

"I'm going to put Sandy in the front seat. You stay here, OK?" I said into his trusting blue eyes.

"OK," he said, agreeing. He was instinctually cleaning the blood from his teeth and lips with his tongue.

I pulled Sandy out and dumped her in the front seat—she had passed out by now—and rejoined my scion in the back.

"I can see now why you put the whammy on her up front," Gavin said appreciatively. My German was learning quickly.

He started the car and put the long, black, sleek car in reverse and pulled out of the empty lot.

"You put a *whammy* on her?" Brett questioned.

I looked at my scion and saw he was starting to gain clarity from the blood. "I hypnotized her so she wouldn't remember this ever happening," I told him.

"Oh... but she'll be OK, right?" He wanted assurance.

"Yes, you were very responsible," I assured him with a warm smile.

He looked at me, then up at Gavin and back to me again very seriously.

"Why am I a vampire?" He asked pointedly. This was the other million dollar question.

"Because I was not as responsible as I should be…" I confessed. "Do you remember me at your girlfriend's house?" Reminding him.

"Marisol!" he said, suddenly scared for her. He looked up at Gavin.

"She's fine. She doesn't even know there's anything wrong. She thinks you're on a last minute tour in San Diego," Gavin answered him.

"Oh, that's good… How were you not responsible?" he asked me.

"I had been in hibernation for the past 48 years when an earthquake woke me up and you were unfortunately the first meal in my path," I admitted. "I didn't mean to take so much of your blood but I didn't realize I had been asleep so long and therefore very thirsty, thirstier than I anticipated… I did not want you to die," it was important to me that he understood.

"Oh," It was a lot to take in.

"This was my only option at the time," I continued to explain.

He thought about this for a long time. Then the inevitable questions start to arise.

"So… I'm immortal?" He looked slightly buoyed by this.

"Yes, unless someone burns you to dust," I answered bluntly.

He cringed at that and formulated another question.

"How much blood will I need to drink?" He asked.

"More in the beginning... It's a good thing you have a lot of fans," I said encouragingly.

He looked shocked. "She's a fan?"

Gavin answered this question. "Yeah, she was eager to come. Course she didn't know you'd be drinking her blood…" he said as he barked a laugh.

"That's not right," he chided himself.

"She won't remember and she'll just be a little tired for a couple of days," I assured him.

He thought about this for a minute and looked back up at Gavin. "What do you have to do with all this?" he asked.

"I guess I was just in the right place at the right time," Gavin smiled. He smiled at me quickly in the rear view mirror.

He tried to digest this without success. "… What does that mean?" clearly confused.

"I walked into Marisol's just after she'd drained you buddy. You didn't have a lot of choices left at that point," He explained.

"Where are we going?" He suddenly asked.

"We're going to drop her off at the Rainbow, then back to my place," Gavin explained.

He thought about that for a minute then looked resigned. "OK," he said as he leaned back and looked over at me with a mix of concern and comfort in his eyes.

As we were driving down Hollywood Blvd. from the strip my scion looked off at something to the left. Gavin noticed this.

"You probably can't live there any more… too many people who can't know," he said.

"Why can *you* know?" Brett asked.

"I don't know. Why don't you ask your sire there?" He flashed another grin at me in the mirror… "I guess as long as I don't blow it I'm OK," he answered for me.

"There are advantages to keeping him around," I admitted. I gave him a sly smile back.

We pulled up around the corner from the Rainbow Bar & Grill and I got out of the back seat and went around and opened the unconscious girl's door.

I picked her up quickly by the waist and brought her to a standing position. I slapped her face a couple of times and she groaned a little. I took her around to the front door and flashed a dazzling smile to the door attendant, Steve. "Iris, remember?" I said. I think he remembered me.

"I think she's had too much to drink and her friends are in there," I told him.

"OK, go ahead," he cocked his head toward the door.

I dropped the semi-conscious girl at her table and gave the same excuse to her friends and exited the restaurant as quickly as possible.

When I got back to the car I got into the front seat this time and slid over to my handsome German who put his arm around me. I turned back to my beautiful new scion and found him processing this new information. "Everything's going to be OK, you know," I assured him.

"Is it?" He looked a little worried.

With that we drove off toward the Fleur de Lis with my new scion's first day to contend with. At that moment, with my stunning new vampire child and my gorgeous German, I did believe everything was going to be OK.

Six

When we turned down Whitley Ave. from Franklin Ave. we were fortunate to find a large enough parking spot right in front of the Fleur de Lis. We parked and, although it was not difficult at all to lift my new scion, I was glad we could all now walk into the building of our own accord. There was always a chance that some nosy neighbor would see me carrying him in unconscious.

Gavin stopped and got Brett's guitar out of the trunk before going in. I put my arm through my new vampire's arm to allow him to escort me in. Really, I wanted to make sure I was close at hand should a human get too close and tempt him into bad behavior. As we were walking up to the corridor I decided to make a suggestion. "Why don't we walk at full-speed?" I said as I looked up at him. At that, I led him toward the door at lightning fast speed to show him that he could. When we arrived in one-fifth of a second his face was enraptured.

"What happens if I…" I put up my finger to my lips to quiet him.

"Let's wait until we get inside," I suggested. I gave him a knowing smile. It would probably take years to satisfy his curiosity on all matters vampire.

Once we got to the apartment door I pulled the key from my pocket, unlocked the door and, when he finally arrived, handed it back to Gavin.

The round clock on the wall said it was 2:00; lots of time left in the night. My scion would be sleeping through the days for a while. Since he was now mostly transformed I could sleep too if I wished.

"Was I here earlier?" he asked, maybe thinking he was.

"Yes. You were in the closet mostly," I clarified.

My beautiful, new scion was gliding around the room noiselessly, adjusting to his new, expanded perception.

"I still feel… thirsty," he admitted.

"You will for a while," I told him.

He continued to glide around the room. He spotted the guitar case Gavin had brought in and decided to play. He picked up the case, removed the guitar and moved at full speed to the couch. He looked up at me and smiled like a little kid on Christmas. He strummed and began to pick out something classical at a very impressive speed.

"Wow, you just became my favorite client," Gavin said, smiling at the possibilities.

"It doesn't feel like I'm moving fast. It's like everything else is in slow motion," he deduced.

"Yes," I agreed and smiled at him. As I walked over to the sitting area and sat down opposite him he put down the guitar. He looked as though he had a couple hundred questions on his mind. My German had chosen a record of a soothing male singer to play and joined me on the couch.

"Who is this singer?" I asked.

"They're called Roxy Music," He replied.

"Like that club next to the Rainbow Bar & Grill," I remembered.

"There's no connection there... but yes," he agreed. It looked like Brett was surprised that he wasn't the only one who had questions.

"So you've actually been asleep for 48 years?" He wondered aloud.

"Yes, unfortunately. I only planned to sleep for 20 years," I said.

"What happened?" He asked, concerned.

"That's a very good question. One I plan to have answered starting tomorrow," I answered in a way that didn't actually satisfy his curiosity.

"Well… you know how since I made you, I am your sire?" He nodded. "My sire, Heinrich, was tasked with coming to wake me up in 1952 and never showed up," I said with a worried expression.

"What could have happed to him?" Brett asked.

"He's either trapped somewhere or he's nonexistent," which hurt to say.

"What's more likely?" Gavin asked.

"I'm not sure. It's very difficult to kill a vampire, especially one as old as Heinrich," I told both of them.

"How old is he?" Brett asked.

"He was changed in 1790 at the age of 32. He's been a sea captain most of his life, even after his ascension to vampirism," I told them.

"How did it happen… for him?" Brett asked.

"I guess you should know everything since this is *your* blood line now too. You should be proud; it's a very noble bloodline," I assured him.

As I said, Heinrich, Captain Heinrich Fredrickson, originally from Vienna, was a Sea Captain who worked for a trading company based out of Portugal. While on a voyage to import sugar and coffee from Saint Domingue, which you probably know as Haiti, he made land in 1790. The revolution had broken out and he was made a vampire in the chaos. His sire, Jacque St Domingue—obviously not his original name—was a vampire who lived in a remote village who had come to take advantage of the chaos and kill as many slave traders as he could. He had mistaken Heinrich for a slave trader. When he discovered his mistake he brought him back from the brink as one of us. They have since become very good friends and usually keep in contact when they can. Heinrich still travels the seas almost constantly—at least he did—and although I've never met Jacque St Domingue, I'm told he likes to stick to the Caribbean and South Pacific Islands, but travels to the continents occasionally," I explained.

Gavin spoke up, "So, you're OK with this Heinrich, your *sire*, right? And he's German, right? So why don't you like Germans?" Gavin wanted to solve this little puzzle.

"I'm actually getting to that. And he's Austrian, not German," I corrected.

"So, by 1790 Heinrich was a vampire and still in Saint Domingue with his boat and cargo and needed to get back to Europe. He stayed with his sire for a while to learn how this could be accomplished and put together a crew, as his crew had mostly been wiped out in the revolution. Jacque helped Heinrich find natives who knew just enough of the legends to not ask questions and hired them for the journey. Heinrich also became attached to a large, native woman whom he brought with him and supplied him blood. Between her, the animals on board and the varmints, he had enough of a blood supply to last a long voyage. He's been sailing the seas ever since then," I told them. It made me sad to think maybe he wasn't still out there, somewhere.

"How did he find *you*?" Gavin asked. He seemed to be asking all the questions.

"So Heinrich shipped coffee and sugar, silk and spices and whatever else needed to be moved from one place to another. When America began colonizing in the early 1700's and 1800's Heinrich also began to ship people over from Europe. That's where he came across me," I began.

"My parents were Jewish, as was I, and they didn't like the climate brewing in Western Europe at the time, and on most of the continent for that matter, for our people. The Germans being the most antisocial…" I looked at Gavin for emphasis. "Just before the turn of the 20th century, my parents made a plan to ship me over to America to stay with some relatives in New York until they could make the journey themselves. My father had some business to wrap up. The year was 1898, I was 19 years old. I was thrilled to be making the exciting journey and to be on my own for the first time," I reminisced.

"I was booked for the voyage on Heinrich's ship, the Josephine and would travel in the winter and early spring. I brought one large trunk which I still have today," I continued.

"Heinrich would allow only a certain number of vampires on any one voyage at a time but his ships were obviously a draw to our kind who wanted to make the trip. Unbeknownst to me at the time, on this trip three very young German vampires would be making the voyage with us," Again, I looked at Gavin to emphasize.

"I don't know who their sire was, or the circumstances of their change, but Heinrich says they were brazen and sloppy during the entire voyage; accidentally killing a couple of the passengers and scaring some enough that Heinrich was busy helping passengers forget. I pretty much kept to myself but I was a young, pretty 19 year old girl on her own, so I guess that caught their attention," I admitted.

"One night they cornered me and pushed me into an empty cabin and forced themselves on me in a few different ways," I was starting to squirm with retelling this part. It was still unpleasant to remember this part of my history. Gavin didn't seem to like this part of the story much either.

"They left me there to die when Heinrich happened to pass by close enough to smell me and bring me back as I am now," I eased a little at the brighter part of the story.

We all sat there silently for a few minutes. "Heinrich has since said he'd like to have turned them all to dust but, even as old as he is, he was outnumbered and didn't want to create a scene on the ship," I explained.

Brett spoke up, "What does being old give you as an advantage?"

"More strength, more speed, more enhanced senses, more enhanced anything that you already had to begin with..." I detailed.

I smiled up at my new scion to lift the mood. "In a couple of hundred years you will likely be one of the fiercest musicians on the planet," I told him. This brought new wonder to his cobalt blue eyes.

We sat in silence for a couple of minutes. Gavin got up to flip the record over to the other side.

"So, do you think Heinrich is maybe just out to sea and somehow couldn't get back to wake you up?" Brett asked generously.

It was nice that he wanted to think the best of Heinrich's circumstances. He was family now after all.

"It's hard for me to believe he would be 30 years late by accident. I think something must have happened and I'm going to find out what," I said, determined.

"For someone who's all over the map, where would you begin to look for him?" Gavin asked.

"I'll start with the safe-houses and the Embassy," I threw out there. Here was some new information that registered on both their faces. They both just stared at me inquisitively, not thinking they had to ask. I smiled.

"Currently—well last time I checked—we have embassies in most major cities and countries around the world. There are safe-houses—places where vampires can come and wait-out or sleep-out the day—stashed all over the place. You would check in with the embassy to get the locations. I have a key…" I added.

"Is that what that key is you keep carrying around with you?" One mystery solved for Gavin.

"Yes, we are supposed to always carry it with us so they don't fall into the wrong hands. It has my name engraved on it," I added.

"Can I see it?" Brett wanted to see what he would someday need and Gavin would not—at least not yet. I took the Bronze skeleton key that was forged with my name on the handle out of my trouser pocket and handed it to my inquisitive new scion.

"How do I get one of these?" He asked.

"We need to go to the embassy and talk to the ambassador," I informed him.

"Where is it?" he asked me.

"Oddly enough, it's within walking distance from here. The new LA Embassy is on the 13th floor of the Fontenoy Building, 1811 Whitley. Well, I guess it's not new anymore; it was last time I was here. It opened when the building was built in 1929. I assume it's still there anyway. They put in state of the art rolling metal doors that closed from the inside for daytime hours and had a live human guard during the day," I boasted.

I pointed my finger at my inquisitive German. "YOU, don't know about any of this."

"What? I'm not going to say anything!" He protested.

"No, you can't let any other vampires know you know this information or you could be in danger, at least of being given the whammy, as you put it," I warned.

"I got it," he relinquished. He looked annoyed at being the one left out; the only fragile human in the room.

In exhaustion and probably in exasperation he yawned. "Well, I'm pretty tired. I know that's so passé." He said as he got up and held his hand out to invite me to come with him, although it was more of a directive. I happily put my hand in his but looked toward my new scion with concern.

"I'm OK," he reassured me. "I'll just read or play music with the headphones. I have plenty to think about," which really was the case.

"When dawn arrives, go into the closet to sleep, OK?" I directed. He nodded and I leaned over and kissed him on the head like the innocent child he was to me. "Good night," I told him.

My German led me toward the bedroom but he stopped me at the entrance to the kitchen. "Hold on..." he said and he went in and pulled out a long rectangular box and the strong silver tape again. When we went into the bedroom he opened the box and began pulling out long strips of tin foil and carefully taping it to the window.

"Brett's a big boy now. You can stay and snuggle with me now instead," he decided possessively. I just smiled at him, happy to be possessed.

While he papered the windows with tin, I pulled my safe-house key from my pocket and put it on the nightstand, pulled off my shoes, the leather pants and fuzzy sweater then laid down and stretched on the very large bed in my underwear. When Gavin was finished he removed all his clothes except his underwear and lay down to face me. His kiss was very long and sweet.

"I want to be like you," he said to me, his face so close to mine. It sounded more like a wish than a request, although I knew he meant for me to change him.

I pushed my nose into the fold of his neck and breathed in deeply. "Don't take this luscious blood away from me yet," I pleaded.

I was running my tongue and lips along the top of his shoulder where I had taken blood from him earlier; the marks were almost invisible now. "Do vampires drink from other vampires?" He asked.

"Yes, but it won't sustain us… it *is* very bonding…" I admitted.

"So bond with me…" he insisted. His heart rate was increasing and he was pushing his pulsing neck toward my thirsty mouth. He was doing to me what I'd done to him; taunting me.

"I won't be the one to change you… it doesn't work if we want to stay together," I warned.

"Why not?" He sounded like a spoiled child who wasn't getting his way.

"There's too much control for the sire. I would end up knowing everything you're thinking, feeling, I could control you if I wanted…" Not that I couldn't control what he was feeling right now.

"Hmm, so maybe Brett can do it?" he suggested.

"He's too young. It's not a good idea," I vetoed.

"So just…" he started to maneuver.

"Wait, don't rush. Give me a little more time with you like this. You have a choice, I didn't. Take your time and think about it," I advised.

He grumbled but let it drop… for now. I had also succeeded in distracting the lower half of his body by this time. If he was determined I would want to enjoy his human blood while I could. So I did.

Seven

After a perfect day of waiting for the sun to set, encapsulated in my lover's bedroom with the very large bed, the evening started out with a surprise.

After making love early in the morning, and once more mid-day, Gavin and I talked and told stories from our lives that were completely divergent, yet not really that different. He related stories about his childhood; including how he discovered he had a sister in his teens and the fractured family that formed him. He told me of his pursuits in music and how he had devised ways to make money using what he had; which was his natural charisma, but he didn't put it that way. He told me of crazy, funny things that had happened while on the road with his musicians, although I'm sure leaving out some of his more philandering pursuits.

I'd told many of my stories including before I was changed into the vampire I am today; my parents dreams for me, my dreams for myself. I told of the fun I'd had during prohibition, frequenting the Jazz clubs and speakeasies and the friends I had. I left out details of former lovers as well, although my lack of chastity did not seem to be a concern for him. This was not usually the case fifty years ago. In that respect, times must have changed. I also skirted over the darkest days of my betrayal, not wanting to dip the mood below the blissful perfection we had achieved for the day.

That perfect mood came to an abrupt halt just before dusk with a knock on the front door. At that particular moment, I had my teeth sunk into Gavin's delicious femoral artery; I'd finally gotten him to agree. Without letting go I looked up at his questioning face. After a minute he widened his eyes as if to say I'd have to let go for him to see who it was. I did so very reluctantly, though I tried to do a good job of sealing it off so that I might get another opportunity soon.

I stayed in the bedroom as he threw on a pair of jeans and went to the door. He closed the door tight but I got dressed in the meantime and sat down to listen. Brett was in the closet but that area was not visible from the front threshold. Of course, I could hear everything as if I was standing right there next to him.

"Heather!" I did know that name by now. Out of respect we didn't go into detail about our former lovers but we sketched the outlines of our most recent relationships, not that anything was recent for me. He'd mentioned her as someone he'd dated on and off for the past few months but that she was not important to him. We never touched on that we were exclusive now; especially since it had only been a few days, but if a new relationship had promise, I believe we had that.

"Hey, baby," she said with a little testiness in her voice. There was a short, pregnant pause, "aren't you going to invite me in?" She asked sounding annoyed.

"Um… sure…" Gavin responded. I could hear her stomp in. *Baby, huh*? The sound of her voice and her carriage made me believe she must be angry. Could she know I was here? I got up and stood at the foot of the bed, ready.

"So, Marcy came by the shop today… She said you were at the Rainbow last night," she said with venom. Oops. Oh well, this would get her out of the way sooner, thankfully.

"Yeah, I was going to call you tonight," Gavin said weakly. Some silence passed.

Gavin went on, "I, uh… I need to be fair to you," he stammered. His voice had moved further into the main room.

"You want to be fair huh?" her voice had escalated. A second later I heard something crash into the wall. "Yeah, let's talk about fair!" she shouted. I could hear her heart was racing and lots of adrenaline had made its way into her bloodstream, and also Gavin's.

Why not? I decided to make my entrance. I could feel the sun had set now. I opened the bedroom door and walked out into the main room. The moment I arrived the bitch hurled something toward my face. I caught it with my left hand. It was an ashtray made of some type of marble. This made me angry. What if I was a human and it had hit me in the head.

She was startled; not only to see me, but to see I'd caught the item she had flung in her fury. I, of course, was completely calm.

"Please don't break Gavin's things," I said calmly, although I was fighting the urge to fling the ashtray right back; and I would not miss.

"Who the fuck are you?" Classy.

"My name is Iris. Who… are you?" I said evenly. I thought about swearing back at her but I decided I was above that, although I already knew who she was, of course.

"I'm Gavin's *girlfriend*, Heather." She said to me then looked over at Gavin and screamed, "Why is she wearing my clothes?" This brought new rage. Gavin was rapidly losing control of the situation, not that he'd ever had it.

I could tell he wasn't sure how to answer this so I responded, "oh, are these yours?" I said innocently, and then began to strip off the pants and sweater in question, dropping them in a pile on the floor, adding a distasteful look to my face as I did. I don't think it helped her mood to see my comfort at being in a state of undress in front of *her* boyfriend.

She fumed at him before she stomped toward the clothes, "it's so over!" she picked up the clothes on the floor. "I want the rest of my stuff too." By this time she was weeping and screeching. She kept on going toward the closet. "What's with all the blankets and tape anyway!"

I'm not exactly sure why it didn't occur to me to stop her before she was headed into the closet and toward Brett, my brand new thirsty scion. I guess I had it in my mind to let her get it out of her system. She actually did have some cause to be upset. But once she had ripped off the makeshift curtain to the closet, Brett was on her before I could stop it. The fresh heartbeat and the smell of the blood and adrenaline must have overwhelmed him.

He's sunk his canines into her jugular viciously and was straining to get as much down his throat as fast as he could. She let out a silent scream as he's placed his thumb over her voice box and held it there. She made gurgling, chocking sounds. I hadn't even taught him that yet.

"Stop him!" Gavin yelled helplessly.

"Brett, Brett, look at me," I implored. His eyes were rolling into the back of his head as he swooned with his second meal.

I snapped at him harder, "Brett! Don't kill her, *Brett*!"

"Back off!" I turned and shouted at Gavin, who was getting a little too close. I didn't want Brett to make an exchange. I think he heard me loud and clear since he did so immediately.

"Brett!" I grabbed a handful of hair and pulled him up enough to make eye contact. "Obey me," I told him evenly.

Once he locked eyes with me, it took a second but his jaws opened and he let go of Heather and dropped her on the ground. She'd passed out by now but it sounded like her heart was pumping enough blood to get her through this.

Realization crossed over Brett's face as the full gravity of his actions dawned on him. As his facial expression started to cross into self-loathing I tried to stop the descent. "It's OK. It's not your fault, it's my fault. I should've stopped her sooner… You can't be blamed and you stopped in time," I rushed out all at once. Then I said, "She's going to be OK," as I looked up at Gavin and his face changed from terror to some relief.

When I looked back at my scion he'd backed into the furthest corner of the closet faster than a human's eyes would be able to see. He seemed disgusted with himself. Still, it was a good idea for him to remove himself from the situation.

"You'll gain more self-control with time," I tried to assure him.

"How much time?" Brett asked, heavy with humiliation.

"Yeah, how much time?" Gavin asked, still looking pretty alarmed with the recent events. "What are we going to do about Heather?" He shouted at me.

It hurt to hear him say her name. I stood up and turned around to face Gavin. "I'd be happy to finish up what Brett started," I charged. "You know, you're not exactly blameless here," I told him. I was fuming. He was trying to stay serious but his face was straining to not smile. I guess it might be hard to take me seriously while I was standing there in my underwear. He attempted to get back on my good side at that point.

"So, I need your help, baby? What should we do?" he said as sweetly as he could. I could tell he was thinking about approaching me but only wavered.

I whizzed back into the bedroom and put back on my dress, grabbed all my things and was back in the room in approximately three seconds; and that included stockings.

"It seems we have quite a large agenda for this evening so we'd better get a move on." I softened a bit. I guess I should try to let it go. "Gavin, you should get all her things together and we can drop her at her apartment once she wakes up. I'll make her forget," I conceded.

"Can you make her forget a few other things?" He said opportunistically.

"What do you want me to tell her?" I said with a sigh.

"Just tell her that she broke up with me a couple of days ago and that maybe she came by earlier and got her clothes." Hmm… that was actually kind of gallant. He was making it hard to stay mad.

"OK… Does she have a key?" I said with some suspicion.

"No," he protested like it was a silly question, but then he looked a little sheepish. "OK… she may have a building key." He opened her purse which was still sitting by the door and fished out her keychain and removed the one that was his. I picked up the girl, licked off the extra blood and set her down on the chase lounge. We met in the center of the room. He took me by the waist when we got close enough and looked into my eyes seriously.

"Look baby, how could I know I was going to meet someone like you?" He already knew how to get to me.

I pouted a little bit. "I know," I admitted but now I would have to arrange my day around the ex. Oh well, at least she was the ex.

I let him kiss me to close the discussion. He made it a good one.

I nodded my head toward the closet to let him know I had something else to worry about. I wandered into the closet and let myself down opposite my new vampire and looked into his deep blue eyes. He was sulking with his face in his hands. I stayed there silently for a minute to let the blood tie sink in a bit and I hoped it would gave him some reassurance.

"You know, it won't be this bad always. In a couple months you'll be able to control yourself even if you haven't fed for the day and in a couple of years you won't even need to feed every day," I hoped I sounded encouraging.

He wasn't ready to respond yet.

"In the meantime, we'll make sure to find you your meal first thing in the evening so you can feel somewhat normal and very soon you'll be able to be around people as long as you've fed," I assured him.

"How soon? He's got gigs," Gavin asked from a couple of steps outside the closet door.

"We'll work on that, first things first. Go get washed up and get dressed." He looked at us then took another look at his unconscious ex-girlfriend and quickly took my advice. I would've liked to take a shower too, of course I didn't need to; I don't sweat and neither does Brett now, but it feels nice and sometimes dirt or blood does get into my hair or on my skin. But neither of us had changes of clothes and we had a full agenda for the evening. So once Gavin was dressed and Brett had put back on his clothes we prepared to leave.

Gavin went down and pulled the T-Bird around to the rear entrance and once I heard him pull up, I pulled Heather up to a standing position, told Brett to go on ahead of me and locked the door once again with the spare key Gavin gave me to show my importance over Heather. I also inherited Heather's building key. I found a key ring in one of the kitchen drawers and put the house keys and my safe-house key on it together. If your collection of keys symbolizes your life then mine was starting to come together.

Brett was in the back seat and I put Heather down on the front seat and Gavin strapped her in with the seatbelt, then I got into the back with Brett. I lifted his arm and put it around me, attempting to give him a comforting look. He gave me an appreciative look back. Gavin drove down toward Hollywood Blvd. and took a right. By the time we got to Highland Ave. Heather was starting to come around. I started chatting mid-story like I'd been talking for some time. "So anyway, there we were and no cab in sight… well, we were a sorry sight!"

"Well hey, are you feeling better?" I had interlaced my hand with the one Brett had draped over my shoulder. I leaned over and looked into her eyes. "Remember, we met when you stopped by Gavin's to get your stuff." Her gaze was immediately locked since she'd never gotten the chance to get her will back so I started right in with the lie she would believe. "You'd broken up with Gavin the night before over the phone, you'd just had *enough*, and stopped by this evening to get your things. You won't remember me or Brett being there, or us dropping you off but Gavin understood and now you can both move on," I said convincingly. I looked over and smiled at my sexy new boyfriend; I think I can call him that now.

Once we got to Heather's house, Gavin got the bag with her stuff from the trunk where he'd put it and walked her to the door. Once she was on the doorstep he gave her a quick kiss on the cheek and turned and came back to the car. He may have been worried that she would remember that but I gave her explicit instructions so she wouldn't. I'm glad he wasn't crass about it. I hoped her wounds would heal quickly enough so she or someone else wouldn't notice them. Brett was pretty savage but I put in a lot of healing time afterwards.

Once Gavin was in the car I moved into the front seat with him. He grabbed my hand and kissed it and said "where to?"

"Your sister's house," I said immediately. This had them both startled, for different reasons.

I sighed, "If you must know, my sleeping chamber, and all my stuff, is in a secret enclosed room behind your sister's garage. There's a trap door in her closet," I confessed. I got stunned looks with this.

"Well, that explains a lot," Gavin said. The look on Brett's face said he agreed. Then we sped off towards the bungalows at Yucca & Ivar.

We pulled over on the way to make sure his sister was at work and not in her apartment. He phoned her at work from a payphone. She was there and it sounded like she had a lot of questions, I couldn't blame her. Ever since I'd named our destination Brett had an increasing look of misery seeping into his expression. Even though we'd stayed in the car, we could, of course, hear both sides of the conversation they were having and this seemed to deepen the misery for him. She was asking about Brett and, even though she didn't say it specifically, there was the lingering question of why he had not called her himself.

"You know, you can *call* her without there being a danger," I encouraged him.

"I know… I want to, of course, but I'm not sure what I should say," he looked conflicted.

"Personally, I think we should bring her into our confidence. It's not like she could stand to lose you *and* become estranged from her brother too; which is what would eventually happen if we stay together and she stayed in the dark," I said logically.

"I can't stand the thought of losing her… we just found each other… but I don't want to inflict myself on her like this. Not after my behavior today…" I could see he was still deeply ashamed of what happened with Heather and the thought of losing control with someone he truly cared about was tormenting him.

I wasn't sure what I could say to comfort him. "Don't worry. I'm going to help you get a handle on your new life. I promise… Then *soon*, we'll find a way for you to be together…" I was feeling resolved about this.

Gavin was getting into the car and heard the tail end of that. He gave us a disapproving look. "No way, man," he frowned at Brett.

Brett wasn't going to argue with him but I would. "Why not? Once he's under control it shouldn't be a problem," I argued.

"No way. She's not like me, or you," he said to me. She's… kind of, you know…"

"Yeah, I'm sure she's not like you, or like me. She's probably more like him," I indicated the miserable new vampire slumping into the corner in the back seat.

I could tell he didn't want to have this conversation. "It's OK for you but not for her?" I was feeling a bit incredulous now.

His lack of response and facial expression was telling me that this conversation was over.

"This conversation is not over," I said defiantly, since he was going to let me have the last word anyway.

We pulled up and parked blocking the garage that was the façade for my home for the past approximately 50 years and climbed the back stairs to my old apartment.

Once we were inside we headed straight for the bedroom. Gavin sat on the low bed and Brett lingered in the doorway. I moved away the things that were strewn on the floor of the closet, removed the wood circle that hid the lock and used the key that fit, not only my hiding place but all the safe-houses around the world.

I gracefully let myself down onto the bed platform, then down onto the floor and pulled the trunk forward to open it. Until I had a permanent place of my own or had officially moved in with Gavin I would leave it here.

"Can you drop down the bag?" I had borrowed a cloth duffle bag from Gavin and he'd brought it in. Instead of the bag, Gavin dropped himself onto the bed platform, a little less gracefully but still impressively, and was surprised at what he found. He looked approving until he noticed the rotting rat corpses in the corner.

"Sorry, I didn't have time to tidy up."

He handed me the bag but stayed up on the bunk because there wasn't much room and I'm sure the rats smelled almost as foul to him as they did to me. I opened up the trunk, which was quite large and very old, and started to load some clothes and shoes into the duffle. I also opened up a paper bag that was stuffed into the bottom of the trunk and loaded in some bundles of cash. When I looked up at my gorgeous German he gave me the eyebrow again and I gave it back to him with a smile.

"Look how much I trust you… You can come down here and rob me blind anytime you want now," I teased.

"Yeah, but then you could pretty much find me anytime you want and drain me dry like those poor rats in the corner." He didn't look like he was in fear for his life.

"That reminds me… why were you not scared or skeptical when you first found out what I am?" I was curious.

He caught the duffle as I swung it up to him then I swung myself up and let him catch me. "Well, first of all, your demonstration skills are pretty explicit…" He started doing a little demonstrating of his own.

After a minute, "also, I have a friend who insisted that vampires were real and that she knew some. 'Course she was high on acid when she told me those things but she had quite a description," he admitted.

"Hmm," I guess that made sense, although I wasn't sure what acid was.

"She told me she was a witch," he added.

"Oh, a witch, that explains it," I said.

"So you're saying that she really is a witch?" Gavin asked.

"I don't know if she herself is a witch but there are real witches, of course. I suspect if she has knowledge of vampires she must have something going on," I surmised.

"Interesting… My sister should know about that," he noted.

"You said your sister communicates with spirits, right?" I remembered.

"Yeah, all her life," he responded.

"Maybe she should look into witchcraft, but if she became a vampire her psychic strength would instantly be enhanced," I thought he should know.

He gave me a look like he wasn't going there again. Then he said "are you ready to go?"

"Yes," I sighed. He then reached up and pulled himself up through the trap door. When I pulled myself through after him I noticed that Brett was sitting on the low bed, facing toward the dresser with his back to us. Gavin left to go to the bathroom and after I'd secured the trap door I sat down next to my new scion. I realized he was looking at a picture of himself lying on this very bed. He looked handsome and human and happy.

There were more pictures sitting on the dresser. Another one of him leaning over a railing topped the stack. He returned the one of him in this bed by pushing it between the small gilded mirror and its frame for display.

"You know, I don't see any reason in the world why you can't be together once we have you under control," I offered. I could see blood tinged tears forming in his eyes. One escaped and I caught it and showed it to him. "Careful, you don't want to stain anything," trying to lighten the mood.

He steadied himself. "Gavin's not on board with that," he sounded defeated.

"Oh please, what a hypocrite. He already wants to change too," I said.

"He does?" This surprised him.

"Yes, but I won't do anything until things get more settled. And I'll need someone else to change him anyway," I added.

"Why wouldn't you change him?" It was a good question.

"Because it's never a good idea to be the sire of your mate… long story." This didn't satisfy him. "You'll see over time how my insight into your mind would make it impossible for that type of relationship to exist for us." I gave him a warm smile.

Gavin returned just then and ignored our touching scene.

"Where to next?" He asked.

"First we have to go to Brett's for his clothes then to the embassy," I related. I figured I'd better prepare Gavin for disappointment. "You know, for obvious reasons, only Brett and I can go into the embassy," I said to Gavin gently.

"Why? …Well that sucks," he'd answered his own question. We stopped at Brett's apartment and, because of his roommates, Gavin went in by himself and loaded up another duffle bag with Brett's clothes and things using the excuse of another tour or something to that effect. The roommates didn't even question this. Once we'd stopped at some restaurant that specialized in preparing food quickly for customers to eat in their cars, he called it a fast-food restaurant appropriately, we made a stop at the drug store for some things I needed, makeup, etc. and then we went back to the Fleur De Lis.

Once Brett had showered and changed into some fresh clothes I did the same. I knew I would take longer and offered for him to go first. I decided to wear a white, mid-calf halter dress that looked good with my dark hair and a pair of red pumps. I matched the red with my new lipstick and Gavin showed me how to use the hair dryer so my hair was now stick straight. I trimmed it with some scissors I found in the drawer to be right at chin length. Unless a vampire is hibernating and refraining from drinking blood, our hair grows at an astonishing rate—about an inch a week. I finished up with some eyeliner and mascara and was ready to make my re-emergence into vampire society.

As I walked back into the main room I announced "Brett, are you ready to go?"

Brett was sitting on the end of the couch where the telephone was. "Not yet. I'm going to call Marisol first," he sounded resolved.

This caught Gavin's attention and just as he was about to protest Brett cut him off.

"Look, no matter what your opinion is of us… I can't just disappear. I don't know what's going to happen but she doesn't deserve that," he told him. He had a point. I was wondering when he'd notice that the power structure had shifted between him and Gavin. There was still a need there on his part but the weight had definitely moved in his direction.

"What are you going to tell her?" he asked. Gavin wasn't going to push his luck.

"I was thinking I'd say that my Mom's sick and I'm going back home for a while, or something like that," he surmised.

We were all silent at this and after a minute Brett picked up the phone and asked "Can I have a little privacy please?" He was nice about it. I guess he was done flexing his new status muscles for the moment. Gavin followed me into the bedroom.

Once we got inside and shut the door I aired my beef, "What's your problem here?" It was hard to not take it personally when a vampire wasn't good enough for his sister.

He came up and took my face in his hands. "I have NO problem with you and me…" I stood and waited for the other shoe to drop. "But I've always been very protective of her. I know it's stupid…" he admitted.

"Don't be a hypocrite. He loves her. *You* put them together," I emphasized.

"I know," he said, knowing he was being unreasonable.

"He'll still be the same person he was before, just… different physical needs," I defended him.

"I'm just afraid she'll want to join him... change," he admitted.

"*You* want to," I reminded him.

"I know. Just give me a little time…" At that he laid back in the bed and I laid back with him. After too short a time, Brett knocked softly on the door.

"I left her a message. We can go now," he said through the closed door.

With that I got up and offered my stubborn German a hand which was more help than he expected, gave him a quick, light kiss that wouldn't smudge my lipstick and joined Brett in the hallway. "Let's go then," I said to

Brett as I flashed him a big smile and hooked my arm through his. Then we strode out the door and down the hallway toward our destination.

Marisol

Eight

What had started out as one of the best weeks of my life quickly turned into a real dud. After that magical night that brought us together, Brett had been sequestered by my brother for an out of town road gig. They'd left Sunday night but now it was Wednesday and I hadn't heard from anyone but Gavin. I was starting to worry that maybe he regretted our night together and wanted to back off. This explanation would be the least surprising to me even with all the evidence to the contrary.

Brett had actually said the words; that he loved me. Even though I never actually said it back I was sure he'd understood I felt the same. Maybe he didn't. I obviously had issues making wrong assumptions and I should probably just lay it all out there. I would love to do that if I could just get the chance. When I'd woken up this morning I pretty much resolved to do just that; I'd tell him explicitly that I was totally in love with him, I had been since the very first time I laid eyes on him and that wasn't going to change any time soon. Even if he'd completely changed his mind about me (which, on some insecure level, I was sure he had) I would be brave and put it out there anyway.

After leaving work on Sunday I floated home on a cloud of well-being until I'd gotten home and heard the message from my brother, effectively deflating the balloon of my expectations for the rest of the evening. I'd hoped I'd get a call the next day… or at least the day after that from Brett personally. When that didn't happen I pretty much sank back into my hobbled lack of self-esteem and made it through my work days with all the enthusiasm of a zombie.

On Monday night after work I left a message on Gavin's machine, answering his message. I didn't get a response but he probably wouldn't check it until he got back. On Tuesday night Arial stopped in the shop, expecting to hear a breathless, victorious love story with a happy ending. I wished I could have given it to her. We'd had our somewhat awkward but sweet beginning, the incredible middle, but the end wasn't turning out exactly as expected.

"So, maybe your brother has him playing all night and there just haven't been any phones anywhere that he's been…" She was stretching to give him a reasonable explanation, and I wished there was one I could think of that jived with what I knew of their plans, but I just couldn't. Obviously, if he'd wanted to call me, short of complete incapacitation, he could have found a phone booth somewhere and called me if he really wanted to.

"Listen, I have something to do tonight but why don't you come by my house tomorrow after work and you can help me with my curse. That should cheer you up," she suggested. It was hard not to be cheered up when she had that infectious, wide grin stretched across her face, which was pretty much all the time. "Maybe we can do some divination and get some answers for you."

"Yeah, OK," I conceded. If I was still in the dark tomorrow I would need someone to pull me out of my slump. It was bad enough already. After Arial left I realized I was tired of not doing anything toward finding out once and for all what was really going on. Well, I knew what was going on was that my brother and Brett were in San Diego doing a quick tour, but they should be back by now. I cleared it with Suzanne that if I skipped my break I could leave early. So when 8:30 rolled around Suzanne came up front and took over.

"So, your brother's been out of town, you say?" She fished.

"Yeah, but he should be back now," I said, depressed.

"Good, tell him to bring his cute little butt by the store. I'll be his sugar-momma and he won't have to work so hard," Suzanne offered.

Suzanne always flirted with Gavin when he came by the store. Gavin had always flirted back; it was his nature to encourage female admiration of any kind. It was just a fun flirtation that both of them enjoyed. Suzanne was much older and several pounds heavier than his type. Suzanne's true love was really the little dog in the corner that loved her unconditionally.

After I assured Suzanne playfully that I couldn't wait for her to be my new sister-in-law, I left work for the evening and after fiddling with the club for a minute to get it off, got the VW on the road. I wasn't going straight home tonight; I wanted some answers. First, because it was the furthest away and I would make a circle around back to my place, I drove by Brett's house to see if there was any sign of him. Luckily, my talents allowed me to do my spying without the indignity of searching for a car or peeking into windows, not that I wouldn't if I had to. But Brett didn't have a car anyway and there was no sign of Gavin's car anywhere in sight. There was no sign of any of either's energies or guides either. That made it pretty clear that this was a dead end.

Next I drove past Heather's house. Heather was there but no Gavin. Then I drove into Hollywood and down to my brother's house and parked on Whitley; nothing again. Maybe I was just being stupid and they were doing exactly what Gavin said, playing music shows. Maybe it was tiring and he just figured he'd call or stop by when they got back. But shouldn't they be back already?

I let my mind wander around the neighborhood. The Fontenoy was a couple doors down from the Fleur De Lis where Gavin lived. Arial was home and alone. Then, when I let my mind float up higher I found several dark red energies, like the ones from the Troubadour that night, at the very top of the building. Not all of them were as negative as the energies at the club but the three that Arial was alarmed by seemed to still be there. I would occasionally see this redish type of energy, in all different places, but not regularly and not usually in groups like this. I made a note to ask Arial about it tomorrow night when I came over. Maybe she would know something more about her neighbors that would enlighten me. She did say she'd tell me more later.

I decided it was time for my night of being a stalker to come to an end. I started up the bug and drove home for another night of zombie misery. When I got home, the lack of messages confirmed the misery I had planned but instead, Julian enticed me to come over and meet his new boyfriend-of-the-moment, Brian. We smoked a little pinner joint Gavin had given to Julian the night of the party and before too long we were laughing and having a pretty good time. It actually got me out of my slump for the hour or so I spent there. Julian wanted to know details about the other night but I let him know I wasn't quite ready to talk about it yet and he let it go, mercifully.

After that I unceremoniously dumped myself into bed and let myself drift into oblivion and was thankful for the mind-silencing buzz.

When I woke up the following morning it occurred to me that I had not heard a single peep from the mystery entity in the past two days. It was like the bar-be-cue had worked some kind of exorcism on that spirit. I reached out with my mind but it was just not there anymore. I had gotten used to its presence and I was thinking I'd miss it. Also I was annoyed that now I would probably never figure out where it came from or why it was here.

I spent the day busying myself with mundane tasks like cleaning the apartment and going to the Laundromat. I'd decided to put all my Brett questions out of my mind and wait until tonight when I went to Arial's since there wasn't much I could do anyway. At least I'd be in the proximity then and maybe she could tell me some things to solve some of the other mysteries in my head.

When I got to work I had a client come in for a reading first thing. Emily was a regular customer; a woman of about 30 who worked as an assistant for a producer at one of the studios. She had thick glasses and spiky hair and smoked incessantly. She liked me to use the Tarot cards and usually wanted me to give her information about her career. She was an aspiring screenwriter but never got up the nerve to put her screenplays into anyone's hands that could actually do something for her. Most of the people who came in for spiritual guidance really just needed some type of counseling. Normally when I pulled her cards I would interpret the cards along with the pictures her guides were sending me to encourage her along the path that she was on because, according to what her guides were showing me, she was really more suited to her current position and her screenplays were not quite ready for primetime. But this particular evening I think my frustration with my own situation must have leaked into my reading because I found myself stretching the meaning of the cards and signals to put extra push into her to either do something about her writing or stop whining about it.

I recognized her increased panic and ended up toning it down toward the end of the reading. She seemed quite relieved after I was finished to be continuing along with her current status quo. I still secretly hoped she might someday shake up her existence and take a chance on her dream. Probably she would end up marrying some grip and having three kids.

At least she had a dream. My dream was to maintain a life with myself and my brother and avoid any disasters that may threaten any of the current stability I'd attained since leaving home. I guess I shouldn't be too hard on myself for not having a long-range goal. During the time when I would have been thinking about college and the future, I was losing my father, then my mother and in the wake of that, establishing an uneasy relationship with my new brother while trying to avoid mutual and self-destruction.

The evening wore on and when Suzanne went out to walk Dino the phone rang; it was Gavin.

"Hey, it's me," Gavin shouted from some payphone.

"Hey, where are you?" I asked.

"We're still in San Diego," he shouted.

"So, how's it going? Are you coming back soon?" I wanted to know.

"Yeah… soon." He obviously didn't feel like talking, so why did he call?

"How's Brett? Is everything OK?" I asked.

"He's fine, busy. We've just been really busy…" He said unhelpfully.

"What do you mean, busy? Are you coming back tonight?" I was getting annoyed now. What does that mean, busy?

"Yeah, maybe tonight or tomorrow. I have to go now, gotta run," quickly.

"OK, well, call me when you get back or…" Click. He'd hung up. What the hell was that? He was acting really strange.

Now I was pissed. Maybe Arial had a curse I could use for irritating brothers. The rest of the night dragged now that my mood was set in the acutely aggravated zone. Finally it was 9:00 and I was out the back door and in my car. I decided just to go straight over to Arial's, rather than stop at my apartment first.

When I got to Whitley Ave. and parked, I was stunned to find that my brother was home and in his apartment, alone. No Brett. I guess it's possible that he could have driven home in the three hours since I talked to him at work and maybe he dropped Brett off at his house but, at that time he didn't seem set on coming home yet.

I thought about going in and banging on his apartment door but I was just too pissed off to see him right now. The curse idea was starting to resonate.

Instead I walked into the Fontenoy and pushed the button for the elevator. It took a long time for it to make its way to the ground floor. It sounded slow and old. When it arrived I got in and pushed 11. The elevator was not only old; it was quite small for a building of this size. Really only four, maybe five small people could ride in this thing together comfortably. In that way it kind of reminded me of my VW. It had bad, florescent lighting that flickered against the wood grain wallpaper; a stark contrast to the elegant, art deco lobby. I wondered how people moved in and out, loading all their furniture into this small enclosed space. Maybe there was a service elevator somewhere in the back. As my mind was racing through all these nonsense questions I think I was starting to sweat.

When the bell finally rang for the 11th floor I was relieved to get off. The moment I did I realized I hadn't been reaching out to get the location of any entities yet. The small dose of claustrophobia had distracted me. Now that I was on solid ground I scanned around. Besides Arial, I immediately reached up to see what was on the top floor; one, two, three, four entities. There was a reddish tinge to three of them but nothing negative.

I decided not to loiter in the hallway any longer and knock on Arial's door. But before I could actually knock, something caught me by surprise. It was unbelievable to me but the spirit that was reaching out to me was my mystery entity. There was no mistaking the flower signature. It too had taken on the more reddish tinge of all the entities that seemed to cluster on the top floor but was still non-threatening. Then, if that wasn't enough, if I was reading this right, Brett's guide's signature was greeting me… with a little bit of insistence, this time with the added red aura like the rest. I was leaning up against the hallway wall and had my eyes squeezed shut trying to concentrate on what they were sending me. It was a massive jumble of things I'd seen before and it was very fast and too confusing to figure out.

It was being made more confusing by the roar of the Harley Davidson bikes pulling up. I went back to the elevator and pushed the button. I was going up there. No matter what was going on I was tired of being in the dark.

Impatiently I pushed the button a couple more times. The old engine groaned as it came down from the top. The car passed my floor (I had pushed the up button) and made its way down to the bottom before starting the trip back up again.

When the elevator finally landed on my floor, I was not entirely surprised to find the three German biker/musicians from the Troubadour in the car staring back at me. Even knowing it was coming by this time, it was still a bit of a shock when the doors opened and I looked directly into their gaze. They were pale and alert but made no move to let me in for the first couple of seconds. I would not be deterred; I forced myself to speak directly into their expressionless faces "Going up?"

They immediately stirred to make room for me in the cramped space. One of them looked at me and smiled in a way that came off as entirely insincere. I smiled back at him with just as much sincerity but probably tinged with a little fear.

As we rode up the last, painful two floors to our destination, I realized that Brett's guide and the mystery entity were becoming more faint; moving away from the building. Had I missed him? It was looking more and more likely. Maybe I could get information from the resident of the apartment on the 13th floor. I was already here.

When the door opened the three Germans insisted that I go ahead of them. I wasn't really sure where I was going but I didn't want to appear hesitant. When I started to move forward I realized there really wasn't a choice to be made here. There was one hallway leading to one door straight ahead. Apparently the penthouse encompassed the whole top floor. When I reached the door, the doorman (there was a doorman) asked who I was there to see. He was a big guy, about six foot two with burly, muscular shoulders and a buzz cut. Since I had no clue who to ask for, I gave him the only name I knew that had been in the place.

"Hi, I'm looking for Brett Carson."

"I'm sorry Ma'am, he just left… Sorry you can't be admitted," he said politely but sternly.

I was going to ask why not but I was actually dropping in without an appointment or without even knowing whose place this is.

I gave him my best smile. "Can you tell me who lives here?"

He didn't budge. He could have been a guard at Buckingham Palace except that he wasn't English. "Sorry."

When I turned around, the three German guys were frozen in a sort of formation, staring back at me. The tall, blonde one was in front with the other two flanking him. I knew they were there, of course, but I expected that they would move past me to enter once I had finished with my questions. Instead the one in front looked at me intently. He told me that he knew the man I was looking for and, if I liked, they would be happy to take me to him.

Now, I can't tell you why because not a minute ago I was terrified of these guys and was reluctant to even get in the elevator with them, but at that moment I was awash with trust and believed him completely when he said he would take me to see Brett.

I agreed and he led the way back to the elevator and out to the front where their motorcycles were parked. I felt completely comfortable getting on the back of the bike of the tall, blond German guy and letting him drive off with me toward my meeting with Brett.

As we rode my thoughts were completely docile. I thought of nothing and just allowed myself to be driven to our destination. We drove up and over the Cahuenga Pass and into the Valley. We ended up on Ventura Blvd. and eventually turned right on Colfax. After that we weaved into one of the neighborhoods and eventually pulled up into the driveway of a nondescript valley tract house. Once we parked I stood up and waited for them to give me direction.

"Let's go in the house, OK?" The tall German directed me into the house.

Once inside, I didn't pay much attention to what they were saying or what was going on. One of them had gone outside a couple of times and came back. After about… I wasn't sure how much time had passed, the bald one said for me to come with him and that he would be taking me to Brett.

I followed him out into the back yard of the house and waited while he moved away one of those free-standing basketball hoops to reveal a metal door into the ground. He unlocked the door and pulled open the heavy, metal door with a bang.

Apparently there was someone inside because he yelled down into the hole, "Wake up Captain, it's dinner time!"

Then he looked back at me and said Brett was down there and he was going to lower me into the enclosure in the ground. This seemed perfectly logical to me so I allowed myself to be lowered in.

Once I hit the ground the door closed behind me and I heard the German lock it from the outside. When I looked around, it wasn't completely dark; there was a single light, a bare bulb enclosed by a metal cage-like fixture. It was a fairly large underground room with not much inside. There was a white bucket in one corner. Against the far wall, there was a man tied up in metal chains. He was lying on the ground and when he rolled himself over to look at me, he was startled when his eyes found my face.

"Don't come near me child, stay where you are!" He said with a slight German accent.

I was suddenly shocked into awareness by my circumstances.

I was dumbfounded by the scene around me and looking at this man with new interest, although I was still feeling pretty calm.

"Good, look at my eyes… promise you won't come near me," he said evenly.

"I promise." I knew I would do as he said.

"Who are you?" I asked quietly.

"Fucking Germans," He said to no one in particular. I wasn't sure what he was getting at. He spoke again.

"Look at me again, right here." He was gesturing to his eyes with two fingers then continued. "You can forget everything the German guys told you. Let yourself break away from their influence completely." It was like he was speaking directly into my soul.

At that moment I felt something lift from my being and suddenly the panic kicked in. My eyes got wide and my heart started beating quickly. I was looking all around and up at the metal door with terror.

"Good, you're back. Unfortunately, you're stuck here," he informed me.

"Where am I? Who the hell are you?" I yelled.

"I'm Captain Heinrich Frederickson, vampire. That's the reason you can't come near me. Where you are is in some shit hole somewhere in the valley. Do you remember the trip here?" He said in one breath.

I was in full panic mode now. I was starting to sweat and I pushed myself as far as I could into the far corner. I flipped over the white bucket and sat on it. That was too much information to process at one time. The trip here, yes, I remembered the trip here on the motorcycle. "*Why* did I get on that motorcycle?" I hadn't meant to say it out loud.

"Don't beat yourself up. They're vampires too. They hypnotized you into oblivion to get you to come with them. I just removed their influence so that's why you're panicking now," he answered. He had a sort of gruff voice but it wasn't unpleasant. I could appreciate his frankness. This didn't stop the panic though.

"Vampires! You're all vampires? Vampires are real?" But somehow, I didn't completely disbelieve him.

"Sorry you had to learn about it this way," he said sincerely.

I'd pulled my knees up into my chest. I had both my hands over my mouth to keep myself from screaming. I had a fleeting, trivial thought that I was glad I'd warn the bicycle shorts and cowboy boots today, rather than a dress.

I looked over at the man chained to the wall and realized that, although I was in a very, very bad situation, I was not in immediate danger and should get a hold of myself. I took a few deep breaths to calm myself.

"So, you're a vampire?" He nodded. "Why are you down here?" I asked.

"I was captured by those German assholes; I don't know 20, maybe 30 years ago." He seemed to drift off for a minute.

"Why would vampires want to capture another vampire?" I was puzzled.

"Because they're immature leaches, that's why," he said angrily. He paused for a moment then lowered his tone. "As I am much older than them, they drain my blood and drink it. It gives them more strength and sharper senses," he explained more thoughtfully.

I didn't know what to say to this for a minute. "If you're older and stronger why can't you get away?" It seemed like a logical question.

"There's a lot of silver in these chains and they starve me. That's why you can't come near me. They starve me to the point where I would drain my own mother and then they take my blood when I'm weak," He said as he dragged the chains a little across the floor.

I was having trouble forcing myself to think logically. I seemed to be in fight or flight mode and logical thinking wasn't a part of that description. "Why am I here?"

"I'm sorry to break this most unpleasant news to you Miss, but you were put in here to feed me." My eyes got very wide at this. "See that empty bag over there in the corner?" I forced myself to look. It was an empty blood bag, the kind they hang on metal rolling racks in the hospital. "They threw that in yesterday as an appetizer—you're supposed to be the meal," he said with some shame.

"I thought they were starving you?" I asked hopefully.

"My last meal was about five years ago, I think. Its puts me into a hibernation state," he said, which was new information for me.

Every time he answered one of my questions the answer would shock me into silence. He continued.

"They need to feed me when I start to dry up; when the blood becomes too thick to draw anymore... Just from that one small bag, I feel more alert today then I have in a long time." I sat there still stunned into silence so he went on.

"But, as I said, you must not come near me as a very big part of me wants to suck every last drop out of your young body... But I don't want to do that. This is not who I am."

"Why is it not who you are? You're a vampire too, right?"

"Not like them. They're monsters. The vampires I normally associate with and those in my bloodline don't kill indiscriminately. We don't have to, of course. Only murderers enjoy killing. Being a vampire doesn't mean you're a murderer."

"So, you're a nice vampire?" I said in a slightly sarcastic tone.

"I'll let you form your own opinion."

I sat there in silence for a while until I wondered what we were waiting for. "When will they come back?"

"Unfortunately, they probably won't come back for a couple of years."

"What! What are we going to do?"

"Their plan is to wait long enough so that it's actually the humane thing for me to drain you dry, rather than let you die of thirst."

This new information made my head swim until I thought I would throw up from the nausea; until I remembered that I would want to hold on to any liquid I had in me at this point.

"So, you've been through this before?"

"Yes, unfortunately. The first time I tried to turn the unfortunate man into a vampire so he might have the stamina to wait for them to return. I wasn't sure how long it would be that first time. But the duration was too much for the young vampire. When they finally returned they heard his inhuman screams and staked and burned him before he ever tasted human blood." That didn't sound like a viable plan.

"The second time I couldn't come up with anything else and after a time, she begged me to release my influence and allow her to die."

"What do you mean, influence?"

"As I did when you arrived, I inhibited your ability to approach me with hypnotism. If you had run over to me right away this discussion would not be happening right now," he explained.

"You can't control yourself?" I asked him.

"I have very good control under normal circumstances. But if someone prevented you from all hydration for days and then put a glass of water under your nose, could you resist drinking it?" he said as a comparison.

"No, I guess not, but I don't think the glass would mind as much."

"No, probably not." He smiled a painful smile. "What's your name, child?"

"Marisol."

"Marisol, that's a lovely name. Is that Spanish?"

"I really don't know… my mother was Swedish."

"Hmm. Yes, you look Swedish." I was starting to calm down and then I remembered my doom. I closed my eyes. I began reaching out into the neighborhood with my head. "They're not here anymore," I pronounced.

"I didn't hear the motorcycles leave," he reasoned.

"I didn't either but they're gone. No one is in the house," I assured him.

"How do you know?" he asked with heightened interest.

"I have a… sensitivity. I can sense non-incarnate spirits… receive information from them," I explained hesitantly.

"You're a receiver? Extraordinary! They don't know that, do they?" he seemed heartened.

"No, I don't think they do," I couldn't see how they would.

"Excellent!" He pulled himself up to a sitting position now and it looked like his brain was working on how this could change our situation.

"I can't send. What good can that possibly be if I can't send out an SOS?" I told him.

"Are you sure you can't send?" he looked desperate.

"I've only tried a couple of times but I might as well be trying to talk to a cat," I said disparagingly.

"Some people can talk to cats," he said seriously. I was looking at him like I wasn't sure what this odd little bit of information was going to do to help us. After a few minutes I laid down on the floor and let the cold concrete touch my cheek.

I could feel my eyelids getting heavy. All that mind manipulation and the emotional upheaval were taking their toll on me. I thought about how, just a couple of hours ago I was happily joking with Suzanne and completely safe and happy. Well, not completely happy, but safe. I thought about Brett and how I'd gone from blissfully happy to the cold misery of this damp floor in less than a week. I thought about my brother. It made me sad to think that the last thing we would say to each other was that inane conversation we'd had from the San Diego payphone. I thought of my last night's sleep following a cherished hour with my friend. I let the tears roll down my eyes and onto the cold floor until I finally dropped off into oblivion.

Brett

Nine

I could smell the blood. I was coming into consciousness, not exactly like waking up had been, more like going from a void of no thought into conscious thought. Dreams were a thing of the past. I've learned that my senses would always be aware, even if I wasn't.

The human blood smell was mixing with something else now, something more urgent, more delicious and my mouth was filling with a liquid; with what I wasn't sure yet. My new, stronger heart was beating harder and forcing me to react to its own desires.

When the curtain came flying down and the overpowering smell wafted over me I reacted by instinct, no thinking or even momentary consideration clouded the decision. Once I'd made skin contact and the sweet and salty blood splashed into the back of my throat, nothing else in the world mattered. I couldn't get enough.

Some part of my instinct knew a way to silence her and I could feel her struggle as she gagged.

Tuning out the voices I pulled harder on the stream of pure life coming into me. "Don't kill her." The voice was far, far away.

"Brett!" The movement broke my concentration. I was suddenly looking into a beautiful, pale face and very large green eyes.

"Obey me." Everything that I was now told me I would do as she asked. I dropped the gagging girl at once. I could hear her heart beating a little lighter than before but still strong. While I licked the last of the blood dripping from my teeth I realized where I was and what I had done.

I instantly pulled myself all the way back into the closet that had become my daytime home for the past few days. I was revolted as I recognized the object of my fixation was my manager's girlfriend, Heather, and that I'd drained her to the point of losing consciousness.

Iris began to make excuses for my monstrous behavior but no words could change what I'd just witnessed of myself; the truth of it. She said it was a matter of time. How much time would I be a captive of these uncontrollable needs of this new life. I already knew the answer.

I could hear they were making plans to clean up my mess. It's not that I wasn't grateful. None of this was Gavin's problem. I was thankful for him sticking his neck out for me.

To Iris I would be eternally grateful. By my most recent example, it was even more crystal clear that what she did to me could not have been prevented by her. It was only her strength that kept me from certain death.

Iris, my gentle, petit benefactor had come to console me away from my morose reflections. Her job would be a tough one as my most important loss was a sudden and profound one, and had nothing to do with my own personal loss of humanity. Although I must admit, I was finding it hard to look into those large pools of optimism and not be somewhat uplifted. She had a gift in that way and I was in no position to resist her.

I got up and got dressed, determined to do my part to clean up the mess I had made. I'd always found it difficult to accept the help of others but since my move to this city, and most especially since Iris changed my life forever, I had done nothing but rely on others for my very existence. I could understand how Iris was obliged to educate me on the life she'd pulled me into. I could even understand how Gavin, my manager would think of me as his responsibility, even through this unanticipated turn of events. And of course I would be forever grateful to both of them. But I would never be completely comfortable until I could at least hold up my end of the equation; stop being a burden.

I went out and joined Gavin in the car while Iris brought Heather down after us. Obviously, it was too soon for me to be trusted with humans in close proximity.

After Iris planted an appropriate story in Heather's head to replace the truth, we dropped her off at her apartment.

Our next stop, unbeknownst to me, would be Marisol's house. Gavin's sister and my one true love; destined to by my brief one true love I'm afraid.

This was apparently the location of the secret chamber where Iris lay sleeping for the past 50 years and why the circumstances of fate decided to change my life forever.

It was too soon to know weather I would gratefully adapt to this new existence of living in the night forever. Maybe immortality would be the best thing that ever happened to me. Maybe one day I'd wish she would have drained me dry that fateful evening, still blissfully happy from the night before. I was not ready to make that judgment, knowing I'd have plenty of time to ponder the answer.

My current preoccupation, besides dutifully adapting to this new life as best I could, was to weigh the decision of weather or not I could expect Marisol to remain with me in my current state. This was a question for which there were many opinions, even just within this car. I'd resolved to remain undecided until I could be sure of the outcome of my ultimate resulting nature.

Even in the wake of this evening's bad behavior, I knew I was becoming more knowledgeable and was getting closer to self-sufficiency every day. Whatever the resulting decision is about our relationship, I needed to contact her myself soon. It was not acceptable for me to just disappear without a word. Not only did I want to call her, I was ashamed of the grief I may be causing her in the few days I'd been gone. It couldn't have been avoided, of course, but I would find a way to correct it as soon as I could.

Once we got to Marisol's house, both the depression I was feeling increased and a new feeling of excitement added to the mixture. Whatever the circumstances, I was back where I wanted to be, for the moment.

As I lingered near the bedroom, I could smell her, and the me that was, and everything that transpired that night came back with a new clarity that must be inherent in this new package of my existence. It was overwhelming.

While the two of them were down examining the secret place where Iris slept, I noticed some pictures strewn on a dresser next to the bed. They were of me and more from that night. I remembered the feeling of when they were taken; complete optimism and happiness, the trust. Would it ever be possible to make it back to that place again? There were so many obstacles to that the doubt weighed heavy and I was finding it difficult to be here anymore. I suddenly felt like the intruder I was.

Again, Iris was there, encouraging me to believe that everything would turn out in the end. It was impressive that someone who was over 100 years old could still have so much faith. Maybe things would get better over time and not worse as I would have thought.

Gavin and Iris had obviously fallen into an easy, natural affair. There was something about their personalities that seemed to mesh and work together. Maybe with the right person adversities could be overcome, no matter how extreme. That was my bravest hope.

Next we stopped at my house so Gavin could go in and gather some things for me. Again; no proximity to humans for the new vampire. Although unavoidable, it was humiliating. Tonight I would be introduced officially to the vampire community and I vowed then to do my best to conduct myself in a responsible, prepared way. If this was my life now, I would do my best to make it work. I would apply myself to be good at it.

When we got back to Gavin's house I was able to shower for the first time since my change to what I am now. I was surprised that it wasn't more necessary but most of the human bodily functions that require regular hygiene seem to be nonexistent now. But, I enjoyed the shower and it was good to change into new clothes. I found I was more than ready to find out more about this new life that I was now leading. The power of it was becoming more a part of who I was now; increasing every day.

Before we left, I decided there was no time like the present to take matters into my own hands and decided to call Marisol. I had no idea what I was going to tell her but when they asked, I told them one of the excuses I'd come up with in my deliberations.

Once I had gotten them to leave the room I dialed the number. I knew Iris would still be able to hear me if she was listening but I could hear them arguing in the other room so maybe I actually would have some privacy for this.

Even though it was conceivable that she might be home from work by now, she wasn't and I was reconciled to leaving a message on her machine. Even this was better than the silence she'd had from me up until now. When the beep sounded I just started talking.

"Marisol… Marisol I miss you. I'm so sorry I haven't called you until now. I wanted to. I thought about you every minute. I have no excuse except to say that there were unforeseen circumstance beyond my control… it's too complicated to go into in this message… but most importantly, I love you... I love you and I hope you feel the same and I promise I'll explain everything when I see you…" Beep.

It was clear to me now that I was incapable of lying to her. I hadn't realized this until I'd contemplated doing just that. I just couldn't do it. So now it was also clear that she would be making an informed decision as to weather or not she was willing to accept me for what I was now.

I got up and tapped on the bedroom door to let Iris know I was ready to go. She looked fresh and excited as we exited toward another new experience for me.

Ten

Iris and I walked out the front of the Fleur De Lis for the first time and turned South, going toward the Fontenoy building and my introduction to the vampire community. It was a community—a condition—that I didn't know existed three days ago. Now it would be who I am until… until the end of time or I am somehow destroyed. Iris had said a vampire must be burned to dust to be completely dead. It's hard to say what's more frightening, the inevitability of a painful human death or the impossibility of that ever happening.

I promised myself that I would tackle this new challenge bravely so as we walked I began asking questions that I thought I would need the answers to.

"So, this is the Los Angeles embassy for vampires." It was not really a question.

"Yes." She giggled and gave me a signal to keep my voice low.

"So, what should I expect? What's our goal?" I'd lowered my voice to a level I was sure no one but her could hear. She answered at the same level.

"Well, we'll go in and talk to the ambassador. I'll introduce you as my new scion and they'll record you in the records under our bloodline," she began. We were walking slowly. I'm sure she was doing this to give me a chance to prepare. "We also want to get you your own safe-house key," she added.

"Are there rules, some governing body that makes judgments?" I asked. There was so much I still didn't know.

"Well, yes and no. Our kind are really more keep to ourselves kind of beings. We're not really joiners, per se. There's an inherent distrust of authority," She explained.

She went on. "But, we do have certain understandings amongst ourselves; certain… basic principals. The first understanding would be to not be flagrant. Don't let people know who would be a danger to us. Be discreet," she said. This seemed pretty obvious.

"Two would be don't run around murdering people; kind of an offshoot of not being flagrant. It would draw too much attention and, of course, not be very nice," she elaborated. This was not something I aspired to anyway.

"Three would be to do no harm to our fellow vampires. This one would seem obvious but you don't want to experience vampire vigilante justice, trust me," she warned.

I couldn't imagine Iris doing any of those things. Of course, I would adhere to these simple rules; it really was just common sense, if such a thing is possible for vampires. Granted, we'd both come close to murdering someone, albeit by accident.

"What's the general consensus on accidental manslaughter?" I asked for obvious reasons.

"Well, it's frowned upon, of course, but our fellow vampires' main concern would be in how it was handled. We have to be conscious of not bringing attention to our existence to those that are unaware. So, I guess what I'm saying is, it's unfortunate, but it does happen from time to time. There was a phone number you could call in an emergency back in my day and someone would come out and help you if you needed it. I've been gone for 50 years so I don't know what's changed since then," she elaborated.

At this point we were walking up to the front door of the building, then into the art deco lobby. We rang for the elevator and waited for the ancient car to descend from the top. You would think if the vampire community needed to use this elevator on a regular basis they would have it replaced with something more modern, faster. Maybe they didn't want to draw attention to their presence. Maybe they mostly took the stairs.

It finally arrived and took us slowly to the top floor. Once there, it was a direct line down the hallway to the one entrance into the penthouse suite. The guard at the front stopped us at the door. He seemed to be human.

"ID?" Iris opened the little bag she'd brought from her stash of things and pulled out her keychain, picked out her safe-house key and showed it to the guard.

"Who's this?" He indicated me.

"This is my scion, Brett Carson. He doesn't have ID yet," she answered cheerfully.

He looked me over. "How old?" he asked.

"Three days," she answered.

"He looked back at me and said, "Don't bite me, I'm going to touch you." With that he slowly took a hold of my arm to assess something about my current state. I would be glad when people stopped treating me like I would break into a homicidal fit at any second.

"He's cold. You can go in," was his assessment. With that he stepped aside and let me open the door for Iris.

When we got inside I could see that most of the place was open into one big, loft-like room with lots of tall square windows open to the night. The door opened into the middle of the unit and the space wrapped around the hallway like a large U. There were many groups of conversation areas with chairs, chase lounges and tables and lots of bookcases packed with books against the walls. There was a small kitchen area, if you could call it that. It had one very big refrigerator. That was newer. It must not have been here when Iris was here last.

"What would be in the fridge?" I asked.

"Blood," she answered matter-of-factly. Of course, stupid question. But she said it in a way that wasn't making fun of me.

The lighting was low and centered on the conversation areas. This made it easier to see the view out of the windows; the city lights and the stars. There were metal doors that were rolled up on the inside for all the windows. They resembled the industrial type doors you'd find at a warehouse. Those would be for the daytime hours, of course.

She still had a hold of my arm as we slowly made our way around the room. There was music playing softly in the background. It was a very soothing atmosphere. I was wondering about the human who let us in.

"Why would they trust that human at the front door?" I wondered.

"Oh, I'm sure he's had a suggestion or two about what he remembers when he's not at work. I'll bet his memory of us starts to fade once he starts down that elevator after his shift," she hypothesized.

"Hmm. So you can be that specific about what you suggest?" I asked her.

"Sure. We've also learned a thing or two from the witches," she offered.

When we got to the back of the room there was a door to a small office that was slightly ajar. As we got closer, a small man appeared in the threshold.

"May I help you?" He asked. He was maybe five foot five, soft looking and balding. He was wearing a hounds tooth suit; pants and a vest, warn loafers and had a on a white shirt with rolled up sleeves and a bow tie. He was also pale and luminous and his eyes shone amber in the dim light.

Iris recognized him. "Harold, is that really you?" she exclaimed warmly.

It took him a minute but then he remembered. "Iris? Oh my, where have you been? It's been decades!" His voice revealed a posh, British accent.

"Literally it has. But that's a long story. First I want to introduce you to my new scion, Harold this is Brett Carson, Brett; Harold McKinley," she seemed to take pride in introducing me.

"Nice to meet you," I said. We shook hands and stood there for a minute while he marveled at Iris, presumably since she'd been gone for so long. He looked me over pretty closely as well. Then he remembered his manners.

"Oh, I'm so sorry, please come in," he offered. We followed him into his little office. It was conventional enough, a desk, chairs, bookshelves—there were lots of books crammed into this little space—a telephone, fax, etc.

"Please sit down," he gestured. He went behind the desk and we sat opposite him.

"Please remind me, from whose bloodline are you?" He questioned.

"Jacque St Domingue," Iris stated.

"Oh yes, of course," he responded. He went back into a closet and came back with a large binder that was labeled "St Domingue" and opened it up somewhere in the middle.

"Let's see… Iris Stein, Iris Stein… here you are," he discovered. He looked at it for minute and then looked up at Iris. Then he said to her delicately, "You're starting fresh, is that right?"

She looked thoughtful. "Yes, Brett is my only scion, currently."

He quickly moved on. "So, when did the change take place?"

She looked up as if to think back and said, "three days ago…" Then she looked at me, "what was the date three days ago?"

"Um…" I thought about it for a minute then said, "It was Sunday… May 26th."

"Very good." He scribbled something into the book and then looked up at me. "You're very young so I'm going to let you do it, but we need a drop of your blood and a finger print right here," he indicated a spot next to where he wrote my name.

He handed me a safety pin and held up his thumb. "Right thumb," he clarified.

I took the pin, opened it and quickly stuck myself in the thumb. It was odd, it didn't actually hurt in the same way it would have when I was human. It was more like I registered the intrusion intellectually; not pain exactly, although I did feel it go in. Harold made an indication with his head to move me on to put my print in the book and after I had done it, he blew on it for a minute then closed the book and went to put it away.

I licked my finger to clean the last of the blood. It did taste wonderful but not quite as good as human blood, definitely different, it tingled on my tongue.

When the vampire returned, Iris began making small talk with him. "So Harold, what have you been up to? Didn't you have a plan to read every page of English Literature ever printed?"

He laughed. "Yes. I've been through most of the seventeenth and eighteenth centuries. I learned French and now I'm working my way through French Literature," he related.

"Fabulous. My French is a little rusty. Although, it is my first language you know," she revealed.

"Really? I wouldn't have guessed," he said genially.

"I was educated in England and moved here to the states when I was still a teenager… That was 80 years ago." This was new information for me as well.

"It was all the rage to lose your accent once the talkies started. I wanted to sound just like Barbara Stanwyck," she had an enthusiastic look on her face.

There was a pause when no one responded. "I know I really sound more like Shirley Temple," she conceded. She pouted at this admission.

She decided to get back to business. "So, actually I was hoping we could get Brett a safe-house key as well," she said moving on.

"Oh, of course," Harold replied. He popped up and went back into the closet and we heard him rustling around a little bit then he emerged with a key and another binder.

He pulled out a modern, brass key, maybe a little longer than a standard key. It was attached to a round, flat key ring by a brass chain. One side of the keychain was embossed with LA (I'm assuming for Los Angeles) and on the other side had a serial number engraved on it. As he scribbled into the book Iris fished in her bag and pulled out the old skeleton key she'd been carrying around and set it on the table in front of her.

Once he was finished and handed me the key he looked at Iris' key and exclaimed, "Goodness Iris, is that the only key you have? Where have you been for the past 50 years?" He asked not knowing.

"Hibernating, actually. I laid down in 1932 and was shaken awake only three days ago," she reported.

"Oh my, well no wonder I haven't seen you around here. Let me get you a new key," he offered immediately. He got up and went into the closet to retrieve another key. Once he got back and started scribbling again, Iris continued.

"You know, when I went to ground in 1932 I only planned to sleep for 20 years. My sire, Heinrich; Heinrich Frederickson, was supposed to wake me in 1952 but I only woke up by accident three days ago… the earthquake you know. I'm worried about Heinrich. Have you seen him or heard word of him?" she inquired.

"No, I'm sorry dear, I haven't. But isn't he the sailor? Maybe he's not made it to land in a while," he offered politely.

"No, I don't think so. We made a plan and he's 30 years late. That's more than an oversight, don't you think?" she suggested.

"Of course it is Iris, I'm sorry to hear it. Did you say you went to ground in 1932?" He reiterated.

"Yes, October," Iris answered.

"You know, the very next year, 1933, we started a new service to let those of us going into hibernation register their place of rest and expected rise in the case that something might go wrong. You're a prime example. I wish we'd started a little sooner," he said regretfully.

"So do I. Who knows, under different circumstances I might have laid there for the next thousand years," Iris exclaimed.

"Yes, that's exactly the problem. Too many of us have just disappeared over the years; your sire being another unfortunate example of this," he shook his head at this.

"So, you'll let me know if there's any news." Iris said.

I'll be sure to ask around. Do you have a contact phone number in case I hear anything?" he asked as he handed her the new key. She added it on to her key ring as I gave him Gavin's home phone number.

"I'll be sure to ask around. Who's his sire? Maybe they can help," he asked.

"He's a direct Scion of Jacque St Domingue," she said proudly. He looked impressed.

"Oh, well, I've unfortunately never met him. I don't think he's ever been here… but I'll put the word out," he offered helpfully.

At that we all stood up and shook hands again. Iris thanked him and he welcomed me to the community. It was like joining a private country club.

As we were walking out I asked Iris if anyone ever stayed here for the day. She walked me around to the opposite side of the big U-shaped facility and showed me that there were two other private rooms that could be used for that purpose. We walked out to the elevator and rang for the car. The doors opened immediately and we got in. Once we were inside the smell in the elevator immediately caught my attention. I was sure the scent was Marisol but I was so new at this I could be mistaken. I turned to Iris and it looked like she was recognizing the scent too.

"Do you smell that? I'd swear it was Marisol," I said with conviction.

"Yes, it does smell similar to the scent in her apartment, but I can't be sure. I've never actually caught her scent in person," she said.

We were both silent for a minute while we tried to make a more definitive judgment. She continued, "Why would she be here though? What business would she have here?"

"I have no idea," I said as I thought about it. As we were descending the sound of motorcycles pulling up in front of the building diverted our attention. The elevator stopped at the bottom and when the doors opened, the three bikers that I'd seen that night at the Troubadour were waiting for the elevator to ride up. Iris gripped my arm a little tighter when she saw them but kept a pleasant expression on her face. Although I took them to have a possibly frightening appearance—it was clear to me now that they were vampires too—I wasn't sure how she could be afraid of them considering she was also a vampire. They stood aside as we walked through the lobby toward the front door and out.

After a few minutes, once we were halfway back to the Fleur De Lis and they were on their way up to the 13th floor, Iris turned to me and said, "That was them, the three Germans who attacked me that night." She had a horrified look on her face that I'd never seen on her before. Of course the story was still fresh in my mind.

"Oh my god, really? Why didn't they recognize you?" I moved her forward toward home.

"They didn't turn me, remember, they only drained me. To them, I'm just some girl they raped and killed 80 years ago. I'm sure I'm not the only one…" she said as she became more agitated. She was now visibly shaken and her eyes were filling with pink liquid as we walked into the Fleur De Lis. Since there was nobody in the lobby I urged her to go full speed to the apartment door and we were inside in a split second.

Once we were inside, Gavin looked up with an expression of amused curiosity but that quickly changed when he saw Iris' face. "Baby, what's wrong? What is it?" She collapsed onto him; pink tears streaking down her cheeks.

He picked her up and was walking with her over to the couch. She was inconsolable. He looked up at me and asked in a more insistent tone, "What happened?"

"Everything was fine until we were leaving... then we ran into those three German guys from her horror story the other night," I told Gavin.

He looked back at me with rage in his eyes. "Seriously, they were here? I'll *fucking* kill them."

Iris, who had her face buried in Gavin's neck, popped her head up in alarm, "No! You don't know what they can do to you. They'll rip you into teeny, tiny little pieces. Promise me you won't," she implored him.

Gavin looked like he couldn't speak at that moment. I'm sure he realized he wouldn't stand a chance against them but the rage wouldn't allow him to let it go. He held Iris tighter as she let her head fall back onto his shoulder.

"I have to do *something*," Gavin seethed. Just then we also heard the Harleys pulling away.

"It was those same German bikers we saw the other night at the Troubadour," I added.

"Oh... yeah, the ones that made Marisol's hair stand on end," he remembered.

Bringing up Marisol's name casually in conversation had a sweet and sour quality to it that socked me in the gut. But we were worried about Iris right now so I let it pass.

"Marisol's friend... Arial... seemed to have some knowledge or insight about the Germans," I'd remembered from the club that night.

"You know she lives there, at the Fontenoy on the 11th floor," Gavin said.

"So, you knew her before, you're friends with her too?" I asked.

"Yeah, she moonlights in... she sometimes sells hallucinogenics," he admitted. Iris again popped her head up to give Gavin a disapproving look. Gavin kept his eyes on me but smiled a little.

"You know, Iris and I think we may have caught Marisol's scent in the elevator there on the way back tonight," I told Gavin. I couldn't see how this would be pertinent but it still bothered me that she was there and he should know.

"She was probably there to see Arial," Gavin added. "Maybe we should go talk to Arial tomorrow. See what she knows," he suggested.

"Tomorrow I'm going to see Marisol," I stated. It was not a suggestion. "You can come with if you like." I was done hiding out. I'd already made my decision. It was time to carry it out. Of course, I would need him to drive me. But I was sure he wouldn't want me to go without him anyway.

"You think you're ready? Don't forget what happened with Heather," he worried. He looked skeptical and a little angry.

"I'll be ready." I would be. I knew what I needed to do to prepare.

He was fighting the urge to argue with me on this point and decided against it. "Well, it's three AM so unless you guys are thinking about working on your tan, I think it's time to call it a morning," Gavin said as he got up and carried Iris with him into the bedroom. She seemed completely content to be where she was in his arms. "See you tomorrow night, man," he offered before disappearing.

Once they closed the bedroom door I grabbed my duffle bag of clothes and went into my place in the closet. I would need to think about what I was going to do for a resting place in the future. I couldn't continue to stay in Gavin's closet. I thought about the secret room under Marisol's closet and daydreamed about staying with her and using that place for my daytime hours. I let myself think about that incredible night we were together and went back over every detail with my new, sharpened memory. I imagined what it would be like for us now that I was different and how she might feel different to me with this new body.

I lingered on this pleasant fantasy for a while until I decided to let my mind clear and suspend all conscious thought until I would awaken tomorrow evening.

Eleven

My eyes snapped open as I went from no thought to complete lucid consciousness in a split second. Nothing but the instinctual awareness of the sun setting had roused me. I closed my eyes to remember the feeling of this knowledge.

I got up and got dressed in a pair of black jeans, combat boots and a steel gray silk sweater Gavin had brought from my apartment and pulled my hair back with a band I'd found in a drawer in the bathroom. I could see in the mirror that I looked different than I had. Every day that passed I appeared to be a little more pale, more luminous. I doubted humans could see with as much detail as I could. I would feel cold to them. I didn't feel cold to myself but the humans I had touched since that night did feel very warm to me, like they had a fever. My eyes were the most explicit to me. They had a glow that I could see but I didn't think registered with humans in regular lighting. I turned off the bathroom light to see the effect. In what would be complete darkness to a human I saw as distinct, low-light images. The bright, glowing eyes of a cat, shaped like my eyes, stared back at me. This would be how I could see in the dark, of course.

My hair seemed to be just a little bit longer than it had been. It all fit back into the band. I looked closely at my face. My beard didn't seem to be growing. This seemed like a contradiction. I looked at my teeth. They were very white, whiter than they'd been before, and I examined my canines. They looked to be the same shape that they were before. I could feel they were sharper. When I touched them I accidentally sliced a small cut into my finger. With the sight and smell of my blood, I detected a small extension of them; a small movement. It's like they were reaching out for it, ever so slightly. It happened with both the top and bottom canines. I was completely fascinated by it. Just as I was about to lick the drop of blood off my finger Gavin knocked.

"Come on buddy, some of us actually have to use the toilet… well, just me really."

I swung the door open and his smell blew over me. I grimaced but stood my ground. "You might want to back off. I haven't had breakfast yet," I warned him.

"Right," he took my advice and backed all the way out through the closet and went back into the bedroom and shut the door. Once he was inside I went out into the main room.

I heard Gavin go into the bathroom and start the shower. Iris came out of the bedroom. She was wearing a fitted black calf-length skirt that flared out at the bottom with low black heels and a white, cap-sleeved button up shirt with a colorful scarf tied around her neck. Her hair hung in a soft wave around her face. She looked like she was headed to a USO show.

I smiled at her. "You look like you feel a little better this evening."

"Yeah, it's hard to stay in a bad mood around Gavin," she smiled back.

"That's true." Just then the phone rang. I looked at Iris.

"Gavin told me not to answer it," she said. We watched it ring five times before the machine picked up.

"This is Gavin. Leave a message." Beep.

"This message is for Iris Stein. This is Harold McKinley calling. I wanted to let her know that the person she was looking for…" Iris was looking at me in an urgent way that told me she was unsure of what to do in this situation. I picked up the phone.

"Mr. McKinley?" I said.

"Yes," He answered.

"Mr. McKinley, this is Brett Carson. We met last night," I reminded him.

"Yes, good evening Mr. Carson," he greeted me.

"Mr. McKinley, I have Iris right here. Would you like to speak to her?" I asked.

"Yes, please." I handed the phone to Iris. She looked thankful.

"Harold, hi. Have you found Heinrich?" When Harold answered, of course I could hear every word.

"No, I'm sorry Iris, we haven't. But, the most extraordinary thing; we've heard from Jacque St Domingue and he's on his way here. Apparently, he's been looking for you too," he sounded excited.

Iris looked up at me and she looked as surprised as I was.

"When will he be here?" She asked.

"He's on a flight coming from Hawaii now but he won't be arriving until just before dawn this morning," he relayed.

"I would offer to let you come to the embassy and stay for the day but at this point we'll be completely booked up with Mr. St Domingue's people." I wondered how many "people" he was bringing.

"No, that's fine. Will you tell Mr. St Domingue that I would be enchanted to meet with him on Friday evening first thing? I'll come by the embassy then," she said with her own excitement showing.

"Yes, of course Iris. I'll tell him the moment he arrives. Will you be bringing Mr. Carson with you?" He inquired.

"Yes, he'll be with me." She looked over at me to confirm.

"I'll let him know. We are all very excited to meet Mr. St Domingue here. Everyone's buzzing. See you tomorrow!"

"See you, Harold," she said as they hung up.

"Wow!" Iris went over and sat on the couch just as Gavin emerged from the closet. He was wearing black jeans, red creepers and was pulling on a black button down shirt that had some red embroidery detailing on the front.

"What's wow?" Gavin said as he went and joined her on the couch.

"Jacque St Domingue is on his way here and he's been looking for me," She said.

"Why's he looking for you? You've never met him before, right?" Gavin asked.

"No but he must be looking for Heinrich too. He'll give us a big advantage in finding Heinrich, being his sire," she said, encouraged.

"How can he help, exactly?" Gavin asked, I was wondering too.

"Well, you can always sense the well being of your scion so he'll know for sure if he's alive or not. He must be alive or why come here? It's encouraging to me that he's coming." Iris did look visibly cheered.

"That's great baby. See, we'll find him," Gavin said in a touching way to Iris. He took a hold of Iris' hand and squeezed. She smiled at him warmly.

"He also should be able to know if we're on the right or wrong track; if we're headed in the right direction. He's also very old so who knows what else he'll be able to do." Her eyes were bright with the possibilities.

I had to admit, the prospect of meeting Jacque St Domingue was becoming an intriguing one to me. This was a man… a vampire, whose blood now ran in my veins. He was a part of who I was now.

The excitement of it had my blood flowing and I noticed that with the proximity of Gavin my mouth was watering again. I consciously backed up away from the couch a few feet.

"Oh Brett, I'm so sorry. I wasn't thinking about how thirsty you'd be by now. Let's go find you a meal," she suggested.

"Then we're gonna to go find me a meal. I'm starving! This chic's sucking all the vitamins right out of me," Gavin said sarcastically as he grabbed Iris' hand and we all headed out to find a meal.

So we got into the car, destination unknown at this point, and headed out. I had not forgotten my one important goal for the day; to pay a visit to Marisol and tell her everything. It would have to wait until she got home from work, after about 9:30, plenty of time to feed and get some food for Gavin.

Gavin had cut down to Sunset Blvd. and was cruising slowly down the street.

"Why don't we get one of those street walkers there?" Iris indicated one of the many hookers that lined Sunset Blvd. from dusk 'til dawn.

Gavin looked back at me then over to Iris. "They cost money," he complained.

"I have money," she offered. She lifted up the little white vinyl clutch purse she'd brought with her.

She looked back at me. It wasn't the hooker I objected to. "I don't want you to have to pay for me," I protested.

She frowned. "Oh, please. I have plenty. I'll have a little too if it makes you feel better," she offered.

I shrugged. I didn't like it but I knew I needed to feed soon or Gavin would be missing a few more vitamins. Iris scanned the lineup and picked out a victim for us. "Ooh, how about her?"

Iris had picked out a large, black prostitute wearing a skin-tight red Lycra mini-dress, fake fur and black pointed pumps. "She's nice and plump," she said with enthusiasm.

I didn't object and Gavin pulled over toward the curb. He was starting to look quite amused with the turn of events for the evening.

Iris started to roll down her window and I interjected. "Iris. Why don't you let me?" She looked back at me warmly.

"You want to solo?" She looked pleased as she rolled up her window and settled in to watch the exchange.

I rolled down my window. As the prostitute leaned down to see inside, Iris quickly turned on the car's dome light.

"You looking for a date?" the woman asked. Once she saw my face she looked surprised; she amped-up her game. "Hey baby. You gonna tell me you can't find a date you don't gotta pay?" She was adjusting the dress to display a little more of her rather large breasts.

I smiled at her and caught her gaze. "How much for the whole night?" I inquired.

She held my gaze and began to relax. "What do you need the whole night for?" She asked playfully.

"I don't need the whole night but I thought you might want to take the night off after we're done," I offered.

She was starting to sink into a more meditative state. "Just you?" she asked.

"Maybe the girl too," I said truthfully. I smiled at her again. "So, how much would you typically make on a Thursday night?"

"I don't know… maybe $500.00," she lied.

Gavin interjected. This was his territory, negotiation. "$300.00 tops," he told her. She didn't look up at him. She seemed to be completely under my spell at this point.

"Would $300.00 be sufficient? I won't take but an hour of your time?" I asked respectfully.

"Move over sugar," she decided. She opened the door herself and got in next to me. Once she looked at me up close she said, "Damn, I'll pay you $300.00. You're the prettiest white boy I ever seen," which was flattering.

"Thanks… Iris?" Iris handed me three, crisp $100.00 bills.

"What's your name?" I asked as I handed her the money.

"People call me Sunny," she said as she smiled at me suggestively.

"Hi Sunny," I said as I handed her the hundreds. She took the money and stuffed it into the pocket of her fake-fur jacket then took it off.

"Thanks… Now, what can I do for *you*, baby?" She put a hand on my thigh and rubbed. Gavin pulled the car around the corner on Hudson and parked behind the Hollywood Athletic Club.

At the same time I held her eyes and started to suggest.

"Sunny?" She fell back in easily. "Sunny, you're going to tell anyone that asks that you gave me a blow job, I paid you $300.00 for it and said it was the best blow job I'd ever had," I suggested.

She was mesmerized. "Damn straight."

With that I sunk my teeth into her neck and started to drink. Iris reached over and lifted Sunny's wrist up to her mouth and joined me.

She was a robust woman with a strong heart and her size let us drink our fill without even softening the rhythm of her heart. Once we were done and had cleaned her up Gavin pulled around to where we had picked her up and dropped her off.

"Sunny, that was the best I've ever had. You should take the rest of the night off," I suggested again. I helped her into her fake-fur jacket and she got out of the car.

"I think I will," she said and ambled over toward the Copper Penny and went inside.

"She's probably starving now," Iris said.

"I know I am," Gavin said. He pulled out into traffic and headed down toward Melrose, then West.

"Wow, look at all these fun stores. I need to go shopping," Iris observed excitedly.

"We'll go shopping soon, baby. Hey Brett, you have a gig on Saturday night. Do you remember?" He reminded me.

"I thought I had a gig on Tuesday night," I recalled.

"You did. I cancelled it, obviously. I haven't cancelled Saturday yet, I wasn't sure," he was asking.

"I don't see why not," I thought. I was feeling like it had been a really long time since I played.

Gavin turned up Fairfax Ave. and pulled around to the side parking lot of Canter's Deli. We walked around and went in the front.

"Oh, I've seen this place. Although I've never been inside," Iris recalled. She was holding on to Gavin's hand with both of hers and trailing behind him. All of their obvious affection was making me impatient to see Marisol.

They sat us in a booth near the middle of the main room. Although I'd been here before, it seemed like an intense shock of bright, florescent lights and tacky colors. I noticed I could actually see the florescent lights pulsing. The smell of dead meat was somewhat sickening.

When the waiter came Gavin ordered potato pancakes, a corn beef sandwich, a bowl of chicken matzo ball soup and a chocolate shake. I ordered a coffee and Iris just asked for a glass of water.

Once the waiter left I said to Gavin, "Hungry?" sarcastically.

"I'm friggin' starving. She sucks it all out of me," he complained. But they were leaning back, gazing into each other's eyes when he said this.

I leaned my head back and stared at the mind-blowing fall-scene ceiling that was back-lit by the florescent lights and thought about what I would say to Marisol; how she might react.

The waiter brought Gavin's' food and our drinks. I used the coffee to warm my hands. I didn't feel cold but the warmth was nice. I used the spoon to stir the coffee a couple of times and blew on it to make it look natural. Iris sipped her water, swished it around her mouth and spit it back into the glass. The water turned a little pink from that. She gave me a smile and a shrug.

As Gavin wolfed down every bit of food the waiter brought for him, Iris crinkled her nose and looked at me. "It's disgusting, isn't it?"

"It kind of is," I had to agree. The dead meat smell from this proximity was even stronger and more sickening.

"Do you mind?" Gavin said with a full mouth. I laughed.

Iris looked contrite, "I'm sorry baby; I know you're doing this for me. I'm buying," she offered.

He looked at her and thought about it and said, "OK," still chewing.

He leaned in to kiss her but she pulled back in disgust. This amused him so he tried harder. She put her hands over her mouth and leaned out further. He eventually went back to finishing his meal. When he was done Iris handed him another water glass the waiter had brought and wordlessly instructed him to swish out his mouth, as she had done.

Before we left, some people Gavin knew stopped by the booth and said hello. Gavin introduced Iris and chatted a little. "Hey guys. Brett has a show Saturday night at the Biltmore. You should stop by," inviting them.

"Hey, yeah thanks, Gavin. Maybe we will. Good to see you Brett," they said as they left and the waiter brought over the bill.

Iris pulled out another hundred and paid the bill up at the cash register. We left and went around the side to the parking lot and got back into the T-Bird.

I looked at Gavin and said pointedly, "Marisol's," again, not a question.

He grumbled but didn't argue, put it in gear and headed out.

Once we got there he parked blocking her driveway, as he always does, and headed for the back stairs. I stopped him, saying we should probably go up through the front. He was a little exasperated but followed me around.

We walked up the front stairs and through the landscaped courtyard to the back. The curtains were open but I didn't see anyone inside. I couldn't smell her very strongly either. We knocked.

No one answered so Gavin used his key to open the door. He walked in, then Iris, and I walked in last. I didn't like intruding into Marisol's house again without her permission.

"Shouldn't she be home by now?" I asked.

"Yeah, it's 10:30. Maybe she stopped somewhere," Gavin theorized then he noticed the blinking light on her answering machine and pushed the button before I could protest.

Beep. "Marisol… Marisol I miss you…" It was too personal. I walked over and hit stop and looked up at Gavin, ready to protest.

"That was a new message," he said. Meaning she hadn't been home to hear the message. This sent a chill through me.

"Where could she be?" I was the one panicking now.

"There're more messages," he said and when he hit play my message started to continue until Gavin hit the skip button.

Beep. "Hey Marisol, it's Arial. You said you were going to stop by last night. I hope everything's OK. Call me."

Beep. "Hi Honey, it's me Suzanne. You're probably on your way but I wanted to check to see that you were OK. Call me."

Beep. "Hey Mar, it's Suzanne again. You're starting to worry me now. I'm hoping you just had such a great night last night that you're sleeping now. I'm gonna call Gavin just to check." Beep.

"Shit. This means she's been missing since yesterday." I was really starting to worry now.

"She must have gone somewhere straight from work yesterday," Gavin was trying to say calm.

"It sounds like she was supposed to go to Arial's and never made it," I was starting to lose it.

Iris chimed in now, "Brett, remember we smelled Marisol in the elevator. She obviously made it to the building…" she said, trying to be helpful.

I looked up at Iris, stunned. All I could think of was those three, murderous Germans. From the look on Iris' face she had the same thought. "Let's go," I insisted.

Gavin spoke up. "Wait. I have to call Suzanne first," he stopped us.

I paced while Gavin called Suzanne and explained that Marisol was missing and that she had been since she left work yesterday. Her boss seemed to be genuinely horrified and asked to be kept informed of any developments.

Next, Gavin called Arial to let her know we were on our way and again, that Marisol was missing. He kept it brief and said we'd be there in just a few minutes.

Before Gavin could even hang up the phone I was out the door and heading quickly for the car. I could hear Gavin scrambling to lock up the house and keep as close behind me as possible. Iris was as fast as me but Gavin was fumbling with the keys and visibly upset.

When we got to the car Iris offered to drive.

"No, that's OK. I got it baby. Thank you, though," he seemed genuinely grateful for her support. Gavin was lucky to have Iris at this moment.

"It's probably better you drive anyway. It's been a long time since I drove…" She started as Gavin squealed in reverse out of the driveway and then floored in down the hill.

It wasn't that far away so we were there in a flash. We pulled up and parked in a spot half-way between the Fleur De Lis and the Fontenoy.

We walked silently up to the Fontenoy and through the lobby to the elevator. Once it came and we got in, Gavin pushed the button for the 11th floor. As soon as we'd boarded and it started up I looked questioningly at Iris.

"I don't smell anything new, do you?" I inquired to her.

"No, her smell is almost gone," Iris said sympathetically.

Gavin was looking at us with a desperate look on his face.

Once the elevator finally arrived at the 11th floor we got off and walked down the hallway to the right to find unit 1103 and knocked.

Arial answered the door almost immediately and, once she had a look at Iris, then Brett, a large nervous grin spread across her face and she sort of froze in place. Gavin spoke up.

"Arial, can we come in?" he said impatiently.

"Of course, come in." She backed up to let Iris in, then Gavin, then me. As I passed her she said to me, "You're different…" This was followed by a nervous giggle.

Her apartment was a fraction of the size of the penthouse suite but the style was similar. Her apartment was one square room with a small dining room and kitchen in the far corner and a bathroom and dressing area off the entrance hallway. She had her bed pushed into one corner and several large pillows gathered around two low tables. There was a stereo in the corner with hundreds of LP's stacked against the wall on cinderblock shelving and some original art on the walls. The lighting was wall sconces on a dimmer and many candles. There was a small dining room table and four chairs in the small dining area near the kitchen.

Gavin cleared his throat, "So Arial, this is Iris, my girlfriend," Gavin said as an introduction.

Iris smiled brightly at Gavin and squeezed his hand. Maybe she hadn't had that label attributed to her until now. Manners always impeccable, Iris turned to greet Arial, "It's nice to meet you Arial."

"You too. Would you like to sit down?" she offered.

She gestured toward one of the low tables. We all went and sat down on three big pillows. Arial sat on the fourth. From the position of my seat and it being so low to the ground, I could see that there was a pentagram painted under her bed.

"Can I get you…?" She then looked at Gavin and spoke just to him. "Can I get you a drink?" holding her smile.

Gavin smirked. "No thanks, Arial."

Just then, Arial remembered why we were here. "So, what's up with Marisol? Where is she?" she wondered.

Gavin spoke up, "That's the problem, we don't know," looking and sounding deeply concerned.

"She was supposed to come by last night," Arial said.

"I know, that's what you said, but she never showed up right?" Gavin asked.

"No." Arial conceded.

"We were here last night and could smell she had been in the elevator. Her scent was there only on the way down so she must have gotten here when we were upstairs." Iris explained.

Arial looked over at Iris, "You were here to see Harold?" more a statement.

Iris looked surprised. "You know Harold?"

"Yeah, he lets me be the door person sometimes… I keep odd hours." Arial giggled.

"So, why was she coming to see you?" Iris asked.

"Well, we're friends. She seemed kind of bummed out the last couple of days so I wanted to cheer her up." Her eyes flashed over to me. "I asked her to come by to help me with my curse," she added.

"It's obvious now why she hasn't heard from you in the past couple of days," Arial said looking back at me. I didn't think I could feel any worse, but apparently I was wrong.

Iris spoke up, "It wasn't his fault… it was my fault," she offered.

"It was an accident," Gavin defended her.

"I don't blame you, Iris... and I'm fine now," I consoled her. I didn't want her to carry around guilt. She smiled at me in appreciation.

"Whatever, it's not my business," Arial said, her valley dialect kicking in strong.

We were all silent for a minute.

Iris spoke first, "So, who were you trying to curse?" she asked.

"There have been three... *visitors*… upstairs who are bringing down the energy of the whole building. I don't have anything against vampires but…"

Iris cut her off. "No, it's OK. Feel free to curse them," Iris said venomously.

"You know them?" Arial asked.

"Long story," Iris replied, fuming a little.

"Well, I told Harold I wouldn't work the door until they were gone. He understood. I put a protective spell on myself so they couldn't hypnotize me but even with that, I wasn't comfortable. I've been working on a repellant spell; I think it may have worked last night," Arial explained.

"Why do you think it may have worked?" Gavin asked.

"Because they haven't been back since," Arial responded.

A monstrous thought was forming in my imagination. I needed to put it out there. "They have her, don't they? Those monsters took Marisol!" I didn't mean to shout it, but I did.

No one knew what to say because there it was; the most probable answer.

"Shit." I leaped across the room and pounded my fist on the wall. Luckily it was concrete and not plaster. I may have frightened Arial.

"He's really young. Has he fed today yet?" Arial was a little concerned.

Iris answered, "Yes, don't worry," trying to sound assuring.

"What are we going to do?" Gavin was getting upset too.

"Brett, come with me. Let's go talk to Harold and find out what we can about these three German assholes."

Marisol

Twelve

As I came into awareness out of the dream I was having, the nightmare actually, I realized there wasn't much difference from my reality. In my dream I was trapped in a small, enclosed space lying down and I was pounding on the walls to get someone's attention. I was screaming but no one was hearing me. I heard myself really scream as I sat up; someone heard me this time.

"Child, child, it's OK," the vampire consoled me.

As the reality of my situation seeped back in, I was at least thankful that this enclosed room was on the larger side; still uncomfortably enclosed, but not so small that I couldn't prevent myself from panicking. I know his intent was to console me, but the outcome of my present circumstances would most likely end in a way that was not OK.

"Heinrich?" The gentle, friendly vampire who would surely end up being the instrument of my death comforted me with his presence.

"I'm here… I'm not going anywhere," he said with unfortunate certainty.

"Yeah, me neither." I lifted myself up off the cold floor and scooted into the corner. I was starting to feel thirsty but I tried not to think about it.

I sat there for a long while clearing my head. He lay facing me on his side. Now that I was looking at him closely, aside from the drawn look, which must be the toll of imprisonment, he was rather beautiful. Of medium build and quite muscular, he looked like a man of 30 when he was still, but when he smiled the crinkles around his eyes and mouth suggested he was older than that. But his skin shone a perfect pale white and the salt and pepper hair that hung to his shoulders was shiny and thick. He had a single tattoo of an anchor on his left forearm.

The shackles and thick chains holding him were fastened to the wall with extremely large metal grommets. A vampire's strength must be immense to warrant such a precaution.

"Does the silver hurt on your skin?" I asked. He didn't look like he was in pain exactly.

"Yes and no. We don't feel pain in the same way you do. We register pain intellectually, so yes, in that way. But mainly the silver sucks the energy out of us; makes us weak," he explained. He did look weak.

"I'm so sorry… when did they bring you down here?" I asked.

"It was 1951 when those German leaches staked me and dumped me into this pit." This made him think. "What year is it now?"

"It's 1980," I reported to him. This news seemed to depress him.

"So it's been almost 30 years… almost that long since I should have been there to awaken my beautiful Iris," he sulked. There was pain in his face.

"Who's Iris?" I asked softly. This registered déjà vu for some reason.

"Iris is my beautiful vampire scion… child," he clarified.

"I fear it will be her destiny to slumber in a void of emptiness for eternity," he said despondently. That sounded ominous.

"Once we're deep into our hibernation, something we need to do from time to time, we lose the ability to rouse ourselves and must rely on our family to do it for us," he continued.

"Iris went to sleep in 1932 after a bad stroke of luck, to… sleep it off, you might say. I am the only one who knows where she is," he said sadly.

"I'm so sorry," I offered. We let that sit out there until it dissipated a bit.

"So, you said they staked you." I started, somewhat delicately, "In the movies—I know, that's all probably bullshit—but in the movies when they stake a vampire, they always die," I stated, curious.

"Well, I wouldn't say it was total bullshit because when you stake a vampire they do *appear* to die. But if you pulled out the stake and re-hydrated the poor soul they would reanimate; be released from the void," He explained. Interesting.

I asked gently, "So, they did that to you?"

"Yes, I was caught off guard. I was immediately plunged into the void of nothingness. When I reawakened I was here," he recalled.

"That really sucks," was my assessment.

He laughed. "I've never heard that phrase, but I like it." That made me laugh too.

"So, you seem to dislike Germans but… aren't you German?" He definitely had what sounded like a German accent.

"I'm from the Austrian Republic. It wasn't always an official country but I consider myself an Austrian," he clarified.

I was pretty sure Austria had been a country for a very long time. "How long have you been a vampire?" I asked.

"Since 1790, it was the year of the Haitian Revolution," he said with conviction. I'm sure there must be some significance for him.

"That's a long way from Austria," I pointed out.

"Yes, well, I'm a sailor, remember? Chances are if a waterway leads to it, I've been there," he said with a far away look in his eye.

"That sounds incredible. I've never even been out of the country. Actually, I've only been to three states," I realized.

"I'm sorry that in all probability, that may be the extent of your travels during this life. But, if you can find a way to communicate our way out of here, I would be more that happy to put my vessel at your disposal to take you to the farthest destination of your choice, anytime you wish," he offered, his eyes glinting and he gave me a hopeful look.

I wished I could find a helpful spirit who could communicate to someone that we needed help down here. It, of course, didn't work that way. Not being a sender I could only project out my reception and hope that someone else out there could communicate to their guides like I could. So far, the neighbors' guides were being unhelpfully aloof.

"So Heinrich, tell me about being a vampire…"

Heinrich told me about what it feels like to be a vampire, what it tastes like to drink blood, how your senses are heightened, what it was like when he changed, where he'd gone and the things he'd done when he was free. He told me about his… "sire," Jacque, and how their relationship had grown through the years. He told me about Iris, his "scion," and how he'd found her; how our captors had drained her and left her to die on the voyage to Ellis Island so long ago. He told me about his ship that he'd left docked in port but that must have been sold off or commandeered by the leaches by now.

I told him about my life in the modern world he'd missed for the last 30 years. I'd gone over some of the things that had changed and new conveniences we now had. I told him about my life and family, about my father's confession, about my mother's suicide, and my relationship with Gavin. I told him about Suzanne and my job, my new German car (not impressed) and the brief, extraordinary love of my life; Brett.

"You know, when you've been in here for 30 years, three days hardly seems like a fair amount of time to put something in a past tense," he began, "I know, maybe everything is in the past now but, I don't know… I can't shake this hint of optimism you seem to have brought down here with you," he said generously.

I wish I could feel the same way. I did feel like, if I had to die in here, it would be some consolation to give what blood I had to Heinrich so he might one day get out of here and back out to the sea he loved.

"Heinrich, before I pass out you have to lift the hypnotism… I don't want to die for nothing," I resolved.

Neither of us spoke for a moment. "Let's cross that bridge when… *if* we get to it," was his reply.

Yucca & Ivar

Iris

Thirteen

When Brett and I left Gavin at Arial's I felt so bad for Gavin I almost couldn't leave. I took him aside and spoke optimistically that we would surely find his sister before anything bad could happen to her. I wanted to believe this. But I knew all too well the brutality and disregard for human life and humanity in general that these monsters harbored.

Brett was waiting in front of the elevator while Gavin and I hovered near Arial's front door. I reached up and kissed him sweetly trying to give him the boost that he would surely need at this moment. The he lifted me up on my toes and held me tightly. "Don't stay up there too long," he whispered in my ear before letting me down, putting a kiss on my forehead and turning swiftly to go back into Arial's. I could hear him hover at the door until we got into the elevator and the doors shut.

When we were on our short way up I took Brett's arm again and gave him an encouraging smile. He attempted to return it. I was horrified that the very monsters that had terrorized me when I was young and vulnerable would now be terrorizing the two people I'd come to love during this new chapter of my life. I would not let this happen to them and I was resolved I would do everything in my power to stop it.

When the bell rang for the top floor and the doors opened, I noticed the guard at the front door was the same as last night. When I approached him I had my own questions this time.

"Good evening, I'm Iris Stein and this is my scion, Brett Carson, from last evening, do you remember?" I began.

"Yes, ma'am, you can go in," he answered blandly and stood aside.

"Excuse me, can you tell me your name?" I asked.

"Um…sure, my name is Mike, Mike Johnson," he replied tentatively.

"Nice to meet you, Mike… Mike, were you here all night last night?" I continued.

"Yes, ma'am," he answered dutifully.

"Did you happen to see a young, human girl here last night? She would have looked like…" I looked to Brett for the description I didn't have. He immediately jumped in.

"She's about five foot seven, long blonde hair, blue eyes, quite beautiful…" His eyes pleaded with Mike for some help.

"Yeah, she was here… She didn't come in though, obviously, she was human, like me," he reported, unintentionally crass.

I could see Brett's face flash to anger. If she would have been allowed in maybe she wouldn't have been taken.

"What did she want?" He asked, raising his voice a bit.

"She was looking for some guy… *you*, I think," as recognition crossed his face.

This flashed pain in Brett and he turned to me with questioning in his face; which I'm sure was how she would know to look for him here.

"She asked for me?" He reiterated back to Mike.

"Yeah, Brett Carson, right?" He reiterated.

Brett continued, "Was anyone else here? Did you see anything else?"

He looked sheepish, "I don't know if I'm supposed to give out that kind of information. I'm not sure…"

"Tell me," Brett shouted at the doorman and was attempting to push a load of influence in through his eyes. I was pretty sure that anyone guarding the door would be protected from this type of manipulation. Mike's jaw dropped but he said nothing.

I attempted to revert to the charm offensive as I squeezed Brett's arm, "Mike… our friend is missing and we believe she may have been abducted. Surely you don't believe that Harold… Mr. McKinley would object to your assistance in our search for our friend. You can clear it with him if you like," I smiled imploringly.

He was looking a little agitated, "No, I'll tell you. Just don't tell them I told you." He lowered his voice an octave. "Those three German vamps, they were following her when she came in. When I had to tell her she couldn't come in, she left with them," he admitted. He was crossing back into sheepish again. "Just so you know, I didn't have a choice, I couldn't let her in, you know that," he said with an apologetic tone. "You know, it looked like maybe they used their influence on her," he concluded.

I looked over at Brett and he was seething at this. I decided it was time to make our entrance.

"Thank you Mike, you've been very helpful. You don't have to worry; we would never disclose your confidence to the Germans," I assured him as I quickly ushered Brett into the embassy. Mike closed the door behind us.

The soothing atmosphere of the embassy wasn't doing much to calm my scion's agitated nerves. I took his arm and urged him around to Harold's office. He'd heard us come in and was waiting to greet us.

"Harold," I smiled as he greeted us.

"Iris, Mr. Carson, it's a pleasure to see you again so soon. To what do I owe this unexpected visit?" He took my hand and nodded to Brett.

"Harold, I'm afraid something terrible has happened," I began.

"Oh, well, please come inside and tell me about it," he said as he sensed our dismay. He quickly went behind his desk and cleared away something he was reading and gestured for us to sit.

"Does this have to do with Captain Frederickson?" He asked.

"Actually, no, but I'm still worried about him too. Yesterday a friend of ours, actually Brett's girlfriend..." I gave Brett a half-smile and his arm a quick squeeze, "...stopped by here to look for him," I began to explain.

"His girlfriend, Marisol James, is human so Mike at the front door couldn't admit her. Well, I know that's the policy but unfortunately, when she was leaving she ran into those three Germans who apparently have been hanging around lately and it's our understanding that they abducted her," I concluded.

"Oh my, I'm so sorry if that's the case. I have to say that those three have not been the best behaved visitors. They've been scaring the human employees and drinking all the stocked blood. That blood's for emergencies and dignitaries," he complained.

"Harold, I must tell you that I have my own history with those three. I don't think you know this but, they were the ones responsible for draining me before Heinrich discovered me and had to change me in order to save me from death," I recalled painfully then lowered my voice, "taking my blood wasn't the only thing on their agenda that day," I added. I didn't like dredging it up but it was important he understand the full brutality of these monsters.

"Oh... oh, Iris, I'm so sorry... I must say it doesn't surprise me though. Those three are nothing but trouble," he commiserated.

"Who are they, why are they here?" Brett asked, still very tense.

"Well I can tell you their names; they're Godfried, Markus and Claudio Horst. I don't believe they're all brothers, maybe they are, but nevertheless they all go by Horst. They only stop by occasionally, every few years or so. I don't know where they live permanently, maybe they are nomadic, but their keys indicate they were based in Berlin, at least in the beginning," he related helpfully.

"They were on a ship from London to New York in 1898..." I added with contempt. "Which one is which? Which one is the tall one with the long hair?" I was morbidly curious.

"The tall one is Godfried, the bald one is Markus and the one with the short hair, the musician, is Claudio," he listed for me.

It didn't help to know their names but it was probably good information to have. This time Brett took a hold of my hand and squeezed it a little, bless his heart.

"I'm sorry I can't think of anything else that might be of more help than that. Perhaps when Jacque St Domingue arrives he might be willing to help with this disappearance as well. He is of your blood; your sire's sire. I hear his people are remarkable trackers," he suggested.

I looked over encouragingly at Brett, then back at Harold. "Well that would be great, if he could help us. When is he slated to arrive again?" She asked.

"His plane is arriving at 3:00 AM. He should be here by 4:00," Harold replied.

"Would you mind if we came back to speak with him then? I know there will probably be nothing that can be done tonight but we are desperately concerned about our friend… I wouldn't require sleeping quarters but I know Brett would," she appealed to him.

"Yes, I think it would be appropriate for someone of his bloodline to greet him upon his arrival. We may not be able to accommodate Mr. Carson though, so perhaps, just you? I'm sorry but I don't know how many are in his party or what their sleeping requirements are," he said regretfully.

"No, I understand," Brett said. He looked at me and asked, "You don't think I can stay alert?"

"No, sweetie, I don't think so. It's too soon," I had to say. He looked visibly frustrated.

"It's OK; I'll go back to Gavin's. I don't want to be an imposition," trying to be stoic.

"Gavin needs support too, so I'm really glad that you'll be there for each other tonight. I'll just be relating all our information tonight and tomorrow I'll be so proud to introduce you to them," I said as I smiled warmly at him.

We both looked back at Harold and then at each other and after a minute it was clear we couldn't think of any more questions to ask.

"Mr. McKinley thanks so much for all your help." Brett stood up and they shook hands. I stood up and took Brett's arm.

"Harold, I'll see you later," I smiled weakly. Harold stood up, nodded to us politely and then we left.

When we got back down to Arial's I could hear Gavin pacing the floor from the elevator. We knocked and after a second Arial opened the door. Gavin was close behind her. I stayed in the doorway. "Arial, thanks so much for your help. You're probably tired so why don't I just grab Gavin and get him home," I offered.

"OK. Did you learn anything?" She asked.

"A little more about the Germans; the Horsts. I'm coming back tonight at around 3:30 and staying at the embassy tonight. Some important people are coming to help," I said. Arial smiled hopefully. Gavin looked torn.

I said to Gavin, "Are you ready?"

"Yeah," Gavin said as he walked out past Arial and slipped his arm over my shoulder. "Thanks Arial. I'll let you know what's happening," he said to her as he swung around.

"OK, be sure to call me because maybe I can help," Arial offered.

"Definitely, we need all the help we can get," Gavin replied back as we started toward the elevator.

We walked at Gavin's speed back to the Fleur De Lis and went inside. It was about midnight by this time.

When we got inside Brett asked Gavin, "Hey, do you have any pictures of Marisol? Maybe it could help with the search," he said hopefully.

"Actually, if you have anything with her scent that would definitely help," I added.

"Yeah, I have a picture I think..." He looked through some papers and came up with a black and white print he said he took of her with her camera. She was quite pretty; she looked quite a bit like Gavin. "I don't think I have anything with her scent though..." he was thinking.

Brett spoke up, "Why don't I go over to Marisol's and get a piece of clothing... I can give you guys time alone," he offered generously.

"You don't mind?" Gavin asked.

"No, I haven't had any time to myself since this whole thing started. I think I can do this one thing..." He said, trying to alleviate some of his obvious frustration.

"Alright, thanks Brett, here," he fished out and handed Brett his keys. Brett grabbed his leather jacket, probably out of habit, and said he'd be back in a couple of hours.

Once we were alone I went up and folded myself into Gavin. We just swayed for a minute then he picked me up and took me into the bedroom. He stood me on my feet at the end of the bed and when he sat down he pulled me down next to him but then pulled my top leg around his hip. I laid my head down next to his with my nose practically touching his. We just laid there looking into each other for a minute before he leaned in to kiss me, slow and lingering. We made love like one of us was going off to war tomorrow. I hoped this wasn't the truth.

Fourteen

It was 3:00 AM. I heard Brett come in just a few minutes earlier. Gavin had been sleeping for about 20 minutes by now and as I attempted to untangle myself without waking him, he woke up anyway.

"Don't go," he said, his lips brushing my face as he spoke. He defiantly held on to my waist without opening his eyes. I obeyed for a couple more minutes of pure indulgence then was adamant that I needed to change for my meeting.

"You need to sleep anyway," I told him as I got up and went to the closet to find something appropriate to wear. I took a quick shower—I smelled so much like Gavin I was sure they would mistake me for a human—then fixed my hair in the new straight way and picked out a peach colored knit suit; back-slit skirt just below the knee and a cute flair at the bottom of the jacket. I added a little of the gold jewelry I'd gotten out of the trunk including a diamond star hair clip I fastened to one side and was ready to go by 3:30.

Once I'd blotted my lipstick by planting a kiss on Gavin's cheek and said goodbye to Brett I was out the door. Since it was so late and unlikely anyone was watching, I decided to high-tail it and was in the elevator at the Fontenoy in less than a minute. Once the door opened on the 13th floor I was surprised to find it was Arial attending the front door this time.

I walked up and greeted her, "Hi Arial."

"Hi Iris, back to the crazy hours. I figured it was safe to work here again; what with the spell working… and the Haitians on their way…" She giggled as she rambled a bit. She was dressed in flowing skirt of bright colors, a coordinated blouse and a pair of wooden-soled slip-on heels. She had dressed up for this.

"Are they here yet?" I asked.

"Not yet, but Harold said they're on their way," she said as she opened the door for me to go in. "Good luck."

"Thanks," I said as I walked in to the soothing atmosphere of the embassy. I noticed there was what sounded like island native music playing softly on the sound system; Harold's attempt to make our visitors feel at home.

Just as I was about to head around the corner toward Harold's office, he appeared and joined me in the lounge area.

"They should be here any time now," He said as he gave me a quick kiss on the cheek.

I heard Arial's giggle as the door opened and the Haitians came in. There were three of them; the first one who entered was a tall male, about six foot three with short, neat dreadlocks and very dark black skin. His cheeks and lips were a beautiful magenta color and his teeth and the whites of his eyes shone very bright. His eyes were black except for a striking blue circle around the outside of his pupils. He wore a dark grey suit that looked very modern with a black shirt and tie. I assumed this was Jacque St Domingue. With him were two female vampires. The first one was quite tall, maybe six feet tall with light coco color skin and green eyes. She was lean and had long, straight black hair that shone like glass. She wore a copper colored suit and heels. The second female was a little shorter and darker skinned, slightly more plump and wore a more modest floor-length skirt with a black bodice and sandals. She had the same blue encircling her eyes and her many long braids were streaked with golden highlights.

"Welcome," Harold greeted them.

"Good evening, thank you for the reception. I am Jacque St Domingue and these are my traveling companions, Celestine and Arelia," He first indicated the tall vampire then the shorter female.

"I'm Harold McKinley your ambassador here in Los Angeles and this is Iris Stein, she is the scion of Captain Frederickson's that I spoke about on the phone," he greeted.

"Mr. McKinley," they shook hands. "Yes, of course. I could sense there was family here from outside of the building. It's a pleasure," he said as he held out both hands for mine and kissed the back of my hand in greeting.

I nodded warmly to the women and replied "It's wonderful to meet you too. I've heard so much about you from Heinrich," I said, feeling the genuine affection of our bond.

This brought the main reason for our meeting front and center. Harold directed us to a seating area in front of one of the windows and we all sat.

Jacque St Domingue spoke first. "As I'm sure must be obvious to you considering your recent history, we must acknowledge at this point the disappearance of my trusted friend and scion Heinrich." His voice was smooth and thick with a French Creole accent. He looked at me, "...and, of course, your sire mademoiselle," he acknowledged.

He went on, "Of course, I can sense that he lives," he said quickly. This was welcome information. We all breathed a sigh of relief. "We are here to do whatever we can to help track and find him. Mademoiselle Stein..." he started.

I interjected, "Please, call me Iris," I insisted.

"Iris," He smiled and continued. "The story Monsieur McKinley relayed to me over the phone regarding your unplanned lengthy hibernation is... disturbingly familiar," he empathized.

"Is it? It was my first one so... I guess I'd still be down there if we didn't have that earthquake," I said honestly.

"So, it was an earthquake that finally roused you from your long sleep?" He asked.

"Well, yes and no. I believe there had been other earthquakes during my sleep, but luckily my sleeping chamber was compromised by this earthquake and some rats came in through the opening and…"

"Blood," he surmised.

"Yes, blood instinct did it," I confessed.

"Well, I'm very glad you found your way out Iris. Unfortunately, your story has been duplicated in different ways all over the world. This problem of hibernating vampires becoming unaccounted for… lost, has been an enduring and chronic one for our kind. This is of concern to me and many of the older ones who have seen this first hand for hundreds of years," he informed us. We were all pretty riveted.

"I applaud the embassies for doing what they can and instituting the program they have for keeping track of those that sleep. This was a step in the right direction and will help to prevent this type of thing from happening to us going forward," he continued. He'd obviously thought quite a lot about this.

"Even with that, there is still the problem of those that have been slumbering for decades… millennia… that lie and wait under a blanket of nothingness," he said ominously. This hit close to home for me and my eyes welled up a bit in horror.

"I'm sorry Iris, I know you've only been back for a few days," he sympathized. I think he could feel as well as see my reaction. I pushed myself to feel grateful. He smiled back at me.

"This is where my new purpose lies. I have been putting together a team to find and release those trapped in this purgatory. I don't know if Heinrich is trapped this way but this is why I brought Arelia. Arelia is a psychic receiver. She can sometimes pick up psychic signatures of spirits and entities out in the other dimensions. She did not have this talent as a human but it has shown itself in immortality," he informed us.

Arelia smiled and spoke for the first time, "I am still working on it; honing my skill." She said modestly.

"She has improved greatly but she is still… hit and miss," he said with affection.

"Arelia is a descendent of my human bloodline as well and my immortal bloodline," he added. You could definitely see it in the eyes.

"My other companion, Celestine, is a powerfully skilled tracker. She brought this skill with her from her human life and has sharpened her senses over the past millennia. Celestine is also my wife," he related and smiled warmly at his wife of hundreds of years.

"So, I have now tired of my own voice," he said with good humor. "I would love to hear if there are any clues to the whereabouts of our Captain Frederickson," as he looked at me.

"Well, this is what I know: Heinrich was the one person I told I was going to ground. This was in October, 1932. The last time I saw him was October 2nd. He promised to return in 20 years to wake me from my sleep…

and I believe his plan was to sail to the Tahitian Islands… but that was so long ago," I fretted. It was sad to remember.

"Has anyone seen him since 1932?" I asked.

Harold answered. "The alarm bell only sounded once you rose a few days ago, of course, but I put out the word to all the other embassies and he did indeed check in at the Tahitian embassy in January of 1933 but there are no records after that of him having been anywhere else. Even out on the seas, he would presumably dock at some point and check in," he offered. We all pondered this.

"Actually, it would not be unusual for the Captain to go… off the grid for long stretches of time," Jacque informed us with a bit of a wistful smile.

I had an idea, "What about his ship? Do they track things like that? Maybe we can find the Josephine," I offered.

"That's a capitol idea, Iris. I'll have all the embassies check with their port authorities and I'll check with ours." Harold said enthusiastically.

"Excellent," Jacque St Domingue said. "I know there has been very little time to get the search started. We are prepared to stay as long as we are needed. Monsieur McKinley has been kind enough to provide us with one of the safe houses for the duration of our stay."

He looked over at me, "Iris, I know you also must have your hands full. Monsieur McKinley says you have a newborn scion," he inquired.

"Yes, but he is adapting very quickly. My only real concern is to make sure he feeds first thing in the evening," I said and I was sure he could feel my pride. I thought I should confess. "He was the unfortunate product of my unexpected rise. But I couldn't have been luckier with my accident of fate," I said with affection.

"That's wonderful, Iris." Jacque St Domingue said. "Accidents don't always work out well," he added. "I was also lucky… with Heinrich," he admitted.

"Yes, you and I are both lucky to have Heinrich…" I thought with melancholy. "I've also found someone special. We're thinking about a planned change... in the future. We're not going to rush it." I beamed.

"I'm very happy for you Iris." He did not judge me for the short time period as I was sure he could feel everything that I was feeling at that moment.

"Mr. St Domingue?" I started to ask.

"Please, call me Jacque. We are family," he interjected.

"Jacque, may I tell you about another disappearance that has happened recently?" I asked.

"Of course, my dear," he said affably.

"Gavin, my boyfriend, has a sister named Marisol, Marisol James. She is also my scion's girlfriend." I paused because this was a little convoluted but he seemed to be following.

"She went missing a few days ago—three days ago, and we believe strongly that we know who took her and that they are up to no good." I was speeding up in my explanation as I went on.

"Well, I know this is not your problem because she is a human and not your concern but the three German vampires who took her were the ones who abducted me before Heinrich found me and saved me with his blood, and now they're back terrorizing poor innocent people. Both my scion and my boyfriend are beside themselves with fear for her welfare and I feel strongly that the Germans should not be allowed to continue to terrorize unsuspecting women…" I was out of breath and starting to well up again.

"Oh, child…" When he looked into my eyes his eyes were also filling with a pink liquid. I realized the connection to our scion bloodline must strengthen with the passage of time. "What concerns you concerns us. We are here and we are more than happy to help you find this person who is so integral to your life," he said with true feeling.

"Thank you," I said and one tear escaped my eye as I smiled my gratitude.

"You say three German vampires. Why do I have the feeling this smacks of the Horst brothers?" He said with distain.

"Yes, that's who they are. I only learned their names from Harold today," I said. "They were coming here regularly but the witch at the door cast a spell to keep them away, so now we don't know where they are," I explained.

"So the human at the door is a witch?" Jacque asked.

"Yes, and you should know, apparently she's also a sender. She said that she was able to send messages into Marisol's head and Marisol received them loud and clear. Marisol's a receiver; a medium," I said and took a breath.

"So, the woman who's missing, Marisol, she's a receiver?" He was becoming more intrigued.

"Yes, she's a human, like I said, but apparently she's quite a powerful receiver," I answered.

"Interesting... this could help us in locating her. Does your scion have interest in changing her to become his mate?" He asked.

"I don't know, maybe. He loves her very much. He hasn't seen her since his change. We thought it would be better to keep him under wraps for a while…" I said with regret.

I continued, "Then she was gone. Everything that's happened… all that's transpired… it's only been since Sunday that all this has happened." I stammered.

"Oh, child… you slumbered in dark nothingness for 50 years and all this has transpired in less than a week. You do know how to make up for lost time," he said as an understatement.

"Do you have this Marisol's scent?" He asked practically.

"Yes, Brett went and got something from her house last night. I didn't think we'd have time tonight to do anything so I thought maybe, if you don't mind, we could all meet up tomorrow and see what we can find?" I was right about the time since the sky was starting to brighten and Harold had gotten up and started to lower the metal blinds.

"Monsieur McKinley, can we assist you with that?" Jacque asked him.

"Oh, no, please stay seated. This will only take me a second," he protested. He did seem to have the roll and tie pattern down to a science.

Once he was done he came back to the group. "Mr. St Domingue would you and your group like to use our rooms for daytime sleep?" He asked.

"I know Celestine and Arelia have been awake for several days and could use the downtime. And, though I don't require it, I have been going for several weeks without a rest so I wouldn't mind joining them," He said.

"Iris, do you have a place to rest?" Jacque asked me.

"Oh, I don't think I could rest… I've been resting for fifty years!" I realized. "I'll be fine out here with Harold. We need to catch up," I said and smiled at Jacque warmly.

"Before you retire, I wanted to let you know, we have a refrigerator stocked with fresh blood. Please feel free to help yourself," Harold told them, and then got up to show them the kitchen and their rooms.

"Good Morning Iris. It was lovely meeting you," Celestine said.

"Good Morning," Arelia echoed her.

"Good Morning Celestine, Arelia, Jacque. See you tomorrow evening," I replied.

Once they were gone I chatted with Harold and read until about 9:00, until I thought it was late enough in the morning that Gavin might be up.

"Harold, can I use your phone?" He was sitting in a big, leather easy chair near one of the big bookcases.

"Of course, Iris, use my office," He offered and went back to his book.

I went into Harold's office and shut the door to give myself the illusion of privacy, since I knew Harold could hear everything I said if he chose to. I hoped he would be concentrating on the book and try not to listen.

I dialed Gavin's number and waited. The phone rang five times and his message machine answered. "Hi, this is Gavin, leave a message." Beep.

"Gavin… this is Iris… I know you can hear me… wake up sleepy boy…" It was fun for me to talk to the machine for the first time.

I heard a click and a fumbling sound. "Baby, is that you?" he sounded a little groggy.

"Hi… I was talking through your machine…" I giggled. I'm sure I sounded like a silly girl.

"I'll save the message so you can hear yourself," He already knew me so well.

"I miss you… my sleek and modern new boyfriend," I whispered.

"I miss you... my pint-sized little blood sucking monster," He breathed back into the phone.

"Mmm... When are you coming home? I have all this extra blood... sloshing around... no one to suck it out of me..." He knew my kind of dirty talk.

"Mmm," I responded.

"So tell me how it went, baby. Do you like this Jacque St Domingue?" He asked.

"Yes, he seems like a very decent vampire. I really like him. He brought two other vampires with him, his wife and another woman who is his scion and descendent. She's a receiver like your sister. His wife is a tracker," I told him.

"So, he's going to help you find Heinrich?" He asked, but I'm sure he was thinking more about Marisol.

"Yes, and he's agreed to help us find Marisol too. It may take more time to find Heinrich, he's been gone so much longer and we have less of an idea where he is," I added.

"That's great. So, he's agreed?" He seemed encouraged.

"Yes. He seems to feel what I'm feeling. I think it's because he's so old," I told him.

"So... should we come there tonight?" He wanted to know.

"I don't think they allow humans in the embassy. I was thinking that maybe... we could come there?" I suggested.

"Yeah, OK... Uh, I guess I should clean up a little," He admitted.

"That might be a good idea," I agreed.

"I told Jacque about your sister's ability and about how Arial could project to her. He seemed to think that could help us... Later on, could you call Arial and see if she'll help us? She worked the night shift on the door last night so she's probably sleeping right now," I relayed.

"Yeah, OK. I'll call her a little later," he said.

"I have a good feeling about this. I can't imagine we could fail with this kind of team working together. Jacque seemed to know who the Horst brothers were so he must know they're no match for him," I said.

"I'm so glad to hear you say that. Brett was pretty depressed last night. I think spending all that time at Marisol's last night had a mixed effect on him. I think it mostly bummed him out," Gavin said.

"Oh, Brett, tell him we're optimistic... So, bummed him out means it depressed him?" I deduced.

"Yeah, sorry, new slang," he apologized.

"No, it's OK, I need to learn it," I admitted.

"So baby, I could talk to you all day and all night... but if I have to clean up for company..." Gavin said reluctantly.

"Oh, OK," I pouted. "It's OK. I'll just go read or something. Harold says he has a thing called a television. It's supposed to be like going to the pictures," I said, expectantly.

Gavin laughed. "Yeah, that might preoccupy your time for a little while." He laughed again.

"I don't see what's so funny... See you later, OK?" I said.

"OK, bye baby." He said, still laughing.

"Bye." We hung up and I went out into the lounge to see if Harold would show me the television so I could see what was so funny.

Brett

Fifteen

I could feel the sun setting. I knew with my eyes still closed, the direction in which it passed beneath the horizon. I took a deep breath and sat up. I wondered if I was breathing during my suspension–like sleep or even if my heart was beating; more questions for Iris.

I sat up and reached for the plastic shopping bag that held the items with Marisol's scent. Trying not to think about how I must resemble a pervert who steals women's clothing, I put my nose in the bag and took a deep breath. It was more intimate sensory information than any pervert could hope to cull with their forbidden loot.

I brought a few items that I had picked out of her laundry, feeling exactly like the burglar pervert while I took them. Since there wasn't much in the basket, I ended up with a Siouxsie and the Banchees concert t-shirt and a pair of thick, white socks she would have probably warn to bed. I also grabbed her towel and hairbrush from the bathroom. I wasn't sure if we would need more than one item.

I got up and came out into the main room, energized that today I would be able to participate more directly in the search. Gavin had been busy while I was asleep. Gone were the blankets and tape that had been up since mine and Iris' arrival and in their place were new velvet drapes, hung properly on rot-iron rods and pulled back with silk ropes, making our dark-day options more permanent and less unsightly. A couple of the dining room chairs were added into the arrangement of the living room seating area and the whole room seemed to have that freshly cleaned glow. Gavin had even filled a glass vase with fresh purple and yellow irises for the coffee table. He was clearly a goner at this point.

"Good, you're up." Gavin came out of the bedroom and had a box of something he was bringing out to the closet in the living room to store.

"I needed to get in there," he said as he quickly passed me to go into the big closet where I slept to grab Iris' duffle bag and bring it into the bedroom.

"What's up?" I asked as I followed him into the bedroom. I was mostly holding my breath since Gavin seemed to have forgotten my morning thirst again.

"I'm making room so Iris can put some of her stuff away. I want to surprise her," Gavin said as he began to pull dresses out of the bag and hang them up in the long closet in the bedroom.

"Oh… OK. What about the search?" I clarified.

"Oh, Iris is bringing the Haitians over here. Apparently, we humans aren't allowed into the embassy," He said with a little bitterness.

"When are they coming?" As I asked there was a knock on the door.

"I don't know. That could be them now," Gavin said as he went to get the door.

Since he had stepped away I took a breath in. I knew it wasn't them, but a human… Arial, who was here now. The reach of my senses seemed to be expanding with every day that passed.

"Oh, hey Arial, come in," Gavin said as he closed the door behind her.

I came out into the main room to greet Arial. "Hi Arial," making a point of not breathing in within close proximity of her.

"Hey Brett… or, should I say *Good Morning*." She giggled.

I smiled at her. I wasn't too sure what to say to that.

"Hey, you guys hang here… I have a couple more things I want to do before anyone else gets here…" Gavin said as he quickly dashed back into the bedroom, presumably to continue putting away Iris' things. He seemed to be in full last-minute preparations mode.

Arial sat in one of the chairs Gavin brought in from the dining room so I sat at the opposite end of the couch, as far from Arial as I could get.

I had a question floating around in my head for her, "So Arial, you were saying that you could push your thoughts into Marisol's head before… Was that what you were doing that night in the Troubadour when the Germans came in the bar?" I asked.

"Yeah, it seemed to work really well," she answered enthusiastically.

"Have you tried just throwing out a message randomly to see if you can reach her?" I asked hopefully.

"Well, I've only been able to do it so far with direct eye contact and a reasonable proximity. And, even if she could hear me she can't send anything back so I'd never know if she was hearing me," she added.

"Hmm… yeah, that's kind of a problem," I pondered how this might work.

"What I was thinking was, if the trackers get us close enough by using her scent, I'll *try* to send out randomly in the vicinity and maybe if she hears me she'll know to make noise so we can find her or something," Arial said, answering my unspoken question.

"That sounds like it's worth a shot," I said encouragingly.

Just then Iris came bursting through the door. "Gavin, I'm home!" She said in a strange put-on accent. Iris strode forward into the living room and when Gavin followed her in from the bedroom, she backtracked to him and he picked her up and swung her around.

"Did I sound like Ricky Ricardo right then? You know… I *love* Lucy!" She was clearly her vivacious self and happy to see Gavin. She'd also apparently discovered television.

After a more intimate greeting she dropped a paper bag on the coffee table and said to me, "Fast food today sweetie. We don't have a lot of time."

I was having trouble reconciling the smell permeating the room with the bag on the table until I opened it and saw the hospital issue bags of blood she'd appropriated from the embassy.

"I've eaten; it's all for you," she said as she was taking in the changes to the room.

I took the brown paper bag into the kitchen and dropped it on the counter then got out a glass and knife, punctured a bag with the knife and poured the aromatic contents into the glass and downed the first one. I took a moment to close my eyes and let it permeate. Then I filled it a second time, put the rest into the fridge and came back out into the living room.

Even while I was in the kitchen I could hear Iris gushing about the preparations Gavin had made to the apartment. They were in the bedroom now and I could hear that she was doing the same regarding her new status as an officially moved-in member of the household.

As I sat down I could hear the more personal noises of her gratitude and smiled at Arial a little awkwardly. I was hoping her human ears couldn't hear quite as clearly the smacking and cooing going on in the other room. Her wide plastered grin was ever present so it was hard to tell.

"So Arial, can I get you something to drink?" She flashed a quick look at my beverage so I qualified, "I think Gavin has some sodas."

"Sure, OK. I'll have a soda," she said.

I went back to the kitchen to get her a soda and a glass and brought it back to her. When I got back Iris had returned to the living room, she had changed her dress. She said to me, "So, the Haitians are going to be here at 9:00."

I looked at the round clock on the wall and it said 8:22.

When I looked back at her she was eyeballing me intently. "Is that what you're planning to wear?" She asked me.

"Um… yes?" I had a feeling my answer should have been no.

She grabbed my hand and took me into the big closet and picked out a nicer button down shirt and a black suit jacket to go with my jeans and boots. It was an improvement.

When she was done with me, we returned to the living room and I took the opportunity to take a couple of big swigs from my glass. She began flipping through the albums looking for something to play then she moved on to look through the cassettes. She picked one and said "Gavin says these hold music too. How do you play them?"

When I got up to help her she was holding one of the cassettes of mine that Gavin had made for demos. "Is that really the one you want to play?" I asked skeptically.

"Definitely," she said smiling at me, so I put it in the player and showed her which buttons to push to play the tape. I turned the volume down to background level. She would have no problem hearing every minute detail of the recording. I myself could hear every distortion and piece of static on the tape. I couldn't resist adjusting the equalizer a bit to try to balance out what now sounded to me like a rough cut of the song.

When Gavin came out it was clear that he'd gotten the memo to dress up a bit too; he had put on a dark gray flannel suit with a cranberry color button down shirt. He had his blonde hair gelled up and back and was futzing with it in the hallway mirror. Iris was standing behind him watching him primp when they knocked. She squeezed his arm and said "I'll get it baby."

Gavin turned toward the door and put his hand in his pocket and he actually didn't look nervous at all. Even though our expected guests were ancient vampires, entertaining and taking meetings was really still his comfort zone.

Iris opened the door. "Jacque, Celestine, Arelia… please, come in," she said enthusiastically.

"Good evening Iris. Thank you for having us," Jacque St Domingue said warmly as he entered. The two women greeted Iris and I stood up as they all filed into the living room.

Iris introduced Gavin first and the two men shook hands and he nodded and greeted the women. Then Iris introduced Arial and then me. "This is my new scion, Brett Carson, Brett this is Jacque St Domingue."

"It's an honor Mr. St Domingue," I said as I shook his hand. I could really feel this ancient vampire's power at this proximity and unexpectedly felt quite humbled in his presence.

"Please, call me Jacque. We are of the same blood," he said generously. We might share the same blood but he had been in possession of that blood a lot longer than I had.

Everyone sat down. I moved around to take one of the appropriated dining room seats as an automatic thing and gave the Haitians the couch. Arial was already sitting on the other dining room chair and Gavin sat on the chaise lounge with Iris next to him.

"So, Monsieur James, it is your sister we are seeking, yes?" he said getting right to the point.

"Yes, Marisol. I have a picture," Gavin offered as he got up and grabbed the picture from the bookshelf and put it in front of the Haitians. "I know a picture won't be of much help but I have it…"

The shorter woman, Arelia spoke then, "No, it may help me. When I'm looking for signatures, sometimes I get pictures," she said as she looked thoughtfully at the picture then up at Gavin, "You cannot mistake the resemblance," she smiled at him.

He smiled back at her then the taller woman, Celestine, spoke, "Do you have something with her scent?"

"Yes, I'll get it," I answered her. I dashed into the closet at full speed and returned with the plastic bag in less than a second but slowed down as I approached to be polite. I handed the bag to the vampire, Celestine.

She opened the bag and inhaled the smell of the contents, nodded, then closed the bag. "Harold had a few linens that were used by the Horst brothers so I have been apprised of their scent already. They travel by motorcycle so their trail, although cooling over the past couple of days, would be uninterrupted by their entrance into a vehicle. This is some good news," she said encouragingly. We were all visibly brightened by her optimism.

"It would be best if I could follow the scent on a motorcycle myself or maybe in a type of open air vehicle," she suggested.

"I have a convertible," Arial chimed in.

"Good, I will ride with the witch. We will lead," Celestine declared and we realized this was our cue to get up.

As we were all filing out, Gavin explained that he would be going out the back entrance to get his car and Arial would need to run back to the Fontenoy parking lot for hers and we would all meet out front.

When the cars were finally pulled around front it was revealed that Arial's convertible was an old Volkswagen Thing. I was hoping that it was not too disheveled inside since both the Haitian women had decided to ride with Arial so the psychics could practice sending and receiving. Gavin opened the back seat door for Jacque St Domingue and I swung around and opened the passenger door for Iris before taking my seat beside the ancient Haitian.

We waited for a minute to let Celestine pick out the fading scent of the Germans and when she was ready they pulled out slowly and we followed. We pulled up to Franklin, took a right and made our way slowly east. It was Friday night and traffic was thick so we would be going slow weather we were tracking or not.

When they got to Cahuenga, Arial turned left and we followed the pass up and over the hill. We crossed over to the West side of the pass at Barham and continued into the valley on Ventura Blvd. When we got to Lauren Canyon, Arial made a right and circled around the block and was now heading back East on Ventura. We turned left on Colfax and after a couple of blocks we turned right on Woodbridge. We drove around the block and ended up back on Woodbridge where we started and Arial stopped and pulled over. Gavin and I got out of the car and went over to see what was happening.

Celestine had gotten out of the car and was trying to pick up the direction. "It's somewhere in this development because the vampire's scent is coming and going through this area. The direction of your sister's scent has been obscured any further by the vampires coming and going. But her scent comes in up to this point for sure. We should park and walk from here," she suggested.

Jacque St Domingue and Iris had joined us at this point. We were all circled around the Thing.

Celestine continued, "Arelia and Arial have been attempting to communicate. They have been successful with eye contact and had some success with Arial looking at Arelia from behind. Arial is going to attempt to send out to Marisol by concentrating on her face with her eyes closed and let her know she's with a receiver. We are hoping that Arelia and Marisol can make a connection. Arelia will be searching for signatures," she summed up.

This all sounded very confusing and convoluted to me but I was hoping it would work somehow. I was ready at this point to go door to door and start shouting her name.

Arial was sitting in the driver's seat with her elbows on the steering wheel and her fingers to her temples with her eyes closed, concentrating. Arelia was sitting next to her doing the same thing. I was wondering if this might be easier for them if we weren't all staring. Gavin went back to the T-Bird to lock it up in case we had to take off quick then came back and resumed staring at the psychics with the rest of us.

After a minute Arelia said "Oh… is that…" The she looked up at Arial just as Arial looked up at her and said, "Oh, is that you… sorry," she apologized then they went back to concentrating.

I went back to starting and waiting for some sign that might lead us to Marisol.

MARISOL

Sixteen

The vampire had been out for some time now. He had said it would be harder for him to stay conscious during daytime hours. So I guess I could assume it was daytime now. I had no way of knowing. I'd totally lost track of the time of day. Since this is the second time I'd lost Heinrich to what he called the black void, I had to assume today was Friday. At least that was what I had decided.

It did seem like he was out for much longer this time. Or maybe I was just thirstier today than I was yesterday. I knew I was, in fact. I unfortunately had realized what the bucket's real purpose was and quickly disposed of its contents through the drain in the floor, thankful at this moment for the vampire's lapse in consciousness.

At some point during the day I had tried to stand on my tip toes on top of the bucket to see if I could reach the metal door in the ceiling. There was still another two feet between myself and any attempt I could make to escape. Not that the door looked in the least penetrable. I also tested the boundaries of the "suggestion" Heinrich had given me while he was out and I found I could not make myself get within about six feet of him without profound loss of will pushing me back.

Of course the majority of my time—the time that I wasn't spent daydreaming about the people and the life that I loved and would miss profoundly—was spent mentally searching to the limit of my parameters for some entity that would possibly be able to help me out of this predicament. Plenty of the neighborhood guides and local haunts noticed my nosing around but they apparently had their own agendas. What could a normal human spirit do anyway? Most people did not have open communication with their spirit guides and would not pay attention even if an entity tried to help.

Heinrich's guide had changed since I arrived. It went from the red entity that I'd recognized as some I'd seen in the past (like the Germans) to a white or colorless entity like most others. This was an important observation because if I chose to accept my own hypothesis, this means that the red hue indicates a vampire's guide, at least one who had had enough blood to stay conscious. The implications were staggering since this meant that in all likelihood, Brett had somehow become a vampire and the entity from my apartment complex was also a vampire. This thought is one that circled my head until I felt as though I was spinning and I needed to lie down again.

Some of the things Heinrich told me about being a vampire and Heinrich himself had eased my fears about Brett and his likely new fate. But no matter how forthcoming Heinrich had been about fielding my questions; I still had so many more.

For another few hours at least I drifted in and out of sleep. Lack of food had sapped my energy to such an extent that sleep was something I could access at will. Without Heinrich to keep me company, I had resolved to let myself sleep only to wake up periodically to scan for… whatever, and then let myself slip back into unconsciousness.

It was during one of these pointless scans when I sensed the cluster of both vampire and human entities at my outer perimeter. There were five deep red vampire guides and two humans. When I reached out for more information I was instantly assaulted with information that grabbed my complete attention. Gavin… there was no mistaking it; human, thank god. Brett's guide with the new, red signature, Arial was there as well, the other human. The mystery entity was the last of the vampire group that was familiar to me.

"Heinrich!" Please let him wake up for what could be our only chance at discovery. I got as close at my mind would allow and yelled at the top of my lungs as he lie there… nothing.

I went back to the corner and sat and closed my eyes and focused all my concentration. Who would be able to respond, Gavin? I hadn't ever been able to get any manifested response from his guide in the past and I'd played with this several times for silly reasons; get him to pick up some milk on the way home, make him forget to ask for my part of the rent, with a zero batting average. Heinrich's guide was the only vampire guide I'd tried to manipulate but even though I'd tried for quite a while, we couldn't find a way to make it work. Arial; I'd never tried to work with a witch's guides as far as I knew. Let me see… I seemed to have her complete attention already. Then I began hearing something… faint words. *Marisol… receiver… send message…*

Even if I was getting it loud and clear this seemed like an obvious directive. What I needed was some way to attract attention to our location. They must be within a mile or two. I did the obvious thing first and screamed my head off toward the metal door. I'm sure it was totally futile. With that thick door it was probably very faint even standing right on top of it and as yet no cavalry.

Think, think… my instinct was saying that Arial must be the key here. I sent her guide a request for a spell. I had no idea if the guide of a witch would have any of the talents or abilities of their charge but it was worth a shot. I sent her a series of pictures trying to convey that I wanted her to light up the spot where I was and that she could get the location from my guide. She seemed to be responding positively but if it was working, who would see it; other disincarnate entities that would not be able to help?

Hmm… maybe the vampire guides would have some way to make the vampires see the magic. Hadn't Heinrich said that it was magic that ran in the vampires' veins and kept them animated for centuries? I first found Brett and sent his guide pictures of the image of Arial's guide and the vision of my glowing presence. *Show him.* Once I believed I had communicated this as clearly as I could, I focused on the mystery entity and repeated myself. This guide, at least, was one I knew and trusted. I left it with those two; if it was going to work they would see it.

I kept going back and forth between the three, Arial, Brett and the mystery entity and waited. I slid down to the floor to lie down, kept sending and waited. I was fighting sleep but the adrenaline was wearing off and the weakness was pulling me under.

Brett

Seventeen

I stood helplessly watching Arial and Arelia concentrate on their task until I couldn't just stand there and do nothing anymore. I think I was really considering my door to door prospect at this point when I said, "I'm going to look around," and started walking. I was only walking at human speed so after a few minutes Iris caught up to me easily.

"What do you think you can do?" She asked.

"I don't know… I'm trying to find her scent right now," I answered hopelessly. "It's all I can think to do."

We continued to walk slowly through the neighborhood, both of us trying to find a scent trail that was beyond our ability after three days.

When we got to the end of a cull-de-sac I stopped and turned and backtracked to the corner at full speed. I let out a quiet exclamation of frustration just as Iris had caught up. She put her hand on my shoulder and I stood quietly and listened.

I could hear dozens of routine, commonplace discussions happening inside the typical suburban houses. As I ruled them out I would tune out and move my attention out further. Just then I thought I heard a scream then it stopped.

"Did you hear that?" I asked Iris.

"No, I was listening out the other way. What did it sound like?"

"I don't know it could have been anything, maybe a kid screaming or something," I said a little dejected. It was just the tail end of something.

"Let's go in that direction, why not, right?" Iris said as she pushed me on.

We started walking in the direction of the unidentified sound at human speed and had been walking for a couple of minutes when I saw it.

"What's that?" I asked with some amazement. There seemed to be a glow coming from the distance; like stadium lights but more concentrated in a smaller area. I stopped and tried to figure out how far away it might be.

"What's *what*, Brett? I don't see anything," Iris complained, she was trying to see what I was looking at.

"You don't see that light? It's so bright… right over there," I pointed straight out at where I was seeing it.

Iris leaned in to follow my finger to the spot I was indicating but when she couldn't see it she sighed, "I don't see anything."

I was suddenly enlivened, "If you can't see the light then that means *only I can see it*," I impressed upon her.

She suddenly understood this meant something. She looked at me and then back at the spot I was indicating. "Wait! I'm seeing it now…" she said as her eyes got bright when what I was seeing was showing itself to her too.

Just as I was about to take off she said "Go! I'll get everyone else," then I took off at full speed toward the light in the distance.

It took me about a minute total, it would have been a little longer but I jumped a couple of fences to shortcut going around some curves in the streets. The neighborhood dogs were complaining loudly in my wake.

When I got to the nondescript house I realized the glow was coming from the back yard. No one seemed to be at home so I jumped over the fence and went into the back. This was definitely the place. It was like daylight in this backyard; something I may never see again.

I couldn't understand where she might be. This was a typical valley back yard, patio, picnic bench, basketball hoop. Was this some type of trick? No, I could clearly smell her. From the scent pattern she should be right here.

With frustration, I threw the basketball hoop toward the back of the garage and it broke the backboard right off but the effort wasn't wasted. There on the ground was the metal door of some type of… bomb shelter, maybe?

When I twisted the lock with my hands it snapped off easily. I threw the door open like it was made of cardboard and dropped down into the space. There she was, thank god. My only thought was to immediately scoop Marisol up and get her out of there as quickly as I could. I did get a quick glimpse of what I recognized as an unconscious vampire before I jumped up and caught the edge with my free hand and easily lifted us out.

"Brett, Is that really you?" Marisol was awake. She was holding on tight.

I dashed full speed toward the house and kicked the door in with my foot before rushing into the kitchen and sitting her on the counter.

I stopped and held her face and kissed her.

She pulled back and said in a gravelly voice, "I'm so filthy…"

"I don't care about that, you're alive," I said thankfully, but she did look tired and… "Oh my god, you must be so thirsty!" I had a glass in my hand and was filling it up in less than a second.

She drank down the whole thing and I refilled it. I was moving at full speed and she didn't seem to be questioning it. She must be delirious and not trusting what she was seeing.

I heard the cars pulling up then after a second the front door burst open. Iris came through the door first followed by the Haitians, then Gavin and Arial. Gavin entered the kitchen first.

"Marisol!" Gavin looked incredibly relieved as he scooped her up off the counter and hugged her tight. "Shit, don't ever do that again!" I wasn't sure what she'd done besides push Gavin into a rare display of brotherly affection.

When Gavin set her on the ground he stepped back and said "You smell terrible," then flashed a grin at her.

At the next moment Iris appeared at the door just as Marisol remembered something. "Heinrich! Don't hurt him," Marisol said. Iris' eyes got very wide and Jacque immediately appeared at the door behind Iris. Even though she must know they were with us I could feel her getting a little intimidated.

"Child, do you know where Heinrich Frederickson is?" Jacque attempted to ask gently.

"He's passed out. He wouldn't let me near him. He doesn't want to hurt anyone," then to Gavin, "You can't go near him!"

"I assure you, there is no one who is here right now who wishes Captain Frederickson any ill will. He is my scion… my good friend and we have been searching for him," he explained quickly. At this point he no longer needed Marisol's help. Iris already had her nose in the air and was heading for the opening in the wall where the door had been.

I was near the refrigerator and smelled blood and remembered something. I opened the door and there were several bags of hospital blood inside. "Here," I shouted towards Jacque. He stopped just before stepping outside and looked over at me. I motioned for him to catch and tossed him a couple of the bags. Celestine and Arelia came in and got several more bags and followed Jacque and Iris out into the back yard.

"Oh, thank god! Is he going to be OK?" She asked.

"Yes, he'll be OK now," I said, looking back at Marisol. This was too much interaction for her to be deliriously missing what was going on here. "Do you know what they're going to do… what Heinrich is?" I asked carefully. Arial was dragging Gavin out of the room to give us some space to talk.

She looked back at me and took a hold of both my hands, "Yes. Heinrich and I had lots of time to talk about things down there," she confessed and it seemed like she wasn't finished. Although now she was looking down at our hands, "Also, I can see certain signatures… you know, the way I do… and I can tell which ones are human and which ones aren't," she said then looked up for my reaction.

The resolution I'd made two days ago… so long ago, to tell her what I was the moment I saw her next, wasn't going to be necessary. She already knew. She didn't seem to be repulsing either. When she realized I understood her meaning she leaned in, tightened her arms around me and put her head on my shoulder. "I thought you were sorry," she whispered.

When I realized what she meant I said, "No… I was… unconscious, for the first two days. I wanted to see you, Gavin kept saying later…" I explained.

"Figures," she said with mild contempt.

"I left you a message but you were already gone," I said remembering our sad discovery. I picked her up again and put her on the counter; she had been sinking down a little.

Iris came in the back door and called for Gavin then turned to us, "Hi Marisol, I'm Iris. It's nice to finally meet you," Iris smiled brightly at Marisol.

"Oh… *Iris. You're* Iris," she exclaimed as Iris looked at her with surprise. "I've sort of been in communication with your… unseen entourage," she said a little embarrassed.

"I have an unseen entourage?" Iris asked, puzzled and impressed.

"It's really just like… your guardian angel has been hanging around my house… for a *really* long time…" Marisol wasn't sure how to explain herself.

"Well I guess that's possible. *I've* been hanging around your house for a really long time," she laughed.

Gavin was in the doorway. "It's OK. She'll be hanging around my house now for a while," he interjected as he came up and joined us and slipped his arm around Iris.

Iris looked up at him and said, "Baby, why don't you and Brett and Marisol catch a ride home with Arial and we can drive your car back when Heinrich's ready. I was thinking Jacque would drive since I still need to practice…" she said, looking up at Gavin as she put both her arms around his waist.

"Yeah, OK. We'll probably take Marisol home first. She needs a shower," he said as he made a face, "Arial can take me home after she drops off Marisol," Gavin said, paused, then looked at Marisol, "Unless you think you need to go to the hospital or something…" he said, remembering she could be in worse shape than she looked.

I looked at her questioningly too, although I could hear her heart was beating strongly and didn't sense anything serious… "No, no. I'm fine… just really hungry and dirty," she said, trying to look stoic. This seemed to distract her from the surprise of her brother and his new little vampire girlfriend.

Gavin fished out his keys and handed them to Iris then, after they kissed enthusiastically he said, "Don't be too long, OK. No staying at the embassy tonight!"

This brought surprise back to Marisol's face to the point of her mouth falling open. Gavin looked at her and laughed at her expression, "Get used to it," he said to her. Marisol composed herself then looked over at Iris with interest but couldn't seem to form any questions.

Iris spoke up, "I'm sure we're going to be great friends. I'm already so grateful to you for helping us find Heinrich," she beamed.

"Heinrich's going to be alright, isn't he?" Marisol asked her, concerned.

"Thanks to you, Marisol. I can't thank you enough," Iris answered sincerely.

"Well I… I was also saving myself," Marisol said modestly.

"All the same…" She turned to Gavin, "You guys go. Even though he's had a lot of the bagged blood I don't want you here when we release him," she warned.

"Enough said," then he turned toward us and said, "Ready?"

"Yeah…actually, Iris, can I borrow your key?" I asked her, hoping she'd understand without me having to go into a lot of detail.

"Of course sweetie, what's mine is yours," she said as she pulled the skeleton key off her ring and handed it to me with a wink.

Arial?" I looked up to see if Arial was ready.

"I'm ready when you guys are," Arial giggled.

Eighteen

The four of us got into Arial's car and, once we'd stopped at Kentucky Fried Chicken and picked up a giant family meal meant for ten people, we drove back to Marisol's house and went inside.

Both Marisol and Gavin ate like they'd been starving for days. Because of the repulsive smell of the food, I was keeping a good distance from their meal. I busied myself by playing DJ with the stereo. Arial ate a reasonable amount of food and she and Marisol talked about how Marisol had gotten Arial's guide to create the glow and gotten mine and Iris' guides to show them to us. I was amazed at the ingenuity she put into this; like her life depended on it, obviously.

Knowing that Marisol would want to shower and regroup after her ordeal, Arial suggested she and Gavin should get going soon. Gavin reluctantly took the hint, "Are you going to be OK?" He looked at me as well as her.

"I'll be fine… You should just pity my hot water heater," she joked.

"OK, well… call me if you need anything…" he said, then to me, "Oh, you have a gig tomorrow night, don't forget."

"Wow, right. OK." It would be a much better gig now that Marisol was back.

"OK..." Gavin said as he kissed Marisol's forehead. "Be careful," Gavin directed at me again.

"Don't worry," I told him and he and Arial left out the back door.

After they were gone I tried to pull her in to me but she pulled back. "Go, take your shower… I'll clean up," I offered.

I could hear the water running as I started to package up the rest of the food and put it in the refrigerator. Once I was done I washed the smell off my hands and came into the back.

She'd been in there for several minutes so I peeked my head in and said, "Marisol?"

"Yeah?" She didn't sound unhappy to hear me come in.

"Can I come in?" I asked quietly.

"Yes," She said sweetly as she pulled the curtain open a little. Although, I didn't see her there; it was not a see-through curtain.

I quickly shed my clothes and got in slowly, so I wouldn't startle her. She was waiting and we both sighed as we fully embraced under the stream of warm water. I think she finally, fully relaxed for the first time since this whole ordeal started because we both stayed there locked in the embrace for a long time and I could smell the salt of the tears that were falling from her eyes behind me.

I just let it happen like that for a while but soon I couldn't help myself from trying to sooth her out of it. I kissed her face where the tears were but soon we were kissing passionately and urgently. I didn't want to push her so I slowed it down and reached out for the towel. I dried us off and carried her into the bedroom wrapped in the towel and laid her on the bed gently.

We lay sideways facing each other on the bed with her still wrapped in the towel for a while as I was stroking the wet hair away from her face and kissing her softly. After a while she was getting more insistent, kissing me more deeply, and then suddenly she stopped and looked at me.

"I need to say… I love you too," she said then she slid her cheek next to mine and continued to say, "You said it, but I didn't… I wasn't sure I'd ever see you again…" She had come back to the urgent kiss and I couldn't resist her anymore. With this new body of mine I was already holding back as much as I could but now I found myself unwrapping the towel and pulling her up onto me.

It was everything it was before and more. The intensity of the smell, the feel and the sound of her excitement was amplified to be more than anything I'd ever experienced before. The desire for her blood was there as well, pulling and twisting inside me but I wouldn't give in to that.

After the first incredible peak and she was catching her breath, I realized that the normal rest afterwards, time to recharge, was no longer something I needed. It wasn't something my body required anymore, like sleeping and eating. But that was just me and I would want to wait for her.

Without breaking our connection, I shifted her over beside me, but after a few minutes things escalated and I pushed her under me and without ever really stopping we were continuing where we left off.

The blood lust was building and I could feel my canines twisting and reaching for her pulse. I think she could sense something when I slowed down a bit and was pulling my face away from hers. She reached her hands up into my hair and brought my face to hers. I didn't open my eyes when she breathed into my mouth, "Do you want… is it… my blood?"

I opened my eyes to her now and said "I don't have to… I can fight it."

She let my head drop down on to her shoulder and enveloped me with her whole body. She said slowly as she moved my face around into her neck, "I want to… I want to be everything you need…"

The proximity was intoxicating and I couldn't keep from running my tongue against the skin where it was beating. I cut her skin quickly to minimize any pain and once her warm blood had fallen onto my tongue and was slipping down my throat I let out an uncontrollable groan of ecstasy. She was there with me and we floated out into a place I'd never been before. When we were finally back and she was still shuddering, I ran as much of whatever my saliva was now on her neck to heal where I'd sliced her.

"I'm sorry… I wasn't going to…" I started to say.

"Huh, uh... you are *not* going to apologize right now..." She protested.

"Um... no... I guess sorry isn't *exactly* what I'm feeling right now... I just didn't... want to push you right now," I explained.

"I've never been better... seriously, than right at this moment," she said and I felt exactly the same way.

Marisol

Nineteen

I was waking up, in a way that was definitely my new favorite way, being kissed awake by the man I was madly in love with. It was very early and still dark outside.

"Marisol… Marisol, I have to go…" Brett whispered to me.

"Don't go… where're you going?" I was still half asleep.

"Um… I can show you… I can't stay here… the sun's coming up," he reminded me.

I found myself trying to convince him not to go but, although he was responding as I would expect, he continued to protest.

"I really, really wish I had that kind of time but… I don't think I do," he said softly as the situation was starting to come clear again. I opened my eyes and saw his glowing back at me. Without my little lamp from my nightstand on it was almost completely dark in here.

"Oh… wow," was my response to the golden glow that was emanating from his usually blue eyes.

"Oh, right, sorry," he said as he reached over me and flipped on the light and looked back at me. "It's a little weird, I know. The first time I saw it…"

"It's like a cat," I said with fascination.

"Yeah, that's how cats see in the dark," he said with obvious implications.

"Cool…" I was wondering what other surprises I could expect besides his obvious speed, strength, ability to see in the dark and, of course, endurance...

He rolled over and put on his pants so I got up and put on a pair of underwear and my silk robe. He opened up my closet and said, "You wanna see?" I wasn't sure what he meant.

"See what?" I was pretty sure I was familiar with all my own clothes. But he was moving all my shoes out of the closet from the floor and removed a small circle of wood to reveal a keyhole. This caught my attention so I moved in closer and hovered right behind him to see what this was. He pulled a large skeleton key from his pants pocket and inserted it into the lock and turned. It clicked and he used the key to pull the invisible trap door open to reveal a secret chamber below.

"Are you kidding me?" I exclaimed when he pulled on a string to illuminate a single bulb as he dropped down onto a satiny platform below.

I started to look down inside but he came back up with a look of distaste on his face and said, "Ooh… ah, sweetie can you go grab me a garbage bag first? Please?" He asked.

I was really curious but I said, "Sure," and ran to the kitchen and got a Hefty and handed it to him. He dropped down even further and put something into the bag and tied it in a knot and brought it up.

He quickly ran out and was back before I could take a step to follow him. I did hear my back door close.

"Don't look inside. Just throw the bag in the dumpster when you go out, OK?" he said.

"What is it?" I wanted to know.

"Dead rats," he admitted.

"I have rats?" This was disturbing news.

"Not any more," he said with some amusement. "Long story..."

"Here, come on." He dropped back down into the secret chamber and onto the platform again. From that position the floor was about level with his shoulders. He was holding up his arms to indicate he would help me down into this place.

I was still standing and peering over him into the room wearily. It looked a little tight to me. He was looking at me inquisitively.

"I'm not very fond of small, enclosed spaces," I confessed.

"Oh… really? OK," he said as he let his hand fall to rest on the edge of the floor.

"Can I just see from up here?" I asked as I got down on my knees and peered down in.

"Of course… It's not really that small in here though," he said as he jumped down from the platform to the ground below. I laid down on my stomach to get a better look.

"This has to be… behind my garage!" I realized as I looked around and took in the vintage wallpaper and the fancy bedding.

"Yeah, this is where Iris was hibernating for the past 48 years," he said as he reached down and pulled something from under the platform. I could see it was an antique trunk. "This is hers," he said as he looked up at me then he pushed it back under.

"Wow, why did she… is that normal to hibernate for that long?" I asked. I didn't even know vampires hibernated. I didn't even know there were vampires until a couple of days ago.

"No, not really. Heinrich was supposed to wake her up in 1952," he informed me as I remembered the story he told me down in that hole.

I was looking around the little room and it didn't seem too threatening. "You know, I think I can come down there… as long as the door stays open," I qualified.

He jumped up and sat on the bunk and as I lowered myself down he guided my legs onto the platform. I tentatively sat down next to him but kept an eye on the trap door above. "It's not too bad," I responded to his concerned face.

All of Iris' frilly décor reminded me of her. "So… Iris is Gavin's girlfriend? That seems a little fast," I suggested. I wanted to know more.

"Yeah, she's even moved in… He's crazy about her," he elaborated.

"Really? *Gavin*… is crazy about *her*? You're talking about my brother Gavin, right?" I asked, unconvinced. It was usually the other way around with his girlfriends and his vested interest was mostly in getting them naked. They never lasted.

"Yeah, I know, but really… it's like they were made for each other," he said, seeming convinced.

"Huh…" I guess I'd have to learn more about the little vampire that could turn my brother's stone heart into something warm and gooey. I leaned over and he put his arm around me as I dropped my head on his shoulder.

"Marisol, I hate to say it but… I have to close that door really soon…" He said reluctantly.

"Oh, OK. How will you know when to get up?" I didn't know how this all worked yet.

"I'll know… I'll be up right after dusk."

"OK." I leaned in and gave him a really heartfelt kiss. "OK, well… see you later." I wasn't sure what the greeting should be for this situation.

"OK," he smiled at my awkwardness. Then he leaned in and kissed me again.

Then we both stood up and he easily lifted me out to sit on the floor above. He had me hand him the key and before I closed the door, through the couple of inches of opening I told him that I loved him. He pulled the string for the light and coming from the direction of two, glowing cat's eyes he said that he loved me too as I shut the door.

I went to the kitchen to get a glass of water and on my way back I noticed that I had four messages even though the light wasn't flashing. I pushed play and heard Brett's voice coming from the machine:

"Marisol… Marisol I miss you. I'm so sorry I haven't called you until now. I wanted to. I thought about you every minute. I have no excuse except to say that there were unforeseen circumstance beyond my control… it's too complicated to go into in this message… but most importantly, I love you... I love you and I hope you feel the same and I promise I'll explain everything when I see you…" Beep.

I pushed stop. I was stunned. I wondered exactly when he left this message and how I must have missed it. He did mention something about a message. I played the other messages left by Suzanne and Arial and erased them afterward but saved the message from Brett. I was going to try to never erase it. Maybe I could just buy a new tape for the machine.

This reminded me, today was Saturday, my traditional day off, but I would need to call Suzanne and let her know where I'd been and see if she needed me today. Since it was 5:00 in the morning I made a mental note and went back to bed for a few hours.

The sound of the telephone ringing woke me up this time. I reached over and picked up the Trimline.

"You're home… oh, thank god!" It was Suzanne.

"Gavin called me late last night to let me know you were home, he knew I was worried. Are you OK? He said you were OK but I needed to hear it from you," she said, out of breath.

"I'm OK. Thanks, Suzanne, I'm fine," I reassured her.

"Good. Are you sure? Gavin said a group of biker guys took you but they didn't touch you. They didn't touch you, did they? Are you sure you're OK?" She was out of breath again.

"No, I'm OK. They didn't touch me. I just got a little hungry, that's all. But I've eaten since then so I'll be fine…" I tried to assure her again.

"OK… Oh, I was so worried. So was Dino. You were worried, weren't you?" She was now speaking to the dog.

"Thanks Suzanne… Do you want me to come in today? I'm sorry I missed so much work?" I offered, although I really didn't want to go in today.

"No, are you kidding? You stay home. Get some more to eat. You're too skinny as it is. We'll be fine here. You stay home tomorrow too if you need to," She offered.

"I'm sure I'll be able to work by tomorrow. I'm fine, really. Thanks, Suzanne. I'll see you tomorrow, OK?"

"OK, honey. I'm glad you're OK. See you tomorrow," she said before she hung up the phone.

All the talk of food had made me hungry so I went into the kitchen, pulled out the left-over mashed potatoes and gravy and was eating them out of the Styrofoam container as breakfast when Gavin came running up the back stairs.

After he'd let himself in he opened a paper bag he was carrying and pulled out several bags of what looked like hospital blood and tossed them into the fridge.

"Iris said if you're going to be around when Brett wakes up you should have these on hand," he said as he finished putting them away. When he was done he shut the door and looked back at me, "Don't get too close until he's had a couple of these," he said sternly.

Then, when he saw my choice of morning meal his face changed and he laughed and said, "Hungry?"

"I'm still starving! I don't know why…" as I shoved another spoonful of cold potatoes into my mouth. This made him laugh again. He lifted my hair up to one side and lifted one eyebrow when he saw the faint mark that Brett had left on my neck.

"Um hmm." He let my hair drop back down and leaned back against the counter with his arms crossed looking at me.

I'm sure I turned a little red when I realized he probably knew exactly how I got that mark and this must be why I was still so hungry today. As I was polishing off the rest of the potatoes I said to him a little defiantly, "So… where's your mark?"

"Nowhere you need to see it, little sister," he smirked.

That was somewhat interesting… and a little creepy to think of it in the context of my brother. "You know, you're less than a month older than me," I protested.

"Yes, but so much wiser," was his comeback.

After I'd tossed the empty potato container into the garbage I fished in the fridge for the chicken bucket and brought it out so we could both have a piece.

I wasn't done, though. I had some ammunition this time. He'd had the upper hand in teasing me for so long I couldn't pass up the opportunity.

"So Brett says that you're totally into that little vampire chic," I said with amused anticipation as I bit into a chicken leg.

I noticed him turn a little red. This was a first. "She's cool… We're hanging out for now," he said as he pretended to be cavalier and licked his fingers.

"Brett said she moved in," I chided.

Gavin grabbed a paper towel and went into the living room and tried to change the subject. "So, you should call Suzanne," he shouted from the living room.

I got a paper towel and followed him in, "I talked to her this morning, she's fine."

"So, you're off today?" he asked.

"Yeah."

"So, Iris was saying that Heinrich got back to the embassy OK," he said.

"Good… That's good," I said sincerely.

"So… how was it down there? Did you guys talk?" He was curious.

"Yeah. He's a really good guy. I'd like to see him again before he leaves," I thought out loud.

"They're still looking for his ship. He may be here for a while," Gavin informed me.

I sat down on the velvet chair and Gavin plopped onto the couch. He seemed like he was thinking of a way to say something.

"So, Iris said the Haitian, Jacque St Domingue, wants to meet with us to discuss something." There it was.

"Meet with *us*? What do you think he wants?" I asked.

"Iris said he's interested in you maybe helping him with this project he's working on. Something about finding sleeping vampires…" he said.

I smiled a little. "So he wants to talk to *us* about this or he wanted to talk to *me*?" I already knew the answer.

"Hey, you know I'm always looking out for your best interests," he said a little defensively.

"So, what? You're *my* manager now too?" I said half-jokingly.

"Whatever, you know you'll want me there anyway," he said, confident. He knew he was right. I guess if I needed any negotiating done he would be the person I'd want to do it. When I didn't protest he went on.

"Brett has that gig tonight so I arranged with a friend of mine who works down at the Dresden to let us use the place to meet after hours," he reported.

"So, it's all arranged?" He was on it, I'll give him that.

"Yeah, I called the embassy to let them know. They're also interested in finding those German ass holes who took you. You don't need to be involved in that, though," he'd decided. Gavin was in that odd, protective mode again.

"Why shouldn't I help them? They helped us, right? I'm safe now. I have lots of vampires on my side now to protect me," I smiled at my own, unfathomable statement.

"We'll see... I don't like it," he grumbled.

"Didn't they also mess with Iris a long time ago?" I remembered Heinrich telling me the story of how he found Iris drained by them and saved her. This got under his skin. He looked like he was ready to join the lynch mob himself.

"Yeah… I'm not saying I don't hope they get these guys and tear them into tiny little pieces… But Marisol, you got off easy. There's more to Iris' story than you've probably heard," but I could guess. This made my stomach turn and I did feel fortunate.

"Look… I'll only help them in any *safe* way I can, OK?" I told him.

"I'll decide what's safe then," he said, exercising his control freak muscles.

"So, I have to go out and promote the gig tonight. You wanna come?" he asked, predictably.

"Mmm, I don't think so. I feel like I just want to be at home today." I didn't want to say that I would feel bad leaving Brett all alone down in the basement... Plus, it *was* good to be home.

"OK, well, tell Brett I'll bring his equipment. You can bring him in your car if you want," he said as he got up and was walking toward the back door.

"Have him there by 11:00, OK?" He said as he left out the back door and didn't stop for my answer.

Twenty

I was waiting for him right as the sun went down. I'd spent part of the day hanging out with Julian, he made me lunch. I told him I'd been visiting friends down in San Diego for a couple of days. I read a little and I also took a pretty good disco nap. I had a feeling this could be a long night.

A couple of hours before dusk I started puttering around my bedroom, straightening up. I took a shower, shaved my legs, did my nails, fixed my hair and put on some makeup. I picked out a cute, black mini-dress and paired it with some platform sandals.

So when dusk came, which in California in June is a little after 8:00 at night, I was ready. The door clicked and opened and I was sitting on the side of the bed, as far as I could be from where he was coming out.

He popped his head out and immediately pulled himself to sit on the edge of the floor and looked over at me. "Hey…" He smiled, took a breath in and then put his hand up and said, "Stay there, OK?" He looked a little worried.

"Hey," I said as I took one of the bags of blood and slid it across the wood floor toward where he was. He smiled back at me with obvious relief. He picked up the blood then looked at me self-consciously.

"Are you sure you want to see this?" He asked.

I scooted a little bit forward on the bed, leaned down and rested my chin on my hands and was adamant about not looking away. He needed to get over this idea that I might repulse at some point.

He accepted that I was determined and moved his attention to the bag. He smelled it deeply first for some reason then punctured a hole in it using one of his teeth. Then he poured it into his mouth as it spouted out and squeezed it until it was empty. Then I slid another one over to him. He smiled at me and repeated the process.

"Is that enough… enough for you to not jump me like a rabid dog?" I asked teasing him.

"I'll always want to jump you like a rabid dog… but I think you're safe now," He said as he smiled and got to his feet.

I scooted around to the end of the bed and tried to let my miniskirt and heels do the talking. I think he heard what I was saying because he walked up, kneeled down on the floor in front of me and slid his hands up my legs starting from my ankles. My time in the bathroom had not been wasted.

Instead of joining me on the bed he stayed down on the wood floor and when his hands made it to their destination he removed my underwear and followed the same path up with his lips then traced his tongue up my inner thigh. I thought he might be looking for whatever the vein was that Gavin was talking about but he made this encounter all about me.

Once I was sure I'd alerted the neighbors completely he did finally come up on the bed and kiss me passionately. We found a couple of other ways to indulge ourselves before I had just enough time to put myself back together and get him to the club.

We made it downtown a little after eleven. I parked the Bug in the parking lot of the Biltmore and made sure to lock the Club in place before we went inside. I have to admit; in the somewhat shady neighborhood of this downtown club I had never felt safer than I did tonight with my gorgeous, lethal vampire boyfriend as an escort. This beat the switchblade I sometimes carried in my pocket at night.

Brett grabbed my hand as we went directly in the front entrance of the enormous, gothic hotel, passing the line of equally gothic club goers, and weaved our way through the cavernous hallways and extravagant ballrooms that had tragically seen better days, looking for my brother and the area of this venue that Brett would be performing in. It was a stroke of genius acquisition of the club promoter to persuade the owners of this disheveled, historic hotel that allowing an endless stream of punk rock and new wave kids to invade the place on weekends to see live bands and puke in the hallways was a good idea. I don't think you could actually ever fill the place, it was that big. I'm sure Gavin would give his eye teeth to have been the one to have made that deal. Well, maybe not his eye teeth.

Industrial, gothic and punk music blared over the voluminous sound system but the scale of the place made it fade in and out from room to room. You would hear the Dammed, David Bowie, Sisters of Mercy, Love and Rockets, the Clash, Richard Hell, Iggy Pop, Blondie and any other current artist whose sound would fill a room, depending on what room you were in.

We just kept walking from room to room until we happened upon a smaller—what was once a ballroom that now had low sconce lighting and some round tables near the front with black tablecloths and candles and a small stage up front. We both spotted Gavin at the same time. He was up near the stage talking to a guy wearing a tailored suit with no shirt, black eye makeup, lots of jewelry and a spiky, black hairstyle. Gavin himself had his hair slicked back and was wearing a white tuxedo jacket over his black shirt and jeans and also had some eye makeup on, which he did on occasion.

When we got close I could hear that Gavin was talking business. He always got a certain cocky tone when he was speaking with someone of consequence regarding his clients. When he spotted us he stopped to introduce Brett to the promoter.

"Hey Gray, have you met Brett yet?" Gavin asked the spiky haired guy.

"No, not yet," he answered and turned toward us.

"Gray Burke, Brett Carson and this is my sister, Marisol James," he was in full schmooze mode.

The two guys shook hands; I just gave a verbal greeting. Gray seemed to absently shove his hands into his pocket and take a step back after touching Brett. His cold grip may have triggered something.

"Hey, I gotta go check on some other things. I'll stop back by and try to catch some of the set. Nice to meet you guys," Gray said to Brett and I. Gavin and Gray shook hands again and he jetted off.

Gavin turned to us and said "I'm trying to get Kevin booked here next week." Kevin was Rocksteady Freddy, Gavin's Ska band. There wasn't a Freddy but Kevin didn't rhyme with Rocksteady so Freddy it was.

"I have to go find his partner and talk him up a bit. Why don't you guys go keep Iris company, she's got a table up front. Brett, you're stuff is already in the wings, you' got about 10 minutes…" Gavin's said, his eyes already darting around looking for the partner he needed to accost. I scanned back toward the ring of small tables clustered at the front of the stage until I spotted the tiny vampire that had managed to find her way into my brother's impervious heart. When I looked at her she smiled and waived so I did the same back. When I turned back around Gavin was already walking off so I tugged on Brett's arm and we made our way over to Iris' table.

When we got to the table she stood up and gave us both a kiss on the cheek before we sat down. She seemed like she was in a really good mood.

"Hi, you two. Wow, this place is incredible, isn't it? I've been here before but that was back in the 20's and actually, I have to say, the place looked much better then. We used to come here to go dancing to the swing bands. No one seems to dance to this new music. Although, there was this girl in the hall dancing by herself but I think she was on something…" Iris chattered on.

I have to admit, she looked fabulous. If someone was physically made for Gavin, she was it. She was wearing a skin tight, red satin strapless dress with black stiletto heals and black elbow length gloves. Her hair was formed into perfect finger waves around her face and the classic silent-era glamour makeup perfectly accentuated her very large green eyes and little bow mouth. She looked every bit the Hollywood starlet, which would have been suspicious anywhere else except in this crowd. A bit of a costuming effect was the norm.

"Hey, I better go keep an eye on my stuff and get set up," Brett said. "I'll see you in a little bit," he said as he gave me a quick, heartfelt kiss and squeezed Iris' shoulder as he passed her on his way to the stage. She gave him an affectionate smile as he passed. I was actually a little intrigued to get to know this person who had so obviously captured the affection of the most important people in my life.

"So Iris, is this the first time you've ever heard Brett play his music?" I asked to break the ice.

"Well, this will be the first performance I've seen. I've heard him play his guitar a little and we played one of the little square tapes of his, but I'm really looking forward to this," she said enthusiastically.

I smiled at her, not sure where to go next. She looked like she'd remembered something and started digging in her purse. She pulled out a pack of cigarettes and said, "Hey, I got these from one of those girls over there," she pointed toward the cigarette girl wearing one of those trays that hung over their shoulders by a strap. "You want one?" She fished in her purse again and came out with a black, Bakelite cigarette holder and put one in it at the same time I pulled out mine and said, "Sure," as I laughed a little.

She laughed too as she handed me one and lit both of them with a book of stick matches the club put on the table in the little ashtray with their name on it.

"So, I'm happy that Gavin has found someone that he really cares about… Brett says you guys are made for each other…" I said with not too much skepticism, I hoped.

"Thanks, that's so sweet of him to say that… I have to say that I am pretty crazy about your brother. We just clicked right away," she said with a wistful look in her eye.

"Most girls can't keep up with him. He can be a little bit… strong willed," I said delicately.

"Oh, well, I don't scare easily," she said with a sly smile.

"So how is Brett doing? You guys seem happy as two peas in a pod." She asked.

"Oh, he's… great," I couldn't help but gush. I blushed a little as my mind inadvertently flashed back on some of the more intimate moments of the past 24 hours.

"I know, he's doing really well. I don't think it will be too long before he'll be relatively safe first thing in the evening," she said, thankfully ignoring my more personal inference.

She leaned in and put her gloved hand on mine, "You know… he was really miserable having to be away from you. He didn't like not telling you the truth," she said emphatically.

"Yeah, that's a part of Brett's character that I really appreciate," meaning his honesty.

"You're very lucky… and I'm very lucky to have him as my scion," she said.

I remembered what Heinrich had told me about the Sire/Scion relationship. He'd said romantic relationships never worked between a sire and a scion, not that I was worried about Brett and Iris; they didn't seem to have that type of connection at all. Heinrich had said it's more like having a child, except you would know everything the child was feeling if you wanted to.

Of course Iris would be incredibly lucky to have Brett as her scion/child, someone with whom she could feel what he was feeling. He was so easy going, such a great guy, but I was pretty biased.

As a funny thought, I pitied the vampire who would decide to be responsible for Gavin, should he choose to go that path. Easy going was actually the antithesis of what he was. There should be a picture of Gavin next to the word difficult in the dictionary.

Just then the lights changed and you could hear the piano warm up music. I scooted my seat around next to Iris to face the stage. Brett was starting with a song that I loved that was just him with the piano. Iris leaned on one arm and seemed to be enthralled with Brett and the song.

Gavin came back and joined us after a couple of songs. Brett had switched to guitar and back a couple of times and a friend of his that plays the cello joined him for a couple of songs, as he sometimes had different musicians join him. The cello gave the music a haunting quality that was just right for this room.

When he was done he thanked everyone and when the lights came up Iris seemed to be completely taken. "Oh my gosh, he's incredible!" She gushed. There might be another level of experience that someone who could feel what he's feeling would have in a situation like this. Although, he did seem to be really 'on' tonight.

"I think Iris may have improved his game a little," Gavin said with a self serving undertone.

"The A&R guy from A&M was here tonight. I'll call him tomorrow and see what he thought," Gavin said, meaning a record executive who may want to sign Brett to a deal and consequently make Gavin lots of money.

Gavin went back stage to help Brett with his equipment and after a few minutes they joined us at the table. I stood up to greet Brett when they got back and he picked me up by the waist and planted a good kiss on me first thing. I selfishly thought of half the girls in the room becoming disheartened by this display.

Gavin was saying that he needed to take Brett around and introduce him to a few people, as usual.

"Why don't we all go, Gavin?" Brett suggested. It was so sweet for him to not want Iris and me to have to sit here and wait while Gavin paraded him around, which he clearly didn't enjoy very much anyway.

"Yeah, OK," Gavin said as he pulled Iris up from her seat and slipped an arm around her from behind.

Brett and I followed Gavin and Iris around and mixed and mingled for a while until Gavin was mostly satisfied with the introductions he'd made. Iris had bought me and Gavin a drink and then Gavin bought us another, out of pride I think. Iris had warned Gavin not to drink too much because she didn't like feeling that tipsy. I gathered that it transferred with blood… more interesting trivia.

We wandered around, got separated for a while and Brett and I made out on a staircase for a while until Iris found us and excitedly said we had to come with her.

When we got down to where she was dragging us to, a hallway near the front entrance, I saw Gavin standing by a photo booth. Iris was saying, "It's a photo booth! I love photo booths. I've taken hundreds of pictures in these things," she was very enthusiastic. She pulled some pictures out of the slot of her and Gavin. We were looking at them over Iris' shoulder and I realized that some of them were a little personal.

"Oops," she giggled a little modestly and handed them to Gavin who stuck them in his inside jacket pocket.

"Your turn," she insisted as she pushed me and Brett into the tiny booth and he sat on the small round seat and I sat on his lap. I had my hands around his neck and we were just absently gazing into each others eyes when the first flash went off and surprised us. After that we attempted to pose and on the last one we copied Brett & Iris' personal, kissing pose. We stayed a little longer than the picture taking required perfecting that pose, until Gavin said, "Hey, c'mon you guys."

When the pictures came out Iris said the first one was the best and I shoved them into my little purse.

Gavin reminded us we had a meeting with the Haitians at the Dresden and if we didn't want to be late we should get going. So we split up then because Gavin's car was parked in the employee parking lot and I was parked in guest parking and we would meet up when we got there.

We took the 101 to the Vermont exit and pulled around back into the Dresden Room parking lot in no time but somehow Gavin still beat us. It was probably because he was driving a big V8 and I was driving tiny little wind-up toy.

It was about 2:15 when we got there and most of the partiers were gone already. There was one really drunk guy out by his car arguing with his girlfriend that he was fine to drive but she wouldn't give him his keys and he wouldn't get in the passenger seat.

There was a brand new black, four-door Mercedes in the lot with a Hertz sticker on the bumper. I had a thought that maybe that was the Haitian's car. I had only met them that one time and I was pretty out of it then. I at least looked and smelled a lot better tonight, which reminded me to reapply my lipstick before we went inside.

When we got up to the door it was locked so we knocked. A busboy answered and Brett said we were with Gavin's party so he let us in. Once we were inside we walked in and took the first right into the dining room area of the establishment and saw that everyone was already seated at one of the booths. It was a beautiful, compact room with white sloping booths, square tables along the center and the soaring, spiraling sconces twisted up into tree-branch shaped candelabras against the mirrored walls.

Jacque St Domingue was sitting in the center of the booth they had taken towards the back of the room with the two Haitian women on either side of him. Arial was there and sat in the booth next to Arelia on the far side. They had pulled one of the square tables up and pushed it in to join the booth and pulled a few of the white leather chairs around it. Heinrich sat next to Arial at the first seat facing us at the square table and Iris was on the end closest to Heinrich with Gavin next to her. The room was empty except for our party. Heinrich and Jacque stood up when we approached, although

Jacque could only raise up a bit from his booth position. This prompted Gavin to get up since this hadn't occurred to him.

"Marisol, it's so good to see you," Heinrich greeted me first.

"Heinrich... you look great!" Since he was facing me, I could see the health and vigor had returned to his face and he looked bright and happy and somehow younger. He had cut his shiny salt and pepper hair very short into a flat top.

When I got within a couple of feet of the table—I had intended to go around and give him a big hug, I found I had stopped in my tracks and couldn't persuade myself to move any further forward. The chagrin must have registered on my face because he laughed and said, "oh, sorry."

I realized then that the hypnosis he'd put me under must still somehow be in effect. I laughed a little too and looked him directly in the eye to give him the opportunity to lift the effect.

"Marisol, I hereby release you from any and all influence placed on you by me or any other blood sucking creature you may have crossed paths with previously," he said with obvious good humor.

I took a breath and stepped forward unimpeded and circled the table to give the friendly vampire a hug. He lifted me up easily and then set me down and put his arms on my shoulders.

"I am forever in your debt young lady and it goes without saying that I can't thank you enough," he said to me seriously.

"Oh, you don't owe me anything, Heinrich. I was saving myself too, you know," I reiterated for him.

"All the same... And I must say, you look pretty as a picture tonight," he said returning to his boisterous manor.

"Thank you... so do you!" I said.

"Argh... well I feel pretty as a picture," he said laughing. "So this is your young knight in shining armor, isn't it?" He had put his hand out for Brett to shake.

"Yes, this is Brett Carson. Brett this is Captain Heinrich Frederickson," I said as an introduction.

"Captain," Brett shook his hand. "Thanks for taking care of Marisol down there."

"Oh, it was nothing.... Really, nothing, I regret that there wasn't more I could have done to help. But I'm so glad this young lady did find a way to get us out of there," indicating me appreciatively.

"Please..." I indicated that everyone should sit back down. I was getting a little uncomfortable with all the fawning attention.

We went back around and Brett held my hand as I slid in the booth next to the vampire Celestine and he sat next to me on one of the big leather chairs.

Jacque spoke up now. "Mademoiselle James..." he began.

"Please, call me Marisol," I insisted.

"Marisol, we are all very grateful for your help in the location of our missing friend, and yourself of course. You have a special gift," he insisted.

"No… it's just kind of… a glitch really…" I protested. I've always been a little embarrassed of this hocus pocus aspect of myself.

"A glitch, you are too modest," he said as I imperceptibly slunk down in the seat a little.

He may have noticed because the next thing he said was, "but, since we are all here now, why don't we dispense with the more unpleasant business first," he looked up at the group.

"The Horst brothers… after having proven themselves over the years to be a cancer on humanity must be dealt with. With this last unforgivable act, I'm afraid they have sealed their fate and must be removed from society and lose the ability to walk among the living," he said inauspiciously.

He continued, "Those of us who have endured the millennia understand that our continued presence is a gift granted by the generosity of those who live cyclical, temporary lives. It is the brave soul who chooses to walk in the most fragile of states, grow old and die, then return to god, only to repeat this process again and again," he said. I was a little stunned by his philosophical tone, but I guess he'd had a lot of time to ponder the big questions of life.

"When we choose it or find ourselves thrust into this existence of potential immortality," his eyes lighted onto Brett for an instant, "our future is not in any way guaranteed. As the years press down on us, we find we must adapt and expand our awareness internally to withstand the pressure… Without a progression toward enlightenment the weight would eventually crush the soul who holds it," he expounded. I wondered where he was going with this but I almost didn't care. "It is this reason that we have found that those who do not find the true impetus for happiness in this existence will find their lives cut short, with or without any facilitation from outside intervention." None of us could take our eyes of him.

"I do not believe that the decisions of life and death are incumbent upon me to make and I do not relish the taking of life or imposing my will on any other being," he said to us, "but we have a responsibility to stop those of our kind who would seek to harm innocents and reek chaos on the living world," Jacque concluded. No one spoke for a minute, and then he looked toward Heinrich.

"We need to take those bastards out of circulation," Heinrich said bluntly. The change in tone was a little comical.

"When you're trying to kill a snake you always cut off the head first," he said in his own philosophical way. "We were thinking that Godfried needs to be staked and buried for a good long time or *God* as he likes to be called." There was obviously still some resentment here. "Later we give the other two a chance to show penitence, change their ways," he said generously, "then if there's no remorse they can join God in the ground for good," he said as a matter of fact.

Jacque St Domingue spoke again, "The Captain has offered to lead the effort to locate these aberrant beings and introduce them to their self-imposed consequences," he said with his silky French-Caribbean accent.

"Arial has offered her unique services as have Celestine and Arelia," he nodded to Arial. "Iris," he looked up at Iris, "you have unquestionable grounds to add yourself to those of us who claim this authority," he said to her. "Is it your wish to join them?"

With determination she looked at Jacque St Domingue then at Heinrich, then, since he had a hold of her hand and had probably squeezed hard, she looked back at Gavin for what would be his disapproval.

"Why would you... Let them handle it. I don't want you putting yourself in danger..." he was trying to stay in the realm of asking insistently and stop himself from moving into stern refusal, I could tell.

She turned to Gavin and held his hands in her lap, "Baby, it's very unlikely I'll get hurt. I need to see those guys get what's coming to them..." She actually looked a little fierce when she said this, in a Cupie doll kind of way.

"Baby, please don't do this. You're *unlikely* to get hurt? Maybe they can bring you a piece of him or something..." I could tell he was actually holding back from his usual authoritarian style, which would be him refusing to let her go. He had a look like this was genuinely causing him pain.

"Baby, I promise," she put his face between her hands. Everyone else had started to turn away from the increasingly personal conversation but I couldn't look away. "I will not be a hero. I just want to be there when they catch him," she said as she gave him a quick kiss then faced back to the group. "I want to be there," she said to Jacque St Domingue.

"OK, then... Monsieur Carson," he turned to face Brett. "I know you have your own complaint relating to this injustice but I'm afraid your circumstances prevent you from participating in our... little expedition of justice," he said apologetically. I'm not sure Brett really wanted to go on this vigilante mission but he looked puzzled at his exclusion. Jacque saw his puzzlement and continued, "You are at an age we condescendingly refer to as infancy. I do not wish to belittle your claim or you in any way but, I don't believe you are ready for a mission such as this," he said attempting to not insult Brett.

"I am... as aware as I can be of my current limitations. I do feel like I can trust your group to do the right thing, bring them to justice," Brett said humbly.

"I am beginning to see why Iris believes she has hit on a stroke of luck in bringing you into our family tree. I suspect it will be a pleasure to witness your progress in the years to come," he said with a warm expression to Brett.

"Then that's decided. We have heard word that the Josephine, the Captain's ship, has been logged recently departing the port of San Francisco. If the Horst's retained it all these years and it has not been sold off, we will intercept them at their declared destination at the Port of Long Beach. We expect them to make port sometime in the next two days," he informed us.

The Captain spoke up, "We hired a fishing cruiser out of Oxnard to give us some warning when they get close but we'll only have a couple hours once we hear from them to move," Heinrich said.

"I doubt they're traveling during the day. I can't see them having any human friends..." Heinrich glowered.

"So, those of us in on it need to stick close. We'll meet at the embassy when we hear and go from there. I'll bring what we need and we also have the element of surprise," he looked quite menacing.

"I figure we'll just dump him in his own hole until we figure out where to put him permanently," he said practically.

I have to admit, I was taking pleasure in thinking of the big German bully lying in his own makeshift prison.

"We'll stake them all and everyone but God gets a chance to make their case in a reasonable number of years," He'd definitely thought this through.

No one spoke for a moment until Jacque changed the subject, "So this brings us to the more pleasant item on our agenda..." he said changing the tone.

He turned toward me, "Marisol... as I was saying earlier, your talents are most impressive... and are not diminished by your obvious modesty," he said genially. He seemed to notice that I was about to protest.

I'm not sure if your family here has related my ambitions to you yet..." He looked to me for acknowledgement.

"They mentioned that you are interested in... unearthing hibernating vampires..." I said somewhat tentatively.

"Yes, exactly. Many of us, through no fault of our own, have been laid to rest never to be reawakened," he went on.

"Like our Iris here; her unfortunate mistake was in telling only one person where she slumbered and when to awaken her, only to be left in an eternity of blackness when he was made unavailable to fulfill his mission," he reminded me. I did feel sorry that Iris missed so many years.

"We now have a program in place to prevent this from happening in the future but I have now made it my mission to find those that would be forgotten and give them the chance to escape the blackness and live once again," he said with purpose.

Everyone looked at me, "That sounds like an incredibly noble cause but... I'm not sure how I can help," I feigned, although I had a feeling.

He smiled, "I admit, our plan is still mostly improvisational as yet, but I had a thought that maybe you could use your talent to locate... spirits, I'm not sure of course exactly how you do what you do, but for you to use your talent to locate those that slumber so we might free them," he said respectfully.

He continued, "May I ask you, what is it that you perceive, as you sit here now, that you might demonstrate how you see what you see," he asked with curiosity. Everyone waited.

"Well... OK..." I closed my eyes. "Like... if I didn't know, or I was outside or something... I would be able to tell that there were six active vampires and three humans in this room, including myself.... I can see that there are two humans in the back room... probably the busboys, I don't sense malice..." I opened my eyes and looked at Jacque St Domingue.

"Interesting, what did you mean by *active* vampires?" he asked. Good question.

"Well, I've noticed, with Heinrich and also with Iris, that if a vampire hasn't had blood in a very long time... I think long enough that it would be impossible for them to stay conscious, their guides appear clear to me, rather than their usual deep red color," I said rather awkwardly.

"That's quite fascinating. Tell me, can you tell the difference between the guide of a slumbering vampire and a human's guide?" he asked.

"Well... yes and no. There's no perceptive difference, but there are behavioral differences..." I was sure I would have to clarify.

"Like with Iris... hers is a single entity, sometimes there are more than one. I knew she wasn't a ghost, which is sometimes the case with single entities, because she was lucid—not illogical or lost like a ghost. She just seemed... bored. The entity couldn't leave, of course... but obviously there was nothing to do..." I explained badly.

"Hmmm. Do you think you might recognize other slumbering vampire's guides?" he asked now; another good question.

I had to think about that one. When I was experiencing Iris' guide I hadn't know vampires even existed. Now that I did, and I knew somewhat what I was looking for, I think I might be able to catch the signature of a bored, sleeping vampire's guide. It would probably insist on interacting with me once I reached out...

"Oh," I suddenly thought of something. "I think I may know where two vampires might be right now," I said as I flashed back to the images I would see when taking my breaks from work in the Hollywood Cemetery and the two teenage entities... pleading... trapped in the small casket... I was gripping the end of the table with a sudden terror. Why had I not put this together before?

"Oh my god..." I was horrified. "They were sending me trapped signals... pleading..." Brett put his hand on my shoulder in a comforting gesture and was watching me with some concern. I gave him a weak smile to ease his mind.

"Would you be able to show us where these two potential sleeping vampires are?" He looked encouraged.

"Of course," I answered immediately. The thought of someone being trapped in a tiny casket for eternity disturbed me to my core. I'm sure it showed.

Gavin spoke up this time, "Marisol, you don't have to do this if it's that hard for you," I think he was concerned but probably more angling for leverage.

"No, it's OK. I want to see if this really is what I think it is," basically telling him that this one's on the house, don't be greedy.

By this time it was about 3:30 in the morning. The sun would be coming up in a relatively short time and there was nothing to be done tonight.

"Marisol, would you be available to show me where you sense these entities tomorrow evening?" He asked politely.

"Sure. I work tomorrow but it's right behind the shop, in the Hollywood Cemetery. If you want to come by around 9:00 I get off then and I can show you," I said. I was hoping I wouldn't scare Suzanne with my imposing group of visitors.

This time Brett spoke up, "Is it really safe for her to be around when you wake an ancient, sleeping vampire? I don't want her in danger," he insisted.

"Well, she does not need to remain with us while we revive them. Once we've located them her work is done," Jacque St Domingue said.

"What if I *want* to stick around and see them revived?" I know this was totally unreasonable but I knew I would be disappointed to be dismissed early.

"No, Marisol. That's ridicules. Why would you do that?" Brett instantly protested.

"No way, what are you thinking. You're not staying there for that…" Gavin quickly chimed in.

Jacque interjected, "Should you decide to stay, which is not my decision to make, I would be prepared to incapacitate the vampire with a stake, should it be necessary. I do not like to do it but it is a precaution I am willing to take for your generous assistance," he conceded.

He continued, "Monsieur Carson, your having such a personal investment in Marisol's well being I think it would be appropriate for you to accompany her during this process. Your youth shouldn't be a problem without obvious intended malice, like the Horst brothers," he looked relieved to be included.

"What if I want to be there?" Gavin said.

"I don't see how having another human on site could contribute to your sister's protection but, as they say, it's a free country Monsieur James. Although if you choose to come along I cannot guarantee your safety," he warned. I looked at Gavin and was about to protest but Iris beat me to it.

"No, baby, no. That's crazy talk. I don't want you there unless I'm there to protect you," That was a mistake. The last thing you want to do is emasculate my brother in a group setting.

"I think I can take care of myself," Gavin looked defensive. Iris must have noticed she'd stepped in a landmine and stayed quiet. I hoped this was a conversation she might pick back up when they were in private.

Jacque St Domingue, showing no end to his wisdom, decided to completely change the tone and said to Brett, "So Monsieur Carson, I hear that you are an accomplished musician. I was wondering if you might be willing to play us a song or two before we call it a morning. I believe I saw a piano in the other room," he said with a warm smile.

"Ah, sure OK," Brett answered and started to get up and gave me his hand to follow.

Everyone followed us as we went around to the bar/lounge area. Brett sat at the piano and started to play something soft and light. Heinrich went behind the bar and poured drinks for Gavin, Arial and I and everyone else took seats at the small, round tables.

As Heinrich served Arial her gin and tonic he said, "Here you are, for the fairest lady I've seen in fifty years…" She giggled at his backhanded compliment. "Let's make it a hundred because that's not much of a compliment then, is it?" he realized.

She giggled at this too and they continued to chat with each other. I turned on my barstool and took a moment to do one of my favorite things, listen to Brett play. The Haitians seemed to be taken with him too. Gavin and Iris were at the far side of the bar and Iris was well on her way to wrapping Gavin back around her little finger. That situation was starting to suit me just fine. And for the rest of the morning until just before dawn, I was lovingly serenaded by my own personal, immortal troubadour.

Twenty One

I had a feeling the nap I took yesterday afternoon would come in handy but, as it was, I was still exhausted by the time we made it back to my apartment at around 5:00 AM. I had just enough time to kiss Brett goodnight and tuck him in to his little secret chamber, or rather Iris' chamber, below my closet before crawling into bed and passing out.

Brett had told me that Iris actually owned the building when I wondered out loud how she could have expected to maintain the chamber undisturbed for 20 years, which really ended up being closer to 50. I thought about all the rent checks Gavin and I had sent to some management company and was curious about how she might be getting that money. I had an absurd vision of dropping my rent checks down into the chamber for her to retrieve at some later date.

Since going to bed at 5:00 AM resulted in me not actually getting up until 1:00 in the afternoon, I had just enough time to shower and get ready for work before I had to leave. Again, I felt bad leaving Brett down there all alone, which I knew was totally irrational, seeing as how he was locked inside and, more to the point; he was a lethal vampire and could take care of himself. I had a thought that maybe this feeling was a holdover of when I had left him here alone the first time and things had gotten a little out of hand.

Still, I couldn't bring myself to just leave without doing anything so I settled for putting a note on the end of the bed saying: "*Breakfast in the fridge. See you tonight,*" then I pressed a kiss mark on the page and taped it to the end of the bed where he'd see it first thing. I wasn't sure how long bagged blood lasted but I was hoping what we had would still be OK.

When I got to work Suzanne was more than happy to see me. Even Dino was yapping and wiggling along with her.

"Oh… Marisol, you're a sight for sore eyes," she said enthusiastically and wrapped me in a tight hug. Suzanne was a thick woman who smelled of Jean Naté body splash and menthol cigarettes. She liked to wear tight knit pants paired with billowing blouses to cover her apple shaped figure. She also had very long, sculptured nails that were always creatively painted.

"I'm fine Suzanne, thanks for not firing me," I said half-sincerely.

"Oh, please honey, it's not like I can run an ad for a clairvoyant," she said. I hadn't actually ever thought of it that way before. I guess I must have more job security than I'd assumed. "Besides, only an asshole would fire someone for being abducted," she said bluntly.

"I know. I guess what I'm saying is it's good to be back," I admitted.

"Well, it's good to have you back, honey," she reiterated.

"Is there anything for me on the books tonight?" I asked her.

"Well… I have my regular Sunday night guy but nothing other than that. It's your first day back so manning the register is probably enough for you to do tonight unless we have a lot of walk-ins or something…" she said generously.

That sounded just fine to me but it also reminded me, "Suzanne, I have some people coming in after closing to meet me about something… I'm kind of helping them find a missing person," I hadn't thought about the fact that meeting them here might mean she'd want to get paid a cut for my services. "I'm pretty much doing it as a favor to them; I'm not asking for money or anything."

"Oh, OK, honey. Of course, you do whatever you want on your time. Maybe if you help them they might give you some good PR for this type of thing. Missing persons can be pretty lucrative," she added. What she didn't know is she'd probably have to wrestle Gavin for the negotiation rights to my brain. I was sure she'd be willing to wrestle with Gavin anytime with or without a reason.

So, for the rest of the night I sold incense and books on Tarot reading, etc. Suzanne took her 5:30 appointment and then gave me a break at 7:00. When I let myself into the cemetery I was more than a little curious to make a connection to the teenagers knowing what I thought I did about what they might be.

When I got to my usual bench near the big mausoleum and sat down, I first did my general scan to see what and who was around tonight. It was still light out so I wouldn't expect to find any vampires around yet. The two teenage entities were there and greeted me half-heartedly, as they had come to do since it became obvious I wasn't taking their hints.

Since there weren't any surprises in my initial scan I reached out to the sibling entities with a little surprise of my own. I sent them some questioning signals with pictures of vampire behavior I'd witnessed to see their response. I did my best to filter out the private, R-rated visuals of my own blood sharing scene that had been intruding on my thoughts at inopportune moments lately.

This caught their attention immediately. They were almost giddy, if a non-auditory entity can be perceived as giddy. They were sending pictures of the teenagers and sending back the images I sent them with a positive undertone that could be perceived as confirmation of my theory.

I stood up now, with my eyes still closed, and sent an inquiry of their location. I had a general idea I was close by but wanted to see if I could pinpoint an exact location. From the angle I was facing I could sense the two of them had become centered next to each other approximately fifteen or twenty feet in front of me. I opened my eyes and saw that the big mausoleum was directly in front of me, the right distance away.

I proceeded into the first long hallway through the entrance. It was about 100 feet across and there were three hallways on each side that branched off into other areas of the mausoleum. The ceiling was almost entirely made of glass skylights running the length of the main hallway. The crypts were stacked seven high and each one had an urn attached to hold flowers but most of them were empty. I was hoping that the siblings were not on the top bunk, although it would be Jacque St Domingue's problem to work that out if that was the case.

I closed my eyes and sent out a request for further direction. I could sense the giddy spirits approximately fifteen feet ahead on the right. With my eyes open, that would bring me to the center of the second section, after the first hallway. Once I was there I turned in the direction they had indicated and closed my eyes. This time they seemed to be down low to the ground (thank god) and a little to the left. I sat in front of where I had thought they were indicating, between two crypts on the bottom and closed my eyes again. I seemed to get euphoric confirmation of my destination. I opened again and saw that the crypts' occupants should be Sid and Phyllis Goldstein. I had a feeling that these two were not Sid and Phyllis Goldstein but at least I had identified our target for tonight. I briefly wondered what had happened to Sid and Phyllis and felt bad for their displacement.

By this time my break was over. I started to head for the shop followed by the insistent entities eager to have their vampires freed. I tried to send them assurances that I'd be back; clocks telling them a couple of hours, after 9:00, etc. I was pretty sure time and space didn't exist on the other side but I hoped they would understand.

When I got back to the shop Suzanne had said the night was turning out pretty uneventful and that she and Dino were going upstairs and I could lock up after close. I had a feeling that uneventful would not be how the evening ended up.

Around ten to nine I went out back and was waiting for my visitors to show up. Finally, just before nine, the T-Bird turned up the alley. When they pulled up Brett got out and I indicated for Gavin to park in one of the spots behind Suzanne's next to my VW.

While Gavin was parking Brett pulled me close to him, put his nose into my neck and took a deep breath. He moaned slightly then pulled back and kissed me. I had a feeling the bagged blood wasn't as satisfying as maybe the warm source might be. It surprised me that this gesture made me yearn for it too and I think my kiss may have reflected that.

But suddenly we were back in mixed company… literally, as my brother and Iris were walking up. Just then the black Mercedes turned up the alley and was pulling up towards us. Gavin indicated to Jacque to park next to him and then he and Celestine and Arelia got out of the car.

"Good evening," Jacque greeted us. Everyone echoed his gesture. "Heinrich and Arial are sticking close by the embassy tonight and will come and find us if the Josephine is spotted coming into port," Jacque informed us.

Celestine then opened the Mercedes' big trunk and pulled out a pretty good sized duffle bag. Both Jacque and Arelia pulled out a similar large bag themselves and Jacque closed the trunk.

I couldn't think of what would be in the bags until I saw both Brett and Iris pull in the scent like it was the best perfume they'd ever smelled and instantly knew that they had brought blood to revive the sleeping siblings, of course.

After I went back inside and locked up, I led the motley crew out through my gate entrance into the cemetery. It was a fairly good walk to the mausoleum and once we were there and had entered the long hallway I realized I should have brought a flashlight with me. Then, when I looked up and saw glowing eyes, I realized that most of the people with me had super-vision.

"It's hard for me to see but we're looking for Sid and Phyllis Goldstein," I said and Brett immediately took my hand and led me to the right crypt.

Jacque spoke up now, "So this is where the sleeping vampires are interred?" he asked.

"Yeah, their guides are doing everything but flashing a neon sign in front of them. They're pretty happy about the prospect of them being released from here," I said.

"Jacque!" Out of the blue Heinrich was walking into the hallway where we all were.

"Captain," Jacque acknowledged.

"It's time. The ship passed Oxnard about an hour ago. They must have docked just up the coast and left at dusk. We've only got about an hour to get into position," he said quickly.

Jacque St Domingue pulled keys from his pocket and handed them to Celestine. "Go," he said to her. "Are you sure you don't need me?" Jacque said to Heinrich.

"No, the ladies and I got this one. Besides, Arial's got a spell that will mask our scent entirely. They won't see us coming until it's too late," he said with a malicious twinkle in his eye.

Celestine and Arelia dropped their duffle bags where they stood and disappeared one by one out the entrance of the mausoleum with Heinrich backing up slowly in that direction looking toward Iris. This was Iris' cue; she would have to decide now. This was really Gavin's cue to pitch his last-minute case.

"Baby, stay… stay here with me and help us with this… Wouldn't you rather help to *free* someone rather than *imprison* someone, even if they do deserve it? You heard Heinrich, they got this one…" Gavin had a gift for persuasion.

She looked sympathetic but resolved, "Baby, you don't know how long I've been dreaming about shoving a stake into those… those…" apparently none of the swear words Iris knew were exactly right for this scenario. Although, I have to say, I have yet to hear Iris use a swear word.

"Baby, don't…" Gavin pleaded as Iris gave him a quick kiss on the cheek.

As Iris ran off she said, "I have to go now before they leave. I'll be back really, really soon," she said as she quickly disappeared out trailing behind Heinrich.

Gavin turned back to our smaller group, clearly agitated. With this new development that left just myself, Brett, Gavin and Jacque.

Once we had absorbed our new circumstances, Jacque looked at Brett and said, "Monsieur Carson, it might be best if you took your human family and backed up a good deal," he suggested strongly.

"Here," he zipped open the side pocket of one of the duffle bags and handed Brett two sharp wooden stakes. "I wouldn't brandish them blatantly, you don't want to incite anything unnecessarily," Brett handed one of them to Gavin as we backed up all the way to the entrance of the mausoleum.

Once we were in place Jacque said, "Ready?"

Both Brett and Gavin were holding their stakes like they were nightsticks or six shooters, ready for a rumble. "I'm pretty sure that's brandishing." I reprimanded as I rolled my eyes.

"Oh, right," Brett said and they both obscured them behind their backs. Then I said, "Ready."

I thought he would do some neat trick and the crypt would open from the front. Instead he turned around and walked back down the side hallway and I heard something crack and open from around the corner. I heard some more clicking and crunching noises and then the ominous sound of rock sliding against rock.

Then he was suddenly five feet in front of us walking toward us. I started at his sudden appearance and so did Gavin.

"I apologize for my speed... They are there," he looked triumphant. "Two small vampires, they have been staked," he said.

"Monsieur Carson, would you help me remove them from the crypts?" he asked.

"Of course," he said, and then they were both gone. A second later, Brett was in front of us with a small, female vampire in his arms. He was walking past us out onto the grass. When I turned I saw that Jacque St Domingue was already out on the grass with the other one setting him down. Brett must have slowed down purely for our sake.

I was looking at the two young vampires; they must not have been more than 16 or 17 when they were changed into their current form. They were lying side by side on the wet grass and both had thick, wooden stakes protruding out of the place where their heart would be. Both had been staked from behind as the points were currently pointing toward the sky. Seeing it up close like this, it was truly unbelievable that any being could live through this type of impalement, let alone for dozens, even hundreds of years. They did *look* dead, although not decomposed in any way, more… recently deceased.

"Do you have any idea who they are?" I asked Jacque.

"Yes, Monsieur McKinley and I stayed up yesterday and did some searching through the archives. If we're correct, this could be Jean-Pierre and

Amelie Claire Bertrand, Paris based vampires who were indeed brother and sister in life. They went missing sometime in 1851 or 1852 after their ship docked at the Port of San Francisco in July of 1851. We have record of their checking in with the San Francisco embassy upon their arrival and there are no travel records after that. Their disappearance was recorded in September of 1852 at the Paris embassy by their Sire, Jean-Francoise Gerard, another Parisian vampire."

"We have not alerted Mousier Gerard since we only contacted the Paris embassy today during the daytime. The Paris embassy is surely getting in touch with him this evening. In any case, if these are indeed his missing scions, he will no doubt be alerted immediately by instinct, of course."

I looked at the two small impaled vampires lying on the ground. The background he gave seemed to mesh with their appearance. The girl, Amelie Claire, was wearing a long, blue silk dress with petticoats, a tight, restrictive bodice and matching lace-up shoes. Her dark hair was swept up in a twisted chignon style and she wore a beautiful cameo and gold necklace. She had little short bangs like I'd seen some of the punk rock girls wearing down at the clubs. There was dried blood staining the entire middle section of the dress surrounding where the stake entered her body.

The boy, Jean-Pierre, was wearing an elegant suit that would, with my limited knowledge of clothing in the 19th century, seem to fit the time period. His cheekbone-length hair was exactly the same color as his sister's. His midsection was also stained a dark brown now after so many years in the crypt. To me, they both looked like miniatures, developing at a time in history when people were just smaller… and they had obviously not had a chance to grow up completely.

"There are no records of any misdeeds or complaints of any kind regarding the Bertrands in the San Francisco or Paris records. I have not spoken with their sire but I think if there were any justifiable reason to stake these two and put them to ground it would be recorded in one of those archives," Jacque stated to everyone, including himself. "We will be reporting the Horst Brother's removal from society when it is done," he said for our information.

Brett disappeared then suddenly appeared with all three of the duffle bags that we'd left on the floor of the mausoleum and set them down next to the Bertrands.

Jacque St Domingue said, "Monsieur Carson, back up and guard your family." Brett led us about fifty feet away and stood in front of us while the Haitian prepared to revive the first vampire. Brett had put his stake into his back pocket. I looked over at Gavin and he had his in his hand behind his back. I slid in closer behind Brett.

Brett and Jacque nodded to each other and Jacque pulled the stake out of the boy. Nothing happened. Jacque opened the boy's mouth then punctured a hole in one of the hospital blood bags and squeezed a spout of blood into the vampire's mouth.

He began to swallow.

When the first bag was empty he quickly punctured another and repeated the process. By the fourth bag the vampire's limbs started to twitch. By the sixth bag he convulsed up and, although it was a bit too far to see, I think his chest cavity began to close. During the seventh bag I could hear him moaning and see him moving around more fluidly. It was at this point that Jacque began speaking to him in French. Of course, I had no idea what he was saying but I imagined he must be filling him in on what was happening and what we were doing. After he finished the seventh bag Jacque didn't move to open another one. The boy opened his eyes and spoke back to Jacque urgently in French. Jacque answered quickly and the boy demanded another answer. Then the boy shouted "Amelie!"

He lunged over and pulled the stake out of his sister's chest. I don't think this was the plan but Jacque only protested lightly and didn't actually prevent Jean-Pierre from starting to revive his sister. Jean-Pierre grabbed bag after bag and, without finesse, ripped each bag open in succession and poured the contents into Amelie Claire's mouth. She, of course, began swallowing right away.

After finishing her sixth bag she began mumbling in French. Her brother spoke back to her with soft tones and was stroking her face as she came to. Jacque spoke to them both now and the girl sat up and looked around in a daze. Jacque handed her another bag and she slashed it with her teeth and continued drinking.

I was fascinated to the point that I almost forgot that we could be in danger. I was holding on to Brett's waist and shoulder peering around him. Gavin was standing about a foot away, still holding the stake behind him.

It was at this point that we finally caught their attention.

It was the boy who looked at us first. He'd lifted his nose as he picked up our scent. Brett raised his hands in a protective gesture the moment his eyes landed on us. Brett said, "Stay back," perhaps futily, since we didn't know if he spoke English. But his tone was unmistakable.

Then Jacque said something pointedly in French, I'm guessing something along those same lines but he used a few more words to say it then Brett did.

Then the boy protested softly in melodic French; expressing in his tone that he meant no harm.

Then the girl, who had become more lucid at this point, began speaking to her brother and he spoke back. They continued to converse back and forth while the boy slowly moved forward toward us. The boy continued with the melodic, unthreatening tone while the girl's responses were more serious.

When he'd gotten a little too close for Brett's comfort Brett repeated his warning to the boy. Since the boy seemed to be answering Brett in French I had to assume that he did not, in fact, speak English.

Then everything happened in fast motion—the opposite of slow motion—so fast I can only assume that I remember it with any clarity or that it actually happened in this succession.

Once the boy had, in Gavin's opinion, stepped one step too close to us, Gavin suddenly came at the boy with the stake he'd been hiding behind him. The boy turned instantly to Gavin and easily slapped the stake out of his hands onto the ground. This angered the boy or incited his blood lust, or both; the result was the same, and he pounced on Gavin and ripped into his throat with his sharp, extended vampire teeth and 100 plus years of thirst.

The moment the girl saw the stake in Gavin's hand with its intention to be plunged into her brother, her anger or bloodlust was triggered and, since he'd already tackled Gavin, she lunged toward me and consequently Brett. She opened her mouth to expose her teeth and screamed… or screeched, more accurately, at Brett and he growled back at her. Somewhere deep inside my shocked brain this registered as something I'd never witnessed before.

She leaped, then he leaped, or maybe they did this simultaneously, but the result was them crashing mid-flight then falling to the ground together. Somehow the stake was pulled from Brett's back pocket and they both had their hands on it and were struggling with it for what was probably at least a split second.

The moment the girl moved from her location on the ground, Jacque had a stake in his hand and less than a second after she leaped toward Brett he was on her. Unfortunately, the moment he plunged the stake into her was the same moment she gained control of Brett's stake and plunged it into him.

While all this was happening I found time to scream both of their names.

I had no time to make a decision based on any kind of thought-out criteria but at this moment I looked back at Gavin and saw the young, French boy draining the blood out of him and also the stake lying on the ground next to them. Without thinking, I dropped on the stake and reached over with it and plunged it into the boy's back, exactly where it had been before.

The moment it went into the boy's body Gavin's eyes shocked open and I realized immediately that this was not a positive development. I had plunged the stake through the boy, out the other end and into my brother.

I immediately flipped the profusely bleeding and unconscious vampire off my brother and saw that the stake was protruding out of the boy by about an inch. As soon as the boy was off him, Gavin's eyes rolled into the back of his head and he was out. There was also blood pooling in his solar plexus area.

At that moment Jacque was next to me on the ground and had his shirt in his hands and was tearing it into shreds. He put a wad of his shirt on Gavin's bubbling abdomen and said, "Push."

I did what he said and looked into Gavin's face then looked over at Brett and saw that the stake was still protruding from his chest. I'm pretty sure I screamed his name again right then.

Then things got very blurry because while I was looking at Brett he suddenly disappeared and then a few seconds later I saw Jacque leaning over the girl then they were both gone. A few seconds after that he was back, and then both he and the boy were gone. Then he was back right next to me.

"Where's Brett?" I probably shouted too loudly.

"He will be safe. We need to attend to your brother. He is only a human and could actually die," he said.

Strangely, this statement actually did calm my nerves about Brett, shocking me into realizing no matter how bad it looked to me, he was going to be OK. I looked down at my brother who was pale as a ghost then back up at Jacque.

"We should get him inside," he spoke evenly into my shocked face. I probably needed to pull myself together at this point.

"Here," he put one of the two remaining duffle bags on his shoulder and slid one arm under Gavin and took a new rag and replaced the bloody one I was holding and picked him up and said, "you let us in, I'll carry him… quick!"

Once he had him I turned and ran toward the gate and out to the alley. I felt like I was going so slow I might as well be trudging through deep sand. I'm sure that's the way it seemed to Jacque St Domingue because when I finally got to Suzanne's back door he was waiting. I fumbled with the keys and finally got the back door open and switched on the hall light and led the way into the séance room. Jacque laid Gavin down on the Séance table and continued to hold the rag on his solar plexus. I could see with the additional light that he was bleeding from a savage looking gash in his neck where the vampire had bitten into him. I grabbed the edge of the table cloth and pushed it into his neck where it was bleeding.

Jacque said, "Hold this and let me see what I can do about that." As I pushed on Gavin's stomach Jacque began licking the wound on Gavin's neck.

Just then Suzanne came downstairs and walked into the room. Dino had preceded her by a couple of seconds, snarling and growling. She had a small silver revolver in her hand. She looked at me with some shock then when Jacque looked up at her she said, "Shit, vampires."

Iris

Twenty Two

I couldn't help but feel guilty sitting in the back of the big German car heading for our destination. Somehow my desire for revenge had softened somewhat with Gavin's sincere plea for me to stay. I knew he was just using his wiles to get his way but knowing his way was truly just to keep me out of danger, I couldn't help but be touched by it.

Heinrich had driven out to get us with Arial in her convertible and now they were headed out to the docks, but I opted to ride with the Celestine and Arelia in the Mercedes. I had gotten the feeling that the two of them were enjoying spending alone time together and had a pretty good idea where Heinrich's new afternoon meal was coming from these days.

The trip was so fast and quiet I was sure we would beat Heinrich and Arial by quite a margin, and sure enough, once we arrived at the docks in Long Beach we had to cruise around for about ten minutes waiting for them. We used that time to look around and see if we could spot the Josephine. Even with the great variety and scope of the ships coming into harbor here, it wasn't hard to find. There weren't many massive, tall sailing ships currently coming into port.

It was lined up behind several freighters anchored in the line against the breakwater and would undoubtedly not be coming into the docks tonight. We parked as close as we could to one of the pedestrian entrances into the docks.

Heinrich found us pretty easily and both Heinrich and Arial joined me in the back seat while we made our plan. I decided to focus so we could get this done. I found I really just wanted to get back to my new life as quickly as possible.

Arial said she was ready with her scent cloaking spell. Heinrich said he had a simple plan. "Since they're pretty much sitting ducks out there at the breakwater, I say we scale the rocks, stake them, then I'll sail the Josephine back into Marina Del Rey and we can load them up closer to the cars tomorrow night."

No one else offered another plan or seemed to have any objection to this one so we got out of the car and prepared to head out. I wasn't exactly dressed to scale breakwater rocks so I took off my shoes entirely and so did Celestine. Arelia had anticipated the need for more practical shoes and kept her flat sandals on. Heinrich handed everyone wooden stakes except Arial, who was now sitting on the hood of her little square convertible chanting her spell. I tucked the stake into the waistband of my skirt behind my back. I was only the backup but I was ready.

We stood and stared at Arial for a minute or two until she finally looked up at Heinrich and indicated to him that her part was done. Then Heinrich led the way and the four of us made good time silently leaping from rock to rock toward our destination.

Once we got pretty close I could hear them laughing and talking in German to each other. They were reminiscing about the last night's meal and making derogatory comments about the two women who, I'm sure, did not volunteer for the pleasure. This put a little bit of skip back in my stride.

Heinrich was motioning everyone into place based on the sound of the German's voices. They were all out on deck which would make our job easier. The four of us silently leapt onto the ship and scaled the ropes up the hull of the old clipper ship and pulled ourselves up to the edge. I felt exactly like a pirate at that particular moment.

Heinrich motioned a count to three with his fingers and without a sound we all swung up on deck. In less than a second, three stakes met their marks and the German vampires slumped to the ground as their blood spread silently out on the floor of the deck. Exactly like we planned, they did not see us coming. As I watched them lay there unconsciously bleeding I thought about how anticlimactic it all was.

Heinrich broke the silence when he started to sing an old German folk song, or maybe it was a sea shanty, and began walking around running his hand along the railing of the ship. He suddenly moved over to the tall, thick mast of one of the big sails and hugged it earnestly. "Oh, Josephine, I'm back… I'm back; I missed you so much…" He was now moving from place to place caressing the different parts of the ancient wooden ship. "Look at those disgraceful knots!" he exclaimed as he begun to correct them. It was a touching reunion.

The three of them picked up the drained Germans and took them down into the hold. Just before they returned to the deck I suddenly doubled forward in pain. Pain was not a common occurrence in our kind. It was like someone had kicked me in the chest and I could feel it like a human would. I heard myself yell loudly as I fell to my knees. The others were with me on deck instantly and Heinrich was at my side. "What is it child?" He looked very concerned, like he might have some intimate knowledge of this type of thing himself. Then more pain. It felt like my throat was on fire and someone had used the same boot to kick me in the gut this time. I heard a blood curdling scream and after it was silent I realized it had been me.

I looked at Heinrich with terror in my eyes. I remembered this feeling all too well. Heinrich said, "Something's happened to her scion," and I knew it before he said it.

I didn't wait for confirmation or consensus; I instantly scaled back down the ropes and started leaping from rock to rock toward where we'd come from. The length of the breakwater was about two miles so eventually the Haitian women caught up to me and were keeping pace. When we'd made it to the car I climbed into the back seat and closed my eyes. Once the Haitian women gave Arial a quick explanation of what had happened, Celestine got in and squealed out of the lot and made her way back to the highway as fast as she could.

I could feel it, something had happened to my beautiful scion. His heart was not beating… but I couldn't sense the horrid, memorable feeling of final death. But there was something else… mixed with the terror was my memory of a scent… Gavin's scent. I concentrated on the feeling of Gavin's essence and found that a lot of the pain was laced into it. I shuddered as pink tears were streaming down my face and I tried to will the very fast car to go faster.

When I looked up we were racing down the modern highway, I think faster than I can ever remember traveling by machine. Other cars were a blur as we went by. By now it must be midnight and the traffic had thinned considerably.

By the time we got off the highway in Hollywood I estimated that Celestine had shaved another five minutes off our already record time, but it still seemed like an eternity. When she squealed up the alley behind the psychic shop and stopped, I immediately got out before she parked the car.

All the scents were coming from the psychic shop now except new, unknown vampire scents coming from the trunk of Gavin's Thunderbird. None were Brett so I immediately pushed through the back door of the shop and headed for the scents of Gavin, Jacque and Marisol.

I flung back the curtain to the small room where, there he was, my Gavin, bleeding from all the places I could feel it on the table in the middle of the room. I jumped up on the table next to him and immediately began to examine his wounds. It was clear that Jacque had done his best to begin the healing process. He'd even managed to transfuse him with some of the blood he'd brought with him. There was a bag hanging from the chandelier that was attached to his wrist that was half-full.

Even though I could hear full well that the crisis was probably over and he would be OK, I still put my ear to his chest and listed closely to his heart. Looking down, I could see the wound in his chest was slowly sealing and not bleeding anymore. I still took a minute to lick around the edges and spit some of my saliva into the small cavity to add my assistance to the healing process before making my way up to his neck wound and concentrating on helping that heal.

"Did she just spit on him?" A voice from behind me asked. I think I registered a large woman with a small gun as I passed into the room on my way to Gavin. The voice came from that direction, not that any of that mattered to me at this moment.

"Yes, it will help the healing," Jacque answered the voice.

"Iris, Jacque says Gavin's going to be OK," Marisol said softly to me. I looked up at her and took her hand. I could smell that she'd had her own share of terror since this happened. The adrenaline mixed with salty sweat was pungent.

"Marisol, where's Brett?" I tried to ask delicately. I was still sitting on my knees on the table next to Gavin. Celestine and Arelia had joined us by then.

Her eyes got watery as she said, "he got staked."

"Where is he?" I asked.

Marisol looked up at Jacque to answer so I did too, "I removed the stake and placed him in the crypt where the Bertrands were," Jacque said, "he has more than a dozen bags of blood to revive himself once he becomes aware of them." This made me feel a little better.

"The Bertrands are in Monsieur James' trunk now but I will be moving them to my car before we leave," he added. There seemed to be a lot of shame registering in his face.

"Why did this happen?" I wanted to know.

Marisol answered, "The French boy got a little too close to us for Gavin's taste and so he pulled a stake on him," I said, in a nutshell.

"The truth is, Jean-Pierre only wanted to thank Marisol for her efforts in freeing them but… he did get closer than he should have and I shouldn't have allowed it. Or, I should have translated what they were saying and headed off the confrontation… In truth, I should never have allowed humans to be there when they were revived," Jacque said regretfully.

"Gavin pulled a stake on a vampire *to his face*?" This is the part that I was stuck on.

As I looked at Marisol I could see that she was fighting off the look of amusement on her face while perhaps trying not to say 'I told you so'.

I had heard enough and went back to licking Gavin's neck wound while Jacque changed the blood bag to a new one.

After a few minutes the woman in the corner with the gun, who had thankfully deposited the gun on a bookshelf a little while ago, spoke up, "I think he's… starting to perk up," she said.

I hadn't moved from my position kneeling on the table beside him. As I continued to lick the wound, I could feel his hands working their way up from my back side to the top of my back. He let out a low moan, "Mmm," as I felt him unzip my dress from behind. I stopped licking and froze.

Marisol spoke up as she re-zipped me into my dress, "Gavin, unless you want to burn my eyes and give Suzanne a heart attack you might want to chill out a little," she said.

When I turned to look back at Marisol I noticed what the woman meant about Gavin "perking up." Apparently, all the blood he'd gotten in the transfusions had made its way into his pants.

When I looked back at him with renewed appreciation he slowly opened his eyes and took in all our faces. I couldn't help myself, even though I was slightly irritated with him for playing vigilante, I was so happy to see him conscious that I grabbed his face and planted a good one on him. He responded enthusiastically, although a little less intimately then before. After a minute I pulled back and looked at him and said, "Don't ever do that to me again!"

"What did I do?" He looked amused and a little confused.

"You pulled a stake on a vampire, *to his face*," I emphasized.

"Yeah... I'll admit, he kinda got the jump on me there," he said, as an understatement.

As he looked around the room he noticed who wasn't there, "Where's Brett?"

"He took the stake that I'm pretty sure was meant for you," Marisol said.

He looked back at me then, when he tried to sit up, he winced loudly in pain. A stake in the abdomen would probably make sitting up a little uncomfortable.

"Don't try to get up. Just stay there," I said firmly.

"If Brett took my stake then what's that?" He said looking down at the wound on his stomach. No one answered him right away and a look of remembrance slowly crossed his face as he looked toward Marisol.

"You... staked me!" He said with amazed conviction.

"I staked the vampire that was sucking you dry... you just got in the way," she protested. "Look, I'm sorry... I didn't mean to push it all the way through to you... obviously," she said, a little contrite. "You're welcome, by the way."

"That hurt like hell!" Gavin complained.

"Yes, it does hurt like hell," Jacque confirmed. "But for us, the pain of being staked is felt by those whose blood created us. Brett didn't actually feel his stake as pain, as much as Iris did, I am sure," he said. "Iris' scion will heal quickly," he added "Unfortunately for you Monsieur James, you get to heal slowly," he said, I think with a little bit of satisfaction.

"I'm sorry baby," Gavin said with new contrition towards Iris. She just shushed him and continued to hold his hand.

"Since you are now awake," Jacque said to Gavin, "I'm afraid we must take our leave. I will take the Bertrands and we will revive them in a safe place. I'm hoping they will forgive the imposition of our first failed attempt. Iris, will you walk us out?" He asked me.

Marisol took over sitting where I was while I walked out after the Haitians. Once we got out to the cars, Jacque transferred two small, staked teenage vampires from Gavin's trunk to the Mercedes trunk then handed me Gavin's keys. "I am truly sorry to have put your scion and friends in danger this evening, Iris," Jacque said with all sincerity.

"Oh, thank you Jacque but it wasn't your fault," I said. He seemed to have something he was trying to say.

"There was a point this evening when the circumstances were such that I would have perhaps had to choose to change him or let him die. I would not have let him die for your sake but when the crisis passed I was glad to not have to make that decision without you," he said relieved. "Would that have been something you would have wanted?" he asked.

"Yes," I said truthfully. "I would not want to lose him, human or immortal," I admitted. "But I'm glad it didn't have to come to that. I didn't want him to not have a choice, even though he seems to be game. I didn't have a choice… Brett didn't have a choice…. I wouldn't change anything about my existence now but, not like this," I could see him relax.

"When you are ready, I would be willing to bring him over for you… If you are interested, also his sister," he offered.

"Oh, Jacque… That is so generous of you. I'm sure they would both… we would be so honored to have someone as… wise as yourself become their sire," I was astonished at his generosity. "I would take full responsibility for their introduction to their new life… if that's what they wanted too, of course," I assured him.

"You may have your work cut out for you with him," he laughed.

"Yes, well… totally worth it," I said sincerely.

I gave all three of them a quick kiss on the cheek and they were off with the Bertrands. I hoped they would forgive Brett and Gavin and that the new found freedom would outweigh the awkward reawakening they'd gotten.

As I went through the back door into the little store, I could hear the woman with the gun giving Gavin and Marisol a mild lecture on getting involved with vampires. When I got back into the room where they were I saw that Gavin was trying to get up from the table and wincing in pain.

"Oh, baby, don't do that," I insisted as I rushed over to him and easily swept him up off his feet. I could tell it was a relief but he looked a little amused and conflicted.

"I'm not sure how I feel about this," he said as he looked at me from his new vantage point.

I looked at him with the new authority of being his official nurse and said, "Be quiet or I'll tie you to the bed and gag you."

He took that in the manner that I would expect and raised that one, cocky eyebrow at me. That never gets old.

Marisol

Twenty Three

I was an hour early arriving to work today but I didn't plan on going inside right away anyway. I had some flowers I'd pilfered from Julian's courtyard garden; some sprigs of night blooming Jasmine and one gorgeous dark red rose. Julian had told me the name of it was a Black Magic Rose. I thought it might be appropriate for today.

It was warm when I woke up so I put on a plaid, pleated mini skirt with knee socks and my low buckle boots topped with a black, sleeveless hoodie. I'd already gotten in the habit of leaving out what was my usual, omnipresent silver jewelry, so had Gavin I noticed. Instead I used what I had that wasn't silver which ended up being mostly black rubber bracelets and some small leather items. I did have a nice collection of lacy underwear from Trashy Lingerie that I'd been incorporating lately.

After I parked behind the shop, I stopped at the liquor store for a bottle of water and walked out to the big mausoleum in the cemetery behind the shop. It was a gorgeous, warm summer day, birds singing, sun sparkling on the man-made lake and tourists milling about, but I was anxious for the day to end and night to fall.

Before I was even close I reached out for Brett's guide, who appeared to me the way it used to before his change, clear or without red hues and with recognition. When I arrived at the mausoleum and located the crypts of the Goldsteins, I sat in front and inquired to Brett's guide which one he was in. Since I was feeling the pull to the left I took it that Brett was currently residing in Sid's crypt and scooted over and sat in front of it.

I arranged the flowers I'd brought in the little urn attached to Sid's crypt and emptied some of the water bottle into it. I wasn't expecting that Brett would be conscious inside, it was daytime after all, but there was a part of me that was hoping that he might have gotten to some of the blood before day broke this morning and there might be some red in his guide's profile by now. As it was, he was in the same position Iris had been all those years, pretty much dead for all intensive purposes except the difference being that he had a large, gaping hole in his beautiful chest and Iris did not. I didn't know if that would begin healing itself without the blood first, I thought probably not.

I leaned over and let my forehead rest against the cold marble and closed my eyes. It reminded me a little of my time down in that hole in the valley, except I was pretty much the only one who had not been in peril this time.

I called Gavin this morning to check on him. Iris had taken him home last night, promising to call if they needed anything. She seemed to have matters well in hand at that point. Although, on the phone this morning he mentioned she'd dented a rear fender trying to park the car. He said something about her needing a little more practice driving before she drove his car again. I'd offered to stop by but he said that neither one of them could really answer the door today and that he would be fine; Iris had gotten them everything they needed to camp out in the bedroom for the day, including blood, which he was in no position to give right now.

I had spoken to Iris too and she promised to meet me here at first dusk. She'd talked to Jacque and assured him that between the two of us, we would be able to get Brett out of the crypt safely; I would know if he was ready and she would actually be able to free him from where he was.

Jacque had told Iris that the Bertrand siblings had been revived safely at the embassy and were grateful for our efforts. Jean-Pierre had said, roughly translated, that once he understood that Gavin was trying to protect his sister, he could relate to that and had forgiven him. He also did not mean to drain Gavin to the point that he had. Iris could probably relate to that.

I'd also learned that apparently the thirst does not disappear completely until the vampire has had the opportunity for blood directly from a human source. The bagged blood can only satisfy to the degree of being able to manifest self control. This actually explained a lot, when I thought about it. They had brought in two donors to help transition the Bertrands into a satisfied state; Mike the doorman and a friend of his. Iris had learned that Mike was a regular donor and companion of Harold's and he didn't have a problem helping out. Now that they were completely under control, the Bertrands said they were anxious to meet and thank us in person for all our help. I'd have to wait and see how Brett felt about that before committing. I *was* pretty curious why they were in Sid and Phyllis' crypts in the first place.

Iris had also said something else pretty interesting, when she said she was doing everything in her power to make sure Gavin healed faster than any other human had, I was curious and asked her what she could do beyond what she had already done. I was aware of the healing properties of a vampire's saliva but not much else.

She said that besides the giant deli platter of dead animals they'd picked up from Ralph's on the way home (her words), she was donating her own blood to the process. Over the protest of Gavin who yelled in the background that this was more information than I needed, she said that a vampire's blood held some healing power and some other advantages for humans and that it also created a bond. She said that unfortunately, it was a one-way bond for the vampire but that was how she knew that Gavin was hurt when it happened.

When she told me this I immediately thought about Brett, of course. It was just a thought. I couldn't automatically assume that Brett would want to give me any of his blood and, in any case, Brett didn't have enough blood for himself right now, let alone me. But it was something else I would file away for future reference.

Somehow, as I sat and reflected on the past day's events my hour had gone by and it was time to go to work. Suzanne had already given me permission to leave early so I could help revive Brett. I had no idea that Suzanne knew anything about vampires but I guess it made sense in her line of work. She knew about witches. She had said it was an "occupational hazard," and wasn't fond of associating with vampires. She had trust issues she wouldn't elaborate on. When I explained that Brett had only been a vampire for a short time, she said that wasn't necessarily a good thing and to be careful but that "I was a big girl and could make my own mistakes, err… decisions." That's one of the things I loved about Suzanne, she didn't judge… not really.

When I came in the back door I stopped in the reading room first to put away my things then checked the séance room. There was no evidence of blood left but the green table cloth that usually covered the séance table was gone, for obvious reasons. Without it, you could see that the table could conveniently morph into a poker table or other types of gaming tables. Although handy, I don't think this is the motif Suzanne was looking to project to clients.

When I made my way out front, Suzanne was there with Dino and I said, "Suzanne, I want to pay for the damage from last night."

"You're too late, honey. Your vampire pal Jacque sent a check over this morning," she seemed pleased. "He was pretty generous… the rest of his community could learn a little something about positive PR from him," she commented.

"Really? See, Jacque's a good guy… they're not all bad," I pointed out.

"I never said they were all bad… just to be careful. I shouldn't have to tell *you* after your ordeal with being abducted by a gang of them…" she reminded me.

"There're plenty of bad human beings too," I argued.

"Yeah, but they can't hypnotize you along with a whole lot of other things," she came back. She had a point there.

"If this guy… Brett… really loves you he'd trust you with some of his blood…" she said mysteriously.

"What do you mean… *trust* me with his blood?" I was puzzled by this.

"I can't believe you don't know this… once you've had a particular vampire's blood they lose the power to hypnotize you… forever," she said ominously.

"Seriously?" Iris did say "healing power and *other advantages*" regarding the power of vampire blood for humans. Maybe Gavin didn't know she'd given that possibility up. "Gavin's had Iris' blood," I confessed to Suzanne.

"Well… I guess that's good. But he should just come to his senses and realize he has everything he needs right here," indicating herself in a somewhat flamboyant way.

"I'm sure it's just a phase," I assured her. But I liked the fact that Iris trusted Gavin enough to give up that possibility. I knew that Brett hadn't ever and would never try to hypnotize me but I was becoming intrigued by the idea of this blood exchange thing more and more.

The day went by quickly. A group of four women, a wedding party really; the bride and three bridesmaids, came in as a gift to each other and I did tarot card readings for all four. It was fun and I felt better about leaving early since I had given the shop a good earnings day in the short time I was here.

I was done with the women at around 7:00 so Suzanne said to go ahead and go early. I gave her a hug, grabbed my bag and flew out the back door and out into the cemetery.

It was turning out to be another spectacular burnt orange and gold sunset that reminded me of that night at the bar-be-cue which ended up being the first night Brett kissed me, among other firsts. It was hard to believe that it was just a little over a week ago. So much had changed since then. If I could go back and change anything I wasn't sure I would. Some things I could have done without but if it meant giving up the rest I think I would just live with the whole mess as it was.

When I got to the mausoleum I went directly to Sid's crypt and sunk down on the floor in front of it. I slid down and laid my head on my bag but then I remembered something. I reached into my bag and pulled out the strip of pictures we'd taken in the photo booth the other night and tucked the edge of them behind the plaque with Sid's name on it, then resumed my position with my head resting on my bag. I adjusted them to my horizontal angle and admired the incredibly handsome guy with me in the pictures. Iris was right; the first one was the best. I looked, in the picture, like I always feel now in his presence… completely in awe. The look on his face is the unlikely reason for my awe; he looked like he was really in love with me. It's still hard for me to buy. I've just never been that lucky.

As the sun began to set I was anxiously watching Brett's guide. I didn't think I'd hear anything but you never know. Waiting… watching… listening… Because I was inside the mausoleum I wasn't sure if it was exactly at the moment the sun went down but at about that time I did hear… *something* from inside the crypt… or so I thought. If there was a noise, it was very faint. Suddenly, not gradually, I noticed that Brett's guide was a transparent shade of red… then just as suddenly it was redder, then redder. Since I don't get sustained images anyway, just flashes, I would see it as sudden changes weather it was gradual or not. So… he was conscious.

I wondered if he might be confused or panicking in that small space; I know I would not be a happy camper in there. As a matter of fact, when I was in a similar place in a dream my thought was to claw my way out with my fingernails, although it always seemed to be ineffective.

Even though I really couldn't hear him, he would probably be able to hear me. I sat up and put my face close to the crypt.

"Brett... Brett, it's me, Marisol," I started whispering but then raised my voice a bit so he wouldn't have to strain to hear through the thick rock. The place seemed to be pretty much cleared out anyway. If there were still some people around they could just go ahead and think I was mental.

"Brett... you're in the crypt where the French brother and sister were... Don't worry, Iris is on her way and we're going to get you out of there very soon," probably the most important information he would be looking for.

"There are a lot of... bags... in there with you..." In case someone was still around that could hear. "Drink as much as you can, OK?" A directive he probably didn't need me to give him.

"Brett... I'm so sorry... this is all my fault. You were right when you said I shouldn't stick around just because I was curious." This was truly my guilt to own. Gavin started it being Gavin but he was really only there because I insisted on staying.

"I promise... no more stubborn self destruction. My behavior is selfish and dangerous sometimes and I don't want you to have to pay for my stupid decisions," I confessed. I hadn't really thought about it. I was really just saying it aloud as it came clear to me.

"I... I don't know what I'd do if something happened to you..." I was speaking more softly again. Even with the wall of rock between us, it was still difficult to speak about the depth of feeling I had for him.

Then it occurred to me, "I guess... something did happen to you... several things have happened to you... but what I mean is... I'm so... relieved that you're going to be OK. But I guess it would be almost impossible for you to *not* be OK at this point..." I was really starting to stumble around now.

"I hope you're OK in there..." I didn't want to stay silent in case he was freaking out in there, I would be. "The though of being in that tiny little box... it just makes me want to vom..." What was I doing? Trying to freak him out more?

"I'm sorry, forget I said that," I changed my tone, "I'm sure you are totally fine in there... Iris will be here any minute..." I reassured him.

"I'm here right now," Iris said as she strolled up the big hallway.

"Oh, thank god," I said truthfully. "If he wasn't freaked out before he must be now," I admitted.

"Hah..." she chuckled. "Don't worry our kind have a tolerance for small spaces. We don't have to breathe and it's quite comfortable for us in a place like that," she assured me.

"Are you sure? I can't imagine I'd ever be OK with that," I shuddered.

"Oh, you probably would be if you were changed," she said.

"So, what do you see? Is he awake?" She asked.

"Yeah, about twenty minutes ago… right when the sun went down… his guide turned red," I reported.

"Hmm," she pondered it.

"Should we wait? Do you think he's ready?" I asked.

"Well, there's really no point. Once he found the blood I'm sure he swallowed as much as he could," she deduced. "Waiting won't bring him any more."

"Why don't you stand back a little…" she pointed toward the entrance. I grabbed my little strip of pictures and put them back in my purse before going to stand where she indicated.

Then I said, "Ready." Last time I said that we weren't exactly ready.

Iris swept back behind the crypts and after I heard the same grinding, cracking and rock against rock scraping, there was silence.

Then Iris shouted, "Don't come back here…"

That was ominous. What could be happening?

Then I heard Brett say, "Don't say that, she'll think something's wrong."

"Something *is* wrong… look at you," she said mysteriously.

"Marisol, it's OK… I'm just a mess…" he said. He rounded the corner as he was simultaneously removing his shirt and using it to wipe off a whole lot of spilled blood from his upper torso.

"Brett!" I started to go towards him but slowed down a little at the sight of him drenched in a lot of the bagged blood.

"I'm a freak show… hold on," As he was mopping the blood from his face, hair, neck and chest I noticed that I couldn't see any kind of mark where the stake had entered his body. I couldn't help myself and went up and touched the place where he had been impaled.

He put his hand over mine and when I looked up at him he said, "I'm OK," and gave me a reassuring smile.

I tried to return the smile but my face betrayed me by pulling down the corners of my mouth and forcing my eyes to fill with tears. I couldn't help remembering the moment it went in.

When he saw this he said, "Oh… shh," and pulled me up in a tight embrace.

He let me sniffle for a minute but I was determined to pull myself together.

"OK… I can see my work is done here," Iris said tactfully. "I have a giant baby to wait on back home," she complained. "Are all men that… *needy* when they're not feeling well," she asked.

This made me laugh. "Welcome to Gavin's world," I snorted.

Brett let me down and I wiped my eyes.

Then I thought about what Gavin had said about the car, "Iris, how did you get here? Do you need a ride home?" I asked.

"Oh no, it's not far. I came on foot. It's much faster… and probably safer for me to walk," she said. I thought about how fast they all were and realized she'd probably beat us home by a wide margin.

"Are you sure?" I said to be polite.

"Yep," she said as she gave us each a kiss on the cheek and disappeared. She reappeared at the entrance of the mausoleum and said, "see you tomorrow," and was gone.

I blinked for a second at her quickness then let myself turn around and lean my head back against Brett's chest. "So, can you see her when she moves that fast?" I asked out of curiosity.

"Sure... it looks like regular speed to me... everyone else is moving in slow motion," he explained.

"That must be frustrating..." I hated to think of him following me, the turtle, around.

"No, it's fine," he protested. He could probably tell I was thinking of it in the context of me, the slow human.

Where we were in the main hallway, the moonlight and a couple of the night security lights reflected into the mausoleum through the ceiling of skylights giving the marble a purplish glow. He was mostly silhouetted but his hair and skin glowed with the reflection of the light shining off of it.

When I was this close to him all of our most intimate moments would come crashing back into my brain and make it impossible for me to resist him. My lips began tracing up the line of his neck where my head was on his shoulder. I could taste the remaining blood he wasn't able to wipe off and the thought of tasting his blood sent a wave of desire through me.

He stayed still while I traced up to his ear and over the line of his jaw, over his chin then stopped as our lips barely touched. His only movement was his deepening breath and his involuntary, growing desire.

When I let go of my resistance and the kiss went deep and intense, I knew we wouldn't make it home before this would become more.

We both gave into it and soon the desire was overwhelming. He picked me up as I wrapped my legs around him and he pushed my back up against the crypt wall. I remembered that there was a bench around the corner in the side hallway and he must have remembered it too because at that moment he carried me around the corner and gently laid me down onto it.

It was a narrow, hard stone bench so to save me from it he put one hand under my hips. I sat up a little and pulled him closer as he moved my underwear to the side and he came down into me.

We laid back as the relief of being together again rippled over us. It was overwhelming and breathtaking as he lifted my hips up to meet his. With my tongue, I could feel... movement, in his jaw. I ran my tongue up next to his teeth and his eye tooth lowered slightly and cut my tongue a little.

"Ah," I started a little and pulled away slightly.

"I'm sorry... I'm sorry," he said as I pushed my hands on his cheeks and kissed his closed mouth to stop the apologies.

"Shh," it was my turn to shush him. "No, it was just... a surprise," I said. Then I was resolved.

As I kept eye contact, I unzipped the zipper on my little, hooded jacket and pulled it and my bra strap off one side to expose my neck and shoulder completely. I let my head fall back down to the bench and lifted up my chest and arched my back in a gesture that was so overtly blatant that it couldn't be mistaken.

He was in no position to resist. He let his lips, and his now slightly extended canine teeth brush across my skin very slowly from my shoulder, up my collar bone, into the hollow with his tongue then up to my neck.

When he clamped down it was sudden and so quick I didn't realize it had happened until after and only his lips held the blood in place. He lingered there as I could feel it trickle out into his mouth slowly then he drew once hard to pull more out. When he did this my lower body tensed in and the feeling sent such an avalanche of pleasure that my screams brought us both quickly to the breaking point, which ended up being longer and more drawn out then ever before.

I relaxed into a puddle of Jell-O while he licked the spot he'd punctured like it was chocolate frosting and pulled himself and me back together.

After more than a few minutes I spoke.

"I, um… I learned something today," I said cryptically.

"Mmm, what's that?" he said between frosting licks.

Without warning, he lifted me up with his hands that were still placed under me in their strategic positions to be straddling him upright as he sat on the bench. He took a moment to breathe in deeply at my neck, then continued licking. He lifted me up so smoothly and easily it was a little disorienting.

"Oh… um, well… Iris told me that… and Suzanne mentioned that… if a person, a human would… drink the blood of a particular vampire… then there would be… certain results…" I stammered.

He stopped mid-frosting lick.

After a minute, "What kind of results, exactly?" then he continued to lick.

"Well… Iris said she knows… she feels how Gavin's feeling at any given time because of their blood bond," I started.

"Gavin has had Iris' blood?" he asked. He had stopped and was looking at me now.

"Yeah, well that was news to me too," I replied.

"So… what does that mean? That I'd be able to feel what you're feeling?" He was the first one to put it in the 'him and me' context.

"Um… yeah, well that's part of it," I said. I figured I'd just spit it out at this point, so to speak.

"So… there's a one-way bond, for the vampire… there are heeling properties for the human and… also it prevents the vampire from ever hypnotizing the human, not that anyone's worried about that here… but if you're considering it then you should know everything," I blurted out.

He smiled at my awkward explanation and said, "Do you want to?" Then he pushed my hair back and kissed me softly.

I said, "Do you want me to?" thinking it was weird for me to be asking him… but he didn't know so…

He didn't answer but instead dropped his head down and scraped his bottom canine against his shoulder. It left a deeper slash than I would have thought as red blood pooled then cascaded over the cut. It was a little shocking as he looked back at me, touched my cheek and said, "Only if you want to."

I looked back at his shoulder and the blood was starting to run down his arm. I suddenly couldn't let it drip to the floor and caught it at the inside of his elbow and followed it up to the source. It tingled or maybe… vibrated on my tongue and slid down my throat like silk. It didn't even feel like I was swallowing. As I took all that was there my mouth closed over the slash where it was coming from and I couldn't stop myself from trying to pull more out.

My head felt like it was floating and Brett was getting aroused again. After a few more minutes, I forced myself to stop and all of this must have had an intense physiological effect on Brett because he kissed me hard with his blood still in my mouth and pushed himself into me. It was fast this time.

After allowing me some recovery time, Brett rearranged us again and as I watched and touched the cut on his shoulder as it closed up right before my eyes.

"All this and it would heal you too if you needed it?" he asked as he saw what I was looking at.

"Iris is using it to heal Gavin from what happened yesterday," I answered.

"Oh yeah… what happened to Gavin?" he asked as he slowly stood up with me and sat me gingerly on my feet.

"Oh…" this would be a long story, "why don't I tell you about it on the ride home," I suggested.

"That sounds good to me," he said and steered me toward the way out. As I grabbed my bag, he noticed the flowers that were on Sid's crypt and reached down and brought them with us. Then he took my hand and led me to the VW so I could drive us home.

BRETT

Twenty Four

The sun had set. Reminding me of the sound a candle makes when you extinguish it with some spit on your finger, I could almost hear the sun being extinguished behind the horizon.

It was unfathomable to me that I could feel as perfect physically as I did now. After the French girl… Amelie Claire, had gotten control of my stake and landed it with precision directly into my heart; it was lights out. But once I'd consumed enough of the rescue blood I instantly healed in a way that can only be described as miraculous. Although nothing, nothing compared to the experience of having Marisol's blood… and her having mine. It was going to be difficult to think of anything else now that I knew this revelation was something that could be repeated. I could feel my jaw shifting just thinking about it.

I pulled the long chain on the single-bulb light fixture in Iris' little sleep chamber and sat up. As feminine as it was, I did like the way she'd fixed up the little space with the wallpaper and fancy linens. It immediately reminded me of her and gave me a warm feeling the minute I became conscious. Iris had said she'd gotten lucky with me. Of all the extreme things I had to endure since I'd been changed into my new form, Iris was the one shining light of hope regarding what my new existence could be. I had definitely been the one to luck-out.

Since today was not Saturday—Marisol's one day off and consequently my new favorite day—I would be alone in the house. I pulled the key out of my pocket and unlocked the trap door, opened it and pulled myself up to sit on the edge of the floor. I closed the door, locked it and replaced the wood circle then put the key on top of Marisol's dresser next to her camera.

Even from a distance, when I took a breath in and smelled the overwhelming sweet smell of Marisol my first thought was to dive into the bed and let the smell overtake me. Instead I went to the kitchen to find some of the leftover bagged blood to calm my thirst a bit.

I walked through the living room, past the thick velvet drapes that were drawn over the windows, and continued to the kitchen and opened the refrigerator. I picked up a bag and put it to my nose and took a breath to ignite the blood instinct and extend my canines to open the bag. But the smell, although not bad really, was weak—seemingly too weak to move my jaw in any way. So I got a knife from the drawer behind me, punctured it and poured it into a glass.

It was somewhat satisfying but I had a realization that the longer blood had been separated from its source, the less satisfying it would be. Regardless of my lack of desire for it, I downed the whole bag and another just for good measure. Lack of self control was something I couldn't abide in myself and I would do what I had to.

I went back into the living room and threw open the drapes on the city side then the courtyard side of the apartment. I flipped open the latch on one of the pulley windows and pushed it open. The aromatic smell of the Roses, Gardenias and Jasmine mixed with the human blood smell coming from the other bungalows was dazzling my senses and held my attention for more than a minute.

A sudden breeze told me that Iris was close by and less than a second later I could hear her little shoes clicking on the steps coming up the front. She was coming at full speed but when she stepped between the units into the courtyard she slowed down to human speed. I had plenty of time to get up and open the door to greet her.

"Hey, what are you doing here?" I asked with a friendly smile.

"Hey you," she said as she breezed by me into the apartment. She let me close the door and she stepped over and closed the window before she continued, "I thought maybe we could share a meal…" she said. "Gavin's still recuperating and Marisol's at work, right? So…" she insinuated.

"Yeah, I…. I did have a couple of those bags of blood that came from the embassy, but…" I hesitated.

"Pretty satisfying, huh?" she said sarcastically. "They've been dormant for a while now… but I'm glad you're being precautionary," she praised. "Let's go take a walk, shall we?" she suggested.

"Yeah, OK. Let me just get dressed," I said as I ran back into the bedroom and opened the bottom drawer of the tall dresser. Marisol had sweetly cleaned this one out for me. I pulled out a faded black t-shirt of some kind, pulled a belt through the jeans I was already wearing, put on my motorcycle boots, then put my hair into a band and rejoined Iris in the living room.

"We'll just go somewhere quick because Jacque called and the Bertrand siblings asked if we could meet them tonight. They wanted to meet with Gavin and Marisol too so I suggested we all meet at the Brown Derby," she said excitedly. "Everyone used to go there in my day. Harold says it's still there…" she went on as we left out the front door and I locked it behind us. I'd gotten the key at the same time as the drawer.

As we walked down the courtyard path Julian opened his door and greeted us, "Hey Brett," he said. We'd met at the bar-be-cue.

"Hey, Julian," I said a little surprised. He smelled tempting but I could control myself. I was glad at this moment I'd had the bagged blood, "this is my friend, Iris," I said as I introduced them. "Iris is Gavin's girlfriend," I added.

"Oh, hi Iris, nice to meet you," he said, giving her a good look-over.

"Hi Julian, nice to meet you," Iris said back to him. "I'm also a friend of Marisol's, she says nice things about you," she added.

"Oh, that's sweet," he said. "So Brett, are you living here now?" he said with more than a little curiosity.

"Oh… I guess, yeah," I said a little uncertainly. I really felt like I didn't live anywhere since I'd gotten my stuff from the shared apartment I was living at. We never actually said it but the key means something.

"That's nice," he said, and I think he meant it. "Stop by anytime… you too Iris…" he said as Iris pulled on my arm to get me moving down the walkway.

"See you," we all said as Iris and I pushed our way down to the street and out of sight and sound proximity.

"So, where are we going?" I asked Iris when we got to the street.

"I don't know, let's just walk down to Hollywood Blvd." she said as we sped to the corner. "We only really need to slow down in the lit areas, I think," she said. We slowly crossed Yucca Street and sped up between Yucca and Hollywood then turned right. Once we hit the sidewalk we slowed and as we walked she was looking at the stars on the ground and into the store windows.

"This place has really gone downhill," she said, disappointed.

"Yeah, it's a little trashy down here," I admitted. We walked and she spotted a smoke shop and decided we should go in. The smell of pipe tobacco and clove was strong and pleasant.

We went inside the narrow store and were greeted by a chubby, twenty-something guy with blonde wispy hair and a goatee that wouldn't quite grow in completely. He had a tattoo on his forearm of a Celtic cross and a nose ring. He wasn't exactly what I'd expect in a pipe tobacco shop but then I remembered something. As Iris was perusing the cases of lighters and golf knick-knacks I looked at the clerk and asked him if he had any other 'types of pipes.'

This surprised Iris and she looked up at me then the clerk. Then the clerk said, "Sure, in the back," as he walked the path behind the cases toward the red velvet curtain in the back. I led Iris toward the back and through to the head shop section of the establishment.

Iris couldn't help herself, "Ooh, decadence," she cooed softly as we entered and she saw all the bongs, pipes and paraphernalia. "You know, Gavin would probably like something from here," she said as she eyed the goods in the case—as if we were really back here to shop.

She pointed into the case at something and said enthusiastically to the clerk, "oh, can I see that please," completely forgetting for the moment why we were here.

"Sure," he replied less than enthusiastically as he pulled out a brass pipe shaped like a coffin and set it on the glass in front of her.

On the wider side of the coffin a piece lifted up like an authentic lid would on a real coffin and you would put your pot in there to smoke. When you closed it there was a brass piece that slid up and locked it into place. There was also a little hole in the lower part of the coffin that was used as a carburetor.

"How much?" she wanted to know.

"Um…" he turned the brass pipe over and looked at the sticker on the bottom of it, "$15.00"

"Sold…" when he picked it up and started to head for the register she quickly continued, "but… actually, I think I may need something else as well," she had obviously recalled why we were here. She looked into his eyes and said, "I'll buy that, but also I'm going to give you a big tip for being such a helpful salesman," she was slowing his heart. "The only thing you'll remember is selling us this cute little pipe," he was becoming mesmerized, "but you won't remember anything else," she said as she took his hand and bit into the inside of his elbow. With him behind the counter, I guess that was the best she could do. I took his other arm and followed suit.

It was so much better than the bags… but not as good as Marisol, of course. This was entirely impersonal but very satisfying. He was a big guy so we had a good drink before we cleaned him up, thanked him for his courtesy, purchased the pipe and gave him a nice tip on the way out.

Once we were on our way back Iris got chatty again, "You know, Gavin smokes entirely too much pot…" she began, "but I told him; only if we're not going anywhere… it's not that I don't like the feeling—it makes me totally giggly… like Arial—but I don't want to feel like that all the time…" she elaborated. I couldn't imagine Iris any more effervescent then she already was.

When we got to the front steps of the courtyard I said to Iris, "Wait…" I could hear the sound of a Volkswagen Beatle three or four blocks away and it seemed to be coming this way. It was so distinct I thought I could have heard it as a human… but maybe not so far away.

I heard it turn on what was probably Vine Street then it came up Yucca toward Ivar and then she was turning up the street. When she spotted us she smiled, then turned into the driveway previous to the courtyard entrance and stopped as I approached and leaned in for a kiss.

"Hey," she said low and intimately, and then she spoke up and said, "Hey Iris, what're you doing here?" in a friendly way.

"Hey Marisol, I'm here to get you guys," she said, "the Bertrand's want to meet with us before they leave for San Francisco in a couple of days," she informed us.

"Oh," there was a little hesitancy there, "OK," she'd apparently remembered they had probably become more controlled since the last time she saw them. Nothing registered in her voice so I must be getting this through the blood…

"We're meeting in a public place if that helps," I added with a grin.

She grinned back, "kind of," she answered. "I'm going to park…" she said as we backed up to let her pull into the driveway and back to her garage. I thought about it and I dashed back to where she was and stopped at her window.

She started a little even though I slowed down before I leaned in the window, "Sorry… can I open the garage door for you?" I offered.

She reached into her glove box and handed me the key to the door. I unlocked it and had it open quicker than she would be able to see.

She pulled in slowly and got out. Once she was outside I closed and locked the door and handed her the key just as she was turning back around to face the garage. She shook her head in a bit of exasperation so I lifted her up, swung her around and kissed her. Iris had joined us by then so I grabbed Marisol's hand and led her and Iris up the back stairs.

"So, where are we going and when?" Marisol asked as we were walking up the steps.

"Oh, the Brown Derby and they said they would meet us at about 11:00," Iris said enthusiastically.

"Oh, OK. I haven't been there in a little while…" Marisol responded once we were inside.

"Me neither," Iris said, not even trying to be facetious.

"Maybe we could go a little early and Gavin and Marisol could get some dinner…" I suggested. I noticed that giving blood had given Gavin a healthy appetite. I could also feel that Marisol was a little hungry…

"That would be great," Marisol agreed wholeheartedly.

"I'm sure Gavin would be all for that. Why don't I go home and help him get ready to go. He's almost completely healed now but I think he likes the moral support…" Iris said as she zipped to the front door. "We'll swing by in about a half-hour to pick you up, OK?" she asked as she opened the door.

"Sure, Iris, thanks," Marisol said before Iris disappeared and the door was silently closed.

Once Iris was gone I swept Marisol up for a more intimate greeting. Her response was as enthusiastic as mine but after a minute she protested, "You know, a half-hour is not very much time…" she said as she allowed me to distract her for another minute. Then I led her to the bedroom and plopped down on the futon while she got ready.

She pulled out a pretty, long sleeved black velvet dress with little brass buttons that went all the way up the front and a pair of fishnet stockings. She dressed behind the screen and brought a pair of patent leather boots out with her and put them on. She fished a black velvet ribbon out of one of her small drawers and tied it around her neck like a choker and went into the bathroom.

I decided I better change too and pulled off the motorcycle boots, t-shirt and the old jeans I had on and put on a newer pair of black jeans, a dark red button down shirt and put my motorcycle boots back on. I also found my black leather blazer and put it on. Good enough, I thought.

When Marisol came out of the bathroom she'd put on makeup and done something to make her hair more voluminous and looked gorgeous, of course. I was sitting on the end of the bed and she had stopped in the doorway and leaned against the jam in a pretty appealing way, probably weighing weather or not to let me mess up the makeup she'd only just applied when we heard Gavin honk.

"Saved by the honk," I said with an opportunistic smile.

"For now," she promised as I got up and we left down the back stairs to get into the T-Bird that was waiting in the driveway.

As Marisol and I slid into the back seat I couldn't help saying, "You know… the Brown Derby is so close we could've just walked." It was on Vine at Hollywood Blvd., two long blocks from the bungalow.

"Oh… no, no, no. They have valet parking anyway and it would mess up our entrance," Iris explained, although I wasn't aware we were trying to make an entrance.

Once we'd made the long, arduous two block journey we pulled up in front of the iconic landmark restaurant in line with the maroon color, long awning that ran the length of the sidewalk leading to the entrance. After a minute of waiting, and a lack of a sign indicating service, it became clear that the Brown Derby no longer had valet service and Iris, Marisol and I got out while Gavin went to park the car. This greatly disappointed Iris.

"Is nothing sacred?" she complained as we waited for Gavin to return from the lot.

"Hey, at least it's still here," Marisol consoled her.

Gavin caught up with us again and we walked up the long entrance to the front door. Once we were inside, I think it looked mostly like Iris expected, except maybe a little sadder, or dingier than it was in the heyday, but you couldn't tell too much with the subtle, subdued lighting. The restaurant had Spanish architecture with domed ceilings, arched entries and exposed beams. The décor was mainly wood and brass and still sported the hundreds of caricature portraits of Hollywood stars of the past.

We approached the host stand and Iris spoke, "Hi, we have a reservation for nine at 11:00, but four of us are here early and we would like to sit for dinner… the name is Stein, Iris Stein," she said with panache.

"Right this way please," the host said as he grabbed four menus and led us to a very large booth in the corner. It was almost 10:00 PM so there was only a smattering of people left in the place.

I slid onto the maroon leather booth first followed by Marisol, then Gavin then Iris. The booth was so big we stayed hovered around the far corner. I slid my menu to the side and Iris did too.

Marisol and Gavin studied the menus until the waiter came back for their order. Iris spoke first.

"I'll just have a red wine," she said to the waiter then the waiter turned to Marisol.

"Um… I'll have a Cobb Salad please," she said, and then the waiter looked at Gavin.

"Steak, rare, baked potato, everything on it, salad with blue cheese and a beer… Budweiser," Gavin said.

Then the waiter looked at me, "I'll have a steak, medium-rare with… French fries and… that'll do it," I said as the table looked at me in mild shock. I smiled and handed my menu back to the waiter as he turned and left.

"You're not going to try to eat that are you?" Iris said as a warning. "It'll just come right back up," she said, letting me know what would happened should I try.

"It's not for me…" I confessed as I glanced at Marisol.

"I got something…" she protested.

"Not enough," I decided. Quietly to her, "You'll need to eat more," I said in her ear… apparently not low enough.

"He's right Marisol… eat," Gavin commanded. He would know…

First Gavin's salad came, then the meals. Although it smelled terrible, I cut pieces of the steak and fed them to Marisol in between bites of her Cobb Salad. She ate everything dutifully. Since Gavin ate a good portion of the Cobb Salad I was glad I'd ordered the steak. Iris gave Marisol the red wine after smelling it for a while.

"Don't you miss food?" Marisol asked me while I was feeding her a piece of steak.

"You know, I do until I smell it," I answered honestly. "It really smells awful to me now," I said.

"It tastes awful too… going down… and coming back up," Iris said laughing. The three of us looked at her, a little grossed out, "everyone tries it once…" she said with a giggle.

"I'll take your word for it," I said, not anxious to ingest this foul smelling stuff.

The waiter came and took the empty plates and Iris put water glasses in front of both Gavin and Marisol. Marisol watched as Gavin swished the water around in his mouth and swallowed and did as he did. Afterward I smiled and gave her a quick kiss of appreciation. I was grateful to Iris to not have to be the one to ask.

Gavin and Marisol sipped the last of their drinks as we waited for the rest of our party to arrive.

When the Bertrand's arrived I didn't recognize them until I saw Harold McKinley walk up behind them. Apparently someone had been sent to Neiman Marcus and purchased all the best petite clothing they could find. They looked like they could be modern day French aristocrats on holiday in the states. Amelie Claire wore a white tailored suit with stockings and black pumps and her brunette hair was long and free-flowing, with short bangs in the front. Jean-Pierre was wearing a tailored designer suit with a white shirt and tie. There was quite an expensive air to them. The Haitians entered behind them and everyone followed the host over to our table to join us.

I could see Gavin was looking a little nervous… even more than Marisol. Marisol was feeling pretty calm really. She did have the added advantage of being personally responsible for the discovery and release of the Bertrands. Gavin was just the human brother to pull the stake on Jean-Pierre. He probably should be a little nervous.

When they arrived Jacque made all the introductions. Everyone greeted everyone else but I ventured that this would be the extent of direct conversation as the Bertrands would need to speak through Jacque for his interpretation. The Haitians slid into the rest of the booth with Jacque on the far end while Harold and the Bertrands sat in chairs they pulled up to the outside of the booth; Harold closest to Iris. This put the Bertrands fairly far away from Gavin and Marisol, which I'm sure Gavin appreciated.

As they sat, Jean-Pierre began speaking to Jacque in heart–felt French then looked at Marisol and Gavin and smiled apologetically. Jacque immediately interpreted.

"Monsieur Bertrand would like to say up front that he apologizes for his ignorance of the English language and relays his only excuse is the laziness of privilege. One of his scions had always filled the role of interpreter and they never bothered to learn." Jean-Pierre added something then Jacque added, "Actually, they came to California with the intent purpose of immersing themselves in the culture and language so that they might learn finally. But of course we know their mission was cut short," he added.

Iris spoke up now. Clearing her throat, she spoke directly to the Bertrands in perfect, lilting French. They responded with appreciative, enthusiastic statements and when they were done she turned to us, "I told them I'd be happy to help them with their studies any time. I let them know about how I'd been born in Switzerland, etc., etc…" she shorthanded.

The little French girl, Amelie Claire, looked up at me now for the first time, then over to Iris and Marisol as she spoke. She looked serious and ashamed. Iris responded to her warmly and then translated, "Amelie Claire wanted you to know, Brett that she's sorry for attacking you and Marisol and putting the stake into you. She apologized to me for this as well, being your sire and all. I told her that's water under the bridge and I'm sure everyone's sorry who had to put a stake in someone else…" she said, which somehow sounded better in French. I saw Marisol nudge Gavin right then.

Gavin cleared his throat and said, "I think I should be the one to apologize… I think I may have jumped the gun…" Gavin said as Iris started interpreting immediately. Her explanation seemed to be much more elaborate so I'm sure she embellished a bit for his sake. She also seemed to gesture wildly with her hands when she was speaking French for some reason.

Just then the waiter came for our order. Everyone at the table ordered water except Harold, who ordered a beer and Jacque who ordered a glass of red wine, emulating what Gavin and Marisol were having. I was sure they would switch them out for the empties at some point.

Once the waiter was gone I decided to ask my curiosity question, "So, does anyone know who put them into the crypts in that cemetery in the first place?" I asked. The question was pretty obvious.

Jacque spoke to us in English while Celestine whispered my question and Jacque's answer in French to the Bertrands, "We don't know exactly, they must have been moved there at some point as the cemetery only came into existence in 1899. The last the Bertrands remember, they had gone on an evening tour of the bay in San Francisco, until the blackness took over," Jacque explained. This reminder of the blackness and the obvious extent of the time they'd spent there made me shudder internally. Iris looked over and gave me a reassuring smile.

"So, you don't have any idea who did this?" Iris asked Jacque in English.

"Oh, I didn't say that," Jacque started. Celestine continued to translate, "we have done nothing else since their resurrection but contact other embassies and speculate on who would have done this and why," he said.

Jacque quickly shot a look at Celestine then spoke to us without any interpretation for the Bertrands, "I'm sorry to have to ask such a personal question… but in order for us to speak freely in front of humans we must know your absolute loyalties," he said. I wasn't following yet. He seemed to be uncomfortable with what he was about to ask. "Am I to assume that... both Mademoiselle James; Marisol and her brother, Monsieur James, are blood-bound to yourself and Iris?"

Now I understood. This meant that Iris or I would know if they betrayed any vampire secrets. Not that I would give Marisol up if she did. But of course she wouldn't. "Yes," I told Jacque and looked back at Gavin who shot me a look, although I'm sure he wasn't exactly surprised.

I reached down and took Marisol's hand and interlaced my fingers with hers and squeezed a little. I couldn't see her minding that I would disclose that but it still seemed callous somehow to put it out there without her permission. She squeezed back in a comforting gesture.

"Again, I'm sorry for the personal intrusion but we have some information that could be sensitive," he said.

"We believe there are witches involved," he continued, "the Bertrands didn't smell, hear or sense any menace prior to their incapacitation. And we have seen first hand how a witch can facilitate that," Jacque said.

"The most disturbing evidence is something our kind have never fathomed before this…" he said a little ominously, "somehow… whoever did this managed to find a way to mask or break the blood bond between the Bertrands and their sire," Jacque said as Iris gasped.

"Oh my god, are you sure?" Iris asked, shocked and appalled.

"Well, when the Bertrands were staked, it would normally be pretty apparent to their sire, Monsieur Gerard," I looked over at Iris just then and she had both her hands up at her chest, looking horrified. I realized she must have had instant knowledge of my predicament when it happened.

"But he assures us that had he sensed anything of that nature he would have done a lot more than file a missing persons report, and he would have done it immediately. He only learned of their disappearance when his letters were returned unopened," Jacque explained. "He was surprised that they would go to ground without telling him, which was his assumption, but he trusted the blood bond completely and allowed them their privacy and free will," Jacque clarified.

Jean-Pierre spoke up then. He spoke a few lines then he said something that amused himself.

"Monsieur Bertrand said they would never have gone to ground at that time. They were quite enjoying their time in San Francisco since it was booming with gold and gold seekers," Jacque related. I hadn't thought about it until then. It would have been interesting to be around during the great California Gold Rush. "He says he had a good stash himself since he could actually smell the gold," Jacque added. I looked over in time to catch Gavin raising an eyebrow to that. I noticed his reaction made Jean-Pierre chuckle.

Jean-Pierre continued and Jacque continued translating, "Monsieur Bertrand says that, of course, all of the belongings that they carried with them are now gone, but that this seems like a very unlikely reason to go after vampires such as them," Jacque said.

They had a very strong, imposing presence, at least equal to that of Jacque. I couldn't help but wonder… "Can I ask… how old they are?"

Jacque smiled and did not translate but answered me himself, "Mr. Carson, you could not know this but it is considered impolite to ask a vampire his age… for different reasons then you would for not asking a lady," he said and smiled at Iris. "As a comparison, a vampire's age is so much intertwined with his power that it would be the equivalent of asking someone how much money they have," he explained so I would understand.

"Oh, I'm sorry, forget I said anything," I backtracked immediately.

"It's alright Mr. Carson. It's natural to want to understand your own, new condition. I can truthfully say that I don't know the age of our visitors but I have heard them mention their participation during the hundred year war in France, if that's any indication," he smiled at me, then at the Bertrands. I wasn't sure when the hundred year war took place in France but I was definitely going to look it up when I got the chance. Celestine translated at least some of this now, adding to my embarrassment, but the Bertrands only chuckled.

Gavin chuckled too. He was laughing now but I was sure he would be checking the time period on the hundred year war just as soon as I would.

Harold McKinley spoke up at this time, "Getting back to the crime perpetrated on our guests…" we all pulled ourselves out of our wondering to pay attention, "Mr. St Domingue and I telephoned several of our contacts as well as inquired through official channels and have come up with a hypothesis of who may have done this," he said earnestly.

"We deduced that this person must not only be a witch but also a vampire," he said matter of fact, which surprised me, "to do this it's our estimation that the witch must possess an intimate understanding of the blood-bond in order to attempt to break it," he surmised. "And so we looked through our logs and records to see if someone matching that description had come into San Francisco at the time of the Bertrands' disappearance."

Harold continued as Celestine translated for the Bertrands, "Now, there are those of our kind; outlaws, anarchists, who don't go through regular channels when they travel and don't take advantage of the benefits of living within regular vampire society," he said, "and we do know who most of these vampires are, even if they don't think we do," he said a little menacingly.

"Even though she didn't check in herself, obviously, the witch/vampire Bronwyn was spotted in the city during that time. It was reported by a conscientious observer to the San Francisco embassy," Harold reported. "Her initial change was never reported in the archives and no one ever stepped up to claim her as their scion," Harold continued, "so it's believed that no one currently knows who her sire is, at least as yet," he said then he looked at me, "there are those of us who take our record keeping very seriously and strive to record all the bloodlines for posterity," he said proudly. I could barely fathom the information that had passed in front of this humble vampire and what he must know.

"But with this new horrible development, those of us who keep the records have doubled security on the embassies," he said. "It was never common knowledge who the Bertrands' sire was and somehow, if it was this Bronwyn witch, she must have gained access to the Paris records in order to learn the identity of Mr. Gerard and cast her repugnant spell to break their bond," he said with vitriol.

Iris responded, "Does anyone know where this Bronwyn is now?" she asked the obvious then repeated herself in French.

Jacque answered, "Not yet… but we have a few… persons of interest," he said with relish. "There is no real evidence that the Horst brothers are in any way connected to Bronwyn, except that they are also mostly anarchists. They check in at the embassies but no one knows who their sire was or is. Their response to this question has always been that they don't know; that they were ambushed and left to their own devices," Jacque explained.

"I find it hard to believe that any vampire could sire three scions at once and come away unidentified," he supposed. "Also, the most compelling connection came when Heinrich was initially captured. Although he was held for the duration by means of relatively undetectable hibernation, when he was initially captured they used a stake and I was never alerted," he related.

"In any case, we have them available for interrogation and Heinrich is primed to start the questioning at first dusk tomorrow," Jacque said.

"Wow," Marisol couldn't stop herself from voicing her surprise at this new mention of the Horst brothers. All four of us seemed to tense up at the mention of their names.

Jacque spoke now, "So, you must not concern yourself about us un-staking the Horst brothers. It will only be done one at a time and under strictly controlled circumstance," Jacque assured us. "We'll start with Claudio and work our way up the evil chain," he added.

Jacque changed the tone now, "I'm sorry to deluge you so heavily in unpleasant vampire business, Marisol, Monsieur James.

Gavin answered, "Oh, no… anything that concerns Iris…. or Brett, concerns us," Gavin answered truthfully.

"I'm glad you feel that way Monsieur James as I was hoping to enlist your sister for additional information to help us in our search for Bronwyn and also to help find the other old ones who have gone missing," he said.

Gavin made a grumbling noise, he seemed to have gotten over any intimidation he may have been feeling up to that point, and protested, "Look, I know Marisol's partly responsible for putting herself in the dangerous position that ended up in the mess that happened with the Bertrands," he smiled somewhat sincerely at them then, as Celestine translated, "but it's a lot to ask of her," he said a little vaguely. Gavin was negotiating.

"I understand your concern for your sister Monsieur James," I'm sure Jacque did; at least the smirk on his face suggested so, "I think you'll find that the Bertrands' were more than happy to express their sincere gratitude once your sister has had the chance to visit her work again," up went Gavin's eyebrow. Celestine didn't translate this.

"If we are right," Jacque continued, "then the other old ones who have not gone through regular channels to report their sleep, uncharacteristically, may have been victim to this new, unknown spell and will need to be found and released," Gavin was following, "and, Monsieur James, those of us who have been fortunate enough to last a great amount of time on the earth have also had that much time to accumulate means," Gavin's eyes got wide at this even as he attempted to remain nonchalant.

"Well…" He calculated, "if we can be sure she'll be safe," Gavin responded predictably.

"I want to help," Marisol spoke up now. "If this witch is taking away people's lives… vampires' lives, then she needs to be stopped and the victims need to be found and released from… wherever they are," I could feel her tense inside at the thought of the small crypt where the Bertrands were and I was for that night. I must remember to let her know I was never in a panic in that space. Especially once I heard her voice…

Jacque St Domingue, the Bertrand siblings and Harold all smiled and seemed to appreciate the commitment Marisol was making. The shy, female Bertrand, Amelie Claire spoke now in a soft French lilt to Jacque so he could translate.

Jacque repeated, "It seems, Marisol, that you are beginning to accumulate benefactors. Mademoiselle Bertrand has offered to bring you over to be one of us. Since I have offered the same to Iris, I couldn't tell you who would have the oldest, most potent blood, but it would be a close contest. I believe as we move forward, you will most likely have your pick of sires, should you choose to join Mr. Carson in immortality," he said warmly.

Since Iris hadn't told me or Marisol of Jacque's offer, the shock resonated on Marisol's face when he said this. She looked like she was having trouble forming an answer.

"Thank you so much," I said to Amelie Claire Bertrand, "Marisol is still digesting that I am what I am, let alone had a chance to consider it for herself… If she eventually decides to go that direction… your more than generous offer is one we'll definitely consider seriously," I tried to say with grace, without presuming too much on Marisol's part. Celestine translated and I made a conscious choice right then to not look at Gavin's reaction.

"Well then," Jacque interjected, "since the wait staff is beginning to give us looks that suggest we have stayed past our welcome…" as I looked around I saw he was right. We were the last ones in the place, "perhaps we should let them close up," he said as he got up from the booth and let Celestine and Arelia up. The Bertrands and Harold pushed back their chairs and Iris let the rest of us out the other end of the booth.

Gavin put some twenties into the folder to pay the bill as Iris approached Amelie Claire. She spoke a few words in French and then gave her a hug. I was noticing that Iris was as much of a natural people person as Gavin was, but in a different way.

She also hugged Jean-Pierre, and Gavin shook his hand, crazy enough, as well as Jacque and Harold. I shook hands with Jacque and also Jean-Pierre. I felt I should do something to alleviate Amelie Claire's guilt so I took her hand, kissed the back of it and gave her a smile. She looked a little bit flustered, which I wasn't prepared for, but I don't think she misunderstood my meaning. I could feel Marisol's defensiveness… jealousy really, although there was absolutely no change to her face. I thought about how it was before we got together and I couldn't get a reading on weather or not she was interested. This blood-bond thing would have been handy then.

Gavin approached Jacque and they shook hands, "Monsieur James, I'll be in touch," I sensed that Jacque could respect Gavin's position as spokesperson for Marisol's business affairs. I would never presume to assume that job since it really wasn't my strong suit and he was the person that did that for me as well. But I would be the one protecting Marisol's safety from now on. Gavin was obviously not prepared for that job.

We all exited the restaurant and got in our respective cars and left. Apparently the Bertrands were off to San Francisco soon. I was curious what Heinrich would find out from the Horst brothers tomorrow. I was mainly curious what Marisol thought about the offer from Amelie Claire Bertrand.

Once Gavin dropped us off and we were inside, the back door locked and she was standing next to the sink looking at the view, I wrapped my arms around her from behind and asked, "So, what did you think of the French girl's offer?" I asked, not using her name to soften any jealousy she might conjure. Now that I had my nose in her neck I was regretting the thought of it. I wondered what it would be like if we were both changed.

"I don't know… I… I don't know…" she answered, not knowing any more than I did. She turned around forward to face me.

I responded "I know that… I can't imagine living hundreds of years and you not…" a little awkwardly. I put my nose into her hair, I couldn't resist her scent when I was this close, "I don't know enough about what it means for both of us to be immortal… I wish I could tell you what you could expect…" My nature and her biology were starting to take over at this point.

After a particularly passionate kiss I lifted her up on the counter and she whispered, "I can't imagine… ever being without you…" as I lifted her off the counter and carried her back to the bedroom… where we stayed until just before dawn.

MARISOL

Twenty Five

My internal clock was definitely shifting to match the night centric schedule of Brett… and Iris and Gavin and everyone else I seemed to be hanging around with lately. It was 1:00 in the afternoon and fortunately I had just enough time to get ready for work.

I popped out of bed, filled with energy, which is how I felt all the time since taking some of Brett's blood. I felt like I was ready to take on anything; was invincible, which was probably an illusion but that's how I felt.

For him, it must be like this times ten. I'll admit I was more than a little curious about the opportunity presented to me by the French girl and Jacque. But I needed to know more, I wouldn't want to jump into anything, especially since things were so incredibly perfect with Brett as they were.

If there's such a thing as blood lust for humans I was afraid I was becoming guilty of this weakness. For him, he had to have it to sustain himself. For me, I just wanted it… every time we were alone together now I could barely think of anything else. This didn't seem to bother Brett in any way. There was some small part of me that wondered if there was going to be a down side or if somehow I could accidentally be changed. I almost didn't care.

I jumped in the shower and washed my hair. The hot water and steam felt great and it seemed like every sense I had was on extra alert. Even as I scanned around the perimeter with my mind it was like I could sense further and more accurately than before. I guess that could come in handy if I was going looking for more ancient entombed vampires. I hated to admit it, but it did sound like exciting and dangerous fun. I should probably keep that part of my motivation to myself.

It was pretty warm out today and probably would be tonight as well so I put on a just below the knee, slim black halter dress with a slit up the back and pulled out one of my favorite black and crimson bustiers for over top of it and laced it up just right. I dried my hair straight and parted it sharply to the side and clipped it back in a swept over style and threw on some cute black round toed pumps. It was a little daring but I liked the idea of Brett's possible reaction to my effort.

After I put on some makeup and downed a couple of bowls of cereal, I got in the bug and sputtered it into work.

When I got there we were already busy so I got to work right away and started helping customers. I helped a young goth-guy pick out a pewter and crystal dragon statue for his girlfriend, sold a woman some books on reincarnation and gave a quote for a full reading to an older woman who looked sad. She decided to wander around the store while she pondered weather or not to do it then left after a while. Once it had slowed Suzanne said, "Pace yourself, you're making me feel lazy," she laughed then looked at me more discerningly, "so… where are you getting all this extra energy?" although, apparently she had already gleaned the right idea.

Since she really didn't need me to confirm I said, "I've been taking my… vitamins…" I said in a way that confirmed anyway.

"Hmm," she huffed, somewhat disapproving. "So when do I get to meet your… young man," she said with some distaste and a little envy.

"That's right, you've never met Brett. I really think you'd like him actually," I assured her. "I'll have him stop by the shop one night so you can meet him," I said, knowing she had a thing for cute boys anyway.

"Listen, Arial called in a list. I guess she's going on a trip somewhere for a few days. She said she was going to ask you to water her plants…" Suzanne said.

I said, "Really, where's she going?" as I crossed back behind the register and got the list Suzanne had written down. I didn't remember seeing any plants at Arial's.

"She's got some boyfriend who's got a boat…" Suzanne started. Of course she did… duh. "They're taking some people to San Francisco and she said she'd be back in a few days," she finished. So, Heinrich would be the one taking the Bertrands back to San Francisco. Of course he would be, I thought.

"OK," is all I said as I grabbed the list and started to gather her order. I wondered what she might be conjuring up for this. Maybe some type of protection… who knows. I looked at the list; Conjure oil, Zodiac incense, Obeah oil… I guess I'd have to wait and see. I put it all in a little plastic bag with Suzanne's logo on it and filled out the order form.

After some quiet time passed during what was dinner time for most people and Suzanne had let me take my break at about seven, she went back into her office to work on the books. It was about a quarter to eight when Arial finally showed up.

"Hey Marisol," Arial said as she breezed in, ringing the front door chime. She looked particularly smiley and vivacious in her usual flowing wardrobe. She'd obviously had her hair trimmed because the short side of her asymmetrical hair style was now super short and shaved a little around one ear. She'd added a streak of black down the long side of her platinum do.

"Hey Arial… I can't figure out what you're trying to do with this order…" I asked, out of curiosity.

"It's for you, silly," she said, as if I should have known.

"For me?" I said, surprised.

"Gavin called me today. He said he and your boyfriend decided you needed a little extra protection…" she said, then giggled.

"From what?" I asked, although I could use protection from a lot of things, come to think of it.

"Well… *mind control by vampires, for one,*" she thought at me.

For a minute I didn't realize she'd not said this part out loud; it was so loud and clear. Once I realized it I said, "Oh, wow, loud and clear." It was probably because of my amped up blood… or hers… or both. Then I said, "Wait, let me try…"

"*What's number two*?" I thought at her as hard as I could.

She smiled widely and thought at me, "*Number two is protection from other witches!*" Apparently she heard me.

"Hah! How was it?" I wanted to know.

"It was… understandable… I could hear it, a little faintly, but I heard it," she appraised.

"Awesome!" That was an accomplishment for me.

"So, do you have an altar here somewhere?" she asked. She was referring to a Wiccan altar, like the one Suzanne made me set up in the reading room for show. I never used it and really, didn't know how.

"Um… yeah?" I answered her somewhat tentatively. "I'll show you…" I said as I grabbed the bag I put together for her and led her to the reading room, "I have to listen for the bell," I reminded her.

Arial followed me into my reading room and I showed her the sorry excuse for an altar that had remained untouched since I started working here. There were a few altar candles, an object candle, a personal candle (all randomly pushed into one corner) and various other things had come to rest on this table like matches, different types of incense, dust, a small clock, a couple of random crystals, an empty coffee cup and a little plant.

"Oh, shame on you… no wonder you attract trouble like it's Velcro and you're a cashmere sweater," she said sarcastically. I did feel a little ashamed now that I knew for sure magic was a serious endeavor, not to be taken lightly. I quickly removed the items that obviously did not belong, like the coffee cup, the clock and the plant, and then blew on the table to get rid of some of the dust; which was more prevalent than I thought since it made me cough. Arial's face had the look of an elementary school teacher who had just learned I forgot my math homework.

We quickly finished cleaning the table and, after she placed a cloth over it I had in the drawer and, oddly enough, put the little plant back in its place, she placed the candles in their holders. She put them where she knew they should go for what she was doing, four of them, then pulled up a chair. Then she dug into the plastic bag and placed a vile of oil in front of three of the candles and put the incense in the middle and lit it.

She began to chant, "Protect Marisol from the influence of any vampires that attempt to dominate her mind… and turn away all destructive designs made against her…" she said, over and over again. As she did this she put different oil onto the different candles. After a minute she indicated with her finger for me to come around closer so I scooted my chair around, and then she chanted the mantra into my head. I guess that's about as direct as you can get. I did sort of feel something when she did this; like that goose bumpy feeling you get sometimes… but maybe I was just picking up on the hocus-pocus vibe in general.

She repeated the process then, replacing vampires with "Witches that intend her harm," and replacing influence with magic, etc. This actually took a good bit of time. Just as she was finishing the part where she pushes it into my head the bell rang for the front door. When I looked at the clock I'd displaced from the altar it said 9:00. I was thinking it was too bad I didn't have a chance to lock the door before the straggler came in.

Since we were basically done, Arial made me blow out the candles and once I'd put the chairs back in their place she came up front with me. She strolled to the book section while I went behind the cash register. I was hoping this would be quick. "Hi, can I help you?" I asked. I don't normally harass someone like a House of Pancakes hostess but I wanted to expedite this customer.

I immediately knew this customer was a vampire. How did I know? Just by looking into her eyes. It must have been the blood I'd received, maybe recognizing its own, who knows. But they glowed with a magic that I'd come to see in both Brett and Iris, and all the other vampires who had entered my life recently.

She was a stout woman with course, brunette hair that had streaks of grey and hung to just below her shoulder. She had pale skin, dark brown eyes and wore differing shades of gray and brown, including a skirt that brushed the tops of her feet that were encased in well–worn Birkenstocks.

What would a vampire want from this store? I wondered if Arial could see that she was a vampire too. I was pretty sure she'd had Heinrich's blood. At this point I also reached out and saw that she had a dark red guide (obviously) that seemed to be sending me a warning. This was bad.

The vampire woman looked up at me and said, "I need… four black alter candles and four personal candles…" she began her list.

Shit, this vampire was a witch too. My mind started to reel and I'm sure my heart started to race because she stopped her list and looked at me with interest. I summoned all my new energy and control to calm my nerves and said, "Yes…" as if I only needed her to continue. So she did.

As I weaved my way around the store gathering up her items I looked over at Arial and pushed into the back of her head, *"Witch/Vampire! Could it be Bronwyn?"* I asked. I wasn't sure if she could hear me but I was using all my nervous energy to push. I knew Arial must have been appraised of the danger by Heinrich even though she wasn't at the meeting we had at the Brown Derby.

I suddenly felt exactly like the cashmere sweater Arial had attributed me to and the Velcro had just walked in the front door. As I was quickly gathering her order I "heard" Arial tell me, *"I'll go get help… keep her here!"* she said in my head.

I was suddenly scared out of my wits to be alone with this… person. I drilled my eyes into the back of Arial's head and "said," "*Wait! Don't leave me here alone! Tell Suzanne what's going on first*," I pleaded.

Arial wandered around a bit then approached as I was writing up the witch's order at the register. She asked, "May I use your restroom?"

I said, "Of course, it's down the hall at the end," and pointed towards Suzanne's office.

I realized now that I was close to filling her order that I should probably slow down. I wouldn't want her to walk out the door and disappear now that she was here. I was sure that she would have disguised her own scent so if the cavalry showed up once she was gone it may be too late.

I smiled congenially at her and asked, "Is there anything else you might need?" hoping she might think of something, and also not.

She looked at me curiously and asked, "Are you the psychic?"

Inside part of me wanted to crawl under the counter and scream bloody murder but I held on to my composure and said, "Um… well, I'm not Suzanne but I do readings too," I said without much conviction.

I wasn't sure how much time the cavalry needed but I was pretty sure a psychic reading would fill enough time for someone to get here. She was eyeballing me pretty good and said, "I get the feeling you have some ability in that way… would you have time for a reading?" she asked me.

"Um, sure. I just need to have Suzanne watch the front while I do it," I said as I quickly picked up the phone and rang her office. There was nothing either of us could say that the vampire/witch wouldn't hear so I just acted normal.

When she picked up (immediately) I said, "Suzanne, there's a person up front who wants a reading… can you cover?" Normally she would've just told me to lock up but I was praying that she got the word from Arial and wouldn't abandon me tonight.

"Sure Honey," she said with a knowing tone, "I'll be right up," and she hung up.

When I looked up into the witch/vampire's eyes I was suddenly very, very grateful to Arial for the spell she'd worked for me just in the nick of time. I don't think the witch/vampire had attempted to hypnotize me yet but the night was apparently young—younger than I was comfortable with.

When Suzanne arrived she smiled amicably as I turned to the customer and said, "right this way," and walked back toward my reading room.

Once we were in the room, before she took her seat she looked discerningly at my altar, took a breath in with her nose and let her eyes come back to reassess me. She must know exactly what I'd just done. If I wasn't scared shitless before, I was now.

I grabbed my deck off the table and sat in my chair. I just had to keep her here long enough for someone… the vampire cavalry to arrive.

"Um… what's your name?" I asked. I figured I had cause.

"Bronwyn," she said, "What's yours?" she asked with a little too much interest.

"Marisol… nice to meet you," I tried to sound sincere.

"Do you have a specific question?" I asked her as I shuffled the deck and put it in front of her to cut.

"I am seeking missing persons…" she said. I cringed inside when I thought that maybe she was talking about the Horst brothers. I hadn't heard yet weather Heinrich had gotten any results from the interrogation he was supposed to be doing… right about now as a matter of fact.

She cut the deck and I laid out the first card, "Your present position is;" I turned over the Ace of Swords and looked up at her, "the Ace of Swords… for you, in this position, it's representing that you're struggling to find the truth… but there is a struggle in you between spirit and logic…" I said, and it was true. It was easier for me to relax if I just read them the way I usually did.

I went on, "Your immediate influences are;" I turned over a deep purple card with the face of a woman who looked stunningly like Celestine in my Morgan Greer deck. I was hoping I'd see her soon. "The nine of pentacles indicates you have had the satisfaction of material success and… you may want to take a well deserved rest…" I'm pretty sure I was pushing my luck with that since I was only looking at her immediate influences and ended up giving her unsolicited advice… advice I was hoping she'd be taking soon…

I quickly moved on… "Your life;" I said as I placed a card directly in front of her, "The tower…" I started, "represents upheaval, restructuring… this represents that your life is going through major changes in the present…" I said rather vaguely.

"What about my question?" She asked impatiently.

"That's next," I said, which was true.

I pulled the next card and placed it in front of me. It was Death, inverted.

"I'm feeling that… the Death card represents rebirth; transformation… for you, in the root position, inversed I'm sensing that those you are looking for will not be renewed…" I was getting a strong finality from her frustrated guide right about now. I really didn't feel like giving her a negative reading. "But it does signify that something has not yet run its course…" She seemed a little less annoyed now.

Just then Suzanne passed into the doorway and said, "Honey, I've locked up and I'm going upstairs now… Can you come back quickly? I want to give you your check," she said without a hint as to weather or not she was bluffing.

I said, "Will you excuse me for a second?" and stood up slowly.

She looked in my eyes and said, "Sure, you're coming right back, right?" as I could feel something in me resisting her, maybe not in me but something surrounding me. I calmly responded, "Yes, I'll be right back," as I followed Suzanne out toward the back.

When we got to the end of the hallway, Suzanne turned in the doorway of her office and indicated that I should keep going out the back. Coincidentally, that was exactly what my feet were telling me to do.

As soon as I silently pushed the back door and it swung open, I was immediately grabbed by an arm that pulled me to the side. When I realized it was Brett, relief washed over me instantly. I turned quickly to look and I barely saw two small figures flit by me silently into the building. Then, as I pulled to look back down the hallway I saw the beautiful face on the Nine of Pentacles, Celestine and Jacque moving quickly and just as silently up the hallway from the front. Everyone was armed… no one entered…

Brett probably should have been getting me out of there but I wanted to see what happened and apparently he did too because he could make me leave if he wanted to, obviously. Instead, we held still as mice.

Just then, as I was looking down the hallway, as far as I could see in the building, which was into the shop, against one of the curio cabinets, Arial stepped into view and "said" to me, "*get her to come out,*" in her own special way.

I stared to step forward but Brett wouldn't let me move. I looked up at him and indicated I needed to talk to her and get closer to speak or it would look fishy, or some semblance of that that I could muster without words.

I was mostly behind him already but technically we were really side by side up until then, at that point he faced the hallway and put me completely behind him and stepped forward extra slow. I pushed a little on his back because more time would just make it worse really. He stepped forward a couple of steps with me right behind him.

When we got back inside, Suzanne was still in her office just behind the doorway and had gotten her gun ready. I don't know why that made me feel better, because it shouldn't have. She had the same Starsky and Hutch look on her face that Gavin had in the cemetery.

I realized by then I should be thinking about something to say to get her to come out. I looked up and thankfully Arial "said," "*Tell her you got a phone call and have to leave,*" she suggested.

I was just past Suzanne's office when I finally spoke up, "Um… miss… Bronwyn? I, um… have a personal emergency at home… can we continue this on another day?" she groaned but didn't come out yet. I stepped forward a little bit more and realized it would be weird if I didn't come all the way into the doorway and tried to impress this upon Brett wordlessly so he reluctantly let me pass, "No charge and a discount when you come back," I gave her my best apologetic smile as I stepped into view. As she got up and walked toward me and the door, I did my best to walk back the way I came without giving her any cause for concern. But just in case I kept going past the Bertrand siblings and circled back around behind Brett and let him walk me backwards next to where Suzanne was standing just out of view.

Just as she came into view in the doorway, petite, sweet Amelie Claire lunged faster than I could see and plunged her sharpened stake into the witch/vampire. She had a look of revenge on her face like I'd never seen but could not mistake. The witch/vampire… Bronwyn screamed, or more accurately, screeched in a terrible, high-pitched, blood-curdling way… but she did not fall to the ground unconscious as I expected.

Unfortunately the stake went in just under her left shoulder and missed its mark by a few inches. There was plenty of blood… but not as much as there would have been if the stake met its mark. At this point, I was pretty well versed on the amount of blood to expect with a successful staking.

The witch/vampire let out a new screech at Amelie Claire and pulled the stake out of her shoulder and flung it on the ground in front of her. During the time I must have blinked, three more stakes made their way into the screeching witch/vampire; one each from the other three ancient vampires in the hallway right then.

Although none of these three stakes hit the mark intended, which was her heart by the way, they had managed to nail her to the wall temporarily. By now I could feel I was staring with my mouth wide open.

Stakes in a vampire that were not in the heart didn't seem to have the power to incapacitate the witch/vampire mentally but had definitely released enough of her blood to stop her from responding quickly so someone could take advantage of the moment. To my surprise, that person was my balls of steel boss, Suzanne, who walked up to the witch/vampire and put a bullet into her heart.

No one said anything because I don't think anyone thought that Suzanne's gesture would do anything to really kill or incapacitate the witch/vampire but after a second of staring at the train wreck in front of us, Bronwyn slowly lost consciousness as quite a bit more of her blood ran out of her. By this time all the ancient vampires had matching slack jaw expressions exactly like the one I could feel on my own face.

"Silver bullets," Suzanne said as a matter of fact. She looked around at the ancient vampires and said a little condescendingly, "Protection spell against wood stakes, I'm guessing… she must have placed one on her own heart…" Suzanne summed up. As everyone seemed to catch on she walked back toward her office.

Just then Amelie Claire grabbed her stake that was on the ground and successfully plunged it into the witch/vampire's heart as the blood sprayed out forward onto the lovely new navy blue Neiman Marcus–style suit she was wearing. The bullet must have removed the witch/vampire's power enough to release the spell, at least that was my guess, and must have been Amelie Claire's as well.

Suzanne had stopped at her office door and watched the spectacle as it happened. She mumbled, "Carpet's ruined…" as she turned to go back into her office. Just then the phone rang and Suzanne went behind her desk and answered it as she sat down, "Suzanne's Psychic and Séance," she announced jovially.

I couldn't hear the other side of the conversation but Brett could and something he heard made him enter the office and move toward the desk, "Uh huh… yeah, he's here… can you hold a minute?" she said into the phone and then pressed red plastic hold button. I could see another line was lit up so someone… Arial maybe, must be on the phone in the front.

"So, Marisol, are you going to introduce me to your young man?" she asked, smiling at Brett.

I was still a little shocked from the recent events so it took me a couple seconds to shake myself out of it and answer, "Oh… of course… Suzanne, this is Brett. Brett, this is Suzanne, my boss," I said as introduction.

Brett smiled indulgently at my newly smitten boss and said, "It's nice to finally meet you…" Then, after a pause, he said, "Is that for me?" while he still had her attention.

"Oh, yes," she said as she pushed the line on the phone and handed him the receiver.

"Iris?" Brett answered. Now that I was closer I could mostly hear the other end. Also, Iris wasn't holding back.

"Brett! Oh, are you OK? I was worried. I could feel you getting VERY tense. What happened? Is Marisol OK? Gavin's here with me," she fired off into the phone.

"Yes… everything's fine now... Marisol caught Bronwyn," he added as he smiled back at me. After he said that Suzanne cleared her throat, "and… Suzanne captured her," he added as he smiled indulgently at my boss.

"What!" I heard her say then quickly relay this information to my brother who mimicked her surprise and grabbed the phone.

"Brett, what's going on?" Gavin asked.

"It's fine. No one was hurt… No one on our side," he qualified.

"Our side? Who was on our side?" he asked for clarification.

"Well, Arial was here when Bronwyn just happened to come into the store… and Marisol stalled her while Arial went to a pay phone and called the embassy, then Arial called me," he explained.

"And you didn't call me?" he protested.

"Gavin, I just left immediately, I didn't wait for anything. Jacque, Celestine and the Bertrands were all still at the embassy when Arial called so we had quite a force show up," he explained.

There was a pause then Gavin said, "So, she's OK?" then he said, "Wait, you said Marisol was *stalling* Bronwyn?" his annoyance returning. I held out my hand for Brett to give me the phone, which he did gladly.

"Hey, I'm fine. I had to keep her here or she'd get away. She wanted a reading so…" I explained.

"What the fuck, Marisol? Do you really have a death wish? What if she decided she was thirsty…" he rambled on. Suzanne decided she wanted a chance to take a crack at Gavin and indicated for me to hand her the phone, which I did without a problem.

"Sweet cheeks, your girl did good… and everyone's fine…I put a silver slug into the bloodsucker…" she covered the phone and whispered to Brett, "no offense," as she did her best to calm Gavin and proceeded to relay more of the fun details to him, which distracted him a bit from his annoyance.

I turned toward Brett as he pulled me closer by the waist and tucked a piece of my hair behind my ear. "You did do good," he said as he smiled proudly at me, "I could only feel an instant of panic then nothing… until I was already here," he said then frowned, "You did scare the hell out of me though," he said as he gave me a quick, soft, discreet kiss since we were standing in front of Suzanne, who seemed to be watching us very closely while recounting for Gavin.

"Thanks for the extra protection," I said. "I think it came in handy," I added.

"Oh, we're not done… there's a whole bunch of other things you need to be protected from…" he said as I became completely distracted from what he was saying while I was gazing into his gorgeous eyes…

I was jolted back into reality when Suzanne put the phone down noisily and said, "Hey, I have something for you," as she dug into her drawer and handed me an envelope. It made me recall what Jacque had said to Gavin about the Bertrand's gratitude at the Brown Derby last night. When I opened it I was shocked to see it was a check for $30,000 for me from some group called the Bertrand Foundation.

Brett looked at it over my shoulder and said, "Wow…" then looked at me and said, "You earned it, you know."

I was shocked and didn't know what to say but then I thought, "Well, twenty percent goes to Gavin," just as an aside.

"Doesn't it always," Brett laughed as I folded the envelope and tucked it between my bustier and dress.

I could hear the vampires on our side cleaning up the mess out in the hall and turned to Suzanne, "Suzanne, I'm so sorry I attracted more mess into the store," I apologized to her.

"Oh, honey, this wasn't your fault. Besides, I don't like hybrids," she added. "Plus, I think we can both expect another check soon," she said with greedy expectation.

When we went back out into the hallway I saw that Bronwyn had been removed from the wall and the Haitians' car had been brought around back and they'd probably loaded the witch/vampire into the trunk. There was still plenty of blood on the wall surrounding four large holes as well as more blood puddling and soaking into the carpet. Jacque turned around and spotted us and walked over.

"Marisol, I am very glad you are not hurt," Jacque said as he smiled and decided to give me a quick hug. He seemed to be in a very good mood.

"The cleaning crew are on their way and we have an appointment with the crematorium," he said pretty conclusively.

"Thank you for your assistance Monsieur Carson," Jacque said to Brett as he shook his hand.

"Oh, of course," Brett said. It was pretty clear he was there for me, which I greatly appreciated. "Please, call me Brett," he insisted.

"Please tell the Bertrands' thank you and that they were too generous…" I told Jacque as he was about to walk into Suzanne's office.

He turned and said, "It was nothing for them, really… Tell your brother I will be contacting him," he said with an expression that acknowledged my discomfort with the money aspect of all this.

I turned to Brett and said, "I have to go get my purse, it's in that room," I said as I pointed to the reading room just beyond the river of blood and the death wall that looked like it should have a blue circle drawn around it. He immediately picked me up and slogged through the river and set me down on the ground inside the room.

Once we were there we were confronted with Amelie Claire, standing still, apparently not wanting to touch anything since she was pretty thoroughly covered in blood herself.

"Excusez-Moi," she said to us, "Je suis désolé pour mon apparence," she said as she tried not to drip on the carpet.

I wasn't sure what she was saying so I just thanked her, "Thank you so much for your help," I said with as earnest an expression I could come up with.

"Merci, Marisol," she said, which I understood. "Je ne saurais assez vous remercier pour votre aide," which I didn't, but I assumed was along the same lines.

I just smiled at her because we didn't seem to be getting too far with this. Brett pulled the table cloth off my table and handed it to her, for which I was grateful. She was… how did Brett put it… a freak show. She smiled at him in a way that I was sure would have included a blush, if that were possible for a vampire. As she mopped herself up I tried to squelch my territorial reaction, and thought I'd succeeded until Brett squeezed my hand. I realized he would know how I was feeling no matter what; even if the feeling was a little humiliating. I tried not to look at him right then as I had no problem turning red.

I quickly grabbed my purse and let Brett lead me out the door as we said goodbye to Amelie Claire and also to Jean-Pierre once we got out into the hallway. Just as we were about to turn to go Arial peeked her head around the corner from the front, "Bye guys… Heinrich says good job…" she said. I think she was still holding on to the phone as she was stretching to peer down the hallway.

"Good job to you Arial. You totally saved me. Arial was the hero Heinrich," I said because I knew Heinrich could hear me. Arial giggled and waved and went back to her phone conversation so Brett picked me up again and waded back through the blood river to take me outside to my car. After thanking and saying goodbye to Celestine who was sitting in the rented Mercedes waiting for… the cleaning crew I think, we headed out.

As I was driving home I noticed that Brett looked a little… stressed maybe? He was leaning back with his head on the head rest with his eyes closed. I was looking back at him between clutching and shifting.

"Honey, are you OK?" I asked him as I accelerated and shifted into third going up Vine.

"Yeah, I'm fine…" he said as he lifted his head and looked at me and smiled reassuringly. He still had a look…

After I downshifted and turned left on Yucca and looked back at him, "Are you sure?" I wasn't convinced.

"There was just…. a lot of blood there…" he said as he ran his hand through his hair, "and I only had one bag before Arial called…" he confessed as I drove down Yucca. It was bloodlust I was seeing in his eyes…

As I downshifted and turned up Ivar I pulled quickly into the driveway and parked like Gavin, behind the garage. I turned to him and pulled loose the bow on the bustier I was wearing and dropped the strap of my dress and this seemed to be enough of an invitation that he pulled me tight and sunk his teeth into my shoulder quickly and with desperation.

It didn't hurt but I still gasped at his insistence as he gratefully allowed me to fulfill his need.

After a long minute and a couple of thankful moans, he stopped and licked my shoulder clean but still kept his head resting in the small of my neck. He took a couple of deep breaths and whispered, "Sorry," as he composed himself.

I brushed his hair out of his face and kissed him with the intensity he'd just ignited in me with his need and said, "Why don't we go inside now." And after we quickly put the VW in the garage and made our way upstairs we spent the rest of the morning satisfying needs.

Gavin

Twenty Six

I was lying in the back seat of the Thunderbird with my head on the headrest and Iris was lying on top of me, both of us completely limp, our breath finally slowing. We were both partially undressed which happened quickly and spontaneously, and we both had a drop of blood trickling down the corner of our mouths. Finally, when I began to move again, she pushed her mouth onto mine, mixing the blood together again, slowly and exquisitely. But I'm getting ahead of myself.

Very early this morning, after I got the gist from Suzanne and I was finally satisfied that things were being taken care of by the vampires after the incident at the psychic shop, I told Iris I had a surprise for her. I had been planning to take her to this place and I thought tonight might be a good night for it.

Iris had decided to sleep through the day. I encouraged her to do that more often so she wouldn't need to hibernate as soon as she might—although she was still many years from having to worry about that, at least a human lifetime in fact.

I was using the time to make phone calls and get some business done. It was crazy to me that no matter how loud I was in the other room it wouldn't disturb her, I could have the Pillagers (my Punk Rock clients) rehearse in the living room and she'd still stay unconscious, but if I just touched her lightly she'd wake up immediately. Of course, I never let anyone come over during the day anymore except Marisol; too risky to Iris.

I spend most of my days as I always did, either on the phone promoting or out in the city doing the same thing. Lately, I've been spending more time on the phone since I'd hired a couple of guys to do the legwork. I'd rather not leave Iris alone.

Towards the end of the day I got a call and it was Jacque St Domingue, "Monsieur James, good afternoon," he said as a greeting.

"Mr. St. Domingue, what can I do for you?" I said, hoping there might be another paying gig sometime in our near future. I was also a little surprised to hear from him since it was only 4:30 in the afternoon and still light out. I was aware, obviously, that most mature vampires don't need to sleep during the day, like Iris, but it's still a little unsettling to get the call.

"I wanted to say that we are very grateful for your and your sister's efforts in helping us reach our goals," he said somewhat formally. "I also want to invite both of you to a celebration of sorts at the embassy tonight," he offered, which surprised me.

"I was under the impression that people like me and Marisol weren't allowed into the embassy," I questioned.

"Since you and your sister have proven yourselves to be trustworthy to our cause, we have convinced the powers that be to make an exception," he said. "I have been known to be very convincing," he said, amused. "Also, since you have been named as the person who represents your sister, I have a reward for the capture of Bronwyn that I need to present to you," he added.

"Ah, OK, we'd love to come. The four of us, with Iris and Brett right?" just to clarify.

"Of course Monsieur James, it goes without saying. If you like, we can discuss terms regarding your sister assisting us in finding the remainder of the lost and misplaced souls," he offered.

"Sure, OK," I agreed, exactly what I was thinking. "What time?" I asked.

"10:00. I'll be glad when the days begin to get shorter. See you tonight then," he added before he hung up.

I'd be glad to see the days get shorter too. Not that I didn't have plenty to do during the day, it's just that it would be more fun if Iris was around to do it with me. I could go in and rouse her anytime and she wouldn't mind but I would feel selfish doing it all the time. The truth is I miss her when she isn't around.

I needed to check with Marisol. I wasn't sure if Jacque would call her or rely on me telling her. I dialed her work number. Suzanne answered.

"Suzanne's Psychic and Séance," she answered blandly.

"Isn't it Sexy Suzanne's Psychic and Séance?" I asked playfully.

"Absolutely. This is sexy Suzanne herself," she answered, playing along.

"Everything back to normal there?" I asked, referring to the most recent bloodbath.

"For the most part. The cleaning crew has their part down to a science I noticed. New carpet's going in tomorrow," she said. "I think I'll still have a healthy sum left over… I'm thinking of setting up a section selling sex toys…" she mused. I couldn't decide if she was serious or not.

"You guys get enough freaks in the store as it is, don't you think?" I asked lightly, not sure if I should really be worried.

"I'm just kidding. I wouldn't make your sister sell sex toys. So serious…" she ribbed me.

"So, is my trouble-making sister there?" I asked, a little relieved.

"Here she is," she said as she laughed and handed Marisol the phone.

"So, you don't think I can handle selling dildos and rubber wear, huh?" she said as a greeting.

"Don't say that out loud, you'll burn my ears," I protested.

"What's up?" she asked.

I cleared my throat and announced formally, "We've been cordially invited to attend a soiree at the Los Angeles you-know-what embassy tonight. Bring your own undead," I added.

"Seriously, they're going to let us in?" she asked.

"Jacque pulled some strings. He's got some payment for us too," I added.

"Wow, I never have to work again as it is. It's a good thing I like this job," the ladder being for Suzanne's benefit, I'm sure.

"It's at 10:00 so if you guys want to stop here first we can go over together," he suggested.

"OK. Wow, that doesn't give me much time to get ready," she complained. "Maybe I can get Suzanne to let me off a little early," since she was sitting right there I'm sure she was already considering it.

"OK. Be here by quarter-till," I said and hung up.

I was thinking about what I should wear tonight. I might have to pull out the Armani suit I'd bought a while back on sale. With this newest check I could go shopping for some clothes, for me and Iris. She always looked so elegant and I wanted to make sure I made her proud too.

I spent the rest of the day making phone calls. I called and booked shows for next month; Wong's West, the Whiskey and I even got Brett a gig at Club Lingerie opening for Rickie Lee Jones. I called the flyer guys I'd hired and sent them over to the printer to pick up the order I'd placed and gave them a list of where I wanted them to go. I warned them against skipping any of the stops, telling them I would check up and I'd know if they did. Regardless of the headache of employees, I should have hired someone a long time ago. It saves me a lot of time.

I ordered some Thai food and had it delivered and after I'd eaten enough food for three people I jumped into the shower and when I got out, I couldn't resist crawling into bed… I was already naked anyway.

It wasn't quite dusk but Iris was happy to be woken up a little early for some breakfast in bed before we had to get up and make our appearances.

Once we were up and dressed we hung out in the living room and played music until Marisol and Brett arrived. Iris looked spectacular, of course, she had on a little strappy black dress that had black feathers at the bottom of the skirt, black stockings with garters (pantyhose should be abolished, I plan to keep their existence from Iris as long as possible) and red pumps. She even had a little black sequined hat to match.

When Brett and Marisol showed up it looked like she'd gotten a head start on spending some of the money. She had on a new dress, some skin tight gun metal grey strapless number with a new pair of bondage pumps. Brett had on a pretty slick skinny-tie Beatles-style suit. They looked good.

We walked over dragging the vampires at our speed. I would be glad when my time as a slow, weak, mortal human was over. And I don't mean when I die in the conventional sense. My future's decided. I even have some old-blood donors to do the job. I just need to tie up some loose ends first then it's sayonara sunlight, hello immortality.

When we got inside and called the elevator I saw Marisol start to sweat, figuratively speaking. "You want to take the stairs?" I asked her, teasing her a little.

"No, I'm fine," I saw Brett grab a hold of her hand. I have to admit, he still seemed to be the same guy he always was even now that he was changed. I guess I should probably lighten up a little on them. Not that I really have much of a choice.

Once the elevator started up—actually since they arrived, Iris started chatting to Marisol about what she was wearing, going shopping, who might be there tonight, what was going on next week, and everything else under the universe. It was thoughtful of her to keep her chatting in the elevator; I think it distracted Marisol from thinking about how small and enclosed the space was.

When we reached the top someone I knew but never expected to see in a place like this was at the front door.

"Johnny, you're uh… working the door here?" I said, surprised. Last I knew Johnny was working at a music shop on Highland. He was a good looking guy; kind of a player, dyed jet black hair, and most recently had been dating the guitar player of an all-girl punk band that sometimes played on the same ticket as The Pillagers.

"Hey Gavin… yeah, uh… what are you… are you on the list?" he asked, obviously as surprised to see me here as I was to see him.

"I should be," I said, trying not to sound too pretentious. "Johnny, this is Iris, my girlfriend," Iris did her thing and Johnny seemed to understand. He must have his own insight into the nature of vampires.

"Hey Marisol… Brett," he seemed to register the difference in Brett. "You guys are good to go," he said as he checked the list.

"Thanks man," I said as we walked in.

"Is there anywhere you're not on the list?" Iris chuckled.

Iris' took my arm and we walked into this most exclusive of clubs. I was used to being let into places that most people couldn't get in to, clubs, hotel rooms, concerts back stage, I'd actually been quite successful at it but this seemed like a big step up from exclusive to, I don't know, ultra-exclusive. I wasn't afraid… more psyched.

We walked in first with Brett and Marisol behind us.

There seemed to be a good amount of people in the place. Since I'd had Iris' blood I could tell when someone was a vampire now by their eyes. Almost everyone was, except just a couple of people as far as I could see. There was a tall beefy guy and his tall, skinny friend, one or two others with vampires.

The first people we saw inside that we knew were Arial and Heinrich.

"Iris," Heinrich exclaimed as he picked her up and gave her a big bear hug.

"Heinrich!" Iris giggled as he swung her around and set her back down next to me. They always seemed so happy to see each other. "Hi Arial, welcome to our little corner of Hollywood," Iris said to Arial.

"Hi Iris, thanks," she said as Marisol and Brett joined us. "You know they're changing the rules for people like us," Arial said.

"I thought they were just bending the rules," Marisol said.

"No, they're starting a guest program. Other embassies do it. You just have to be approved and register... see," she pointed to a table behind her, in the far corner where Arelia was sitting. We wandered over while Marisol and Brett chatted with Heinrich and Arial.

Arelia was sitting at a small table in the corner made for playing chess that now had a big logbook on it. She had a pen and a jar of safety pins and a bottle of alcohol with her. I had a feeling I had to do more than just sign in.

"Good evening Gavin, Iris," Arelia greeted us.

"Hey Arelia. So, what do I have to do," I asked her.

"We need a finger print... in blood of course," she said with a smile and pushed the big book toward me.

I turned to Iris, "Baby, why don't you do it. That pin's going to hurt," I complained playfully, of course I knew she'd be happy to.

"I'd love to," she said, as I expected. Arelia indicated my right thumb to Iris. Iris took my hand and looked up at me with her big, green eyes and kissed my thumb before gently putting a tiny slice into it. I placed it down onto the paper and pressed to make my mark. Then Iris took my hand back and put my thumb into her mouth and sucked just a little, which she could see was starting to distract me so she quickly licked it clean and gave it back to me. Then I signed my name and so did Iris as my sponsor then we stepped aside. Marisol and Brett had come up behind us, although Marisol seemed to be trying to not watch up to this point.

Iris and I stepped away but when I glanced back I could see that Marisol wasn't using the pin either.

We walked back into the main room and Iris showed me around. She showed me the impressive metal gates that came down in the day and I made a mental note about those.

A young waiter with pale skin, dark circles under his eyes and slicked back hair, wearing a white waiter's coat approached us and asked if we'd like a drink. She ordered me a red wine (she said she liked that in me) and nothing for herself. He insinuated that what they had was fresh and she declined anyway.

I wondered if she felt like she was cheating on me or something by drinking someone else's blood so I told her, "Are you sure? Do you want something?" I checked.

"No, I'm totally fine baby. I've been awake long enough now that I'm finding I don't need as much anymore," she assured me.

"And why order a hamburger out when you can get steak at home, right?" I added as a joke as I gave her a quick kiss. Iris thought it was funny.

The waiter looked at us like this was too much information and went to get my red wine. A little later I noticed that Brett had accepted the blood in a glass. I wondered how long it would really take to get a grip on the control. Besides the incident with Heather, Brett had been doing a pretty good job keeping control of himself, at least as far as I knew. It still made me feel better to see him with the glass.

As we mulled around, I made an effort to try to remember if I'd seen any of these people or vampires before. I was sure I'd recognized a girl who was a vampire from one of the clubs that maybe I'd seen before I could discern the undead vibe. She looked like she recognized me too.

As we walked around the huge, loft-like place we made our way to the other side where we ran into the Bertrands. Great, more non–English. How do you live to be a thousand years old, or however old they were, and not learn English. I did know they were at least 500 years old. I'd called the library and asked them to look up the Hundred Years' War for me.

"Bonsoir," they both said.

"Good evening," I said in return. That was pretty much it for me.

Iris greeted them in French and began a rapid–fire conversation with them; mostly her talking and them listening. Jean-Pierre, the boy—I guess you really couldn't call a 500 plus year old vampire a boy but he did look young—began conversing with her in an animated way. I couldn't understand what they were saying but I could see that he was becoming a little too interested in her, especially when he kissed her on the hand. I could feel my ears turning red, and I think Iris could too because she backed up a step and leaned into me in a fairly natural way while I put my arm around her. He was short and frail looking but I was pretty sure he could kick my ass, since he'd pretty much already done just that. So I just smiled at him (more of a smirk, really) and kept my mouth shut while Iris said whatever she did to pull us away. Did she always have to be so irresistible to everyone?

When I saw Jacque I squeezed Iris' shoulder and we made our way over to where he was. He was chatting with Harold McKinley, the ambassador.

"Harold." she greeted him.

"Iris," He kissed her on the cheek. "Nice to see you again Mr. James" he said to me as I shook his hand. He held onto my hand for a little too long while we shook and even put his left hand on my arm. I was getting a strongly appreciative vibe that I understood but couldn't actually return in the way he would probably like. This happened to me pretty frequently for some reason and really, I guess it was flattering.

When he finally let my hand go I looked over to the left and noticed that tall, beefy human guy and he seemed to be giving me a dirty look. No worries, guy.

After Iris chatted a bit with Harold I interjected to ask Jacque if he had a minute to talk. This gave Iris the opportunity to continue chatting when we slipped into the office that was just behind our group.

He went and sat down behind the big desk and I took the seat opposite him. There were a lot of books in this room.

"So, first things first," he said as he reached into a drawer and pulled out an envelope and handed it to me. As I started to put it in my jacket pocked, which seemed like the proper thing to do, he said, "Please," and indicated I should open it, so I did.

When I opened it the check was for $50,000. I was honest in my reaction when I said, "Wow," and then went ahead and stowed it in my jacket.

He continued, "Now, I can't promise that every service your sister performs will garner this level of compensation since this sum was gathered from the many who were delighted to see the witch be taken out of circulation," he began, "and, although we are putting together a fund for this explicit purpose, we are expecting that the rescued souls will be the ones to reward their rescuer themselves, as the Bertrands did," he explained. "What I can promise you is that the fund would be willing cover all your expenses and guarantee up to a $20,000 reward for each mission and anything they give you over that is yours to keep, of course," he offered.

I thought about it for a minute. Then I countered, "How about $25,000 minimum and expenses, reasonable expenses for all four of us if we travel?" I asked.

He pondered me for a minute then answered, "That sounds reasonable, Monsieur James," he said as I nodded my head in agreement. "You know, I would feel better if all four of you were immortal and not so… vulnerable," he tried to put delicately.

"Me too, actually," I responded, "and I plan to take you up on your offer in the very near future. I just have some things to take care of first… my mother… covering my business while I'm… adapting, and most importantly discussing this with Marisol," I laid out pretty honestly. "I'm not sure where she stands exactly. I'm a little conflicted about her changing. That's really what we need to discuss," I added.

"Well you can take some time as we plan to stay on in California for a while," he explained, "it seems that Bronwyn spent some time here and up north and this may be where quite a few of the lost are hidden," he informed me. "It seems that the Horst brothers were indeed the scions of Bronwyn and we are trying to find out if there are more and what else they know about her deeds during the last few hundred years," he related.

"Well, that's convenient for us," I said. "So, can I ask you… why did she bury the Bertrands? They said she wouldn't have gotten very much money…" I asked.

"Apparently, Bronwyn wasn't after money so much as she was after status and revenge," he started. "Claudio Horst was quite forthcoming about her practices and motivations." He continued, "Her plan was to break the blood-bonds of old vampires moving up the chain and eliminate them in succession," he told me. "She hated vampires, even though that's what she eventually became, and she even killed her own sire," he explained. That was a statement that Iris would have gasped at, I was sure.

"When she ordered the Horst's to capture Heinrich their plan was to then come after me but apparently they were never able to locate me. The Horst's leached his blood but in the scope of things, Heinrich is not very old, but older than the Horsts so they used him in that way. Bronwyn would have just staked him for good but couldn't until she had found me in order to cast her spell and break our bond completely. Apparently she was able to mask the initial staking but Heinrich tells me it was for a very brief time. Without a spell on me I would have sensed something was wrong eventually. Luckily, I am not the easiest vampire to find unless I want to be found," he said with a conspiratorial smile.

"So, her plan would have been to stake and bury Heinrich then go after you?" I said.

"That is what I am told," he answered.

"So then, they were set to go after the sire of the Bertrands next too?" I added.

"Yes, but apparently Monsieur Gerard can be quite elusive as well.

"Huh… so what was her ultimate goal?" I asked.

"To be the oldest and the most powerful," he said.

"How old was she? I know it's rude to ask but for her…" I figured it wouldn't be rude to ask how old the dead witch was, now that she was completely dead.

"No, that's OK. I think she is beyond taking offense," he laughed. "She became a vampire in 1693 to escape the Salem Witch Trials. She was never charged but it is our belief that many humans were burned for sticking pins into the dolls of those little girls when we have pretty good idea who did that," he said.

"She was a governess in the Parris household where the girls lived and she was quite a powerful witch in her mortal life. She had been bringing up the girls to follow her into the craft when they became unmanageable and Bronwyn would use extremely cruel methods to force their obedience," he explained.

"Other members of her coven were being accused of the crime but Bronwyn initially escaped their suspicion due to her relationship with the girls. As the investigators got closer to suspecting her, she found a vampire willing to turn her and escaped," he said. "She detested vampires and could not abide the control inherent in the Sire/Scion connection so she did something that we consider to be completely against our nature, which is to kill your own sire," he explained.

"Her hatred of the vampires was rooted in them being responsible for informing to the local magistrates of the witches' crimes," he told me. "Those of us that believe as I do in the sanctity of human life and common goodness are most prevalent in our kind, even then," he explained. That was good to hear.

"We don't know how many scions she has created over the years but this is also something we will be investigating going forward. There may be some of them that might want to adapt to vampire society and live within accepted practices… that is our hope," he said.

"As far as we know… she's never bonded with another immortal," he said. This reminded me…

"Mr. St Domingue," I started.

"I think you can call me Jacque at this point," he laughed.

"Jacque… can I ask you a personal question?" I asked.

"You may," he said, curious.

"You're married…" I started.

"For several hundred years…" he smiled.

"Are we going to… Iris and I… will we lose anything… when I change?" He really seemed like the best person to ask.

He appraised me for a minute then said, "You will lose a few grains of sand… but gain the entire beach," he said reassuringly. "You should keep in mind that what you are doing is a very big commitment," he warned. "When two immortals become bonded it is forever and very… unrelenting," he advised.

I nodded. I had a lot to think about. "Thank you… for your candor… and the check, of course," I said as I stood up and put out my hand for him to shake.

"My pleasure, thank you… and thank your sister…" he said, as he shook my hand with his large, cold, five hundred plus year old hand. "I look forward to a mutually beneficial relationship," he added.

I went out into the main room to find Iris and found her talking to Brett and Marisol.

"So, you were in there for a long time talking to Jacque," Marisol said, questioning.

"He was giving me the scoop on Bronwyn," I said. I could see they were interested in the story but, "It's a long story… I'll tell you guys later, OK?" I had an agenda.

"So, are you ready for your surprise?" I asked Iris. She looked at me as if innocently unaware but I knew she didn't forget. She loved surprises. She already asked me where we were going a couple of times tonight but she really didn't want to know. She was only adding to her own suspense.

She said her goodbyes to Brett and Marisol and a few other people, she always kissed everyone, then she said to me, "I'm ready," and let me lead her out of the embassy, the building and out into the night. I think she would have gladly put on a blindfold if I asked her to.

It was on nights like tonight that I really appreciated my old car. All the new cars had bucket seats that I'm sure were safer but they wouldn't have allowed Iris to scoot over and snuggle up while I drove; the way she was now. I would take my chances.

I went East on Franklin until I cut up on Western to go toward Los Feliz Blvd. When I started to go up into the hills I could see her getting excited. She may have even been here before, I wasn't sure exactly when it was built. When I turned into the observatory parking lot I asked her, "Do you know where we are?"

"No, but I can't wait to see," she said. Maybe it was after her time. Since it was after eleven the building itself would be closed (I wasn't sure exactly what time it closed but I'm sure it was before now) but we would be able to see the view, which was the real reason I brought her.

Once I parked and we were walking I noticed that there weren't that many people left here, which worked for me; just a smattering of cars. I grabbed her hand and said, "c'mon," as we got closer.

You could see the lights from the parking lot but once we circled around the walkway that lead to the viewing platform and she saw it she exclaimed, "Wow!" and paused then said, "It's so big now," looking out at a city that was probably ten times the size it was when she was last present. They had those coin-op telescopes but that would be a waste on her.

From the first viewing platform, we moved on to climb the stairs to circle all the way out in front of the observatory. When we got there she decided she wanted to sit on the concrete railing. She didn't need my help but I still held her waist and kept a hold of her when she turned around to see.

I couldn't get over feeling like she was somehow fragile. Which was stupid, I know. She could probably throw me a hundred feet if she wanted to. But there was something about her femininity… her emotional sensitivity maybe, that made me still want to protect her.

She had been looking out for a long while when I said, "So, can you see every detail, for miles and miles?" I asked her. Her seat put her conveniently on the same level as I was. I could put my face right up level with hers. When we were standing I had a good ten inches on her.

"It's amazing… it's overwhelming, really," she said with the same open wonder she considered everything with. She had a gift for appreciating and finding the best in someone or something. She always found the beauty in every day life.

"So, it's a good surprise?" I asked, knowing she was hard to disappoint. I was holding her tight around the waist and was nuzzling into her neck at the time.

She turned toward me and brought my face to hers, "Every day is a wonderful surprise," she said; which was exactly the right answer, then I let her kiss me.

Sometimes… the way she seemed so vulnerable, yet she was the strongest, most confident person I think I've ever known, it would sometimes cut me to my core… push the way I felt about her to a level that scared me…

She slowly stopped kissing, turned her legs around to face me and put her face next to mine and said into my ear, "You know… I'm not upset that I was asleep for so long now…" she started softly, "I think I was asleep for exactly the right amount of time," she said as she pulled back to look at me now. She had a look on her face how I felt; both enthralled and petrified. I kissed her desperately and deeply…

This moment was digging into that intense, scary place that made me want to declare things and keep her from ever leaving me. I knew she could feel what I was feeling… when I felt this way that I did… which was more and more often these days… why did it scare me so much?

"Tell me…" she whispered into my mouth, her cold hands in my hair and on my face…

"You know I love you, baby," I told her; then I showed her.

"I know," she breathed back and the intense, scary, incredible place enveloped us both in its grip. In a very short time I needed her more than I've ever needed anything before.

I pulled away suddenly and lifted her off the wall then grabbed her hand and we ran down the steps and around the big, iconic building as we raced for the car.

I quickly opened the back door of the car and got in and she got in after me, closing the door behind her and finding her place in our kiss again. I leaned back in the big leather seat and pulled her on top of me as things steamed up quickly. We were desperately pulling clothing out of the way and freeing ourselves until finally there was nothing between us and our sudden intense need for each other.

The sounds coming from us were closer to expressing pain or something like it. She bit into her own shoulder and released, then she watched me as I reached down with my mouth and took what she'd given me. In the next moment she clamped down on my exposed neck and it was like I wanted to crawl inside her and stay there forever.

We ended up sliding down horizontally as our now muffled screams took us to the deepest part of this new, scary, intense place together.

Now, being back in the exquisite, blood mixing kiss, I couldn't think of what I was afraid of before. There was only this, nothing else.

Book 2, "**Whitley Avenue**" coming soon…

Visit our website @ www.hollywood-gothic.com

Or, to find us on Facebook, search for DeAnn Price.

www.ingramcontent.com/pod-product-compliance
Lightning Source LLC
Chambersburg PA
CBHW050513260626
47157CB00004B/1310

9780578028903